Phoenix Knights: Journey to Safehold

Milena Delgado Laborde

For my mom Julia and my best friend Trisha. Without you this book would not have been written. I love you both so much.

Contents

CHAPTER 1

THE FINAL BATTLE

It was childish of him to expect a response from a dead man, let alone his dead father. Alanor asked the question out loud anyway, running the tips of his fingers through the dust that had collected on the ornate engraving of the name on the tomb.

"What am I to do now?"

He couldn't bring himself to lie on top of it the way he had when he was a child and it lay empty. Back when they would come down here to get away from it all, and his father would lift him up onto the stone sarcophagus that would eventually be the king's final resting place. His father would hop onto his grandfather's tomb, and they would lie there and joke around. Later Alanor would be sore from having the decorated edges of his father's name dig into his back.

Despite the cold, it used to be his peaceful place, resting amongst his ancestors, his legacy. Until the day that King Octavian was placed in his tomb and a new one with a new name, his name, was placed beside it. Empty. Waiting. He could see it from where he was standing. There was a high chance he would find himself in that box sooner rather than later. Tomorrow even. Would death be comfortable? He found the griminess on his hands unnerving as he rubbed his fingers together mindlessly.

"You always taught me that magic was evil," he whispered, "but magic has saved my life. Do I reward my savior or punish him?"

The title that had been carved underneath his father's name, the Supreme Vanquisher, had been given to the late king during the Great Purification. Had it been purification, or had it been genocide? Alanor had heard sorcerers call his father the Blood King before. He had always chalked it up to the ravings of criminals. It was difficult to grapple with the realization that perhaps he had been wrong. Perhaps his father had been wrong. Alanor knew his father would push him to execute the man who had saved his life. How could that be honorable? But then again, magic always led to death and destruction.

Perhaps magic would twist and distort the soul of his best friend. Would it not then be a mercy to kill him before the magic made a monster out of him? He knew that's what his father would say. He wasn't sure what was right or wrong anymore and now, on the eve of battle, he was even more conflicted.

"I thought you'd be down here."

Alanor turned to see his highest-ranking knight standing in the entrance of the cavernous room, holding a lit torch. As new light filled the dark but not damp room, Alanor realized that his own torch had been burning out. He nodded to the knight. The man was taller than Alanor, but he had similar coloring, with his blond hair and blue eyes. Would his father have preferred Sir Theodore as a son?

The other man looked at him with a wry smile. "You used to come down here to escape training when you were younger."

"Yes, I remember." Alanor felt his face warm at the reminder of his time as Sir Theodore's squire. His father had placed him under Theodore's tutelage, despite the knight being only a few years older than him.

Theodore stepped forward, clearing his throat and taking up a more formal voice. "Your Majesty," he began, "the scouts have returned."

"What did they see?" he asked.

"Kal's army moves directly for the citadel from the northeast. The scouts spotted his forces approaching the Bergen Pass."

Alanor cursed. "We cannot let him get to the citadel. His last attack left us without enough supplies to handle a siege. We only managed to fight them off because of—"

Theodore nodded. "The war council has gathered. They await your final decision, on both Kal and...Nevinon."

Alanor was silent for a moment before looking away. "He has magic."

"Like Moira," the knight said.

Alanor winced, then sighed. "He lied to me. He's been lying to me for years."

"If I may speak freely, sire?" Theodore asked. When Alanor nodded, the knight continued. "It seems that he has been using his magic to protect us, to protect you. He certainly saved our lives against Kal's men. He didn't have to reveal himself like that. And you were already questioning your stance. That's why you decreased the punishments for practicing magic, isn't it?"

"Yes, that's what started this whole mess in the first place." He paused. "Maybe I was wrong. Do you think I'm making the right choice, Theo?"

Theodore looked at King Octavian's tomb. "I do not know much about magic, other than what I was taught. But I admit that I haven't seen any evidence that magic has corrupted Nevinon. Or that it did the Lady Moira, before she..."

Alanor nodded. "Nor can I. And if they have magic and are not evil, there must be others. How can I kill someone for saving my life? All our lives."

"But you have doubts, sire?"

He sighed. "What if I'm wrong and he is the exception? Or it just hasn't had enough time to turn him? What if my father was right? He always said that magic would lead Amari to ruin. What if I'm wrong to oppose Kal?"

Sir Theodore shook his head. "I cannot say if your father was right or wrong. But I can say for sure that Kal is wrong. He has taken up arms against his people, against his king. It is treason. He must be stopped."

They were lost in thought for a while before Alanor broke the silence. "You loved her, didn't you? Moira?"

Theodore stayed silent.

"I would've given you my blessing," Alanor said.

The knight gave a single nod, and Alanor decided to change the subject. He knew speaking of her would bring only pain. "Send out messengers to all the villages northeast between the Bergen Pass and the citadel. We'll evacuate the people behind the citadel walls, just in case."

Theodore looked at him. "The council won't be pleased."

Alanor gave a bitter smile. "When are they ever?"

"And what will you be doing about Nevinon, sire? He did save us from Kal, but the council will push for his execution."

"How can I trust him when everything he's ever said could be a lie? How am I to know what was real and what was fake?"

"I believe the path forward is clear, sire." Alanor sent him a questioning glance and the knight explained, "You must speak with him. To find out the truth." Theodore hesitated before adding, "There is something else you should know."

"What is it?" It was unusual to see Theodore so discomfited.

"There are signs that our allies may not be lending their support for the battle ahead. They are outraged over rumors that you appear to be supporting magic. It seems Kal has been sending messengers to our allies telling them you have a sorcerer fighting for you."

Alanor took a deep breath. "Damn. We can't win this battle without their help."

"Perhaps it wouldn't be such a bad thing then," Theodore said. "To have someone like Nevinon by our side."

"I will keep that in mind," Alanor said.

Sir Theodore nodded and left the room, pausing only to mount his torch onto one of the sconces on the wall, ever thoughtful, leaving Alanor the light. The king steeled himself. He would have to set his feelings aside. There was a conversation to be had with a certain sorcerer.

⚜

Alanor made his way down the stairs to the dungeons after lingering at the top for a while, bracing himself for the cold and the darkness that would meet him. He didn't know if he was slowing down out of fear or reluctance to face his friend. If Nevinon had been his friend at all, that was. Alanor had no idea how long Nevinon had been practicing magic for. Had he always been a sorcerer? Had their entire friendship been a lie? If so, why had he saved them all from Kal and the hunters when they had been surrounded? Why would Nevinon spend years living in Amari as an apprentice, and later a physician, if all along he had the power to be a king? It made no sense to him.

He finally entered the dungeons and dismissed all of the guards. Nevinon would not tell him the full truth with an audience. Alanor walked down the long, dark corridor, scrunching his nose at the strong scent of mildew in the stale air, until he came upon Nevinon's cell.

The moment that Nevinon spotted him, the man jumped up from the bench behind the bars. The brunet sorcerer was dressed in his usual riding clothes and boots, rumpled and dirtied after a few days in the dungeons, not having been able to change since he had been arrested directly after the skirmish. They stared at each other in silence for a few long moments.

"Alan," Nevinon whispered.

"I want to know how long," he said, his voice strained. He didn't even know what he was going to say until he opened his mouth. "I want to know how long you've been lying to me."

"Alan, I—" Nevinon shook his head. "You have to understand. I wanted to tell you."

"But you never did," Alanor said. "Ten years. We've known

each other for a decade. Worked together. Laughed together. Faced every threat together." By the end he had raised his voice. "And you've had magic this entire time? Answer the question," Alanor demanded. Nevinon startled at his harsh tone, and Alanor uncrossed his arms. "I want to understand. I do. But in order for me to understand I need to know the truth, Nevinon. How long have you been lying to me?"

Nevinon looked down at the ground briefly before looking back up at his king. "I was born like this. I was born with magic."

Alanor shook his head before the other had even finished speaking. "That's not possible. I thought magic had to be learned."

"Sorcerers have to learn magic, but I am not a sorcerer. I'm a warlock. There's a difference."

This was new information to Alanor. "Different how?"

"Like I said," Nevinon spoke softly as if afraid of reproach, "sorcerers learn magic, witches and warlocks are born with magic. I've been able to use magic since I was a babe."

Alanor froze. "And this is...usual?"

Nevinon shook his head. "Most of those who are born with magic begin showing signs as adolescents. But I'm the exception, I suppose." He scratched the back of his neck.

Alanor couldn't hold back a huffed laugh. "As per usual then."

Nevinon sent him a sad smile and nodded.

"So the entire time I've known you, you've been able to use magic?"

Nevinon nodded again.

"And you've never tried to stop using it?" Alanor asked.

"Of course I have." Nevinon frowned. "You think I want to have magic? To face a death sentence for merely existing? To have to hide who I am and lie every day? If I could choose, I would choose to be normal." Nevinon sat back down on the bench. "But I can't stop using magic. If I stop for too long, the energy will just build and build until I can no longer control it, and it'll just explode out of me when I least expect it."

"Maybe it's an addiction," Alanor said.

"Or maybe magic is just natural, and not evil," Nevinon suggested.

"All of the magic that I've seen in my life has been directed at either killing me or destroying my kingdom. You know that. You were here for it. How can you sit there and tell me that magic is not evil?"

"Because magic has also saved your life, and not just recently. Do you think this is the first time that I've saved you and the others with magic? It's just the first time that I had to do so publicly." Nevinon sighed. "There is so much good that magic can do. I wish you could see that."

"Have you been using your magic for your duties as a physician?" Alanor asked.

Nevinon shook his head. "No, actually I can't perform healing magic. But I've been using it to help where I can, to save the knights, to save you, and to save your father when he was alive."

Alanor looked at him in shock. "You're telling me you used magic to save my father's life? The man who made magic illegal in the first place?"

"Several times actually. You wouldn't believe how many times the two of you almost kicked the bucket." Nevinon smiled.

"Why?" he asked with wide eyes. "Why would you save my father? In fact, while we're at it, why don't you tell me why you would save me?"

Nevinon recoiled backward as if struck. "How could you ask me that? Of course I would use my magic to save the lives of my friends, and of my friend's family. Of course I would protect my home." Nevinon held the frayed hem of his shirt in fidgeting hands, hesitating before asking, "Will you execute me?"

Alanor threw Nevinon's words back at him. "And how could

you ask me that? You're my friend. And you know that I've lowered the punishments for magic."

"Banish me then?"

"No. No banishment either." Alanor paused before taking a breath. "You say you would use your magic to protect your home. Is that still true? Even after—" Alanor motioned to the iron cuffs on Nevinon's wrists.

"Yes." The warlock nodded. "Always. My magic is yours, Alan."

"I don't know if magic is good or bad yet, but I know that if Kal takes over the citadel, that would be the worst outcome for my people. He has always been a vicious bastard. I can't let my kingdom fall into his hands."

"I want to help," Nevinon stood and walked slowly forward, resting a hand on the bars of his cell. "Let me defend my home. Let me show you that magic can be used to protect as well."

Alanor pulled the key to Nevinon's cell out of his pocket, but he hesitated. "And what happens if I let you out of the irons and the magic begins to take over and corrupt your soul?" He fiddled with the key, pressing the curves into his palm.

Nevinon rolled his eyes. "That's not how magic works, but if it makes you feel any better, if I start to show signs of corruption, whatever that means, you can put me back in the irons."

In that moment, he wished for nothing more than to keep Nevinon in chains for his own protection while he researched the harm that magic could cause him. But there was a long and vicious battle ahead, and Alanor knew that his men would be outnumbered. If Nevinon could use his magic to help them with as few casualties as possible, then Alanor was willing to let him out of the cell.

"You will come to me immediately if you start to feel differently," Alanor commanded. "We leave at first light. We'll be meeting Kal's army at the Bergen Pass."

Nevinon nodded. "I'll need to get my physician's tools ready to bring with me as well."

"I'll send Sir Theodore to help you," Alanor said.

"To watch over me, you mean," Nevinon said. "To make sure I don't become some demon in the night."

"Exactly." Alanor smiled before composing himself. "Promise me that you won't lie to me anymore."

Nevinon's expression slipped into something more solemn, and he laid a hand on his heart. "I promise."

Alanor opened the cell and unlocked Nevinon's cuffs. The king nodded toward the tunnel leading to the stairs, and Nevinon left after sending him one last glance. Alanor sighed and looked down at the iron manacles in his hands. He hoped that he was making the right decision, not just for his kingdom, but also for his friend.

Alanor stood on the steps of the castle courtyard as his men prepared to leave the citadel to meet Kal's army and cut them off. As the first rays of light broke over the trees, he turned to look for his wife. He spotted her walking through the courtyard, instructing the servants and staff who were setting up a medbay area to receive any knights who would be injured in battle.

Instead of wearing one of her dresses in the usual warm tones that complemented her dark skin, Genevive was dressed in dark-colored trousers and boots, and had her curly hair up in a bun. She spotted him and her face lit up as she approached. She bounded up the steps, and he embraced her before meeting her lips with his. A wolf whistle that they both recognized as Sir Cassius's interrupted them and they separated. Alanor sent the knight a mock glare before smiling at the woman in his arms, her form fitting perfectly to his.

"Be safe, Alan," Genevive said. "Do whatever you can to come home."

Alanor nodded. "Don't worry, Evie. I have faith in my men.

We will win this battle and show Kal exactly how traitors are dealt with."

His knights had heard him and gave a cheer in response. Genevive shook her head but smiled.

"Besides," Alanor lowered his voice so that only she could hear, "Nevinon will be with us."

"And for that I am infinitely glad," Genevive sighed before adjusting his collar.

Alanor hadn't commented on it, but Genevive had been quicker to accept the physician's magic than most. It made sense, he supposed, considering the two used to be thick as thieves back when his wife worked as a serving girl and Nevinon had still been an apprentice. The man in question walked into the courtyard with his medicine bag. Most of the knights paused and looked at the physician with trepidation.

Alanor let go of his wife and walked down the steps to address his men. "I know some of you might be nervous about the coming battle and the unique situation we find ourselves in. This will be the first time in over two and a half decades that Amarian knights will be fighting alongside magic. I know this feels new and sudden, but I have in the last few years come into information that might put into question the corruptive force of magic, and recently I have lessened the punishments for the use of it. We all know Nevinon. He is loyal to this kingdom. He has defended us in the past and continues to do so. The tyranny and destruction wrought by Kal and his witch hunters will not prevail. We will see this war finished today."

His men let out another round of cheers, and Alanor kissed his wife one last time before moving to mount his horse. Nevinon pulled up beside him and the rest of his most trusted knights in the formation.

"Nev!" Cassius called out. "I can't believe you didn't tell me you had magic. We could've been having so much fun."

Solomon shook his head and smiled at his partner's antics. "I think that might be part of the reason why he didn't tell you."

"Can you make things explode?" Cassius continued. "Levitate things? Do you think you could make wine with magic? I'll never have to buy alcohol again."

Nevinon sent Alanor an exasperated look and the group of knights laughed as Cassius continued with his long list of questions. As they rode out of the city, Alanor looked back at the sight of his castle, with its gleaming white stone and imposing towers. His home. He did not know what would happen during the battle ahead, but he hoped that he would live to see his city in all of its splendor once more. That they would return home victorious, securing peace for his people for years to come.

THE SOUND of metal clashing and cries of pain and victory rang out across the valley. To the side, on the cliff that overlooked the battlefield, Alanor slid downward toward the ground. With his back flush to a tree, he took a moment to catch his breath. He did not close his eyes though. He would not let his exhaustion distract him from the battle that raged around him.

His breath froze at a nearby sound. A group of knights was passing behind the clearing. Not knowing if they were allies or enemies, he pressed himself further to the tree. Gods, let them pass quickly and not see him. He was in no condition to fight off more than one assailant.

Late that morning, Alanor had led his army onto the field with his most reliable knights by his side. His brothers, his closest friends. Moments into the battle however, he had lost sight of the others. Somehow he had made his way past enemy lines, to the west of the field.

The battle was dying down now, but in order to return to camp he would have to pass through the valley teeming with enemy soldiers. It was a feat that would've been difficult even with his most skilled knights and Nevinon by his side. To do so alone would be a suicide mission.

He spotted a short path that led to a peak that overlooked the field. He checked behind him to make sure the path was clear. The battle had not lasted long at all, but it had been fierce. Kal's army had been made up of many mercenaries and witch hunters. They had been outnumbered by them but Kal's men were not used to organized battle. Even with the added advantage of having a sorcerer—no, warlock, he corrected himself—fighting on their side, the battle had become long and drawn out.

He made his way to the cliff, crouching down so he wouldn't be seen. For several long moments he looked out, frantically trying to catch any glimpse of his friend and physician. But he could not see anything. Nevinon had disappeared from the battle after he had decimated three large groups of witch hunters with a huge blast of fire. Then, in the distance, he spotted Nevinon standing on a hill on the other side of the field, with his hands outstretched. A dozen bolts of lightning rained down upon the hunter army. The light was so bright, Alanor had to look away. When he looked back, Nevinon was no longer on the hill. He felt a spike of worry for the other man. Alanor backed away from the cliffside. He needed to go rejoin his men before he was caught by himself.

A shadow moved toward him from the left, but exhausted as he was, he was not able to lift his sword up in time. A fierce burning sensation washed over him, radiating outward from the wound in his side, and he cried out in pain. The enemy gave a jerk and pulled his sword from Alanor's side. He fell to the ground with a soft thud. Above him stood a man with sharp features and shock white hair.

Kal.

"Finally," Kal growled. "After all of these years watching you, the golden king, decimate our legacy. I finally get to watch you die."

Alanor gritted his teeth, then sputtered at the metallic taste in his mouth. He had bit his tongue as he fell. It was the least of his worries now. "What legacy? A legacy of injustice and cruelty?"

Alanor tried to reach for his sword that had landed next to him but Kal kicked it a few paces too far for him to reach.

"A legacy of strength and victory. We could have freed Amari from the evils of magic. Instead you sided with corruption."

"I only lessened the persecution of those who would use magic for good. I cannot be sure that magic is evil anymore. Not if Moira—"

"Moira," Kal hissed her name, "was weak against the temptation magic presented and the only good thing she did was off herself. For that I commend her."

Alanor spat out the blood in his mouth and glared up at Kal. "She was my sister in all but blood. Don't you dare speak of her. I can't be sure if magic is good or bad but I can be sure of this. You are the evil one. You have betrayed my kingdom and killed my people. And for that you will die."

"The only one who will die here is you." Kal sneered and motioned toward the battlefield. "Where is your pet sorcerer to save you now?"

Alanor tried to muster the energy to get up, but it was futile. He could not die before the man who had murdered his people, his knights. It was unthinkable. He wanted to avenge them even if he died trying. But all of the willpower in the world could not stop his body from failing him as Kal advanced with the sword poised above him ready to strike.

CHAPTER 2

THE PROPHECY

Nevinon picked himself off of the ground with a groan. It took him a few seconds to regain his balance. That last blast of magic had taken a lot out of him, but now was not the time to be lying down to rest. Thankfully the witch hunters had run away from the hill. Those who had survived at least. The warlock looked out over the field, searching for his king. Nowhere to be found. He had lost sight of Alanor quickly and that didn't bode well at all.

He spotted a puddle nearby and crouched down. His reflection gave him pause. His black hair was matted with blood and his face was marred with scrapes and bruises. He watched his blue eyes turn golden as he whispered a scrying spell that he had learned a few years ago, then gave the magic his command while thinking of the image of his king.

"Show me Alanor Erikir Kova."

His reflection warped and images formed in the puddle. As soon as Nevinon could tell what was happening his heart began to race. Alanor was on the ground, thankfully conscious, though lying in a pool of blood. Too much blood. Worse, the man standing above him with a sword outstretched was none other than Kal. Nevinon had to find Alanor. *You'll never make it in time.* Nevinon gritted his teeth. *No, focus.*

He leaned closer to the puddle. There was a rock wall behind them. They had to be on the cliffs on the other side of the battle-field. Nevinon let the image of the two men go and rushed over the hill, blasting away any man in his path. He had to get to Alanor before it was too late. He berated himself for not taking the time to learn a transportation spell of some kind.

He got to the cliffs in record time, though if anyone asked, he wouldn't be able to tell them how he got there. Time had become distorted and Nevinon could focus on only one thing. He got to the clearing he had seen while scrying, only to see Kal above his king, taunting him.

Kal laughed as he looked down at Alanor. "You're a worthless king and Amari will be better without you. You—"

Kal's speech cut off with a gurgle. Nevinon's magic had acted without direction, lifting Alanor's sword from the ground and thrusting it through Kal's middle. Kal collapsed to the ground. The traitor died quickly. It was more than he deserved.

Nevinon ran and knelt by Alanor's side. He pressed down on his king's wounds, warm blood reddening his hands. He knew from experience that Alanor had lost too much blood. The metallic smell reminiscent of rust hit him like a punch in the gut.

Alanor grunted in pain. "So tell me, with all of that magic you have, is there anything you can do to fix this?"

Nevinon shook his head and gave a bitter laugh. "I told you before. I'm shit at healing magic." He also didn't have his physician's tools with him. Alanor was bleeding out fast.

Alanor gave a shallow huff. "Only you, Nev."

"We need to get you back to camp immediately."

Alanor shook his head. "It's too far away, I'll never make it there. If your magic can't heal me, then nothing else will be able to either."

Nevinon looked around frantically for anyone nearby who

could help. But they were alone, and help was too far away. He took a deep breath and held his hands over the wound, pushing his magic into Alan's body. It didn't work. It didn't look like the magic had done anything other than exhaust Nevinon further. His vision became blurry and he could barely pull in a breath. His tears rained down on Alan's face, and his king sent him a pitying look.

"I can't—I can't do anything. I can't fix this."

Alan placed a hand over his. "It's alright, Nev, it's alright. You saved us. You saved Amari and my people." Alan looked over at Kal's body. "It's over. You've ended it."

"But what about you, sire?" Nevinon cried.

"Don't go referring to me by my title now." Alanor smiled then coughed. "If it's my time then it's my time. I'm glad I gave my life to protect my kingdom."

Alanor closed his eyes. The warlock shook him awake. "No, stay with me, Alan." Nevinon tried another healing spell to no avail.

"You'll tell my wife—tell her I love her," the king mumbled.

"You'll tell her yourself when you get back to the citadel."

Alanor pressed something into his hand. "Take it."

Nevinon looked down to see that Alanor had given him his king's seal. "No, Alan, please, there must be some way to fix this. I'm not ready for you to die. There's so much I haven't told you. So much I haven't said. You can't leave me."

Alanor opened his eyes slightly and raised a hand to hold the back of Nevinon's head, "You've been the greatest friend I could have ever asked for." Alanor turned his head to look him in the eyes. A tear ran down his face before his eyes went cold and lifeless, and the hand that had been holding Nevinon fell to the ground.

"No!" Nevinon shook Alan, but the man was so obviously dead that Nevinon gasped in shock and closed his eyes, bending over to press his face against Alanor's chest. Nevinon screamed, and sobbed, and begged, but Alanor did not—would not, could not—come back.

"Please," he shouted to the sky, begging for any god to listen. "This can't be happening. I—"

The sky became cloudy and dark. Lightning flashed and rain began to pour. For a second Nevinon thought his pleas were being answered, but it took only a few moments to realize that the storm was being caused by his own magic, his grief manifesting physically. Nevinon sobbed even more and cradled Alanor's body to him, groaning in pain like a wounded animal. His magic could destroy armies but not perform a single healing spell. Perhaps magic was only meant for destruction after all. Maybe it did corrupt. He never got to tell Alanor, tell him the most important secret of all.

He had failed his king.

Genevive watched from the side of the courtyard as the knights began to pour back into the citadel. Nevinon hadn't arrived yet so the lower town's physician had stepped in and they were making do with the supplies on hand. They had set up several medical tents and cots to attend to the wounded as they came into the city. She spotted Sir Theodore at the same time that he saw her. She rushed toward him.

"Is Alanor with you?" she asked. "I haven't seen him. Or heard any news. I haven't seen Nevinon either. I've been getting worried."

Theodore shook his head. "I lost sight of both of them shortly into the battle. I saw Nevinon at one point summon this crazy storm. The lightning struck down most of the hunters. The rest fled. The storm started up again as we were leaving the field. I didn't see Kal past the opening surge. Honestly, I hope the man was trampled."

The knight took off his cloak and wrapped it around her shoulders. She hadn't noticed how cold it had gotten until she felt the warmth of the wool.

Genevive was about to respond when her attention was distracted by some of the men who were carrying in Sir Solomon. The man seemed to be delirious. His leg was wounded and he was sobbing. The men laid him down on a cot nearby.

"What's happened?" Theodore knelt by the injured knight.

"They killed him. They—" Solomon choked out, closed his eyes, and shook his head.

Genevive felt a stone sink in her stomach. "Killed who?"

"Cass—" Solomon gasped for air. "They, one of the archers—and I couldn't stop it. They killed him." Solomon raised an arm over his face.

Genevive covered her mouth with a hand. Theodore grabbed Solomon's arm. Everyone knew that Solomon and Cassius had been more than friends, more than brothers in arms. The two men had kept it quiet but it was obvious to all who knew them.

"Sol," Theodore said, "did you see what happened to the others? To the king? To Nevinon?"

Solomon shook his head. The physician had finally approached and they backed up a few paces to let the man work on the injured knight.

"We need to arrange for another physician to come if Nevinon isn't here by nightfall. And we need to continue making space for the wounded," Genevive said.

"I'll send out the messengers to nearby towns to see if they can spare anyone with any skills that could help," Theodore said.

Genevive nodded to him and he walked away. She looked at the entrance of the courtyard once more, hoping that she would see her husband. She did not. But the queen could not afford to stand there just waiting for him. She went to approach the physician to see if there was anything she could do to help, and she hoped that her husband would return home soon.

Nevinon pushed the small boat out into the water. Alanor's body was lying in it. He had surrounded Alanor with as many flowers as he could pick from the shores of the lake. As the boat got farther and farther away, he used his magic to set it alight. It was the same funeral he had given Frederick and Moira. Wet tears trailed down his face. He didn't even bother to wipe them away. He had not stopped crying since Alanor had left him. Nevinon's mouth tasted of nothing but salt and blood.

With his blurry vision he looked down at the king's seal in his fingers. A golden medallion the size of his palm with Alanor's royal animal, the owl, on one side and the Amarian crest and Kovian family motto on the other. He let his fingers run over the motto, letting the words and their meaning come to mind. Familia quam omnia. Family above all.

"I swear I will find a way to make this right," Nevinon said. "I cannot live an eternity on my own. Not without you."

Lightning struck the statue of the goddess that lay at the top of the stairs to the temple. The high priestess climbed up the steep steps as carefully as she could, avoiding the water that was rushing down the stone staircase to the best of her ability. The rain had practically turned the hill into a waterfall. She put one hand on her silver coronet to keep it steady while the other hand held her skirts up as she climbed. She made it to the temple doors but did not stop to catch her breath before she pushed one of the doors open and nearly ran headfirst into the initiate who had called for her.

"High Priestess, thank goodness you've come. The oracle has come to. It seems as though she's ready to give a prophecy."

The young girl followed her into the main room of the temple. An open ceiling decorated with mosaics and held up by marble columns protected the inhabitants from the rain, yet still allowed the room to be somewhat exposed to the elements at the center. A feature of the temple that the high priestess lamented now as she tried to get warm despite being soaked to the bone. She would've cast a drying spell if she weren't too distracted and emotional to control the magic within her.

An elderly woman sat cross-legged on a strange chair near the front of the room, her head raised, her eyes glowing with a power that filled the room with white light. A middle-aged woman wearing the typical dress of a priestess rushed toward them. "Perhaps this is a false alarm, Your Eminence. The oracle has not given a prophecy since—"

"You did right to send for me anyway," the high priestess interrupted. "Is the scribe ready?"

The initiate nodded. "Yes. He is here. He went to prepare his supplies. I'll go get him." She left the room.

The high priestess approached the oracle and soon came close enough to hear her mumbling, though not close enough to understand what she was saying. The young girl came back, a man wearing a white tunic trailing behind her. The man bowed to the high priestess, saying quietly, "Your Eminence," before settling down at a nearby table with his quill and ink at the ready. They did not have to wait long.

The oracle spoke aloud in a raspy voice. "The King of Koshmar has been repelled but not defeated. Our victory is shallow and temporary. The shunvora will return." She took a long inhale and her eyes began to glow with golden light as she spoke her prophecy.

"The shunvora will rise.

The shunvora will rise and Alexsantari will burn,

When the godchild sets foot on Pithikarian soil."

The head oracle continued speaking the second half of her prophecy, three more lines, six in total, and with every word dread rose up within the occupants of the room. Eventually the oracle closed her eyes and dropped back into her dormant state.

"The godchild?" the priestess asked. "Does that mean what I think it means?"

"And the part about the shunvora coming back?" the scribe asked. "Pithikar was nearly destroyed last time. How will we be able to defeat them again? Especially without..." The man paused.

The high priestess took a shaky inhale. "The decision is clear. If there is ever a sign that a godchild has been born..." She trailed off in pained hesitation. "The birth of this child heralds the return of the shunvora and the godless, and only his death will bring peace. If born, this child must die before they enact the apocalypse." Even though they had also heard the prophecy the others gasped, but the high priestess nodded as if to convince herself as well as the others.

"For the good of Pithikar and all of its people. The godchild must die."

CHAPTER 3

THE REVENANTS

Nevinon looked up at the full moon. It had taken much to discover the ritual he was going to perform that night. He had searched through all of the kingdoms in the Isles, or what was left of them anyway, from shore to shore. Searching for a way to end this miserable life. The only thing that kept him from sailing to the mainland and searching for answers there was the fact that he could not bear to leave the land where his family had lived and died.

He hadn't aged a day. He had no idea why he had been cursed in such a way. He had tried so many times to end it, in so many ways. Others had tried as well. But any wound he was inflicted healed within moments, and if he died it was only temporary. It tore at his soul. His magic kept on healing him from anything and everything, when at the most crucial moment it had failed to heal his king.

It was the most peculiar thing. He was no one of importance. Why had he been cursed in such a way? Sure he was powerful. He had never met anyone who could cast complicated magic without spells, spoken ones. But that was the only remarkable thing about him. He lived on, even though there was nothing to live on for.

Friends and family, gone. Amari, gone. And the Isles conquered by barbarians and witch hunters.

Nevinon had watched from the top of the hill as the last of the citadel burned to the ground. It was the first time he had returned to Amari after Alanor's death. He had managed to save only a small amount of gold and Kovian family heirlooms in the tunnels beneath the city before the invasion came. But Nevinon would not leave. Could not leave. Where would he go? What would he do? There was nothing in this world for him anymore. And the small whispers of an idea began to form in his mind. There had to be a way, any way, for him to circumvent his immortality and join his family across the Veil.

That idea had kept him going the last few decades. He had finally found the answer. Maybe. He had taken this ritual from a sorcerer employed by one of the barbarian kings. It was the darkest piece of magic Nevinon had encountered in a long while. A ritual that required blood magic as well as a living sacrifice. A ritual that would have been forbidden by the laws of his king. But his king was dead and so was not able to stop him.

The ritual was a bonding spell that would intertwine the lifelines of two or more people. It was often used to enslave servants and sorcerers alike. But Nevinon had another idea of how to use the spell.

What would happen if he were to perform the spell to connect his lifeline to the lifeline of his king? The ritual had never been attempted in that way. Hopefully, performing the ritual on himself would connect his lifeline to Alanor's, allowing himself the sweet mercy of death in the process.

For the ritual to work he had to wait for a night where the full moon coincided with Samhain, when the Veil between worlds was thinnest. But he did not have a problem with waiting.

For his living sacrifice he had chosen an owl that he had captured from the local forest. The ritual had to be performed in a place of increased magical energy. He had chosen the shores of the lake where he had said goodbye to all of his friends. The place had been imbued with his own magic through decades of his grief-induced outbursts.

He left behind all of his belongings at his camp, a bit away from the lake. Not that it mattered anyway. He wouldn't be able to take anything material with him across the Veil. As the full moon rose above the horizon, he killed the owl, wincing and thanking it for its sacrifice. He drew a ritual circle decorated with runes that had taken him years to develop on the ground in blood and stepped inside.

All that was left was to wait for the moon to hit its highest peak before starting the chant that would hopefully bring him eternal rest. It had taken him years to translate the words he had stolen from the library of the barbarian sorcerer. Even longer to figure out how to pronounce them.

When the moon was finally at its pinnacle, Nevinon began to chant the words of the spell. Though the words were spoken in a foreign language, he could feel their meaning in his soul.

Let these souls be bound forevermore.

The circle he had drawn started to glow and a wall of magical energy rose from it, separating him from the outside world with a barrier. At this point, the ritual called for the use of an item of extreme value and high energy belonging to the captor. The item would be coated in the blood of the prisoner, binding them to the captor's lifeline.

Nevinon was trying to bind his lifeline to Alanor's, so the ritual would require something important that belonged to his king. The only thing of enough importance was Alan's king's seal. A seal was supposed to be entombed with its king in the royal catacombs, but Nevinon could never part with it, and he had given Alanor a water burial anyway.

With a knife he had cleansed he made a careless cut on his hand, ignoring the pain, and coated the seal with his own blood. The cut healed. Nevinon smiled. He would not be healing for much longer.

He repeated the ritualistic words a second time. And then a

third time. It was enough. He felt a tug at his magic. The surge of energy that overwhelmed him was enough to bring him to his knees. The seal began to glow.

"Nevinon, stop this."

A voice called to him from beyond the barrier of the ritual circle. He looked up and scrambled backward in shock at the sight of his mother standing on the shores of the lake before him.

"Mom? How are you here? It's true then. You're dead. How did you die?"

"It's more complicated than that." His mother shook her head. "You must stop this ritual. You have no idea what you are doing."

"If you're here, then that means it's working. The spell is reaching across the Veil."

"Nevinon, stop this," she repeated.

"No," he refused. "I won't continue on like this. I can't. Why have I been cursed with immortality when all of my friends, my family, have perished? Do I not deserve to rest as much as they do? Do I not deserve to see them again? What have I done to deserve this endless torment?"

"You have done nothing wrong, my son," she sighed. "But you meddle with powers that you do not understand. There are circumstances that you are not aware of. Your actions will have consequences and those consequences will be vast."

"So be it," he said.

His mother vanished before his eyes and the magic around him surged once more. He was knocked to the ground, winded. When he stood up the barrier of magic around him had disappeared and so had the ritual circle that he had drawn on the ground. The full moon had come down from its pinnacle and had begun its journey to set. And yet he was still here. Still breathing. Still alive. He took the ritual knife and stabbed it through his palm viciously.

It healed.

"No!" he screamed. He threw the knife into the shallow water and screamed again before he collapsed to the ground. His ritual had failed. Nevinon curled up and began to sob. He had truly been cursed to live an eternity by himself, away from those he loved most. Surely the gods hated him, though he had no idea what he had done to offend them so. The exhaustion from using so much magic was catching up with him. With tears on his face, Nevinon sunk into oblivion.

WHEN ALANOR TOOK in his last breath, the last thing he was expecting was to breathe in again and choke on the water that surrounded him. He saw a light above him through the water and kicked upward. He broke through the surface and took in a big gasp of air. Around him he could hear the same sounds of gasping and coughing. He swam forward until he could stand up in the water, with his feet sinking slightly into the muck at the bottom of what he could clearly now see was a lake. The place felt familiar although not immediately recognizable. Had he been here before?

How the hell was he even still alive? He certainly remembered dying just a few moments ago. Checking his side, he noticed that he didn't even have a wound anymore. Not even a scar. In fact, he was missing quite a few scars.

He lifted his head and took in a sharp inhale at the sight of his closest friends around him. They were all standing in the middle of a lake without clothes. He paused when he saw Frederick and Moira. Moira had died only a year ago. Freddie had died nearly a decade ago though, when he had still been a prince.

"Alanor!" a voice cried from the shore. He looked up to see Nevinon rushing into the shallow water. The other man reached him and embraced him. "Is this a dream?"

"Nevinon? What's going on?" Alanor looked around. "Is this where we had Moira's funeral? You found a way to heal me."

"No, I—" Nevinon glanced at the others.

Alanor spotted his wife to the left. She was submerged in the water up to her neck, like Moira beside her, and was speaking with Theodore in quiet tones. Solomon and Cassius had collapsed into the water in a pile of limbs as they embraced and made out with no regards for their audience. Alanor looked away quickly. Moira spotted them and drew nearer, though she avoided his gaze.

"Nev?"

"Mimi." The warlock reached out for her and the old friends hugged. Nevinon seemed to realize that Moira was as naked as the men and he blushed as their hug ended. Moira smirked at the sorcerer—no, warlock.

"We're not supposed to be here, Nev, I can feel it. What happened?"

"I—I don't know. I don't understand what's happening either," Nevinon stuttered.

Alanor was distracted briefly by a shout from Cassius. "Where the hell are my earrings? And my tattoos? Those cost a fortune!"

Then Alanor looked away as Frederick approached and he felt his heart squeeze at the sight of him, whole and healthy and not covered in blood. The man spoke once he was within earshot. "The last thing I remember is stepping in front of an arrow meant for you, sire." Alanor still had nightmares of that day. Of course he wasn't supposed to have a favorite knight. But everyone knew that he did. He clasped Freddie's forearm and felt the man squeeze his arm in return.

"It seems that we've come back to life," Theodore answered as he came forward. "It's good to see you, Freddie." He turned to Alanor. "We were all dead."

"The final battle," Alanor breathed. "Don't tell me—"

"No, we won the battle," Genevive interrupted. "But the only ones to survive were Theo and I... Oh, and Sol." She threw a sad look at Solomon, who was standing next to Cassius. The dark-skinned man had his hands tangled in Cassius's long brown hair. He nodded to the others.

"But we died eventually," Theodore said. "The last of us to die was Genevive."

"I didn't last long after your death," she said to Theodore. "Only a few months." She turned toward Nevinon and Alanor. "We searched for the two of you though. Neither of you came back. Eventually it was obvious that you weren't able to."

Alanor turned to Nevinon. "Did something happen after I—?"

Nevinon shook his head. "I never went back. I couldn't."

"Final battle? Seems like I missed a lot." Freddie frowned. "So we were dead? And now we're back?"

"Sure looks that way," Cassius laughed. "Look, I'd love to stand here in the buff and keep chatting about our deaths, but this water is freezing my bollocks off."

Alanor glared at the man. "There are ladies present!"

"What, like they've never seen a man's bits before?" Cassius shrugged.

Moira raised her hand, smirking. "I haven't."

The shameless knight smiled at her. "Well, would you like to?"

"Cassius!" Alanor scolded.

Moira laughed. "I don't think your man would like that very much." She gestured at Solomon.

"Oh, what, this fellow?" Cassius placed a hand on Solomon's chest. "I'm sure he wouldn't mind, right, Sol?"

Solomon smiled and shrugged. Cassius went to kiss the other knight but yelped and jumped. "Ah! Something touched me. There's something in the water—it's a monster!"

"It was just a fish, dear," Solomon said quietly.

"Oh," Cassius said. The group shared a laugh at his expense.

Cassius stuck his tongue out at the others. "Oi, don't judge me for being suspicious when I wake up naked in some creepy lake after supposedly dying. I don't even recognize this place—where are we?"

"This is where some of you were buried," Nevinon answered.

"Oh wow, thank you, Nev. That makes it much less creepy."

Cassius rested one hand on his hip and the other on Solomon's shoulder.

Nevinon shook his head at his friend's antics then spoke to Alanor. "We really should get out of this water. The last thing we need is for you to get hypothermia."

Alanor nodded but then paused, glancing over at the two women in their group. "I don't suppose you have clothes for all of us?"

Nevinon blushed again. "Um, I think I might have some clothing at my camp, but not enough for all of us. Though there is a town nearby. Stay here and I'll come back with enough clothes for everyone."

"What happened to not getting hypothermia?" Freddie asked.

Nevinon smiled and spoke a spell at the water of the lake. Alanor startled as the cold water turned warm within a few breaths. Alanor relaxed into the water, not having realized how cold he had been. Nevinon seemed reluctant to leave his side but nodded to Alanor. "I'll be back as quickly as possible." The warlock disappeared behind the tree line but not without sending a thousand glances backward.

"No, seriously," Cassius said again. "Is anyone else missing scars?"

†

Nevinon had brought the group back to his camp once he had procured clothes for everyone at the nearby village, mostly through theft, but they didn't need to know that. He wondered what he was going to tell them, about the ritual, about himself. He had promised to never lie to Alanor again, but the thought of his king looking at him like he was some kind of freak or creature made it impossible for him to open his mouth and speak of his immortality.

The group had come back in the middle of the day, around the same time he had woken up on the shore. Nevinon had fallen unconscious, drowning in his sorrows, and had awoken to the sounds of his family having returned to the land of the living. Nevinon felt his heart squeeze. It was too good to be true. What would be the price for this? Either way, Nevinon would pay it gladly.

Once the others were huddled around the campfire, clothed in miscellaneous garments, it was getting dark again. The others had begun to ask Genevive and Theodore about what happened after the battle at Bergen Pass, since they had seemingly lived the longest. Aside from Nevinon, that was, but he wasn't going to say so.

Theodore laid a hand on Alanor's shoulder. "The civil war weakened us. Even by the time I had died, the barbarians from the north were already preparing for invasion. The witch hunters that were left allied with them. We lived for several decades past the battle. We were both in our sixties when we died."

"You look quite dashing for a sixty-year-old man." Cassius winked at him.

"Thanks, Cass," Theodore laughed. "We do all seem to have regressed back into our early twenties if I had to guess. Certainly younger than when we died." There were a few nods of agreement from the group. Theodore turned toward Nevinon. "I understand why you never came back. But what happened? Where did you go?"

"I—" Nevinon hesitated. "I was around. I went back to my hometown for a little while." He wondered what he would say about dying, or his lack thereof. He had obviously lived past Evie and Theo, but to outlive them by a lot would be suspicious. "I think I outlived the two of you. I was there to see it happen. The sack of Amari. The barbarians burned the kingdom to the ground. Not that there was much left. Not even the people. Those cowards abandoned the citadel."

"That's not possible," Alanor said.

"I'm so sorry, Alan. I was only able to save very little by hiding it in the tunnels. Everything else was taken or destroyed."

"And you?" Cassius looked at Nevinon with a furrowed brow. "What happened to you? How did you survive this barbarian invasion? Did—did you die like the rest of us?"

"If he died, why would he have a camp here?" Solomon pointed out in a muted tone.

The camp. How was he going to explain the camp? He opened his mouth, not knowing what he was going to say.

"I died shortly after the invasion happened but I came back before you all did. Maybe by a few days. I was making my way to the lake since...this is where I gave Alanor a funeral. Moira and Freddie were also buried there."

"Not just them." Genevive started. "After the battle, we gave Cassius his funeral at the lake and we both decided we wanted to be put to rest here as well." She nodded at Theodore.

"How long has it been then?" Alanor asked.

"As far as I can tell"—Nevinon could barely look his king in the eyes—"it's been about a century since you died." That was the only way Nevinon had measured time.

There was silence again as the group took in the new information and waited for their king's response. "I need to see it. I'm sorry, Nev, but I just can't believe it. We need to get to the citadel to see what has been done."

Nevinon nodded. "We are still within our borders. The citadel is only a few days' trip away."

"Then that is where we will go next," Alanor said. "I'm not saying that I don't believe you, Nevinon. You know I trust you." The words cut like a knife. "But if Moira and Frederick weren't standing beside us today I would wonder if you were enchanted or something. Dead for a century? But I remember being alive only moments ago." Alanor shook his head.

Genevive spoke up from where she was sitting at Moira's side. "If we're going to start traveling on foot to the citadel tomorrow, we need to get some sleep tonight."

The others agreed and began to make preparations to hunker down, but as Nevinon went to help the others he felt a hand on his arm. He looked up to see Freddie standing next to him with a smile, and the knight pulled him aside from the group. Nevinon hugged the other man who had, up until the day he died, been his closest friend. Freddie had even been the first person he had told about his magic, and the other man had taken that secret to the grave.

While they were hugging, Freddie whispered to him, "Was there anything you didn't tell the others? I noticed you were looking down the entire time you were talking about dying." Nevinon sighed. Freddie always could see right through him. They separated but stood closely.

Nevinon checked to make sure the others weren't listening before blurting out the truth, "I didn't really die."

"What do you mean?" Freddie asked.

"I mean I never died at all."

"You've been alive this whole time? A century? On your own?" Nevinon could hear the worry in his voice and it warmed him to know that Freddie would always look out for him.

He tried to fight back tears as he nodded. "Yeah."

"Oh, Nev, I'm so sorry." The knight gripped his arms. "You shouldn't have had to be alone. Do you know why we came back?"

"I think that was my fault," Nevinon whispered. "I performed a ritual last night. But I wasn't trying to bring everyone back, I was trying to—"

"Trying to what?" Freddie asked.

"Trying to—" Nevinon hesitated. "Trying to...join you all."

It took a few moments for the meaning to sink in for the other man, but Nevinon knew when he realized what that had meant, because Freddie immediately brought him into an even tighter hug. When was the last time he had been held like this?

"Do you still feel that way?" Freddie asked.

"No." Nevinon gave a sad smile. "Not now that I have you all here with me."

"Good." Freddie pulled back slightly. "You come tell me right away if that changes."

"Oi!" They recognized Cassius calling to them as he approached the pair. "Stop hogging my favorite sorcerer."

"Warlock," they both corrected him.

"Sure, warlock." Cassius nodded and gave a sly smile. "Mind showing us some more magic?"

Nevinon laughed and led them back toward the others. "Not right now, Cass. It's bedtime for wayward knights." As they lay down that night, Nevinon looked up at the stars and wondered how he had found himself back in his original situation, keeping something massive from Alanor. He wondered what the look on the other man's face would be when he discovered the truth. It took a long time for Nevinon to fall into a fitful sleep that night, despite the fact that for the first time in a century he wasn't alone.

The being floating in a void of writhing darkness took a deep breath in and opened his eyes. Something had woken him. And the creatures around him. Something was tugging at him. There was a light in the darkness. He moved toward it, then pushed through it. With a groan of pain, he found himself on the ground. As he got up he realized what had happened.

Something, or someone, had set him free. He smiled at the night sky, and his smile grew wider when he realized that he had brought a small horde with him. Now he would have his vengeance. What a lovely birthday surprise for him and his master.

"Friends, let us begin our feast!" the man called out. "I know exactly where we can start."

He was answered by the maniacal laughing and yipping of the creatures that swirled around him. He told them the location of the place he wanted them to take him. He felt a tug and a moment of freezing cold and then he was standing in the middle of a room surrounded by men. He did not know their names, but he recognized them. The shadow creatures circled above them toward the ceiling. The men had raised their weapons.

"Who are you?" one of them called. "How did you enter this place, sorcerer?"

"I am no sorcerer." He glanced at the man's crossbow. "I wouldn't try that if I were you. We're on the same side."

"You're an intruder and you're obviously using enchantments. Why shouldn't I kill you?"

The horde above him began to laugh and shout in joy and anticipation. He joined them and gave the man a vicious smile. "Because I know how to rid this world of the plague that magic brings. Permanently."

CHAPTER 4

THE TOMBS

We feast...we feast.
   Find them. Hunt them. We feast.
Kill. Kill! KILL!

Nevinon gasped awake and shivered at the slimy feeling that the nightmare had left him with. Although it didn't feel like a regular nightmare. This one had felt real. And those voices... There were few things that scared him after all of these years. He had a bad feeling that he had just found another thing to add to the list.

He shook his head as the feeling of fear dissipated. Maybe it was just a side effect of the ritual or all of the emotions he felt yesterday seeing everyone alive again. He wasn't going to be able to sleep anymore so he stood up and got started on breakfast. He still had some food saved, though it would run out much quicker now. He could have it ready before the others awoke. It was only a few moments later that Alanor joined him.

He could feel the guilt drowning him from the inside. "I'm sorry."

Alanor stared at him for a while. "What are you sorry for?"

Nevinon paused, staring at the cooking food. "For not being able to save you during the battle. There's nothing that I haven't regretted as much as that. I should have been able to do it. If I had then maybe none of this would have happened."

"I don't exactly know what this is, Nev. I'm not sure what's happened to us."

"Me neither." The guilt was a rope, wrapping itself around his neck like a noose.

They were silent for a time before Alanor spoke. "You don't have to be sorry about anything. In fact, I should be thanking you. In those last moments I was afraid that I would die before that traitor. That I would leave my family to face him alone. That he would be free to wreak havoc upon my kingdom. Because of you, before I died I was able to see his betrayal punished. And I died in your arms. It was the best death I could've ever had. I'm glad you were there instead of someone else."

"I tried to do what you wanted of me. I tried so hard to protect Amari. But without you the project seemed futile. I couldn't go back. There is no Amari without you." Nevinon's voice became nearly indecipherable. "There is no life without you."

"Oh, Nev." Alanor reached out to grab Nevinon's shoulder. "I know it must have been hard but—"

Nevinon shrugged off his hand. "No, you have no idea what it was like. No one else understands me like you. Knows me like you. Theodore, Genevive, and Solomon were the only others left after the battle. I knew they had each other and I had no one, so I never returned. I tried to keep your memory alive. I wore nothing but black for years. But everyone moved on without you. And without me. So no, Alanor, you have no idea what it's been like to live this long completely alone."

"How long have you lived?"

"What?"

"You say that it has been a century since I died. When did you die exactly? How long ago?"

Nevinon forced himself to not look away the way that he

usually did before telling a lie. It seemed his efforts were meaning-less though.

"The truth, Nevinon."

He hesitated. "I didn't mean to say all of that before."

"I know you didn't mean for me to learn your secrets."

Nevinon looked at Alanor for a long time. "I'm sorry." He looked down at his hands.

Alanor sighed, "I know you are. I just wish you didn't have to lie all the time."

"Me too," he whispered. "I'm trying my best."

Alanor nodded and reached out to place an arm over Nevinon's shoulders, pulling the warlock to his side. "I know, I know. Let's just focus on getting to the citadel for now."

By the time the food had finished cooking, filling the campsite with a savory scent, the others were awake and preparing themselves for the long trek ahead. Nevinon served the others breakfast and felt the noose around his neck loosen just a little.

After eating breakfast, and assuring Nevinon that he would be careful half a million times, Alanor was able to split apart from the group. In other circumstances he would be hesitant to have the group spread out but the last time he had seen his wife had been before the battle when he had assured her that he would come home. Only for him to fail to fulfill his promise.

Genevive had been helping the others pack up camp when Alanor asked if he could speak with her. They moved a little ways into the woods so they would not be overheard.

"Evie, I'm so glad you're alright. I'm sorry I wasn't able to come home." Alanor leaned in to kiss his wife, but she leaned away.

"Alan, I—I can't." She shook her head.

Alanor froze. "What do you mean you can't?"

"The last time I saw you was at least forty years ago. You can't just pretend like nothing has changed."

He shook his head. "Nothing's changed for me. I still love you. You're my wife."

"I *was* your wife."

Alanor took a step back and swallowed. "Is marriage not supposed to be forever?"

"Until death do us part." She nodded. "But death did us part." Evie put her hand up to stop any response. "We should get back to camp."

She walked away leaving Alanor baffled. What had changed? Was it because they were all alive now? Amongst the group was Freddie, who had been Evie's first love. Perhaps now that they were all back, she wanted a chance with him? He did not get to ponder it further before he was interrupted.

"Don't fret, Dollface. If you're looking for a kiss, you can always get one from me." Cassius leaned up against a tree and winked at him.

Alanor scoffed and shook his head. "Shut up, Cass."

"What?" Cassius shrugged. "It was a valid offer."

"Yes, and I'm sure Solomon will accept that as an excuse when he comes to rip out my spine for touching his partner."

"Oh, you know Solomon's alright with me flirting."

"He'd have to be, considering that it's half of your personality." Alanor smiled at him.

"Oi, I resent that."

They shared a laugh before the atmosphere turned serious.

Alanor observed his knight. "So what do you make of this? Us dying at different times and coming back. Nevinon's explanation. Do you really think it has been a century? The forest around us doesn't look that much changed."

"You're not saying that you don't trust Nev, are you?"

"Well, he has a tendency to lie. Do you blame me?"

"He wouldn't. You know he wouldn't. Not about Amari."

Alanor conceded the point. "Maybe not, but still. All I

remember is the final battle against the traitor. But Theo and Evie both say that they lived past that."

"Well, I certainly believe them. Theo is as uptight as they come, same with Evie, there's no way that they're lying."

"What about you?"

"What about me?"

Alanor rolled his eyes. "The others said you didn't survive the battle?"

"Yup. I'm told that I died shortly before you did."

"Oh." Alanor didn't really know what to say. "I'm sorry, Cass."

"I'm only sorry for Sol's sake." Cassius looked at him curiously. "Why are you sorry?"

"It was my job to protect all of you and I failed."

"Don't be stupid. It was our job to fight the enemy and protect Amari. We did that."

Alanor looked down and kicked a small rock. "I'm not so sure we did. If Nev is right about Amari being invaded and destroyed."

"As far as I'm concerned, anything that happened after my death has nothing to do with me."

"I certainly disagree."

Cassius shrugged. "Look, don't get all guilty on us yet, Doll-face. We still have to get to the citadel to assess the damage."

"Very well."

The two knights made it back to camp where the others were still packing. As he approached, he paused when he saw Frederick by Genevive's side. The man with tan skin, tanner than his, and curly black hair to Alanor's straight blond locks. Frederick, who had been Genevive's sweetheart in their youth before he died tragically. Alanor shook his head and ignored the pit in his stomach. He would not let something like this distract him from leading the group home.

They left the camp during the morning hours and started to walk toward the citadel. On horseback they could have made the trip in a single day but on foot it would take longer, three days at minimum. While they were certainly familiar with their surroundings, they were not familiar with the current enemies of the time so they were all being extremely cautious.

Cassius was entertaining them as always with a tale of one of his epic conquests. "The beast was almost as tall as the tallest trees in the forest, and wider than this clearing here, and it had the wings of a demon!"

"Oh, please," Alanor laughed. "It was barely the size of a horse."

Cassius smiled at him. "You're just jealous because you got knocked out early on in the fight, Dollface."

Alanor shook his head and the group continued walking.

IT WAS the night before they would reach Amari's citadel. The group made camp again and Alanor took first watch. A few minutes in he heard a rustling of cloth behind him. He looked up to see Moira brush some dirt off her dress before she sat down next to him. It was strange to see her in such ordinary clothing. Back in Amari her dresses had always been high quality and bold, her wardrobe full of jewels and embroidery and rich colors meant for the nobility. Her long black hair, falling in waves, had always been decorated with adornments. She had always complained that it took hours and the help of several maidservants to style her hair.

Now his sister in all but blood was sitting next to him in nothing but a simple beige dress, the kind that a peasant would wear, and her hair was already starting to show tangles despite her efforts to tame it that morning. Though he was thankful that he did not have to deal with hair as long as hers, he could relate to the unfamiliarity of the clothing he was wearing. There had been several times in his youth where he had dressed himself as a peasant in order to traipse through the lower town without being gawked at, or worse, having the people avoid him out of fear. He hadn't done so since he'd been crowned king.

They sat together in silence for a while before Moira looked at him. "So"—she nudged him—"what do you think we're going to find at the citadel tomorrow?"

He took a deep breath and stared out into the woods. "I don't know. Nevinon says that the citadel was abandoned and later invaded and destroyed. But when I think of the citadel I can only see it the way that I left it. There's a small part of me that's hoping that it's all a joke, but I can see in Nevinon's face that it's not, and that scares me."

She nodded. "I don't even know how we're here right now. When I—" She paused and looked down. "Well, I wasn't expecting to wake up again. And certainly not naked in the middle of a lake."

He laughed. "Neither was I, that's for sure."

Moira smiled at him before her face grew serious. "So, the others have been talking. From what I gather there was a civil war between you and the head of the witch hunters? How did that come about? I thought you were just as against magic as your father."

Alanor looked at her. "I was. Until..."

"Until what?" she asked.

"Until I woke up to find my sister dead in her room because she could not bring herself to tell me she had magic." He swallowed. "And then Nevinon... There was a skirmish with Kal and his men. We were outnumbered and about to be killed when Nevinon just blasted them all away with magic."

Moira looked away. "I had no idea that Nevinon was also magic back then. But I could feel it when we came back just for a few moments when we were standing in that lake. His magic was...intense."

"Mimi..." He hadn't called her that since they had been children. "Why did you not tell me?" he asked. "You and Nevinon both. Did you really think that I could sentence you to die? Am I really so untrustworthy?"

Moira didn't respond, but the look she sent him told him everything.

"You did expect me to have you executed." He sighed. "How could you think that of me? We grew up together. We're family."

"How was I supposed to know? You never showed any signs of being sympathetic with magic users."

Alanor stood up. "Well, maybe that's because all of the sorcerers that I've met have tried to kill me and apparently all of the magic users that were trying to help me were lying to my face every day."

Moira stood up too. "Have you ever thought that maybe the fact that magic was illegal was the cause of that?" She shook her head. "I wish I could have had the courage to tell you about my magic, but I had no reason to think you would do anything other than sentence me to the death of a sorcerer."

Alanor felt the fight leave his body, and he slumped back down against the tree he had been sitting in front of. Moira followed suit and both of them sat in silence for a while.

"When did you even discover that you had magic?" Alanor asked.

"Oh." She laughed. "I started setting random things on fire when I got angry. And you know about my nightmares. It got pretty obvious after that. It was only a few years before Octavian died." She turned away slightly. Speaking of Octavian was a rough subject for many, Alanor knew. His father had been a very strict man and he had been quite feared by his people. Alanor loved his father despite his many flaws, but he had sworn the moment he had been crowned that he would never give the people any reason to be so afraid of him. Apparently he had failed in that as well.

"That was around the time we stopped speaking to each other," he realized.

Moira nodded. "I was trying to distance myself from you and him. I was trying to wait until you became king, hoping that maybe then things would change. But then you were crowned and nothing changed. I didn't want to live the rest of my life in fear"—she shrugged—"so I decided to take matters into my own hands. I mean, if I was going to die anyway..."

Alanor took a breath. "I wish you hadn't felt that way."

"Yeah, me too," she whispered. After a while she stood up again. "I should let you get back to your watch."

Alanor nodded awkwardly and Moira turned to make her way back into camp. He wanted nothing more than to go back in time and make things right again. Everything had gone so wrong, so fast, back then. First his father had died, then Moira, and by trying to lessen the restrictions on magic in honor of her passing it had caused only more war and strife and eventually his own death. Alanor sat there for many hours until his watch was over, thinking over all the different things he could have done that would not have led his kingdom to eventual ruin.

THE GROUP STARED out in shock at the sight that awaited them at the citadel. If it could even be called a citadel anymore. They were standing on a hill that overlooked the walled city. It had always been one of Alanor's favorite places. As a boy and all throughout his adulthood he would return over and over again to this hill to overlook his kingdom. The sight always filled him with pride and a desire to do right by his people. Now all he felt was a crawling feeling over his skin and a sinking pit in his stomach.

Due to the shocked silence, he assumed the others were just as disturbed. There was not much of the city that hadn't been destroyed. The surrounding walls were all broken down completely. The towers had all fallen. In the lower town where the peasants had lived, the wooden houses were all gone. Everything had been burned to the ground.

How could this have happened? He was at a complete loss. His home was completely gone. He startled when Nevinon began to speak.

"When the barbarians came the first thing they did was set fire to everything they could. They used their catapults to destroy the rest." Nevinon stared at the ground.

Freddie spoke up. "Nev, you said that you managed to save some things. Underneath the city in the tunnels?"

Nevinon nodded. "We should be able to make it to the siege tunnels safely if nothing has changed since I've been gone. The last time I checked, the entrance to the dungeon through the main hall was still intact. I layered that part of the castle with as many protection spells as I could. We'll have to pass through the dungeons and then the tombs. I sealed off all of the other entrances."

"Right." Alanor managed to scramble up some semblance of calm. "We'll make our way into the siege tunnels to recover everything that Nevinon was able to save. Then we'll make camp a little ways into the forest. We'll decide what to do once we figure out how much is left from what we had."

Nevinon looked to the side. "I can tell you right now it's not much. Certainly not enough to do something like rebuild the citadel. I—if I had known—I would have done something more to prepare for this."

"Not sure how you would've known we'd all be coming back to life." Cassius shoulder-bumped Nevinon. "Should we all go?"

"Yes," Alanor said. "I don't want us splitting up just yet. Not before we know it's safe. Nevinon, can you lead us there?"

The warlock nodded and the group began to make their way toward the abandoned city. The tunnels were hard to get to. They were able to make it into the courtyard without a problem, but the entrance to the main hall was covered by debris. Nevinon and Moira used their magic to move the debris out of the way, though it seemed the warlock was more practiced. Both of them were winded for a few moments after using their magic. After they had recovered, the group continued. Once they were in the main hall they headed to the dungeons off to the left. Nevinon's protection spells had prevented the tunnels from collapsing. They encountered no more debris as they descended the stairs.

Once they passed the dungeons they started down a narrow staircase down into the royal tombs. Alanor froze before he could pass the entrance. The last time he had been here was before the last battle.

"Alanor, we should get going. It'll take a bit longer to get into the tunnels and we don't want to be walking around here after sundown. We should—" Nevinon was interrupted by a thumping noise. They all paused. The noise came again, louder this time and accompanied by what seemed like muffled screaming. Theodore held out the torch to illuminate the entryway.

"Um," Cassius whispered, "what's down there?"

"The royal catacombs," Alanor said.

"That's...ominous." Cassius leaned to peek over Alanor's shoulder. "This better not be like that time we faced the undead in the forest of Risvall."

"Let's hope," Theodore said before taking a few steps into the cavernous room.

"Is there no other way to the tunnels?" Freddie asked. Nevinon shook his head in response. The group made their way forward slowly as the noises became louder. When they finally found the source of the noise, they all took a step back in a mix of fear and shock. The noise was coming from inside his father's tomb.

CHAPTER 5

THE RESURRECTION

The voice from inside the tomb was too muffled to recognize. The cry for help came again, and Alanor moved forward to push the stone cover off. The knights approached to help him and together they managed it. Alanor was the only one who did not back away in fear when the tomb was open. Instead he stared on, his mouth open in shock as Octavian Kova, his father, sat up, healthy and whole, and gasped in relief.

"Dear gods," his father wheezed. "For a moment I thought I would perish in my own tomb." The man looked around and seemed to recognize Alanor, Moira, and Theodore, but his eyebrows scrunched together as he regarded the other knights. "I don't recognize the rest of you."

"Holy shit," Cassius cursed. The knight turned to audibly whisper to Theodore, "Is that the previous king?" Theodore nodded but didn't say a word.

After taking in big gulps of air, his father looked up at the group again before focusing on him. "Alanor?"

"F-father?" He cursed himself for stuttering.

"What happened? All I remember was the attack... We were drugged, no, poisoned... I couldn't fight back." His father shook his head and raised a hand to his forehead as if to stave off a headache.

"You did fight back," Alanor said in a quiet voice. "We were both attacked by the assassin, and we were too drugged to fight, but you...don't you remember?"

Octavian shook his head again. "Everything is blurry. But I remember you were in danger."

"The assassin came to attack me, to kill me, or perhaps the both of us, and you stepped in front of him. You killed the man but not before he—" Alanor choked, remembering how he caught his father as he fell, with a dagger protruding from his chest, and held the man in his arms as he died.

"I saved you," his father sighed in relief. "That's good."

"Good?" Alanor asked. "You died."

"Yes. It's obvious you thought so considering I woke up in my own tomb." The man stood up shakily. "Perhaps the drug that was given to me only made it seem like I died."

"Father..." Alanor trailed off. It was obvious that his father didn't know that time had continued on without him. It was just like what had happened to the rest of them when they had awoken in the lake. How was he going to break the news of their coming back to life? How was he going to tell the man that he had failed to protect the kingdom?

"How long ago did you wake up?" Nevinon asked.

"Who're you?" His father paused before nodding. "Oh yes, the physician's apprentice, no? I don't know. I wasn't able to tell. There's no light down here. Though it was definitely more than a day, perhaps two or three. I'm just glad you came to check. Any longer and I might've actually died." The man laughed as he got out of the tomb and said to Alanor, "The court will have to be notified of course. I'm sorry, my boy, but you'll have to wait a while longer for the throne."

Alanor felt himself tear up and he turned away but not before the other man could see. If only that had been the case so many years ago. What he would've done for this exact thing to have happened then. Maybe then everything wouldn't have gone to the dogs.

"What? What's wrong? I'm fine. I feel fine." His father hugged him.

"No, you don't understand. You died. In my arms, you bled out."

His father looked at himself. "But I feel fine. I don't have any wounds. Perhaps it was just an illusion."

Alanor shook his head but didn't say anything.

Nevinon spoke up. "You might want to look behind you."

"Behind me?" He turned. "At my—" Alanor saw the exact moment that his father noticed the second tomb. "What is this?" His father approached the other tomb, the one with Alanor's name, and ran his hand over the letters in much the same way that Alanor had his. The man turned back to the group. "What the hell is this?"

"It's been more than a few days since your death, sire," Theodore said.

His father swallowed. "How long?"

"More than a century," Nevinon answered.

"Excuse me?"

"It's a bit of a long story," Nevinon said.

"We were all dead and now we're not," Cassius said.

Freddie spoke then. "We're just trying to get our bearings. Amari was destroyed by invaders, sire. It's been a while since we died." He glanced at the warlock. "Nevinon was able to save some things in the siege tunnels."

His father looked curiously at Nevinon. Alanor didn't know how the man would react to Nevinon having magic, and he knew the warlock wouldn't be trying to hide it anymore. It was a clash waiting to happen. "We don't have the time to explain everything right now, Father. We need to leave by sundown. But before that we need to get to the siege tunnels."

His father started to say something but Alanor interrupted. "Please, Father, I will explain everything later."

The man hesitated and then nodded. "Very well then."

In order to move from the catacombs into the siege tunnels, they had to pass through a section of stone pathways that were quite risky to traverse. To their left was a ledge that had no railing and dropped off into a deep cavern that they could not see the bottom of. The faint sound of rushing water ensured a quick freezing death if any of them were to slip and fall over the edge. Even worse, the stone path had deteriorated over time, leaving many sections where they would have to jump over gaps. The path was so thin that they could only move in a single file line, with their shoulders brushing against the cavern wall.

Alanor led the way while Nevinon took up the rear in order to make sure he could catch anyone with his magic if they fell down. At one point Evie slipped, but Octavian managed to grab her before she fell. His father obviously recognized her as the girl he had taken a liking to when he had been a prince. The man had fought tirelessly against such a match. There was an awkward moment between the two before Evie nodded her thanks and continued walking.

Once they were in the tunnels it was only a little ways until they reached the section where Nevinon had managed to save some of their belongings. It was not much. Enough gold for bare necessities for only a short while. It certainly was not enough for all of them to live on for any significant period of time. Aside from that there were several other family heirlooms, such as his signet ring.

He looked at his father, and with a quick motion he offered the ring, but Octavian shook his head and looked away. Alanor tried not to feel happy and quickly slipped it onto his finger, feeling better already. There were several paintings and vases, which they decided to leave behind.

Out of the corner of his eye, he spotted Theodore and Genevive pocketing a couple of items that looked like gold coins from far away. Alanor wondered what they had taken. Maybe the two were making sure they had enough money for the supplies they needed? The group would have to go into a nearby town for those as soon as they could. In the far corner of the room, Nevinon called Alanor over and offered him a red box with a proud grin.

"Is that what I think it is?" he asked.

"Your king's crown." Nevinon nodded.

His father approached, looking over Alanor's shoulder curiously as Alanor opened the box. His crown had a simple design, a mostly smooth gold surface with a few jewels here and there. It was certainly much less ostentatious than his father's crown had been, though Alanor's was taller. The lessened weight allowed for more height.

"Oh!" Nevinon reached into his shirt and pulled out a medallion and handed it to him. It was his king's seal.

Octavian looked with wide eyes at Nevinon wearing his seal but covered the look quickly and motioned for the seal. Alanor showed it to him.

"An owl?" He hummed in thought before looking at Nevinon. "You wouldn't happen to have my king's seal? Or king's crown? I noticed the one I was entombed with wasn't the one I was coronated with."

"Oh." Alanor winced. "I had you entombed with the crown you wore most frequently toward the end. The one with more jewels than gold." He gave an awkward laugh. "I figured you would've preferred that one. I had never even seen your actual king's crown until..." He cleared his throat. "It seemed very simple compared to your other ones."

"Ah yes." His father nodded. "Amari wasn't in a great state when I conquered it. It was only after many decades of accumulating wealth for the kingdom that I felt it wouldn't anger the people to see me in such a crown. You were right to think I preferred it, but"—he frowned—"it is tradition to be buried with one's first crown. Regardless." Octavian shook his head. "You still have it, don't you?"

"Ah, well, um..." Nevinon threw him a pointed look.

Alanor hesitated. "See, the thing is." He cleared his throat. "I didn't have you buried in your king's crown because I... needed it."

His father gave him a shocked look. "You didn't use my king's crown, did you? That would've been an omen of the worst sort. You couldn't have."

"No, no, I didn't wear your king's crown, but I did have it, uh, repurposed, I suppose."

"What is that supposed to mean?" his father asked.

"Well..." Alanor held his own crown out for his father to examine.

After a bit, his father spoke. "The jewels. I recognize the same jewels from my king's crown."

Alanor nodded. "It's the same gold too, I—" Alanor hesitated. "Well, I had your king's crown melted and reforged into mine."

"You did what?" His father looked at him in horror. "That's —that's...I—" He shook his head. "I have no words."

Alanor quickly tried to explain himself. "It was supposed to be like a symbol of a kind, of a transformation. Like my crown was made from yours, as my reign came from your foundation." He cringed. "It was supposed to be...a metaphor."

"A metaphor?" his father asked.

"Well, I buried you in the crown you loved the most and I got to keep your king's crown to make my own. And you were dead, and this was a way to—to—"

"To what?"

Alanor tried to fight down the blush that was creeping up on his face. "To keep some of your guidance with me, or something, I don't know, look." Alanor took back his crown and returned it to the box and closed it. "What's done is done."

There was an awkward silence until it was broken by Nevinon. "Um, I did keep your king's seal...if it's any...consolation. And we should probably take your crown from your tomb. We need to be out of here soon."

"Who are you to tell me or my son what to do?" his father asked.

"I'm"—he paused to look at Alanor—"the physician."

"Oh." His father looked away. "I suppose Juniper passed?"

Nevinon swallowed and nodded and said in a rough voice, "Shortly after yourself..." He coughed where he should've said an honorific. His father didn't miss the lack, but didn't say anything about it.

"He was a close friend." His father looked at Nevinon closely. "He thought of you as a son."

"And I of him as a father," Nevinon whispered before taking a breath. "Anyway." He brought out another box, smaller this time, since it contained just the medallion. "Your king's seal."

The man took a breath and accepted the box. He opened it to examine his own seal. The Amarian crest on one side and his symbol, the eagle, on the other. His father took the medallion from the box and slid it over his head and underneath his shirt. Alanor did not follow suit. He had put on his signet ring, but something about wearing his king's seal now that Amari was gone felt wrong. Was he even still really king?

Alanor put away his cynical thoughts and focused on the task ahead. They packed up all the money and Alanor's crown and seal in a bag. Each of them, including the ladies, took swords as well as some daggers. Solomon grabbed a pair of crossbows, stating that they would be useful if they needed to hunt. Alanor noticed his father picking up an extra sword that was shorter and thinner than the rest.

In a short while they were back up in the courtyard. Without discussing it, they knew that they would have to decide what to do next. But first they needed to take care of necessities.

His father stared out in shock at the empty courtyard and the destroyed castle. He kept silent as the group moved out of the city, and Alanor worried that his father would have some sort of outburst before they were able to safely make camp. Once they reached the hill overlooking the citadel, his father finally spoke.

"It looks worse than it did after Vasilios sacked and conquered the city. It's...what happened here?" His father turned back toward the group.

Alanor sighed. "There was a civil war. We won the war eventually but Amari was weakened."

"Then barbarians invaded from the north," Theodore said. "They destroyed the city."

"A civil war?" Octavian looked at his son. "What caused it?"

Here was the moment of truth. Alanor swallowed and looked at the group. The last thing he wanted to get into now was this, but there was no avoiding it. He took a breath. "I lessened the restrictions on magic. Or...well, at first I changed the sentence."

"That's ridiculous. Why would you have done such a thing?" his father asked. "I spent my life ridding our kingdom of such evil corruptions and the first thing you do is let them back in again? After everything I taught you?"

"I'm not so sure that you were right, Father. Yes, I have seen magic used countless times for evil purposes, but I know that it can also be used for good. I have seen it used by people who are good people, and who didn't deserve to die." He glanced at Moira. "There were certain people, namely the witch hunters and their leader, who took great issue with that, and it threw our kingdom into war."

"I'm not surprised. Those are the exact disasters that happen when magic is allowed to be used without restriction."

"You've told me all my life that magic will corrupt a person that uses it. But I—I know people who have used it for years and yet they are still good people, so how can both of those things be true?"

Octavian went to speak but he was interrupted by a small voice.

"You lessened the sentence on magic? Truly?" Moira approached Alanor. "You made it safer for my people?"

Alanor nodded. "When I found out about you that morning...that you were no longer with us and it was because of the law, my law, I knew something had to change. So yes, I lessened the restrictions on magic. Kal couldn't accept that, and that's why he betrayed us."

His father took a step back. "Moira? You...you have magic? But why would you learn such a thing?"

Moira gave him a cold stare. "I was born like this."

"Impossible. I refuse to let you be corrupted by the taint of magic." His father shook his head.

"Magic does not corrupt more than any other power does. All your stance did was result in the murder of innocents," Nevinon said bitterly.

"You seem so empathetic to the struggles of magic users"—his father scowled—"I would almost suspect you of being one."

"Maybe that's because I am one," Nevinon spat out. "All your crusade against magic did was ruin Amari. And in the end, Kal and his merry band of murderers weren't just targeting magic users. He was just as willing to murder anyone who got in his way, and he didn't give a damn that he was killing people from his own kingdom. From his home."

His father looked back at Alanor. "Kal? Kal was loyal to Amari. He wouldn't have—"

Nevinon scoffed. "Kal was a filthy traitor. He managed to kill most of the people in this group including your son. He deserved what he got and more."

"No. Kal killed you? That's— I—" His father shook his head and fell silent.

"We can discuss this further tomorrow." Alanor sighed. "We need to make camp." He walked past his father without another glance. He had always known that if he had been alive, his father would have felt ashamed at his lessening of the punishment for magic. But it didn't stop him from feeling the sting of his father's disappointment. Alanor led the group back past the hill and into the forest where they set up camp at a nearby clearing.

"It's already getting dark." Alanor looked up. "Tomorrow we'll head into the nearest town for supplies."

"I'll take first watch." Solomon sat down at the edge of the clearing.

Everyone else settled down for the night. Alanor felt a pit in his stomach. He had no idea what to do or where to go next long term. He had no idea how to get the group to agree on a plan without a fight breaking out between his father and the others. Alanor knew he would have to come up with something. He quickly abandoned himself to a restless sleep.

ALANOR WOKE up to the sounds of some of the others preparing breakfast. From the looks of it they had used the last of their food stores in order to make it. They were going to have to go buy food in the nearest town that day.

"Looks like Dollface is finally awake."

"Piss off, Cass," he said.

"Oh, don't get your knickers in a twist, sweetheart." Cassius smiled. "I did help make you breakfast after all."

His father glared at Cassius. "He is your king, isn't he? Would it kill you to show my son some respect?"

Cassius nodded with a very serious face. "Quite possibly, yes."

Octavian rolled his eyes and returned to ignoring the group. Alanor felt a sudden spike of anxiety. Was his father angry that Alanor was leading the group and not him? His father had been used to being treated as a king. No one in the group except for Sir Theodore would treat him as such. Alanor just hoped that they could make a decision on what to do next before any arguments broke out.

The others glanced at him occasionally as they ate, perhaps to see if he had come to a decision already. All of them except for his father of course, who stayed uncharacteristically silent, and stared moodily into the distance.

He knew he would have to say something eventually.

"Nevinon, you came back first. I need more information on

the current state of the Isles. You said that Amari was invaded by barbarians. What else will we be dealing with?"

"From what I've heard..." Nevinon paused. "The barbarians mostly abandoned these lands after they basically destroyed everything a few decades ago. What we have to worry most about now are the witch hunters that took up the space that they left behind."

His father scoffed.

Nevinon threw an acid look his way. "Something to say, Your Majesty?"

His father looked at the group. "I don't see why we have to be so afraid of the hunters. If anything we should be aligned with them."

"The hunters still idolize Kal. If they realize that we seek to reestablish Amari then they will be against you as much as any witch or warlock."

"What about our allies from before? What happened to the surrounding kingdoms?" Alanor asked.

"All of the other kingdoms were sacked as well." Nevinon shrugged. "The barbarians destroyed everything and built their own kingdoms. But they abandoned them several decades ago. Because of the invasion, so many people died that there weren't enough people to tend to farms and such. Not enough food to go around. So the barbarians left and in their place the witch hunters rose to power. The name 'witch hunter' may not even apply anymore, even though they still do hunt sorcerers primarily. They are more bandits than anything else. And they control all of the Isles, from north to south."

"You seem to know a lot about the current state of affairs for someone who just came back to life." His father gave the warlock a suspicious look.

"He came back just before we did," Cassius said firmly.

His father gave a sarcastic smile. "Of course he did."

Theodore coughed. "So, we have no kingdom, no castle, no allies, and no money. Great. What do we do now?"

Moira spoke up from the edge of camp. "If the hunters are as rampant as you say, and Amari is destroyed, I see no reason for us to stay."

"You mean for us to abandon our home?" Octavian asked incredulously.

"This was never my home," Moira said.

"Of course it was. Don't speak nonsense." His father shook his head.

"Oh, so it's normal for me to live in fear in my home?" Moira asked.

"If you had come to me, I would not have charged you with treason. We could have found a way to fix this."

"My magic is not something to fix." Moira looked then at Alanor. "I say we leave. Perhaps we will be safer on the mainland. The Ruhavian Empire has always been more accepting of magic."

Octavian looked at his son in turn. "It's nonsense. We can't leave everything that we've ever known behind. We could stay here and fight. We could rebuild Amari."

"As much as I am hesitant to leave," Theodore started, "I don't see how we could rebuild Amari. You saw what state the castle was in. We don't have the resources to establish a whole kingdom. At least not right now. And with no allies to lend to us, I—I just don't see it happening."

Evie, who had been standing on the edge of their clearing, came forward to sit next to Theodore. Alanor noticed that she placed her hand on his shoulder.

"I agree with Theo. I think the first thing that we need to do is get to a place where we're safe and then perhaps think about what to do next. Although"—she glanced at Moira—"I am also reluctant to leave the Isles. I don't think any of us have ever even been to the mainland. And sailing the Yazau isn't free of danger either."

"I've been across the sea before," Cassius volunteered cheerily. "It's great over there. An infinity of taverns populated by just as many pretty women. That's all a man could ever ask for."

Solomon rolled his eyes. "The Isles also have taverns and women, Cass."

"Besides"—Freddie elbowed Cass—"you won't really be looking for any pretty women, right?" He winked at Solomon, who shook his head.

Cassius shrugged. "I suppose you're right. I guess I don't really care where we go." Solomon nodded in agreement.

Freddie looked across the fire at Nevinon. Alanor remembered now that the two used to be very close friends in Freddie's early days in Amari.

"I think that considering our party has two magic users," Freddie said, "we should think about getting as far away from the witch hunters as possible."

With everyone having voiced their opinions, the others were silent as they waited for Alanor, who spared a glance at his father before speaking.

"I'm sorry, Father, but I have to agree with the others. This place is no longer safe, especially for Moira and Nevinon, and possibly the rest of us. We are not familiar with the area anymore, and the last thing we need is to go up against an enemy we know nothing about with not enough resources to win. I think that we should perhaps head south, toward Maydon Port. It'll be easier for us to get the things that we need near a port city. Once we're there and we're safe, we can consider whether or not to leave the Isles."

His father threw him a betrayed glance but the others in the group nodded. Despite the sinking feeling that he always got whenever he disappointed his father, he knew that at least he was making the decision that would protect his family the most.

"Well." Evie stood up and started gathering her things. "That's settled then. We'll head toward Maydon Port."

"We can't walk all the way there. It would take too long, and we would be vulnerable the whole way," Theodore said.

Nevinon spoke up. "There's a small village not far east from here. Maybe a couple of hours on foot. We can see if we can buy some horses there. We can sell the horses at Maydon Port if we need to for money."

Alanor nodded. "Then that's what we'll do."

He gathered his things. The others followed suit, and they set off.

✶

WHEN THEY WALKED INTO TOWN, the townspeople were picking up wares and food from the floor and sweeping up broken debris. The town looked as if it had been ransacked. The people stared at the group in open suspicion and hostility as they passed.

Moira approached a woman to the side of the main road who was holding an infant. "Excuse me, madame, has this town been attacked?"

"Raided. Again. It was those thrice damned witch hunters. Said they were looking for a dangerous group of sorcerers. We told them we weren't hiding anyone here, but they didn't believe us."

"A group of sorcerers?" Alanor asked. "Did they say anything else?"

She shook her head. "You should ask down at the tavern. They spent the most time there." She leaned in closer. "If you ask me, I think the tavern owner's daughter is one of them. We've all had our suspicions for a while, but no one's seen her use...magic." She whispered the last word in fear.

He frowned. Alanor wanted to buy their supplies and get out as fast as possible. He certainly didn't want to run into a group of sorcerers, but he knew it was important to know your enemy. They needed to know everything they could about the hunters in order to avoid them. With a glance at the group he could see that the others felt the same except for Nevinon.

"We should get what we need and leave," Nevinon said. "There's no need to go looking for trouble."

"If we're looking to avoid the hunters we should at least find out what direction they went in, shouldn't we?" Theodore asked.

"We should find out as much as we can about this group of sorcerers on the loose as well. I think I would rather run into a group of witch hunters than a group of unknown magic users," his father said in a tone of disgust. Alanor gave an internal sigh. Another argument was on the horizon.

Nevinon rolled his eyes. "Yeah? Wait until they have you hanged for your association with two unknown magic users." The warlock mimicked his father's tone.

"Oh?" His father scowled at the other. "They wouldn't have me hanged if I were the one to report you." He looked at Alanor. "Remind me again why we haven't done that exact thing."

"Because if you reported him then you would have to report me too." Moira glared at Octavian.

His father startled slightly as if he had forgotten for a moment that Moira was also a witch. His father cleared his throat but said nothing after that.

"We'll go to the tavern to find out more about this group of sorcerers and where the hunters went," Alanor interjected before anyone could say anything else.

"So you agree with him?" Nevinon asked, motioning toward his father.

"I agree that we should be worried about running into a group of sorcerers that we don't know anything about as well as running into a group of witch hunters. We should avoid both, and in order to do that, we need information. So we'll go to the tavern to get it and that's that," Alanor said firmly. Nevinon nodded after a moment and the group headed in that direction.

"Well, at least I can get myself a drink." Cassius smiled.

"With what money?" Evie asked, laughing.

"Mmm." Cass nodded. "Yes, that does put a damper on my plans. Maybe they'll give me one on the house because of my dazzling smile?"

Alanor shook his head in amusement. "I think we will have to avoid towns from here on out. Even if we have to hunt for food. It's not worth it if we run into hunters."

Once they reached the tavern they walked inside the empty establishment. A man, presumably the owner, was wiping a table while a young girl, perhaps his daughter, was sweeping the floor.

The two threw wary glances at each other before the man stepped forward. "What do you want? We're closed."

"We heard that witch hunters passed through here. One of the townswomen mentioned that they spent the most amount of time in your tavern. We're just looking for information on what or who they were looking for."

"Well, they were witch hunters, weren't they." The man scowled. "They were here hunting witches as always. A group of them this time. And as you can see there is no group of sorcerers here, so you best be leaving this place."

"Look." Nevinon stepped forward. "I don't agree with what the hunters are doing. Raiding towns and hunting down innocents. But if we're going to avoid them we need to have information on what they were looking for, specifically, and where they went."

Alanor pulled Nevinon back and whispered to him, "We have no idea if the group of sorcerers are innocent. And these people could report us to the hunters as suspicious if we are seen to support magic."

"Yeah, I'm sure that the group is evil, just like all sorcerers, right?" Nevinon scoffed. "These people won't want to call the hunters back to town. Look at what they did to this place."

Alanor glared at the warlock. "Don't put words in my mouth. I'm just saying that those sorcerers could've done something bad to attract the attention of the witch hunters."

"Like what? Being born with magic?" the warlock huffed.

"Not all sorcerers are good," he said.

"Not all of them are evil either," Nevinon snapped. "And I'm getting tired of having to repeat that sentiment."

Alanor jumped when the plates that hung on the wall all cracked through the middle at the same time.

Nevinon gasped. "Was that me?"

"I don't know," Alanor said.

"Yes it was." The younger girl approached them, having overheard. "I felt your magic when it surged. Didn't you?" she asked Nevinon. "You're too powerful to miss."

"I've never been able to sense magic in others," Nevinon explained.

"You lot." The owner was looking at them. "You're sorcerers, aren't you? May the moon shine down favorably upon you."

Nevinon nodded. "And upon you also. Merry meet."

The owner nodded and motioned to the group to come in closer. "I'm not a magic user myself but—"

"I am." His daughter spoke up.

Nevinon nodded. "The townspeople mentioned they were suspicious of your daughter. If I were you I would leave this place soon."

The man nodded. "Yes. I'm afraid you're right. We could never be too careful in these parts."

Alanor cut in. "Could you tell us a little bit more about the hunters that came to this place and what they said they were looking for aside from a group of sorcerers?"

The owner nodded. "They mentioned something about their higher ups looking for a place called Safehold. Apparently they believe that it's some sort of safe haven for magical people. They must be seeking to destroy it. But I've never heard of such a place existing. If I had, I would've taken my daughter there years ago." The man looked at Nevinon again. "Have you ever heard of such a place?"

Nevinon became tense and Alanor recognized the look on his face. The other man was about to lie.

"No I've never heard of it." The look on Nevinon's face was one of bitterness and resentment. "I'm sure if it did exist my mother would've taken me there."

The owner nodded and glanced at the door behind them before speaking again. "There's something else."

"What is it?" his father asked.

The man became visibly afraid and spoke in a whisper. "The hunters have recently begun working with dark creatures. They were here during last night's attack. I couldn't see them very well but they were like something out of a nightmare. I had to hide my daughter under the floorboards. They're warded, you see?" The man shook himself. "That's all the information I have for you. Now I must ask you to please leave. Too many of us in one place for too long will attract the attention of the hunters."

"Wait," the girl said before turning to the tavern owner. "Maybe we should go with them, Dad. We'd be safe in a group of so many sorcerers."

"Or maybe in even more danger," the man responded.

"So many?" Moira asked. "There's only two of us."

The girl shook her head. "No it's alright. I won't tell anyone. I can sense magic in all of you."

"What?" Theodore asked. The girl nodded.

"I think it's time for us to go." Alanor motioned for the group to follow him. "Thank you again for the information. We wish you the best of luck."

The group was barely clear of the entryway before Cassius spoke. "Why would she sense magic in us?"

"Maybe it's magic left over from whatever brought us back to life?" Solomon suggested. "That's not exactly a normal thing to happen."

"And why would the hunters be allying themselves with magical creatures if what they want to do is eradicate magic?" Theodore asked.

Moira huffed, "Haven't you heard? Hunters are the height of hypocrisy."

"Safehold. A safe haven for sorcerers..." his father mumbled. "I haven't heard of a place like that either. If I had..."

"You would've destroyed it and everyone in it?" Moira asked rhetorically. His father did not respond.

Alanor's focus was on Nevinon however. Nevinon, who had definitely recognized the name and then lied about having never heard it before.

"Nev, tell me honestly. Does this Safehold exist? I know you recognized the name," Alanor said.

The warlock shook his head before sighing. "I did recognize the name. My mother used to mention a place named Safehold. But I'd never heard anyone else talk about it or mention it. I had always just assumed that it was a story my mother made up to make me feel better or hopeful. I was quite inconsolable as a child"—he glanced at Octavian—"over not being able to use my magic for fear of being captured and killed."

"A child?" his father asked. "How young were you when you learned magic?"

"I was born with it. Just like Moira," he said.

"Yes, but I only started showing signs of magic when I was around seventeen years old," Moira said. "And from what I managed to read from the few books that survived the purification, that was quite a normal age."

Nevinon nodded. "That's true. From what I've seen on average most magic users born with the ability show signs in their late adolescence and early twenties."

"But you started showing signs when you were a child?" she asked.

"No," he breathed, "I started showing signs of magic the moment I was born. I healed my mother after she gave birth to me, or so I've been told." He glanced at Alanor. "It's the only moment in my life where I've been able to perform healing magic."

"You don't talk about your mother much," Alanor said.

"What is there to say?" Nevinon shrugged. "She raised me and then disappeared without a trace when I was thirteen." He shook his head. "Anyway, it would be nice if a place like Safehold existed, but I doubt it does. The hunters are chasing a myth. We should get what we need and leave this town now." The warlock sped away from the others. Alanor went to follow him but was stopped by Cassius and Frederick.

"We've got this," Frederick said. "He always gets touchy when his childhood comes up."

Alanor nodded. "Evie, Father, Sol, and I will go get the horses. When you catch up with him, go grab us some food. I think the market is in that direction. We'll need enough to last us the trip to Maydon."

Freddie and Cass split from the group and Alanor turned to the others. "Theodore. Moira. Can you find us some tents or at the very least sleeping bags for all of us?" He had deliberately left Theodore and Moira alone for the task. He hoped that Theodore would remember the blessing he had given before they had ridden out for battle.

"Sure." Theo sent Evie a quick glance before departing. Alanor wondered briefly what that was about.

Solomon looked forlornly in the direction that Cass had gone in. Alanor laid a hand on his shoulder. "Sorry, but I think we're going to need your help with getting horses." He motioned to Genevive and his father.

His father patted Alanor on his back and pointed toward the stables at the end of the road. Hopefully they would be able to find enough horses for the group to ride to Maydon. With the witch hunters and apparently a group of sorcerers around, they could not afford to go on foot.

A few moments later they were at the stables, though they were surprised to find them mostly empty. His father was talking to the merchant, both of them irate.

"What do you mean there aren't enough horses? We have the money to buy however many horses you have," Octavian said indignantly.

"It don' matter how much gold you rich folk have. That

won't change how many horses we have. And we only have two. The rest were used for food."

"How are we all going to get to Maydon with only two horses?" Evie whispered to Alanor.

Solomon stepped forward to speak with the merchant. "Do you perhaps have a wagon that we could buy?"

The merchant looked them over and nodded. "I have that there wagon." He pointed toward a rickety wooden wagon in the corner. "It'll cost you twenty gold pieces."

Alanor had to physically pull his father back as Octavian shouted curses at the man. "Twenty gold pieces? For that poor excuse of a wagon? You're out of your mind."

The merchant smirked at them. "Well, I'm the only one in this village with a wagon and horses, so good luck trying to get to wherever you're going without buying 'em from me. Oh, and the horses will cost you an extra five each."

"We have the gold," Alanor said to his father.

"It's a rip-off and he knows it!"

"But we don't have a choice. Not if we want to get to the Maydon Port in less than a fortnight if not more."

Octavian scoffed and walked away. "Do what you want."

Alanor nodded at Evie, who had been put in charge of keeping the gold, to pay the man. She handed over the gold pieces reluctantly, and they took the two horses and the wagon. The merchant walked away joyfully.

While Sol and his father were hooking the wagon to the horses, he went to go and see if the others had gotten what they needed. He was itching to get out of this town as fast as possible. He saw Cassius, Frederick, and Nevinon a few houses over and he walked toward them. They were carrying only one sack. Alanor could tell from a distance that it wasn't even enough food for two people let alone nine.

"What happened?" he asked.

"There's not enough food here for the trip," Nevinon said. "In fact we weren't able to buy much at all."

"It looks like the hunters took most of the food stores of the town. Animals," Frederick grumbled. "They're leaving the town to almost starve as punishment for not giving them the information they wanted on the sorcerers they were hunting."

"That's horrid," he said.

"We were able to find out where the hunters were headed after here though," Cassius said. "It looks like they were heading north."

"Toward the citadel." Nevinon frowned.

"Well, thankfully we're going south," Alanor said. "We'll just have to hunt our food on the way."

"It's getting colder," Frederick observed. "I just hope that we'll be able to find enough game."

"You and me both," Alanor said.

They joined the others and were thankful to see that Theodore and Moira had managed to buy sleeping bags for all of them and a few bags of horse feed. In the end they were not left with much gold at all. At the very least they would not be sleeping on the hard ground anymore.

Though Frederick had a point. Soon the temperatures would be getting colder and they could not afford to be caught in the wilderness. They needed to get to Maydon as fast as possible. If only for shelter, though Alanor had no idea how they were going to pay for it. An uneasy feeling settled in his gut. What kind of a king was he that he could not provide for his family? What kind of man? He shook off his melancholy as the others were putting the supplies into the wagon and getting ready to ride out.

"Does anyone know how to manage one of these things?" he asked.

"I do," Solomon volunteered. "Everyone hop on. It's small in the back so you'll have to squeeze in together, but there's no other remedy."

Octavian threw a disgusted glance at the wagon before getting on after Alanor. He squeezed himself into the corner next to his son. He obviously did not want to get near anyone else in their group. Alanor shook his head. It was a tight squeeze, but they all managed to fit in the back of the wagon, while Solomon rode up front. Alanor settled in, attempting to discreetly cover his nose to block out the dank musty smell of the old wagon. They were in for a long journey.

✟

THE MAN PACED BACK and forth in front of the mirror. The creatures had imbued the mirror with their power, allowing him to communicate through the Veil. At the stroke of midnight, black smoke and red eyes took up the surface.

"Have you captured them yet?" A deep growling voice came through.

"No, my liege." The man knelt down and bowed his head. "I have sent the men and our...friends to the citadel. They will be able to pick up on their trail there."

There came an angry hissing noise before the voice responded. "See that you capture them and soon. They are our only way to enter Safehold."

"Of course, my liege." The man stood. "Those fools don't stand a chance. I will capture them."

The face in the mirror gave a wicked smile, full of fangs, and laughed. "And once you are in Safehold, what shall you do to those fools?"

The man clenched his fists. "Then I'll have my vengeance. I will kill them all."

The voice gave a screeching laugh. "Yes. We shall both have our vengeance. It won't be long now. I have waited so long— Not long, not long..." The voice trailed off as the image in the mirror faded away, leaving only the reflection of the man standing in front of it.

"Not long now indeed."

CHAPTER 6

THE GIFT OF MAGIC

Nevinon helped Genevive set a fire while the knights prepared for their hunt. They were hoping to bag some game before the weather took a turn for the worse. Moira was sitting next to them speaking with Genevive, but Nevinon was having a hard time focusing on their words. He had been thinking nonstop of the ritual and why it had done what it did. He had never heard of something like this. Every time he was forced to lie about having died his stomach turned. And now he was dragging Freddie in this mess too. He tried to push it all down and focus on the task at hand.

Solomon and Cassius were building traps out of wood while they conversed quietly. Solomon had already finished his traps and after giving his partner a quick peck, he left to go and set them when Nevinon walked up to Cassius.

"Need any help setting those?" he asked.

"Sure." Cassius nodded. "We'll check them tomorrow. Hopefully we'll have caught something."

"Well, if the others don't come back with something now we won't be having dinner tonight."

"Well, that would be bad, wouldn't it." Cassius laughed. "We wouldn't want the royals throwing hissy fits when they go hungry, ey?"

Nevinon shook his head. "So Solomon finally let you out of his sight willingly? I thought he was going to glue you to his side."

Cassius shrugged. "I think he's still having issues because of the whole me dying before him thing."

Nevinon nodded. "He must've been pretty distraught after the battle." He looked into the distance where Alanor had disappeared. "I imagine we all were."

Cassius slapped his hands on his knees and stood up. "Well, in that case I'm glad I missed it." He grabbed Nevinon by the arm and began to pull him toward the woods with the traps in his other hand. "Now come on, let's go catch ourselves some food."

"You know hunting is not really my thing." Nevinon smiled. "Not even with traps."

"Can't you just, I don't know"—Cass shrugged—"conjure up some food or something with your, you know..." He wiggled his fingers.

"My magic?" he asked.

"Yeah." Cass smiled.

Nevinon sighed. "Well, it depends. There's lots of theories on magic and creating food. From what I've read, and that's not a lot, by the way, magically created food doesn't contain actual nutrients so even if you were eating, your body would act like you weren't."

Cass frowned. "Well, that's inconvenient."

He gave a sour smile. "There's not a lot about having magic that is convenient."

Cass slung an arm over his shoulder. "So there's no way to fix our food problem with magic?"

"Well, I suppose I could try growing the food. I haven't really tried it before."

"You've been around for almost a century and you've never tried to grow food before?"

Nevinon froze. "I haven't been around for a century."

Cassius raised an eyebrow at him. "I may act like it most of the time"—he crouched down to set the first trap—"but I'm not an idiot. I noticed a few of the supplies you had at your camp would've been hard to come by this time of year. I think you're the one that brought us back. And I think whatever ritual you did must've taken a lot of desperation and a lot of time to find and set up."

His first instinct was to deny the accusation. But he was so tired of lying. Nevinon was silent for a while before he answered Cassius's previous question, trying to hide how shaken he was. He did not want to talk about his time alone.

"No, I've never tried to grow food before. I usually use my magic in battle and complicated rituals and things. I needed to in order to protect Alanor and Amari. But I learned magic mostly on my own and out of order. Most of what I do is instinctual. There's a lot about magic that I don't know, and there aren't many resources that survived the 'purification.' And besides...a lot of what applies to other sorcerers and warlocks doesn't apply to me."

"Why's that?"

Nevinon thought about confiding in Cassius about his magic never working like other magic users. Like the fact that he could do things that would kill a normal sorcerer without breaking a sweat, and the fact that he rarely had to use spoken spells for simple things. But the last thing he wanted was for Cassius to look at him differently. To look at him and see a potential enemy and not a friend.

"Don't know," he evaded. "Anyway, back up. If I'm going to try this, I'm going to need space."

Nevinon knelt down to the ground and put his hands flat over the grass, closing his eyes. He called on the well of magic deep within him and pushed his magic out, feeling the ground beneath his fingers. With his magic he could sense the life within the grass growing out of the ground, and pushing further, the roots of the trees that stood all around them. He could feel the little critters moving around in the dirt. He could feel the bird flying from tree branch to tree branch. He could feel that he was losing himself in it all.

He pulled his magic back so that he could focus on just the ground before him. He knew what he wanted to do, and he envisioned a plant growing out of the earth and becoming heavy with the weight of it bearing fruit. As per usual, he had no spell to work with, but instead used his magic to coax the ground into growing the plant he had envisioned in his mind.

He felt the ground begin to cooperate with his magic, and he heard Cassius gasp as the ground began to sprout with several bushes around him. He fed the ground more magic, before opening his eyes. The bushes around him had grown heavy with several different types of fruit, some of which did not grow from bushes at all.

He stood up from the ground and dusted his hands off on his pants. "Well, that's that, I suppose." He looked at Cassius. "I guess I can grow food with magic."

"Whoa, that's amazing. I think I felt something when you did that just now. Like some sort of energy."

"You did?"

Cass nodded. "Can anyone do that?"

"I have no idea. Anyone with magic I suppose, though from what I've learned from other magic users, most people with magic would need a spell."

"Can I try?"

Nevinon gave him an indulgent smile. "Cass, growing food as your first act of magic would be pretty complicated. Perhaps we should start with something simpler, like...starting a fire? We don't even entirely know if you do have magic, or if you can access it if you do have it."

"How would you know? I don't know, and if I don't know, how could you? How do you even know if you have magic?" Cassius gave him an enthusiastically curious grin.

"Well..." Nevinon thought for a second. "I suppose...because you use it."

"There's no other way to tell?"

"Most sorcerers will accidentally start using their magic. It's linked with their emotions, so..." He trailed off.

"Huh." Cassius smiled. "Well, no harm in trying."

"Be my guest." He gestured.

Cass knelt and put his hands on the ground. After a while, he looked back up at Nevinon. "Um, what am I actually supposed to be doing here?"

The warlock laughed. "If you have magic it should be accessible by pulling the energy up from within you. It's a bit hard to explain, but finding the energy within you is the first hurdle, and once you know how to access it, it'll become easier. It's this warm energy, and you usually feel it in the center of your chest."

Cassius sent him a doubtful look.

"I know it's confusing. I wish I had an introductory book to help but they were all burned and destroyed. I've heard the stories of a few people who lived in Amari before the great purification. There used to be whole groups of magic users, and they trained one another formally. I've always wondered what it would've been like if I had been taught the traditional way instead of having to figure everything out for myself." He looked down.

Cassius nodded solemnly before giving a soft smile. "Well, if you figured it out I'm sure I can too."

Nevinon laughed and shook his head. Cassius never could stand being serious for too long. "Alright, hands back on the ground." Nevinon motioned. "Right so, everything around us has an energy. Its own type of ambient magic. You make things happen by calling on your magic or the ambient magic around you or a combination of both. In this instance it'll be both. You'll call on your magic and mix it with the energy you'll feel in the ground."

Cassius closed his eyes and after a while gave a nod. "I think I can feel something. Warm feeling in my chest, right? Kinda like burning, but it doesn't hurt."

Nevinon blinked in shock. "That sounds right. Now, you'll want to pull on that energy, moving it upward and down your arms and into the ground. As you push your magic into the ground, you need to really visualize your intention. This is the most important part."

"Okay, visualize...got it." Cassius paused for a moment. "How does that work?"

"You have to picture it in your mind. How the plants will look like, how it will feel to the touch, what kind of fruit it'll grow, how they will taste. You really have to picture it happening in your mind, and then will it to happen with the energy you are pushing into the ground and the life energy that's already in the ground to begin with."

"Right, okay...deep breath." Cassius rolled his shoulders.

Nevinon watched on in silence as Cassius focused on the ground in front of him. The warlock had never seen the other knight so focused before. Nevinon felt a slight pull at his own magic in his chest. He watched on in shocked silence as the ground in front of Cassius sprouted another fruiting plant, this time a very small tree, honestly it was more like a thick twig, that then sprouted a single red apple.

Cass jumped up. "I did it! Holy shit, I did it!"

Nevinon swallowed and did not join Cassius as the knight jumped for joy. He had lived in Amari for many years and had known the knights for just as long. None of them had magic during their first lives. Even if he couldn't sense the magic in others, the ability would've made itself apparent eventually, especially in a large group of people.

So if none of the knights, including Cassius, had magic during their first lives, how was this possible? Nevinon wondered if somehow the ritual he had performed had given his returned friends magic. If it had, was that the only side effect or were there other ways that they had changed that they hadn't noticed yet?

He felt a stabbing feeling in his chest. What if their return was only temporary? No. No, he couldn't think like that.

He let the dread wash away. He couldn't let Cassius see him so worried. He would tell the others and then he would have to evade their questions too. He plastered a smile on his face as they began to harvest the fruit.

"Hey!" Cassius looked up suddenly. "Do you think I can grow an apple that tastes like a different fruit?"

Nevinon couldn't help the laugh that bubbled out of him. Regardless of his worries, he felt eternally grateful to have a friend like Cassius.

The knights had split up to cover more ground. Alanor walked carefully between the trees. Back in Amari he had always been considered the best hunter amongst the knights. If anyone was going to bring back food for the camp it was going to be him. Alanor paused and slumped up against the tree.

There was nothing really keeping him in the leader position of the group. Of course he had been king during his first life, but so had his father, who had ruled for many decades compared to his measly five years. His stomach sank low in his gut.

A king protects his people, keeps them safe, and provides for them. So far he had done none of those things for the group. Why should the others listen to him?

His internal monologue was interrupted by a flash of brown in the near distance. He leaned to the side to get a better view, and then crouched down silently. It was a deer. Sized well enough to feed his family, not just until they reached Maydon. A deer like that could last them a while, if it was prepared correctly.

He lifted his crossbow and aimed at the deer. He shifted. He did not notice that he was standing over a weak twig that snapped with the extra weight. The deer looked up and Alanor pulled the trigger, but by the time the arrow reached where the deer had been standing, it had run away. The arrow hit a tree with a dull thwack.

"Damn it," he cursed.

He spent the rest of the afternoon walking through the woods without coming across anything else that he could bring back other than a rabbit that was too small to be worth any real effort. With the oncoming winter it wasn't surprising. But it was certainly disappointing.

The sun began to set and he resigned himself to returning to camp empty-handed. Hopefully the others would have found something. It wouldn't surprise him to see Freddie or Theo walk into camp with a large buck or some such thing. Perhaps he was not the best hunter amongst them anymore. After all, Theodore would have more experience now.

He was almost the last one of the knights who went hunting to return to camp, with Freddie not having come back yet. He noticed that Cassius and Nevinon were also missing.

"Find anything?" Genevive asked hopefully.

Alanor shook his head. Her shoulders slumped in disappointment. "Neither did anyone else."

Moira approached. "It's late and it'll be winter soon. We would've usually finished with our hunting parties a few weeks ago. It's not surprising that you didn't catch anything."

Theodore also attempted to comfort him. "It's also a new terrain and we're in unknown territory. It's no wonder that we didn't come across anything worth hunting down."

Alanor realized then that he had been the only one to see anything that could have fed them for a significant amount of time. And he had failed to bring the animal back because of his own stupidity. He wondered if he should say something, but the deer was probably long gone, and all it would do was show the others that he was not fit to lead the group. He sighed and went to sit by the fire.

Solomon sat next to him. "Well, no big deal, we've survived

such nights before. We'll try again tomorrow. And the traps will probably have something."

Alanor was about to respond when Cassius and Nevinon walked back into camp carrying two large baskets full of fresh fruit.

Cassius was beaming and he walked over and put down his basket. "Well, I guess we can all thank magic again, because we aren't going hungry tonight."

Alanor walked over and picked up a peach. "These are not in season." He looked at Nevinon. "Did you grow these? With magic?"

Nevinon smiled. "Not just me." He pointed at Cassius.

Alanor looked at his knight. "You're not serious."

"Serious as can be, Dollface." He bent to the floor and laid his hands on the ground. "Looks like that tavern girl was right. Look at this." Cassius closed his eyes and bent his head. A few seconds later a small flower bloomed out of the ground. "It's kinda like I can feel the plants, and the trees around me when I really focus, and then Nev told me how to locate my power and use it to grow stuff."

Nevinon nodded. "We tried some other types of magic, but it seems like earth magic, specifically with plants, comes naturally to him."

"Amazing," Moira said. "And you did it without a spell? I can't believe you were able to do something so complicated so fast. It took me months to just get a flame in my hand, and that was with a spell."

Solomon took a strawberry from the baskets and ate it. "Mmm these are good."

Nevinon laughed. "It is curious. Cass wasn't able to do other types of magic with or without spells, but this came naturally. Usually it takes months or years of practice to have that much control to do something so complex. I'm wondering if it would be the same with all of you."

"You think we can all grow plants with magic?" Freddie asked.

"Mm maybe, but perhaps a different elemental magic will come to you as naturally as plant magic did to Cass. We're treading on unfamiliar territory here."

Theo picked up an apple and sat down. "Is this usual?"

"Not at all." The warlock shook his head and seemed to pause. "I'm wondering if it's another side effect of the reincarnation. I'll have to do more research when I can. Either way, at least we won't be going hungry for the foreseeable future."

All of the others took fruit from the basket and began to eat, except for his father, who remained silent on the edge of the camp. Alanor picked up an apple, which he knew to be his father's favorite fruit, and brought one over. He offered it to his father but the man just looked away and shook his head.

"I'm sorry I wasn't able to bring back anything. Please, Father, don't go hungry because of my failure."

"It's my choice and I refuse to taint my body with magic."

Alanor looked up and sent Nevinon a pleading glance. The warlock rolled his eyes and picked up a peach to bring over. "Come on, look. Everyone else has eaten. It's not poisoned, if that's what you're worried about."

Octavian glared at Nevinon. "And how do we know that you're not the one transferring your wickedness to us through the food you grow?"

"Aside from the fact that Cass showed magic before he ate anything I grew?" Nevinon held out the peach again but his father refused once more.

Nevinon huffed and walked away. "Fine. Do us all a favor and starve then." He scoffed. "Out of all the people from Amari that could've been brought back it just had to be you. The man who made my life hell from the first day I stepped foot in the citadel."

Octavian stood up. "Good! That means I was doing my job right. Trying my best to keep your kind away from the people of my kingdom." Alanor placed a hand on his father's shoulder to try to calm him down but the other shrugged him off.

Nevinon turned around. "You're an ignorant bastard and you

have no idea how happy I was the day you died and Alan took the throne."

"Why? Because you knew you could manipulate him into legalizing your corruption?"

"Magic is not corruption. It is a tool that can be used for good or bad. Alanor wasn't blind to the good that magic could bring. He was twice the king you could ever be and twice the man!"

Octavian shouldered past him and lunged at the warlock. Nevinon held his hands up, ready to defend himself, but Theodore stood to hold his father back. Cassius stepped in front of Nevinon.

Alanor moved forward to place himself between the two men. "Please, that's enough." His pleas were ignored. He noticed out of the corner of his eye that the ground beneath Nevinon's feet was beginning to smolder and burn.

Octavian strained against Theodore and Alanor, yelling at the warlock, "You're the one that brought Amari to ruin and you'll bring the rest of us down with you!"

Nevinon laughed. "I'm not the one that trained my son's murderer. And you accuse me of causing Amari's downfall?" He shook his head. "I suppose it's to be expected. After all, the guilty are always the first to point fingers."

Octavian leaned back as if he'd been slapped across the face. He turned and stormed out of camp.

Alanor turned around and looked at his friend. "Nevinon."

"I'm not sorry. He was the root cause of the civil war and the root cause of your death. And that is unforgivable. I don't even know how you can stand his presence after everything he did. After all of the people he killed. People like me."

"He was wrong," Alanor acknowledged, "but he's my father."

Nevinon shook his head and walked away in the other direction, leaving burnt footprints in his wake. Cassius followed him, and Solomon followed the knight. Alanor didn't know who to go after, so he stayed by the campfire. He sighed again. His family was falling apart.

Before anyone could come up to him, Frederick came into the camp carrying several small rabbits. Not enough for the trip but enough for at least a day.

"Saint Frederick." Theodore gave a mock gasp. "You're telling me that you would dare murder innocent rabbits?"

"Shut up." Freddie shook his head. "It was actually really hard emotionally so you should all be very thankful." Theodore laughed.

Frederick handed over the rabbits to Genevive with a shy smile, and Alanor felt a stabbing pain in his chest. Of course Frederick would have been the one to find food in the near wintertime instead of him. He couldn't even keep his family together, let alone feed them.

He felt the frustration well up inside of him and he could not stop himself from mumbling, "Maybe Freddie should be king then."

To his horror, his comment had been audible, and had been heard by both Frederick and Genevive. He blushed in embarrassment and left the camp, walking a little ways into the woods and cursing himself. That was no way for a king to act. He sat down on a fallen log with his head hung. When he felt someone sit down next to him he already knew who it was.

"I'd make a horrible king, you know. I'm much too easily distracted," Frederick said.

Alanor scoffed. "Yeah, distracted staring at my wife."

Frederick gave him a look that was both sad and guilty. Damn those puppy dog eyes. How could he resist such a pitiful look? He sighed and laid his hands on Frederick's and they intertwined their fingers.

"Even though I know you and Evie had a thing, we mourned you when you died. I mourned you." Alanor looked at the other. "Saint Freddie." He smiled. "You were the first man I knighted. I mean, Theodore was already a knight under my father's reign, but you were the first man in the ranks to be my knight. And you were always the most honorable amongst all of us. I've always admired your moral backbone and your patience. I try but sometimes my temper gets away from me.”

“Everyone gets frustrated every now and again. It’s alright,” Frederick said.

Alanor smiled before his face grew serious once more. “You saved my life. And I was never able to thank you for what you did.”

“I was just doing my duty,” Frederick said.

Alanor shook his head. “It was more than that.” He paused. “I know it makes me a horrible person but I wish it had been someone else. I used to wish that you had stood aside and let one of the other knights take that arrow in the chest.”

“But if I had been the type of person to let another get hurt just to save my skin, would I really be me?” the knight asked.

“No, I guess not,” he breathed. He let the silence between them grow for a bit before speaking again. “Freddie, I—” He sighed. “I understand that Evie might want to take this chance to be with you this time instead of me.” He swallowed. “If that is the choice that she makes then—”

“It won’t be. She loves you,” he said.

Alanor gave him a sad smile. “Yes, but she loves you too and I am not a fool.”

Frederick gave his hand a squeeze but said nothing. Alanor half expected the man to offer to back off, just like he had before back in Amari. But he wouldn’t, Alanor realized. Not this time. Not now that they had all been offered what seemed to be a second chance. He sighed again.

“Whatever her choice may be,” Frederick said, “it has no bearing on your worth as a king. We are all loyal to you. You are the best leader we could have asked for.”

“I seem to be doing nothing but failing all of you,” he said.

Frederick shook his head. “You’re too hard on yourself.”

“Perhaps.” Alanor was lost in thought for a second before the silence was broken by a loud ribbit.

“What was that?” he asked.

"Nothing," Freddie responded too quickly.

"Was that a frog?"

Freddie sighed and brought a frog out of his pocket. "It just seemed so lonely."

Alanor smiled, remembering the other man's affinity for animals. "Freddie, we're having enough difficulty caring for ourselves, let alone a frog."

Freddie sighed, "I know. Oh..." The frog wriggled out of his grip and bounded away into the forest.

Alanor laughed and bumped his shoulder to Freddie's before he stood up. "Come on. We should get back to camp. And you should find Nevinon. He had a fight with my father."

Freddie groaned. "Well, it was a long time coming. I'll go bring him back to camp."

They split from each other and Alanor returned to camp to find his father sitting far away from the others again. It couldn't be helped, he supposed. A while later Nevinon came back, having been cajoled to rejoin the group by the three knights who were closest to him. He sent the warlock a grateful glance and the other man gave him a small smile. That night the group lay down to rest, content with their new sleeping bags. They would have to hunt again soon if they wanted meat but that was a problem for the next day. Alanor, despite his many worries, fell asleep without too much trouble.

AFTER THE FIGHT, Octavian and Nevinon stayed as far away from each other as possible, not even looking at each other. Freddie and Cass had taken to sitting on both sides of Nevinon to protect him in case his father tried to attack the sorcerer again. Not that Nevinon needed protecting anyway. Moira had also started avoiding Alanor. The group ate breakfast in relative silence, no one wanting to break through the awkward atmosphere. In the wagon, Nevinon and Octavian sat at either end, each going so far as to avoid looking in the other's direction.

These were the two people he was closest to in the world, and they wanted nothing to do with each other. Alanor had no idea what he could do. They had certainly never been friends back in Amari. Nevinon had had to hide his magic, and he had only become a full physician after Octavian had passed. His father had only ever known Nevinon as the physician's apprentice, and they had rarely crossed paths. Alanor could only be grateful for that. If they had been closer and his father had found out about Nevinon's magic, the man would've been executed.

It was an impossible situation but one that needed to be fixed. They could not focus on getting to safety if the group was constantly torn apart by their bickering and arguing. Obviously his father was in the wrong, having executed many innocents just because they had magic.

When Moira, the woman he thought of as a sister, had ended it all because of his ignorance, his grief had been unbearable. The thought that Moira had been so afraid of him that she had never confided in him, and the thought that he had never gotten the chance to prove himself to her as someone who would do the right thing had broken his heart. Even if he still had his doubts about magic, he wanted nothing more than for his family, including Moira and Nevinon, to be safe.

But despite the fact that his father was obviously prejudiced about magic, and had committed a lot of wrong, he could not bring himself to shun the man as Nevinon and Moira expected of him. Octavian was his father. The man had raised him and cared for him. Alanor loved his father.

When they stopped to make camp again for the night, and everyone had cooled down slightly, Alanor pulled his father aside. "Father, I need to speak with you."

They moved a bit away from the others so that they could not be overheard.

His father looked him over. "Is something wrong?"

Alanor nodded. "You've been pretty silent so far into the trip, other than to disparage magic that is."

"You know what I think about magic," Octavian said, "and of your thoughts to make it legal."

"Yes I do," Alanor agreed and was silent for a while.

"So what's this about then?"

Alanor paused for a moment in order to put his thoughts into words. "All throughout the time that Amari was at war against the hunters, against Kal, I couldn't help but wonder, if you had been alive, if you would have supported them or me."

Octavian stood upright and looked at him with wide eyes. "What kind of question is that? Of course I would support you. You are my son. No matter what I think of your decisions I would not oppose you in such a way."

Alanor exhaled, feeling a weight lifting off his shoulders.

His father continued, "And I can't believe that Sir Kal would do such a thing. You know I trained him myself."

"Yes, well, none of us were expecting it either. Though I suppose we should have, considering how passionate he was about eradicating magic as a whole."

Octavian did not respond for a while. "Is that what you wanted to ask me?"

"Not entirely." Alanor shook his head. "This whole time the group has been treating me as their leader as they are used to, and following my orders."

"You are their king," Octavian said. "It is to be expected, no?"

"Yes, but—" Alanor hesitated. "You are my father and you were king before me. And now you're alive and"—he motioned to Octavian's state—"perfectly well enough to lead."

Octavian gave a bit of a smile. "Yes, it's quite a shock. I actually think I'm a bit younger than I was when I died. Curious, no? I almost forgot what it's like to wake up without back pain."

They shared a laugh. Octavian continued, "But if you're asking me if I would rather be king, the answer is no."

"Really?" Alanor asked.

"You sound so shocked."

"You were always so...adamant about your authority when you were king."

"Yes, well, I'm not king any longer. Nor do I wish to be. My kingdom is gone and these people"—he motioned back toward camp—"I don't know them. They won't respect any orders coming from me. Besides"—he shrugged—"it's a burden I do not wish to bear again."

Alanor nodded in understanding. "Alright then. We shall continue as we have. All I ask is that you keep an open mind. Magic is not all bad."

His father huffed, "And you've seen a lot of good done with it, have you?"

"Unfortunately, because of the war I never had the chance. But I've talked with Nevinon. Seen him in action. Seen him save and defend lives. Magic is capable of many things. I know that it could be used for the good of all."

"Oh, well, if Nevinon says so." Octavian rolled his eyes.

Alanor sighed, "Please, Father. For me. For Moira."

"Alright." Octavian held his hands up. "Just a bit of an open mind. Only for you and her."

"That's all I want."

"And maybe it's a good thing you're leading us," his father said. "I certainly don't think Nevinon would ever accept me as king."

Alanor laughed. "He barely accepts me as king honestly. It's not like he follows my orders most of the time. Though he has seemed less rebellious since we came back."

He sobered when his father sent him a serious look. "Then why do you trust him so much?"

Alanor took a few moments to consider the question. He discarded the first response that came to his mind. His father would never accept such an emotional reason. "Because he has proven his loyalty to me many times over. Because he is dedicated to me and my kingdom." He tilted his head. "Or what's left of it anyway."

His father nodded and was silent for a bit. "How old were you when you…"

Alanor looked down at his fingers. "It was only five years after you. I was just a few months shy of twenty-seven."

His father looked away. "Only twenty-six…"

"Are," Alanor started, "are you ashamed of me?"

His father looked back at him, startled. "Ashamed? No, I'm… I'm sad. You should've had the chance to live a longer life. Instead you were killed by one of ours…one of mine. I—I feel responsible." His father shook his head. "Nevinon was right. I trained your killer."

Alanor laid a hand on his father's arm. "You couldn't have known."

His father didn't respond but Alanor could tell that the man was still feeling guilty. Of all of the places this conversation could've gone, Alanor hadn't been expecting his father to share his guilt so readily. Perhaps what Nevinon had said earlier had had a deeper impact on his father than what he had originally thought.

"I don't blame you," Alanor said. "Kal was his own man. He made his choices."

His father swallowed and then changed the subject. "So, do you really think it's a good idea to leave the Isles?" The man looked into the distance. "Reminds me of when I was a child."

"When you had to flee the citadel? Because of Vasilios?" His father nodded absently. "You've never really told me the story before," Alanor said.

His father gave him a sad smile. "Maybe I will someday."

Soon after, they were called back to camp by the others and joined them in eating dinner. The knights were already having a conversation about Maydon. Cassius interrupted them as Alanor and Octavian approached.

"I know what we need." Cassius clapped his hands together.

"We need a group name! I mean, we can't be called the knights of Amari anymore."

Theodore raised an eyebrow. "Why not?"

Cassius rolled his eyes. "Aside from the fact that it's inaccurate and also a dead giveaway to who we are?"

"It's not inaccurate," Theodore responded.

Alanor huffed a silent laugh and finished his dinner, letting his men talk themselves out. After they had eaten they quickly settled in for sleep. They were getting close to Maydon now. Alanor could only hope that the rest of the journey would be uneventful.

His hopes were for naught however. Alanor managed only a few hours of sleep before he was torn from rest by the sound of a woman screaming.

CHAPTER 7

THE SHADOWS

It took a few seconds for Alanor to recognize the screaming voice. He looked over the camp and spotted Moira thrashing in her sleeping bag. Theodore was already by her side trying to shake her awake.

"What's happening?" he heard his father ask from behind him.

"She's having a nightmare," Nevinon responded.

Alanor looked at the warlock in worry. Moira had always had horrible nightmares ever since she was a child. It was only when he was older, after she had passed, that he realized that sometimes her dreams had come true. Theodore managed to rouse Moira from her nightmare and was comforting her while she sobbed.

"What's wrong, Mimi? What did you see?" Alanor asked.

"It was horrible," she gasped. "There were these creatures. These monsters made of ungodly shadows."

"What happened?" Nevinon asked. "In the dream."

She swallowed audibly. "It was us. We were traveling and these monsters came out of nowhere and attacked us. They...ripped into us with their claws and fangs, and we could not fight them with our swords, everything just went through them. Like they were, I don't know, made out of air or something."

"I've never heard of such monsters before." Cassius spoke seriously for once.

"It could be a metaphor. An omen perhaps?" Nevinon got the campfire burning again and sat down. The others followed suit.

"I'm sure it was just a nightmare. Nothing more. Moira's always had horrible nightmares," Octavian said.

Alanor shook his head. "Those nightmares were not always just nightmares, Father. Some of them came true."

Octavian looked to the side. "More magic, I suppose."

"She's a seer," Nevinon said.

"Perhaps it is an omen and those monsters are stand-ins for the witch hunters," Frederick said. "Maybe it's a sign that we should leave or at least that we are not safe here."

"Yes, we've established that we're not exactly safe already," Octavian said acidly.

"And yet"—Frederick glared—"you would still refuse to leave the Isles."

"This is our home. If you wish to abandon it so easily that only speaks to your character." Octavian looked Frederick over. "And I would expect nothing more from a peasant."

"That's enough, Father," Alanor interrupted. "I will not have you insulting my men. They may have been born peasants but they are each more honorable than the other knights of Amari were combined. Nobility isn't born, it is earned."

Octavian rolled his eyes and said nothing.

"What should we do about this then?" Theodore asked.

Alanor thought for a few quick moments. "I have ignored Moira's dreams too many times to my own detriment. We shall not ignore this one. Because we cannot be sure what the monsters are symbolic of, we shall have to be extremely cautious from here on out." He turned toward Moira. "If you have any more dreams or nightmares, let us know."

Moira nodded. Alanor continued, "We should clear up camp and continue heading south. It's almost dawn anyway." The others did as bid and packed up the camp. They were back on the road in short order.

Kill! Kill kill kill kill!
The Slaughter is coming. We feast.
WE FEAST!

Nevinon gave a shout as he came to. His chest felt like it had been scratched but when he lifted up his shirt there were no signs of any injuries. He let his shirt fall and drew in a shaky breath. That was the second time now that he had had the same nightmare. Just an empty darkness with those horrid voices.

"Nev, are you alright?" Frederick asked.

Nevinon looked up to see most of the group sitting up and looking at him. All except for Octavian, who had rolled over in order to go back to sleep, even though it was almost dawn again. They had spent the whole day before traveling in the rickety wagon and they would be doing the same again in the morning.

"Yeah, I'm fine." He shivered. "It was just a nightmare."

Alanor stood and walked over to him. "First Moira, and now you?"

Nevinon shook his head. "I'm not a seer." He waved Alanor off. "Go back to sleep. I'm fine."

The knights shared a look of concern but Nevinon ignored it and went back to sleep. Or at least he pretended to until the sun rose. Then he stood up to make breakfast with the last of their food stores. Again. If they didn't find a place to stay for the winter they were in trouble. He sighed.

After the group ate breakfast, Nevinon went to help Solomon ready the wagon and the horses. Cassius was already there putting away their meager supplies. Cassius went to lift them all onto the wagon before he dropped three of the bags onto the ground, one of them falling onto his toes.

"Fucking damn it all to hell and back," Cassius cursed as he hopped on one foot.

Octavian, who had been bringing his sleeping bag over, looked at the knight disdainfully. "My god, you have a mouth."

Cass smirked at him. "Would you like to see what else it could do?"

Octavian gave a shocked laugh before climbing into the wagon.

Alanor punched Cassius on the arm as he passed. "Are you really hitting on my father right now?"

"Why not?" Cassius shrugged.

"Well, there's no accounting for taste," Nevinon laughed.

"Oi, I'll have you know I have great taste." He winked at Alanor. "You come from mighty fine stock, Dollface." Alanor shook his head and didn't respond.

Cassius followed the others into the wagon and they were off again. Nevinon was sitting across from Octavian this time, but he tried to ignore the other as best as possible as the wagon lurched from side to side over the rough road. His attention was caught by the man however when the other gave him a look. Not a disgusted look but a concerned one, which was unexpected.

"What?" he asked.

"Your face." Octavian motioned.

Nevinon brought his hand up to his face, under his nose, where he noticed a warm tickling feeling. He pulled his hand away only to see blood on his fingers.

"Nev, I thought you said you were alright." Alanor looked ready to call for Solomon to stop.

"I'm fine." He brushed the other off again. "It's just a nose-bleed." He could see that the others wanted to comment but he turned his head away. They said nothing and he gave an internal sigh. He was not used to so many people having eyes on him. He supposed he would have to get used to it eventually. He let the rhythm of the moving wagon lull him into a light doze.

He spent the rest of the day in silence, and that night he went to sleep without speaking to any of the others. He wasn't quite sure why that nightmare had thrown him so off course. He'd had nightmares before, but this one had felt different. He tried to ignore the feeling of dread that creeped up on him as he lay down to sleep.

ALANOR WOKE up with a shout when someone grabbed his arms and dragged him out of his sleeping bag. He fought back against his assailant and was finally able to get away by kicking the man between the legs. It was a dishonorable move for a knight, but he had no idea who this man was or what he wanted. As he rolled away from his attacker, he heard the others in the group shouting, as well as the sounds of fighting around him. They were being ambushed. It was still too dark to see anything.

"Nev," he called out. It probably wouldn't be a good idea to use Nevinon's full name. "The fire!"

With a burst of light from the other side of the camp, the warlock had heeded the order and threw a ball of fire toward the campfire that had died out at some point in the night. The wood lit up in a blaze strong enough to light up the entire clearing.

Alanor spotted his sword on the ground and he picked it up and unsheathed it. Just in time too, because not a moment later he was attacked by another man. Their assailants were all wearing witch hunter uniforms. Though, due to the lack of stripes on any of their shoulders, these men were of lower ranks.

So the witch hunters thought that they could send their lackeys to take them out? Alanor gave an angry smile as he thrust a sword into his attacker's chest. The hunters were in for a much ruder awakening than the one they had paid them.

The knights had finally organized themselves with their backs to each other. Even though they were experienced knights, they were out of practice and outnumbered. The hunters had surrounded the camp, and the size of their group was more than double the number of the knights. But Alanor grinned. He and his men had beaten worse odds before, especially with Nevinon on their side.

Alanor took on another two hunters. As he parried their blows, out of the corner of his eye he spotted Moira slashing at a man with her daggers before Evie slammed a pot into his head from behind and he went down.

His father took down five assailants in quick succession with his double swords, one in each hand. He remembered then that his father could handle a sword in either hand, and was now making effective use of that ability. It had been rare to see his father fight with a sword in his left hand, as it was not considered proper dueling form for a knight, and he had never seen his father fight with two weapons at once. He was almost distracted enough to miss another attacker approaching from his left.

He quickly dispatched the hunters around him. Solomon and Cassius were back to back, even though Solomon seemed to be trying to keep Cassius away from their attackers. Frederick and Theodore were at the far side of the camp, having been on watch duty before the hunters attacked. Another group of hunters approached Alanor but they were blasted back by Nevinon, who was flinging spells left and right.

At this point, almost all of the hunters had been dealt with. As he took down another hunter, he heard a man call out, "Don't move or I'll kill her."

He turned and froze. One of the hunters had grabbed Moira by the hair and had his sword to her throat. Alanor didn't even have time to think before Moira scowled and stabbed the last one of her daggers into the man's sword arm causing him to drop his weapon. She spun around and put the other dagger in his throat. The knights did not waste the opportunity to take out the rest of the hunters. Alanor thought the fight was over but it was not.

An arrow shot out from the trees. It was headed directly for his father's chest but then it stopped in midair. Another couple of arrows followed the first but they all froze before falling to the ground harmlessly. It must have been Nevinon working his magic. The warlock held his arms out and made a swatting motion. The archer was flung out of the tree he was perched in. The man landed with a severe crack that resounded throughout the camp. He didn't get up again.

Alanor gave a sigh of relief. The battle had been long and hard but it was over now and he took himself out of battle stance. The attackers had taken them by surprise but they hadn't been known as the best knights in the land for nothing.

"I didn't know you could fight with both hands," he heard his father say to Moira.

"I didn't know you could either," she responded.

He shrugged. "I was born left-handed."

She gave a nod before turning to speak to Evie. "Nice work with that pot."

"Thanks! You were great with those daggers." Evie smiled at Moira.

Cassius whistled. "A woman who can fight. Now that's what I like to see." He turned to Solomon. "I think I found my type." Solomon rolled his eyes and nudged Cassius's shoulder with his own, but he was smiling, used to his partner's antics.

"Don't think I didn't notice you trying to protect me from those hunters." Cassius wagged his finger at his partner. "I can defend myself, you know."

"Not always," Solomon mumbled. Cassius gave him a rare sad look before he enveloped the other in a hug. "Look at how this man loves me." He smiled. "You should all be very jealous."

His father came and approached him while the others conversed. "The hunters knew we were here. How is that possible?"

Alanor shook his head. "I have no idea. Maybe they just stumbled upon our camp? It could have been a coincidence."

"With this many men?" his father asked. "I don't think so. They came prepared to face us." His father observed the others with a cool glance. "They fight well"—he sounded surprised—"for a group of peasants."

Alanor glared at his father. "You know I'm the one that trained them, right? And most of them were already better swordsmen than the knights I already had." His father frowned but didn't respond.

Alanor saw Nevinon standing a bit away from the group. The warlock had his hands to his head as if he was fighting off a migraine.

"Nev, are you alright?" he asked.

Nevinon looked up to mumble, "Yeah, I'm fine." But he wasn't fine. He was bleeding from his nose. And his eyes. Nevinon collapsed to his knees with a cry, and held both his hands to his ears. "Leave me alone!" he shouted.

"Nev, what's happening?" Frederick rushed to his side. "Who's doing this to you?"

"The voices," Nevinon groaned in pain. "It's the voices, they're back again. And they're closer."

His father shook his head and took a step back. "He's mad."

"He's not mad," Moira said. "He's right. Something's coming. Something bad. I can feel it."

Not a moment after she had spoken the words, a group of monsters, unlike anything he'd ever seen before, appeared at the north edge of the clearing. The monsters seemed to be almost bleeding into the camp from the shadows of the trees. They all stumbled back and huddled together, facing the creatures.

"What the hell are those things?" Cassius cried out.

At first glance, the creatures seemed to be made of shadows that had coalesced to create their physical bodies. There were four of them, and each was several heads taller than a normal person. They were hairless with black leathery skin and wings like bats. Large, fully black eyes stared at the group. One of them unhinged their jaw to show off a mouthful of uneven rows of sharp, jagged teeth. The creatures had abnormally long arms with huge hands, and long fingers that ended in sharp claws. Their legs gave the image of a wolf standing on its hind legs, with claws that seemed just as sharp as the ones on their hands, and dug deep furrows into the ground as they stalked forward slowly.

The creatures' hissing voices filled the clearing, accompanied by the occasional high-pitched manic giggling and shrieking. Alanor reeled back as the stench of rotting flesh hit their noses.

"There are more of them behind us!" Evie cried out.

One of the creatures launched itself at Solomon. Solomon's sword did nothing against the creature, and when Cassius joined him, the same. All of the attacks went right through it. The shadow creature jumped into the sky right above Solomon and grabbed his knight, lifting him into the air. Solomon groaned in pain and it seemed as if the creature were sucking out a golden light out of him. Cassius tried to get in its way but nothing was working. Whatever it was doing was killing Solomon.

Alanor picked up his sword from the ground but hesitated to attack. It would do no good. He looked for Nevinon but couldn't spot him immediately.

Behind him he heard Evie scream. Theodore gave a shout, "Watch out!"

He spun and saw Theo get thrown by a blast of dark energy from the shadow creature, into a tree where he stayed down. Evie held her hand up to shield herself but it was no use and the thing began to take the same golden light from her and the woman collapsed. Freddie tried to shield her with his body but soon he was under as well.

Another monster shot out from the trees directly toward Octavian and slashed him across the chest, taking him under like the others. Alanor backed up against a tree at the edge of camp in an effort to observe the fight, if it could even be called that. The creatures did not seem to have a weakness.

Alanor finally spotted Nevinon trying to attack the shadow above Solomon. The warlock created another ball of fire and threw it toward the creature. However, the creatures seemed to absorb all the magic that was thrown at them. It was making them stronger. Moira tried her hand at throwing fire at one of the creatures and this time it seemed to hurt the thing, but there were too many of them.

Alanor could do nothing except look on in shocked horror.

One of the creatures near Nevinon began to pull a string of light from the warlock but it was not golden, it was white. Then the thing bit into the light savagely, cutting out a chunk of it. Nevinon screamed and fell to the ground, but managed to throw some spell at the creature that pushed it away long enough for him to stand back up.

"Nothing is working!" Moira shouted.

Cassius called out to them, "There are more coming!"

Alanor could see more shadows moving in the trees and a large group came out after Moira, who couldn't fight off so many at once. They were losing, and if nothing was done they would all be dead soon. He rushed toward Nevinon, even though he knew he would not be able to protect the other.

Alanor felt a surge of hot energy rise up inside of him. A second later a blindingly bright white light blocked his vision. He couldn't see anything. In a fit of panic he raised his sword, but he did not swing it for fear that he would hit one of his group. Just as quickly the light was gone, and Alanor realized that the light had been coming from Nevinon, who was still trying to throw everything he could at the shadows around him.

"Nev," he called out breathlessly, "it has to be you. Only you can stop this."

The warlock shook his head. "I'm trying. The magic is just making it worse. It's attracting more of them!" Nevinon cried frantically.

Alanor looked up and could see a large group of the creatures circling above them. "No, it has to be you. I know it. You've summoned lightning before, try that. You can do it."

Nevinon brought his hands together and with a quick motion shot lightning at the closest shadow, but it was absorbed just like all of his other attacks. Nevinon moved so he was back to back with his king. Alanor could hear the panic in his voice when he spoke. "It didn't work. I don't know what to do."

They were going to die here. There was no way to win against these things. If this was going to be his last moment then he would not waste it.

"Nevinon." He swallowed. "It's alright. We can't win. It's not your fault, I don't blame you, I—" He turned to face the warlock but one of the creatures slashed at him. He twisted out of its reach but collapsed to the ground when he felt a sickening and horrible pull. The creature was taking something from him. He had a frantic thought that maybe it was taking his soul.

"NO!" he heard Nevinon scream distantly, as if he was speaking underwater. "You won't take him from me again!"

Alanor fought against the pull of the shadow creature above him to turn his head and look at his friend. Nevinon's eyes had gone completely golden, and the same blindingly bright light he had seen earlier blasted outward from the man. The light obliterated the shadows that were close to Nevinon, including the ones that had been sucking the life out of them, and pushed away the others. They melted back into the trees and disappeared as if they had never been there in the first place.

Alanor could finally breathe with ease. He stood up on shaky legs and looked over the group before looking back at Nevinon. He startled when he noticed the other bleeding from his nose again. Alanor was about to call out to him when Nevinon collapsed without any warning.

"Nevinon!" Alanor caught him as he fell and lowered the warlock to the ground gently.

"I'll take care of him." Alanor looked up to see Frederick next to him. "Theo's got Evie. Your father—"

Alanor inhaled quickly and looked across the camp toward where his father had gone down. He rushed over. His father was facedown so he quickly turned him over. He was bleeding profusely from his wounds but Alanor could still feel his pulse.

"How is he?" Theodore asked. Evie was sitting up next to him.

"Alive," Alanor breathed. "We need to wrap his wounds but he's alive. And you? I saw you get thrown into that tree pretty roughly."

"I'll live," Theodore grunted.

"We need to get out of here." Alanor startled when he heard Solomon's deep voice full of panic. It was rare to see the other man looking so fearful. Solomon was holding Cassius tightly to his side.

"I agree," Alanor said. "Those things could come back at any moment."

"There is no way we can maneuver the wagon in this darkness. We would have to wait until dawn at least," Genevive said.

"I think I might be able to help with that." Moira held up her arm and summoned a ball of light.

"That works." Alanor nodded. "Let's pack up and get everybody into the wagon. We need to get as far away from here as soon as possible."

As the others frantically packed up the camp, Alanor began to wrap his father's wounds. He wasn't as good at it as Nevinon of course, but it would do for now. Frederick and Cassius had already moved Nevinon into the wagon, as soon as Cassius had been able to reassure Solomon that nothing would happen to him if he left the other's side. When they were done, Frederick came over to help him move his father into the wagon. There was no other remedy for it. They had to place his father next to Nevinon if they wanted to make space for the others. All he could hope for was that they would not begin to fight immediately after waking up.

"What were those things?" Cassius asked.

Alanor shook his head. "Let's just focus on getting out of here." He stepped off the wagon to help the others pack. He had to make a good show about being unfazed in front of the others, but he was also preoccupied by the same worried thoughts. What the hell were those things? And how had they known that the group had been here? Alanor felt the dread cover him with a heavy weight. Those things were still out there and Alanor hadn't been able to do anything to fight them off.

It seemed that he had not been hiding his thoughts as well as he should have been. Solomon came up to him and put a hand on his shoulder, shaking him gently, and motioning with his head toward their meager supplies. Alanor nodded and let the labor of packing up the camp distract him from his fears.

NEVINON GROANED as a rocking sensation woke him up from a deep sleep. Instead of waking up on the cold, hard ground, he could feel rough wood beneath him. Even before he had opened his eyes, he knew that he was in the wagon. The world came into focus. The others were sitting on the benches on the side of the wagon. He could tell it was still nighttime.

"How is Solomon driving this thing at night?" he asked.

Cassius bent down to help him sit up. "Moira's up front with him. She's lighting the way with magic."

He groaned in pain as he sat up. He felt like his bones were aching and the dizziness that overtook him was overwhelming for just a few seconds. When it passed he was able to focus better and he noticed Alanor next to him with his father leaning heavily on his son's side. Octavian was conscious but shirtless. His shirt had obviously been torn to make makeshift bandages for the three bloody slashes across his chest.

"He's bleeding. Please help him," Alanor said.

Nevinon stood and quickly sat down on the bench next to Octavian, still exhausted from the amount of magic he had performed earlier in the night. "You know healing spells aren't my strong suit."

"No, I know." Alanor nodded. "But your training makes up for it."

Nevinon reached for Octavian's bandages when the other gritted his teeth and shook his head. "No. I don't need any help from a sorcerer."

Nevinon glared at him. "You do realize I'm a trained physician, right? You are the one that approved my apprenticeship in the first place so long ago."

Octavian scowled at him. "And if I had known what you really were, I'd have killed you on the spot."

Alanor reached out and placed his hands on Octavian's arm. "Father, please, don't be so difficult. Remember our conversation. You're hurt. You need help."

Octavian sighed and nodded reluctantly. Nevinon searched through his bags and sighed.

"What are you searching for?" Octavian asked.

"I need something to clean your wounds with," he responded.

"Oh, here, take this." Cassius pulled out a flask and handed it over.

Nevinon raised an eyebrow at the other. "Where did you get that?"

Cassius shrugged. "I might have stolen it off a guy."

"Cassius," Frederick scolded him. "That's not proper behavior for a knight."

Octavian huffed and then winced as Nevinon cleaned his wounds. "I don't expect anything different from a peasant. There's a reason I only knighted nobles."

Cassius laughed, "I'll have you know that nobles steal more and more often than peasants do."

"Now is not the time," Nevinon muttered distractedly as he discarded the shirt scraps that had been bled through and wrapped Octavian's wounds using another spare clean shirt from one of the bags.

Meanwhile, the warlock kept an eye on his king as Alanor checked on the others. Aside from heavy bruising on Theo's side, the others were left unharmed but exhausted. By the time Nevinon had finished treating Octavian's wounds, the others had fallen into a dreadful silence. The warlock had a feeling that the cloud of fear had been around since they had left their camp. After a while the sun began to rise and Moira did not need to light the way for Solomon anymore. She switched with Cassius, who joined Solomon up front, cuddling up to the larger man.

"What on earth were those things?" Freddie broke the silence. "They seemed to be made of air. All of our attacks went straight through them. Even the magic wasn't helping."

"It helped eventually. Thank goodness," Cassius called from the front of the wagon.

"I think I may know." Nevinon's admission was met with shocked glances. Alanor motioned for him to continue. He wondered if he was doing the right thing by sharing this with the others. There was a chance that it wasn't relevant and the stories he had heard were just made up. He took a breath before speaking again. "In the town, I mentioned that my mother used to tell me stories of a mythical place called Safehold when I was younger. This place was a safe haven for all magical creatures. It was said that the god and the goddess were more present in that world..."

Freddie moved to sit down next to him and placed an arm over his shoulders, knowing that it was hard for him to speak of his mother, who had passed long ago. Nevinon made it a habit to not speak to anyone about his childhood, even Alanor. But for some reason he had confided in Frederick the day he had met the man, both of them connecting over being orphans. There was something so disarming about the knight.

The warlock took a breath and started to tell the story. "She would only tell me this story about how a long time ago magic was being hunted—I suppose things never change—and so the goddess and the god gifted magical people with a safe haven away from those that would deem magic evil. The goddess gave some of the people special divine powers, and those people were to be the leaders of this magical place. Then the magical people along with all of the magical creatures of the world were sent to this place where they would be safe. She said it was a world that was full of magic. I remember as a kid I would dream about finding a way there."

"What does this have to do with those creatures?" Frederick asked gently.

"She mentioned them a few times, or something like them," Nevinon said. "She called them something. I don't remember what it was. I think it was in a different language. But the way she described them was exactly like the shadow monsters we saw. The story she used to tell me was that not everyone in Safehold was happy, and there were some who desired more power than they were given by the gods. One of them decided that he was going to find a way to defeat the god and become a god himself, so he created these monsters that would consume all of the magic in Safehold and eventually also the magic of the gods."

Nevinon looked down at his hands before continuing. "These creatures were made of darkness, and they were attracted by magic, since that's what sustains them. They had long claws and black eyes. That's all I remember, because as soon as I started having nightmares about the monsters, she never mentioned them again."

"And you never asked her later about these stories that she used to tell you?" Octavian asked.

Nevinon paused for a long time before he spoke. "She disappeared when I was thirteen. She went out to buy food at the market in the next town over, or at least that's what she said she was going to do, and then she just...never came back." Nevinon fiddled with a string hanging off his shirt. "I looked for her many times to no avail. When she never turned up I was taken in by the town's midwife. It's how I first started learning how to become a physician. Aside from the stories told to me by my mother, I had never heard them from anyone else before."

The group was silent for a long time, not knowing how to react.

"You've never really talked about your parents before," Alanor said.

Nevinon nodded. "There's something else. These things hunt magic. The tavern owner's daughter mentioned sensing magic from all of us. That light that was being taken from all of you"—he swallowed—"that was magic."

"That's impossible." Theodore shook his head. "We don't have magic."

"The light that was being sucked out of you says differently," Nevinon said.

"What if that was just our life force or something?" Cassius asked.

Nevinon shook his head. "I know magic when I see it. I've seen magic taken from people before."

"I agree," Moira said. "It was definitely magic."

"So what you're saying is that some of us have magic now." Octavian laughed. "I think I would know."

"I didn't," Moira responded. "I didn't realize until I was older. I spent my entire childhood without realizing that my dreams were more than just dreams. That the weird things that were happening around me were because of me. Even when my powers got stronger I still didn't realize. Not until the evidence overwhelmed my sense of denial. It can stay dormant for a long time. Maybe it's just coming out now that we've come back."

"No," Nevinon disagreed. "None of you had any magic in our first lives. It would've come out eventually the way it did with Moira."

"Is there a way to know for sure? If we have it now?" Theo asked.

"Um..." Nevinon hesitated, glancing at Octavian. "There are certain...tools that can be used to tell if one has magic. Allegedly. I've never actually seen or used one in person."

"Can't you sense it sometimes?" Moira asked. "The magic in others?"

"That is something that many magic users seem to be able to do, but I've never been able to. I don't know why." Nevinon realized what Moira was saying and looked up at her. "Have you been sensing magic from the others in the group?"

Moira hesitated before answering. "A bit... It's kind of new to me. It's harder to sense when we're all around you. Your magic seems to overwhelm any other nearby sources. Maybe that's why you've had trouble sensing it?" She tapped her chin with a finger. "I— It could be possible that somehow some of us that didn't have magic before have magic now."

"How?" Theodore asked at the same time that Octavian protested loudly.

"That's a lie." Octavian stood and pointed at him. "I think that you're the one that summoned those things, or at least attracted them like you said. Perhaps this group would be safer without you."

Freddie stood and blocked Nevinon from Octavian's view. "Hey, he's the one that managed to save us all. I'd say we're pretty safe having him with us."

Alanor threw his father a look and the older man sat down. Alanor turned toward him. "Is it true that some of us can now have magic when we didn't before?"

Nevinon sighed and nodded. "It's possible. I don't know how. But it is. If Moira and I had been the only people amongst us with magic, the shadows would have only attacked us and not you. At least that is what I can conclude from what I remember from my mother's stories."

He could see the emotions warring on Alanor's face. Alanor had been brought up to believe that all magic was a corrupting force and that having it would turn you evil. Which was obviously bullshit, but Nevinon knew that it wasn't Alanor's fault he had been raised to believe such lies. Even so, he was still shocked at what Alanor said next.

"Can it be cured?" Alanor asked.

"Cured? What do you mean by cured? Magic is not a disease." Nevinon tried not to let the hurt show on his face.

Alanor threw him a skeptical look. "I know that you are not

evil, and that you use magic for good. But how can we know if it's because magic isn't evil or if you're just strong enough to fight its pull? What if it actually is corrupting, and some of us aren't strong enough to fight that corruption?"

"Magic is not a corrupting force," he replied.

"But how can you know for sure?" Alanor asked.

Nevinon didn't respond. There was no reason to. No matter what he said, Alanor and his knights would not believe him. They had never experienced the warm, protective feeling of such a pure energy surging within. All they had seen was the outcome of Octavian's "purification" and all of the magic users who had fought against it violently.

"Whether or not we have magic," Frederick said, "we still need to decide what we are going to do now."

Alanor took a breath. "It's already dawn. I get the feeling that those things only attack at night since they were driven away by Nevinon's light. We will rest here in the wagon and try to put as much distance between us and the camp as possible."

"There's something else that we need to discuss," Octavian said. Alanor nodded for him to speak his mind. "The attack by those monsters was preceded by an attack by the hunters. I know that it could have been a coincidence but it felt more like a planned ambush. So how the hell did they know where we were?"

"I don't know," Alanor said. "That's what worries me the most." The king shook his head. "We'll speak more about it when we stop for camp."

"We can't keep going on like this, Alanor," Theodore said. "Constantly on the move. Continuously having to hunt for our food. Winter is coming soon. If we don't find a solution..."

"I know," Alanor said, obviously irritated, "and we'll have that conversation when we make camp."

The knight nodded and said nothing more. Nevinon leaned back and braced himself for a tense day.

A MAN WALKED SILENTLY into the clearing, his pale skin and white hair contrasting deeply with his black clothing. His boots sunk into the muck, the blood of his men mixing with the dirt to create mud. He looked on disappointedly at the carnage.

"How could this have happened?" His face showed no emotion but his voice betrayed his anger. Not only had those filthy betrayers killed almost every last one of his men, but they had even managed to push away his creatures.

He looked to the side to throw a severe glare at the man who was groveling on his knees at the edge of the clearing behind him. The man should've attacked with the others, but instead had hidden like a coward in between the trees.

"We thought they would be defenseless, sir. But they were all armed. And well trained at that. And there was a sorcerer amongst them, no, several. There was this light, and then those creatures, they fled."

"And you thought what? That you would hide away instead of helping your own men?"

The man hesitated, trying to find some excuse. "Well, I—if I had attacked I would have died as well, sir. I thought if I could stay away from the fight, then I would survive in order to tell you what happened, sir."

He snarled at the groveling soldier. "Do not try to pass off your cowardice as strategy. There is nothing I hate more than a coward."

He pulled the dagger from his belt. The man saw and tried to run, but when he threw the dagger it struck true, and the man collapsed to the ground. The soldier died with a gurgling sound that echoed in the clearing. He walked calmly to the body and flipped it over. With quick work and one of his custom knives from his belt, he removed a tooth from the man and pocketed it. He stood and observed the clearing.

"Useless," he complained. "They're all useless." He stared at the blood on the ground and wished it belonged to his enemies.

"I swear," the man whispered, "they will pay for this."

CHAPTER 8

MAYDON PORT

They stopped in the late afternoon. Solomon and Frederick took care of the horses while Nevinon approached Octavian to check his injury. Alanor watched on as the warlock unwrapped his father's bandages and gasped.

"Alanor, look." Nevinon motioned toward his father, who was also looking down at his own chest in bewilderment. There was nothing. The wounds were completely gone. They had not even scarred.

His father looked up at him. "How is this possible? It's been less than a day."

Theodore had followed Alanor over. Nevinon nodded toward him. "How are your bruises?"

Theodore lifted his shirt. "Gone." The heavy bruising that had decorated his side had disappeared.

Cassius, who had approached them, stared mournfully at Octavian's chest. "Wow, what a waste of alcohol." Cassius then ducked as Nevinon threw a small stick at him.

Alanor shook his head in disbelief and turned toward the warlock. "Did you heal us somehow without us noticing?"

"How many times do I have to say that I'm shit at healing magic?" Nevinon said, exasperated.

"Right, because I just magically healed myself. That makes sense," Octavian said sarcastically.

Nevinon shrugged. "Well, it wasn't me."

"Do you think this has to do with us losing our previous scars?" Cassius asked. "I'm still pissed about my tattoos and piercings."

"I lost a piercing as well," his father said. "Who the hell knows what's wrong with us. Maybe this magic has twisted us somehow."

"Yet another discussion to table," Alanor sighed. "Right now we need to discuss what we're going to do."

The rest of the group had already assembled near a campfire that Moira had started. Alanor and the others joined them. There was a stretch of silence as the group waited for Alanor to speak.

"I know we said we would wait until we got to Maydon to make a final decision about whether to stay on the Isles or head for the mainland," Alanor said, "but I think we need to make that decision now. With what just happened with the hunters and those things... I have no idea if that was a coordinated attack, and if it was, then we're not safe here, not even if we head south."

"If they're this active up north in small towns, they'll be out in full force at Maydon Port hunting for any sorcerers trying to flee to the mainland," Nevinon pointed out.

Cassius threw a worried glance at his friend. "So you're saying that we could be headed into the lion's den by heading toward Maydon?" Solomon put an arm around Cassius's shoulders, trying to calm his worry. Nevinon nodded in response.

"If the hunters and those...creatures are hunting us specifically, then it won't matter if we head toward Ruhavia. They'll follow us," his father said.

"Why would the hunters follow us so far away from the Isles?" Theodore asked. "Why would they be hunting us in the first place? We've only been here for a short while. I doubt anyone actually knows who we are."

Alanor caught the suspicious glance that his father threw at

Nevinon, though he had no idea what his father was thinking about the other. Alanor hoped that the conversation would not deteriorate into a fight between them.

"I think that we should head toward the mainland. I know I've already stated my opinion before," Frederick said, "but I think it's even more urgent now. We're not safe here."

"I agree," Solomon said. "What other option do we have?"

"Yeah, what are we going to do?" Cassius asked. "Live in the woods and hunt forever? Winter's almost here and if we don't find shelter, we're gonna be screwed."

"We can find shelter here," his father said, frustrated. Alanor could tell that he was desperate for the others to decide to stay on the Isles. Alanor was also hesitant to leave his home. But his feelings did not change reality.

Alanor looked at his father. "If the hunters have really allied themselves with those things, and it seems like they have, it's only a matter of time before we're caught. Even if we don't all have magic now, we have two powerful sorcerers—"

"Warlock."

"Witch."

Nevinon and Moira both interrupted.

"—in our group," Alanor finished, glancing annoyed at the other two.

"Perhaps then we should leave the sorcerer behind." His father glared at Nevinon. "Then we would not be at risk."

"If you're going to leave Nevinon behind then you're going to have to leave me behind too. Is that what you want?" Moira asked. His father looked away and didn't respond.

Nevinon rolled his eyes. "Besides, are you forgetting the fact that those shadow creatures attacked you too?"

"The suggestion is pointless anyway, if we actually do have magic now," Genevive pointed out.

"We don't know for sure that we do," Theodore said.

Alanor could feel that the others were getting frustrated and it was only a matter of time before everything exploded into a fight.

That was the last thing he wanted. Infighting would only make them more vulnerable to attack. Besides, he had already made his decision. It had been made the moment he had seen those creatures stalk into their camp and attack his family without him being able to do anything about it.

"We're leaving the Isles." The others stared at him, perhaps shocked that he would come to a decision so quickly. "Those things are dangerous, and we barely got out alive this time. I don't want to go up against them again, especially if they bring larger numbers. It's not safe for us here anymore so that's the end of the discussion." He gave a single nod as if to reaffirm his decision to himself and the others. "We'll head toward Maydon as we planned, hopefully avoiding the witch hunters along the way. Once we're at the port we'll see about getting a ship to Ruhavia as fast as possible."

He would not hear any protests about his decision. He felt a bit sorry for his father that the man had been outvoted so harshly, and a bit worried himself about what would happen to them on the mainland, but the decision had been easy. On the Isles his family was in danger and that was unacceptable.

THE MAN with white hair stood at the center of the room, with his soldiers surrounding him. His creatures were amassed at the ceiling above them, waiting for their feast. The men watched the things warily, not sure if they should be trusting the man who worked so easily with such creatures of darkness.

They should trust their instincts, the man thought with a smirk. Those who disagreed with his rule had no place in his army. If they were smart they would've run. Today would be their last day as human beings. Not that he cared. These men were only a means to an end. Only a stepping stone toward real victory.

"My king has told us of a place that is full of magic," the man began to speak, "and there, my lovelies will be able to feast!"

The room was filled with the sound of manic giggling and screeching. Every man in the room felt the dread pool in his stomach except for the white-haired man, who seemed so comfortable standing beneath his cloud of darkness.

"Those of you that ally themselves with us will be remembered as true warriors. As those who fought to rid this world of the evils of magic." The man spoke directly to the crowd. "But those of you who have disagreed with my methods, who have openly expressed your desire to fight me or my horde, will not live to see the day that magic burns." The man grinned. "What say you? Will you join the most honorable fight?"

But the shadows did not wait for the men to respond. They descended upon the crowd in a rush. The man with white hair smiled at the sound of panicked screaming.

KILL! Kill kill mine mine MINE!

The sound of ripping flesh accompanied the voices this time.

WE FEAST! The Great Slaughter is coming!

Nevinon could hear the screams of men along with the manic laughter and giggling in his head. The noise became so loud that he brought his hands to his head and doubled over in his seat in the wagon. The others in the group were speaking to him but he couldn't hear them over the noise. He could feel the warm trickle of blood from his nose over his lips, dripping down from his chin. And then just as the noise had started, it went away.

"Nevinon." Genevive was in front of him, holding him steady. "What's going on? This is the second time we've seen you like this."

"I'm fine," he brushed her off. "I'm fine, it's just motion sickness."

"Motion sickness, my ass," Cassius said.

The others sent Nevinon doubtful glances but they were

distracted when Solomon called out to the group from the front, "I see the city. We're almost there."

"This conversation isn't over, Nev." Alanor sent him a stern look.

"So what's the plan once we get to the city?" Theo asked.

Genevive was counting their remaining funds. "We need to sell this wagon and the horses. Hopefully that, plus the amount left over, will be enough to get us safe passage across the Yazau."

"The city must be crawling with hunters. We'll need to keep our heads down," Nevinon interjected. He hadn't been this far south in a very long time, but he just knew that the hunters would be there to try to stop sorcerers from leaving the Isles without due "punishment." It would be just their luck for them to get caught just before being able to get free.

"Alright then." Alanor nodded. "Once we sell the wagon, we'll head to the docks to speak with the captain of the next ship bound for the mainland."

With that agreed the group stayed silent and alert as they crossed into Maydon. They were stopped as the guards checked their wagon. They stepped off the wagon and stretched their legs. While Solomon went to speak with the guards, asking about where they could sell the wagon, the rest of the group took in their surroundings.

There was rubble everywhere, and cracks on all of the walls that they could see. Everything was in a shocking state of disrepair. Even from just where they were standing they could see several beggars farther down the road. The city was quite obviously poor.

"What happened to this place? It used to be one of the richest port cities on the Isles," Octavian said.

"The same thing that happened everywhere else." Nevinon brushed some dirt off his jacket. "The barbarian invasion and then the takeover of the witch hunters. The hunters only care about killing and ransacking. They don't do anything to help the people. They've destroyed our home. And you founded them."

Octavian went to respond but Alanor interrupted, "That's enough! Like it or not we are in this together. And if the two of you can't be civil then we'll leave you both behind. I'm tired of the fighting and the blame game."

Nevinon shot a betrayed look at his king. "So you're saying it's not his fault that the Isles went to shit."

"I'm not saying he was in the right." Alanor turned to Octavian. "You were wrong to kill so many innocents."

"You and I have different definitions of *innocent*," Octavian said.

Alanor ignored the comment and continued, "The fighting between you two is a distraction we cannot afford right now. We need to focus on getting to a safe place. Once we get to the mainland you can have it out as much as you want, but you will not endanger the whole group by doing it here and bringing unwanted attention to us. Is that clear?" Alanor waited until both men nodded their understanding. It grinded Nevinon's gears to have to be civil to the Blood King but he was Alanor's father.

Solomon rejoined the group. "The guard says that we could find a good price for the wagon and horses at the city stables. He gave me directions. There's just one problem. The stables are right in the middle of the witch hunter headquarters here."

Nevinon shook his head. "We can't go."

"No one else is going to buy this thing or the horses," Theodore said.

"Damn," Alanor cursed. "Well, they don't know our faces. I'll go with Solomon and the rest of you make it to the docks and wait for us there."

The protests rose up immediately.

"You'll put yourself in danger," Nevinon said.

"You can't go." Octavian was shockingly agreeing with him on this one. "I will go in your place."

"No, Father, you lead the rest of the group to the docks," Alanor insisted.

"What if they attack?" Nevinon asked.

"I don't see why they would. And if they do I can protect myself. I'm a trained knight." Nevinon went to argue but Alanor interjected, "Nevinon, protect my family. They need your protection more than I do."

Nevinon looked to the side and sighed. "Fine. We'll be waiting for you at the docks. Be careful."

Alanor nodded. He got onto the wagon again, this time in the front with Solomon. They headed to the stables in the opposite direction of the docks. Nevinon watched them go with an increasing sense of dread. He turned to look at the group and saw his worries mirrored back at him.

"Come on," Cassius said. "We better get a move on." The others nodded and Nevinon reluctantly followed them toward the docks.

When they reached the stables, Alanor noticed only a few stable hands. The place was in the middle of a group of buildings he assumed to be the hunters' headquarters. Hopefully they wouldn't run into any during their exchange, but Alanor was ready to defend himself if necessary. Solomon called one of the stable hands over and showed him the horses and the wagon.

"I'm afraid I can only give you two silvers for the horses and another two for the wagon." The stable hand shook his head.

The knights shared a glance and Solomon spoke. "That's much less than what we paid for the set in the first place."

"Then I'm afraid you were overcharged. But that's as much as I can spend on a set like this. The horses are older than we would normally buy. And the wagon is also used."

Alanor looked back at the wagon. *Used* seemed like an understatement.

"We'll take it," Alanor sighed.

The stable hand called a few other workers over to help unhook the horses and lead them into the stables. Solomon took the chance to ask the stable hand about any outgoing ships from the city.

"There's one leaving soon."

"How soon?" Alanor asked.

"Today. At noon." That was only an hour or so from now. "You better get there quick if you want to catch it."

"When does the next one leave?" Solomon asked.

"Next ship doesn't get here for another three months, and it'll be here for a fortnight."

"Three months?" Alanor looked at Solomon. "I thought this was the largest port city in the Isles?"

"It is." The stable hand nodded. "But things have been rough for many decades. Not just here but on the mainland too."

"Really?" Solomon crossed his arms.

"Mm-hmm, you know with the fall of the Ruhavian Empire, trade has basically come to a standstill. And the droughts don't help much. It's like this place has been cursed or something." The man shook his head.

Alanor sent a worried look to his knight, who turned to speak to the man. "Thank you for the information."

"I'm sorry I couldn't give you more for the horses and wagon."

Alanor shook his head. "Don't worry about it."

They took the money and walked away. Alanor waited until they were out of earshot before speaking. "So Ruhavia has fallen as well? Nev didn't mention that."

Solomon shrugged. "You know how he is. Keeps things close to the chest. Maybe he didn't know. Or maybe he just forgot to mention."

"Yeah, maybe," Alanor responded.

"Either way, we need to find a way onto that ship. I don't think we can wait three and a half months."

Alanor opened his mouth to respond but was distracted when he spied a group of uniformed men walking into the nearest building. Alanor and Solomon were half hidden behind the stables but they had a clear view of the hunters. This was their headquarters, and they were right in the middle. Instead of feeling dread like he probably should've, he felt hope bloom in his chest. This was their best chance of finding out what the hunters were up to and better yet, how to avoid them. He looked around, but the square was empty.

"Come on." He motioned for Solomon to follow. He rushed across the square and around the building that he had seen the hunters enter. There had to be another way in.

"Alan!" Solomon whispered. "What are you doing? We need to get out of here."

"If we can find a way in, we can figure out what the hunters are doing with those creatures. Maybe we can figure out what they're after. This is our best chance," he said.

"Yeah, our best chance to get caught," Solomon said. "We promised the others we would be careful. Trying to infiltrate hunter headquarters is not being careful, it's being reckless."

"Well, if being reckless means that I can figure out a way to protect my family, then I'll do what I have to do," Alanor said. "Now help me look for a way in."

They crouched down and looked in through several windows. "This one looks like a records room," Alanor said. "Help me pry open this window."

"Just so you know," Solomon said, "I completely disapprove of this course of action."

"Noted." Alanor lifted open the window. The room was empty. He dropped into the room and quickly blocked the door with a chair. Solomon followed him. As quietly as possible they began to open drawers at random and flip through their files. Most of them were execution orders and records from sham trials.

"Sire." Alanor turned at the serious tone of Solomon's voice. "Come look at this." Solomon was over at the desk looking through the papers that had been on top. Once Alanor saw what Solomon had found, the dread he had been missing came back in full force.

All over the desk were papers filled with information. Information about everyone in their group. There were files on all nine of them, including their names, ages, physical descriptions, and even drawings of their faces.

Alanor and his family were being singled out and hunted like game. But why?

CHAPTER 9

THE DEPARTURE

"I suppose that solves that riddle," Solomon said.

"How do they know all of this about us? How did they know that we had come back?" Alanor asked.

Solomon shook his head. "No idea."

Alanor took a breath. "Have you found anything with information on those shadow creatures?"

"No, not yet." Solomon opened the desk drawers to begin looking through them. Alanor moved onto the next set of drawers on the far side of the wall. There was nothing on the shadow creatures but there were several files full of correspondences in between hunter ranks.

"Hey, Sol, come look at this. All of these letters mention the same thing. Safehold."

"That safe haven for magical people?" Solomon asked. "I thought Nev said it was a myth."

"Yeah, well..." He trailed off. "Maybe he was lying."

"Why would he lie?" Solomon asked.

"I don't know," Alanor said. "Because he always does." He gave a sour smile. "Maybe because he wanted to keep the place safe from my father." Alanor tried to keep giving Nevinon the benefit of the doubt, but it was hard when the warlock kept lying to his face. It made Alanor wonder whether anything he said was true. Despite that, Alanor knew he could trust the man. Weird how that worked. But trust could only go so far.

Solomon went to respond when they heard someone trying to open the door.

"Oi!" a voice called out. "Did someone lock this door?" Whoever it was tried to jostle the door knob but the chair was blocking the door. It wouldn't hold forever though.

Alanor and Solomon moved toward the window, and at Alanor's signal, Solomon climbed out of the room. Their luck did not hold out however. As Alanor was climbing out after Solomon, the door to the room was kicked in by two men. They instantly recognized them, and one pointed toward Alanor. "That's them!"

Solomon pulled Alanor out the window as fast as possible and they ran past the stables and back into the city. The hunters were on their trail however, and warning bells began to ring from behind them. Someone had sounded the alarm. They had to get out of the city.

"We need to get to the docks now," Solomon called out.

They raced through the city streets, dodging people and jumping over crates. Solomon pulled him into a dark alleyway moments before the hunters sped past them. When it seemed like they weren't coming back, they continued weaving their way through the city streets. They made it to the docks and saw the others waiting for them.

Octavian grabbed Alanor's arm. "Alan, finally. This ship is about to leave. What took you so long?"

Alanor shook his head. "Later. We need to get on this ship now. Did you speak to the captain?"

"Yeah. I told him we were waiting for you to arrive with the money for our passage."

Octavian motioned behind him to a man who was walking across the docks in their direction. Alanor could tell from his clothing and the way that the other men deferred to him that he was the captain. Alanor swallowed his nerves and hoped that he didn't look like he'd just raced through the city.

The captain stepped forward to shake his hand. "Your friend tells me you're looking to make it to the mainland."

"Oh, he's my father," Alanor commented before he could think it over. This was probably not the best time to be giving out more of their information. He cleared his throat and continued, hoping to cover up his blunder. "Um, yes. How much?"

The captain looked them all over before saying, "Two silvers for each of you."

Twenty silvers total then. He looked at Evie nervously. She shook her head. "I only have four silvers. Did you get enough to make up the difference?"

Alanor shook his head and turned back to the captain. "We don't have that much."

"Then you'll have to wait for the next ship," the captain responded simply.

"And when is the next ship?" Evie asked.

But Alan interjected, already expecting the answer, "Please. We can't wait here long. Is there anything that we could do? Clean, cook? We have a trained physician in our group."

The captain paused and looked over the group, focusing on Nevinon without prompting. "A trained physician, you say?"

Alanor nodded and Nevinon stepped forward. "That's right."

The captain motioned to the crew that was boarding the ship. "One of my men has been sick lately and I owe him a favor. Will you look him over?"

"Of course, if me and my friends can get passage on your ship," Nevinon said.

The captain thought it over briefly before nodding. "Alright, five silvers total and the rest of you help out where you can. You'll be assigned your duties. We'll be setting sail in just a few moments."

"Thank you," Alanor said. He turned to the others and motioned them aboard. "On the ship now." He could see in the distance a group of hunters were making their way up the shore toward the docks. "Now hurry," he rushed the others.

Octavian resisted. "Alan, we left some of the bags with our supplies on the shore."

"It doesn't matter. We have what's important," Alanor said sternly, motioning to the bag in his father's hands that held his crown and their other valuables. "We'll leave the rest behind."

Octavian must've seen the look on his face because he didn't argue further before following the others onto the ship. Alanor was the last to make it on. The ship started moving away from the docks just moments before the hunters reached them and started screaming for them to come back.

"What do those blasted hunters want now?" one of the crewmen shouted out.

Another laughed in response. "They want us to dock again."

The first man turned to the captain. "Your orders, sir?"

The captain looked at the group for a moment before saying, "We continue on our course. I'm not losing money by being delayed." He walked away.

Alanor almost collapsed in relief. His father stepped closer to whisper to him, "Who were those men on the shore?"

The others leaned in to hear Alanor's response, but Nevinon cut in, "Those were hunters. What happened? I thought you were going to keep your head down."

Solomon raised an eyebrow at him and Alanor sighed. "We were in the middle of their headquarters. There was no better chance to get more information about what they're doing and what those shadow monsters were."

"What did you do?" Nevinon asked.

Alanor hesitated. "We might have broken into their head-quarters."

"Alan," Genevive scolded him. "You told us you would be careful."

"Look, that's not important." He shook his head. "What is important is that the hunters had all of our information and even drawings of our faces. They were hunting us. They knew exactly who we were when they attacked us."

Octavian looked at the pair with wide eyes. "How is that possible?"

He shook his head. "I have no idea. But we also found a bunch of letters, each talking about finding Safehold. Whether it's mythical or not, the hunters believe that it exists and they're looking to find it."

"Those shadow monsters. Do you think they're connected?" Theo asked. "Did you find anything out about them?"

"No, nothing," Alanor responded.

Nevinon ran a hand through his hair. "I've never heard anyone but my mother mention Safehold before. And I've traveled the whole Isles."

Alanor looked at the others. "Well, whatever this place is, it means something to the hunters and somehow it's connected to us. I don't like how much information we're missing."

Octavian nodded his agreement. "Once we get to the mainland we should comb the libraries for mention of such a place, as well as anything about what happened to us and what those things are."

Solomon looked around and Alanor noticed that some of the crew were looking at them curiously. "For now let's just keep our heads down and do as we're told by the crew. I think the captain is already suspicious."

The others nodded and they sat down on some crates on deck to await their orders. Alanor watched on as the only homeland he had ever known disappeared over the horizon. When he was younger he had dreamed of leaving his castle and all his responsibilities behind. Of getting on a ship toward the mainland and seeing the wonders of the world. Now he could only think of leaving the Isles with unease, even though in the end it had been his decision. He wasn't some young hotshot knight anymore. He had a family to take care of and on the mainland he would have no power to his name that would facilitate that. Alanor found that now as an adult the unknown made him more wary than excited.

Once they had hit the open waters of the Yazau Sea and they had lost sight of land, the captain of the ship approached. However, instead of focusing on Alanor, the man approached Nevinon directly.

"May the moon shine down favorably upon you," the man said.

Nevinon looked at the man with wide eyes. "And upon you also. Merry meet."

The captain turned to look at them suspiciously. "You are sorcerers, aren't you? If you're running from the hunters you must be."

"Not all of us," Nevinon said.

"Nevinon!" Alanor looked at the captain with caution.

"It's fine, Alan," Nevinon said. "This is a smuggling ship, isn't it?"

"That's correct," the captain said. "You don't mind if I ask you for proof? The hunters have been getting increasingly bold as of late. I don't doubt that they will learn of our codes eventually."

Nevinon raised his hand and formed a ball of light that hovered over his palm. He motioned for Moira to do the same. Moira held her hands out and summoned a flame in her cupped hands.

The captain looked at the others. "Only two of you?"

"Um..." Cassius raised a hand. "I can grow plants, but I don't think I can do that here."

The man nodded slowly. "Alright. The name's Jacob." He shook their hands.

Alanor went to introduce himself but the man raised his hand to interrupt. "I don't need to know your names. The less I know the better when the hunters come to question me." He motioned for the group to follow. "Right this way. You'll be staying below deck with the others."

"The others?" Alanor asked.

Instead of responding, the captain led them down several sets of stairs to the bottom level of the ship and toward the back, where there was an open space filled with cots on the floor and hammocks hanging between posts. The room was large but still packed with people. He could see some of them performing magic amongst themselves.

"Magical refugees," Nevinon observed.

"You've got to be kidding me," his father said. Moira elbowed him. "Ow."

"This is where you'll be sleeping." He motioned toward a set of cots and hammocks that were free near the far corner. "We had prepared for more people so there's more than enough space for all of you. You'll all be assigned chores. Everyone has to chip in here." He looked at Nevinon. "My second-in-command has been sick for a while. He's in his room. Can you look him over?"

"Absolutely." Nevinon looked at Alanor and he nodded. The rest of the group got settled in their cots as Nevinon and the captain climbed the stairs.

Alanor and his father naturally chose the beds that would allow them to defend the others most easily. The ladies chose next. An argument ensued amongst the knights about the remaining spots but Alanor tuned it out. All he could think about was the fact that this was the first time he had ever been on a ship, and the first time that he had been so far away from his home. He could tell with a look at his father that the other man was feeling the same. It was hard not to lose a little bit of hope with every moment that passed when Alanor had no idea what they were headed toward.

Nevinon had to come back only a short while after he left. Alanor had asked him what had been wrong with the crewman who he had seen, but the warlock had shaken his head and said nothing. Though he was a bit miffed that Nevinon was still so willing to keep secrets, Alanor wasn't surprised this time. Nevinon had never been one to divulge information about his patients, something he had picked up from his mentor, Juniper.

Alanor spared a thought for the man who had taken care of all his childhood scrapes and injuries, but he stopped himself before he could start thinking of all the people he missed from home. That road would lead only toward despair.

They all settled in to rest. Alanor did his best to seem like he was relaxed even though he was still on high alert. They were surrounded by unknown magic users after all. He wondered how he was going to be able to sleep in such an environment.

A few hours later, some of the crewmen came down with food for everyone. The amount given to them paled in comparison to any meal he had eaten as king or even as prince, but after a week or so of living off the land, the group took to the food like it was a feast. After having eaten, the other inhabitants of the lower deck began to sit in a circle at the center of the room.

"Come." An elderly woman waved them over. "Join us."

Nevinon stood up readily but Alanor held him back by the arm. "What do they want?"

Nevinon laid a comforting hand on Alanor's arm. "I think most of these people must be druids. They share in conversation after meals. It's tradition. Don't worry, they're not going to launch spells at you," Nevinon said sarcastically.

Alanor did not want the others to think that he was scared so he followed after Nevinon and sat down next to him. The others joined them, with his father sitting down last, looking like he would rather be doing anything else. Alanor hoped that the man would not launch into an attack on the sorcerers. Who knew what would happen if they started a fight on the lower deck.

"Let us introduce ourselves." The elderly woman smiled. "My name is Stella. I am the matron of this group." She gestured to those around the circle who began to say their names. Alanor would not be able to remember who was who, but he noticed that most of the druids had names that came from nature.

Nevinon introduced almost all of them but when it came time to introduce himself, Alanor, and his father, the warlock gave a seamless lie. "My name is Nicholas. This"—he motioned to Alanor—"is Ormund and this is Zandros."

Zandros was his father's middle name and as such wouldn't be as recognizable as his first. Alanor wondered what would happen if these people knew they were sitting next to the Supreme Vanquisher.

"Well met. We welcome all of you." Stella nodded.

"Forgive my curiosity," Nevinon started, "but you are druids are you not? Which clan are you from?"

"We are a small break-off group of the White Star clan. We were attacked by hunters about a month ago. We are the only ones who have survived. It has taken us this long to secure passage to the mainland."

Nevinon leaned over to whisper to Alanor, "That was the largest clan of druids on the Isles, numbering over two thousand people. Last I heard they had hidden themselves behind some pretty powerful wards." Alanor looked at the two dozen who surrounded him. It must've been a massacre.

Alanor swallowed. "I heard about the collapse of the empire." Nevinon gave him a surprised look. "How can you be sure that your lives will be better on the mainland?"

"I could ask you the same," Stella responded. "I can't be sure. But I know that if we had stayed, the hunters would have slaughtered us all, the way they tried to before. Our clan was very large. We are all that remain. If we are to ensure that our traditions, culture, and magic survive, then we must survive. We must endure."

Theodore spoke gently. "Forgive me my ignorance, but I did not grow up around magic. There are certain people that believe that magic is a corrupting force. That once a person has access to magic they will inevitably turn to immoral acts. Is this true?"

Some of the druids blistered at the comment and glared at the knight. Theodore continued, "I don't mean to accuse. Only to learn more about magic."

The woman shook her head. "That is a rumor spread by those

who would see magic eliminated that is proven by those persons who have magic and are already immoral or desperate. Magic in and of itself does not corrupt, but magic is power, and power in the wrong hands can be misused. There are those who would use magic for good, and others for evil. Just like there are those without magic who could use a sword for good or for evil." The elder sent a pointed glance to their swords.

"But it is a weapon," his father pushed.

"Only when the user wishes it to be. Magic can be much more than just a weapon. It can be used to heal, to build, to grow." Alanor thought about Cassius and Nevinon growing food to help feed the group as Stella continued, "But if a magic user is attacked they may feel that their only option is to use their magic as a weapon. Perhaps in defense. Perhaps in revenge."

His father narrowed his eyes. "And do you use your magic in revenge?"

"Not at all," Stella said. "The druids are above all a peaceful people. We will not use our magic to kill or to attack. Even if it means our death. Unfortunately, this has caused the extinction of most of the druid clans that used to live in the Isles. We hope to find better lives with our brothers and sisters on the mainland."

"I wish you the best of luck," Alanor said.

Stella nodded. "And you as well."

Cassius leaned forward. "Here's my question, what even is magic? Like I get that it's some kind of energy but what is it really and how does it work?"

Stella looked at Nevinon and Moira. "I couldn't help but notice you have two very powerful magic users in your retinue. They haven't been able to explain?"

Nevinon coughed and ran a hand through his hair. "We've never been formally taught. I've only really learned from a few books that I've been able to find."

Stella nodded slowly. "I see. Well..." She paused and appeared to prepare herself, reminding Alanor of his tutors before they would launch into a lecture. This was one he was keen on hearing however, and it seemed like the others in the group agreed as they all leaned in to hear more. Even his father seemed interested, though he was feigning otherwise.

The matron began, "Everything in existence has an energy. It is the act of manipulating that energy that is referred to as magic. Anyone can learn to manipulate the energies around them through many, many years of study. These people are sorcerers. There are some people who in addition to being able to move the energies around them a lot more easily can also manipulate their own energy. These people are referred to as witches or warlocks. The latter are born with the ability to use internal and external energy. They don't need to study in order to use their magic, only to control it. In general, the term *magic user* applies to all three."

"How can you tell for sure if you have magic?" Genevive asked.

Stella sighed. "There were ways the ancients used to tell for sure, but they have been lost to time. Nowadays, there is no real way to tell other than if magic presents itself naturally. To the untrained, magic will be linked to emotion, and will usually manifest itself as elemental at first. This is because elemental magic is the most natural form of magic, which is not to say that it isn't difficult to master however."

His father spoke. "What causes one sorcerer"—he hesitated and glanced at the druids around them—"ah, or witch and warlock, to be stronger than another magically speaking?"

"No one quite knows why, but the way it shows itself is..." Stella paused as she seemed to think of the right wording. "Think of it as if every witch or warlock was born with a well of magic. And the amounts of magic inside the well are different for everyone. In some instances, individuals can expand their well with time and study, but for the most part, the amount of magic you are born with stays relatively the same. Some people only have puddles of magic, others, like your friend"—she motioned to Nevinon—"have oceans."

Alanor looked at Nevinon, who seemed nervous at the mention of his power. "Oceans?"

Nevinon glanced at him. "I've been told that I am quite powerful. It doesn't matter." He waved it off.

The matron scoffed, "Of course it matters! I've never felt anything like it. Your magic drowns out everything around it." Her face took on a thoughtful expression. "I suspect you might have difficulty sensing the magic of things and people around you?"

Nevinon nodded.

Stella smiled. "Perhaps you'll be able to with practice. You could join us during our stay on the ship for such things."

Nevinon smiled. "I would love to."

"What about spells?" Alanor asked.

"Spells are used as a focus for more complicated magic," Stella said. "Visualizing is a very important part of using magic. Spoken spells can help with that. There are many different spells across many different languages. There are even some debates about which languages are more powerful for magic. Some theories say that the older a language is, the more effective spells in that language will be. On the other hand—"

Stella was interrupted when one of the crewmen walked down the stairs to the lower deck. "Excuse me, hello, all." The man sent a wary glance at the new passengers. "I'm here to assign everyone their tasks for tomorrow. We'll all have to pull our weight here."

"Of course." Stella nodded. With that, the druids began to stand and crowd around the crewman. Alanor and the others retreated to their corner waiting for their turn. Alanor sighed and hoped he would be assigned to a task that wouldn't make him look like a complete fool.

"Say, Dollface," Cassius said with a laugh, "you ever even held a broom before?"

Alanor shook his head and smiled before responding, "I might just smack you with one the first chance I get."

NEVINON WATCHED from his spot on the floor as the conversation between the knights devolved into their usual banter and teasing. He rolled his eyes in amusement. He could swear that sometimes the knights acted like little children with all their back and forth. His attention was caught when Moira sat down next to him.

Moira turned to him. "You know, I wish I had known that you had magic too. Back in Amari," she said in a somber tone, "maybe I wouldn't have...you know. I just felt so alone."

Nevinon nodded. "Yeah, I know what you mean. We could've helped each other learn more." The warlock looked back at his king. "You know it was actually your confession letter to Alanor and his reaction that gave me the courage to reveal my magic to him. It was in the middle of a skirmish, and I was sort of forced to, but it helped."

Moira gave him a brief smile. "I'm glad something good came out of it then." There was a silence before she spoke again. "This all sounds very complicated. The magic, I mean."

Nevinon laughed. "You're telling me." He turned so that he was facing her. "Magic is just a thing that exists but we humans like to categorize and experiment with everything. All of these things are just observations made over time. And we don't even know everything that magic can do yet, we're still learning." He frowned. "And so much of our progress was lost when..." He looked at Octavian, who was sitting on his cot facing away from the group.

Moira all of a sudden had a guilty look on her face. "Nevinon. Have you ever done something bad?"

"Like what?" he asked.

Moira hesitated. "Like...have you ever killed anyone?"

Nevinon nodded. "I have. Only in defense or battle though. Not that it truly makes a difference."

Moira was silent for a while before asking, "Do you think that the magic pushed you to do those things?"

"No." Nevinon stared at her. "Why do you ask?"

"What if I had done something bad in our first life?" she asked.

"Such as?"

Moira shrugged.

"Like killing someone, you mean?"

She shook her head. "Never mind." She stood up. "You know what, I think I'll head to sleep early tonight. We have a long day ahead tomorrow anyway." Moira walked away and climbed into one of the hammocks. He wondered what she could've done that had made her feel so guilty.

Alanor slid the whetstone down the sword in his hands. He and his father had been assigned the task of sharpening the crew's swords and taking care of the other blades in the ship's meager armory room.

"This is beneath us," his father said.

"We all had to do the same thing for our swords back in Amari anyway. Besides we're not kings anymore," he responded. "We should be grateful we were even granted passage in the first place."

Octavian stopped his motions and turned toward his son. "Did we really have to leave? Maybe we could've stayed. If we had told the hunters who we were—"

"They already knew who we were," Alanor interrupted, "and they were hunting us down."

His father looked down and continued his task. "It makes no sense. We hadn't even been back for that long. And we hadn't made contact with that many people. How did they know about us?"

"I keep thinking it over too. I don't know."

"What if—" His father stopped and shook his head. "Nothing, never mind."

"What? What if what?" Alanor asked.

His father's grip went tight around the sword in his hand. "What if we have a leak? In the group?"

Alanor was rendered speechless for a few moments before he responded, "You think that someone in the group is betraying us to the hunters? No, absolutely not. I know you don't trust my knights but I can vouch for all of them."

"Maybe it's not a knight," Octavian said.

Alanor sighed. "This is about Nev again."

"Think about it!" Octavian gestured with his hands. "No one saw him come back. He's shifty and he tells these half-truths. How do we know it's not him?"

"He's a warlock. Why would he be working with the hunters?"

Octavian shrugged. "Maybe he would exchange us for his own freedom?"

"If that's true then why would he let us get on a ship headed away from the Isles? He absolutely has the power to stop us. But he hasn't."

His father just shrugged again and didn't respond.

"Father. I trust Nevinon more than anyone else, and I mean that. He would never betray me. Not ever."

"Believe what you want to believe," Octavian said.

Alanor had to fight the urge to respond in kind, but he knew that there was nothing he could say to convince his father of Nevinon's loyalty. If the warlock's actions hadn't proven it already, then nothing else would. He sighed and continued his task. He wouldn't deny that there was a part of him that wanted to reach the mainland already. Though that would mean jumping into the unknown once again. Still, he was sick of being on the ship and playing the role of a servant when he had been born to lead.

However, despite what his father would think, he had learned in Amari that nobility wasn't born, it was earned. If he had to earn it once more, then he would. He continued with his task and hoped that one day soon he would be able to find a way to lift his family out of the situation they currently found themselves in. If only so that he wouldn't have to hear his father muttering again for a long while.

THEY HAD BEEN on the ship for a couple of days already, each one similar to the last with the only difference being the daily chores that were assigned to them by the taskmaster. The hours had begun to bleed together. Nevinon walked down to the lower deck holding on to the railing firmly. He had spent the day tending to his patient and checking over the other crew members in turn. Last night he had discovered that the crew's second-in-command had come down with a fever due to an infected wound.

This morning Nevinon had cleaned it properly and used the ship's supplies to make the man a salve that would help with the pain. One of the druids had also come up to help the man along with some healing magic. Nevinon fought down the jealousy that surged up within him. A physician with magic who couldn't even use said magic for healing. What nonsense.

Thankfully none of the other crewmen had any illnesses to worry about. It was almost close to dinnertime now. Stepping onto the lower deck, he spotted Octavian and Moira sitting in what he had dubbed in his mind as their corner. When they had been assigned to do laundry together he had begun to panic. Those two got along almost worse than he and Octavian, which was saying something. Not to mention that both of them were nobles who had never done laundry before in their lives. Moira had asked him for a spell that would help, but he told her that he had never used a spoken spell for laundry before, only pure intention. Which was the case most of the time he used his magic honestly.

At a glance they looked fine. "No one seems to be injured. I see the laundry went well."

Octavian looked up at him and scoffed before sending a half-hearted glare at Moira. Moira rolled her eyes and motioned for them to step away, far enough that Octavian wouldn't be able to hear their conversation.

"What's his deal?" he asked.

"I went to the druids and they taught me a spell that would clean the clothes and then another one to dry them afterward. I managed to finish the task in under an hour without even touching the clothes. Octavian got pissed. Says he would've preferred to do it by hand." She scoffed. "Like he's ever actually done chores before."

He raised an eyebrow at her. "You know," he said with a smile, "people in glass houses shouldn't throw stones."

She rolled her eyes but he was saved from hearing her response when they were approached by Stella.

"Hello, dears." The matron smiled at them. "I was wondering if the two of you would like to join us. You mentioned your interest in learning formal magic before. Some of the younger ones were just about to hear a lesson, if you'd like to sit in."

They both nodded eagerly and joined the circle that was forming in the center of the room. It was smaller than the one that had formed before. Nevinon imagined that some of the druids were still busy doing their assigned tasks.

"We'll start today with sensing our internal energy." Stella walked them through the process. It seemed like Moira had no trouble sensing her own magic. But try as he might, Nevinon just couldn't get a grip on his own energy. He quickly grew frustrated with the task.

"It's alright if it takes time to reach your inner energy," Stella said as she sat down in front of him.

He sighed. "It's not that I can't reach it. I can. It's just that I can't really get a sense of its entirety. I can't control it. It just does what it wants. Honestly, I feel like a ten-year-old again. I don't know what's happened to make me lose control like this."

"Is there a chance that your powers have increased recently?" she asked. "It's rare for someone to go through such a rapid increase in power outside of adolescence, but not completely unheard of."

"I have no idea," he said, "but how would I even know?"

"I can teach you a way to sense how much magic you have at your disposal now. But without having done this before, there will be no way to know for sure if your powers have grown and by how much."

Stella spent the next while coaching him through entering a meditative state where he was supposed to access his magic with more ease and precision. But he still couldn't get a grip on the edges of his magic.

Nevinon sighed in frustration, but before he could try again, they were interrupted by the rest of the group clamoring down the steps accompanied by two crewmen who were bringing down their dinner. He and Moira joined the rest of the group in their corner and Nevinon ate in silence as Moira regaled the others with what they had learned.

Why hadn't the method worked for him? Was he destined to always be different? He wished he knew why his magic didn't work the way it usually did for others and spent the night wondering how he would ever master his magic if it kept changing on him.

He was pulled out of his thoughts when Alanor sat down next to him and elbowed him softly. "What's with the face?"

"What face?"

"The 'I'm so alone and miserable' face," Alanor said. "The same face you always have when you're feeling buried under the weight of all your secrets."

He didn't respond but Alanor nodded thoughtfully. Perhaps that was all that needed to be said about that, because the king nudged Nevinon with his closed fist, then opened his hand to reveal a pair of dice. "Come on, let's play. Just like the good old days, right?"

Nevinon felt a smile form against his will. "Where did you find these?"

"Cassius gave them to me," Alanor explained. "I'm pretty sure he nicked them from one of the crew."

Nevinon rolled his eyes. "Honestly that man is going to get us into trouble one of these days."

Alanor scoffed. "Like he hasn't already? You don't remember that time in Benny's Tavern when he—"

"Oh, don't remind me," he interrupted, laughing. "That was one of the wildest nights we had back in Amari. Took me days to recover."

Alanor cracked up laughing. "Me too. I hadn't had that much fun in a while, back then." The mood sobered a bit, with both of them remembering that day. It had been the first moment Alanor had smiled after taking the throne. He had to remind himself to thank Cassius one of these days. "So..." Alanor motioned with his head at a small empty table on the other side of the room. Nevinon nodded.

They sat down and played a few rounds. Nevinon won each, though he might've used his magic to help along the way. Alanor caught on quickly. "Cheater." He threw one of the dice at Nevinon, who caught it in his hand and laughed.

"I used to do that quite a lot in Amari to win against you," he admitted.

Alanor rolled his eyes. "A kingdom where magic was punishable by death and you were using yours to win dice games? Against the king?"

"Not just when you were a king," he said. "I remember beating you as a prince a few times too. Though you were much more of a sore loser back then."

Alanor nodded. "True." He took both dice and threw them again. "I wasn't used to losing at anything back then." His tone turned sour. "I suppose I should be used to it now."

Nevinon reached across the table and grasped Alanor's hands in his. "Losing a dice game isn't comparable with losing a home. Especially to those monsters." He was referring to both the witch hunters and the shadow creatures. "Sadness and fear aren't weaknesses, Alanor."

Alanor sighed and pulled back his hands. "How can they not be?" He looked at the rest of the group. "They acknowledge me as a leader now, but that will change if I can't prove that I am worthy of that position. A leader should be able to take care of his people."

"Alanor, you were born to be our leader. That will never change. We will have your back through thick and thin." Nevinon shook his head. "It doesn't all have to be on you. You can let some of us share the burden too."

Alanor raised an eyebrow at him. "That's rich coming from you."

Nevinon shrugged. "Okay, so sometimes I don't practice what I preach. That doesn't mean it isn't wise advice."

They sat in silence together as Alanor stared down at the table and whispered in a quiet voice, "I'm not the king of anything anymore."

"Alanor." Nevinon waited until Alanor looked up at him. "You will always be my king."

He watched Alanor take a deep breath and clear his throat. The man pointed at the dice. "Well, as much as I'd like to sit here and commiserate with you, I still have to beat you at this game in revenge so..."

Nevinon shook his head. Knights. They were all the same. They couldn't stand an emotional conversation for more than a few minutes. That was alright though. He would just have to keep reminding Alanor that he was worthy of his position. Nevinon picked up the dice. "You're on."

THE NEXT DAY, as dawn crested, Genevive was cutting up some fruit to serve to the crewmen in the galley. Theodore had been assigned the same task and they were alone in the room, floundering in the silence. She had not remembered a silence like this between them since before they had been married so many years ago.

"I think we should tell him," Theodore said.

She paused. "And add to his burdens? He tries to hide it well but I know that he's struggling now with trying to find a way to keep us all safe. I don't wanna make it worse."

"It's not right for us to keep this from him." Theodore gave her a sad smile. "I see the way he looks at you. He still loves you. He needs to know."

Genevive sighed. "Just give me some time. I'm just not sure how to break it to him."

Theodore nodded. "And what about us? Are we still...?"

Genevive looked away. "I—I don't know."

"That wouldn't have anything to do with Frederick being here, would it?" She normally would've been offended at the question but she recognized that teasing tone he used.

She smacked his arm softly. "Shut up." He laughed.

She sighed and put down her knife. "I miss them."

Theodore did not hesitate to embrace her. "I know," he whispered. "Me too." He placed a soft kiss at her hairline.

It was a long while before they were able to let go of each other. They continued to do their chores in silence, but it was not as stifling as it had been before. However, Genevive knew that she would have to make a decision sooner or later.

CHAPTER 10

THE ENEMY SHIP

Moira stared up at the wooden ceiling for a while before she pulled herself out of the hammock and climbed down. Alanor, Nevinon, and Octavian were nowhere to be seen. More than likely they had gotten up earlier in order to take care of their assigned tasks.

Genevive was already awake and sitting on one of the chairs that had been brought down yesterday. The other woman was fiddling with a thin comb, occasionally trying to pass it through her tight curls, to no avail. Moira sat down next to her.

Genevive held up the comb. "The boys bought this comb." She sighed then offered it to Moira. "It would probably work for your hair."

Moira took the comb and began passing it through her wavy black hair. It certainly seemed that the comb was made for her type of hair. She continued to use it despite the fact that she had never been able to manage her waist-length hair on her own before. Genevive tried to untangle her hair with her hands and then silently asked for the comb back to attack a frustrating knot. Despite all of her efforts, the comb just would not pass through her hair.

Genevive cursed. "This thin comb is going to break in my hair."

Theodore, who had sat up a bit before and had been listening, approached them. "I could help you if you'd like?"

Moira looked on with mild shock as he ran his hands through Genevive's brown curls. Moira noted after a moment that his offer had probably been to Genevive exclusively. Moira had noticed the two were closer than in her first life and wondered what had caused the change. She knew they had grown up in the same household, with Genevive being the daughter of one of the Claymore house servants, but Moira thought they had grown apart.

"We'll have to ask the druids for a comb that won't hurt you," he said.

Genevive gave him a sweet smile. "Sure, if you don't mind."

Theodore smiled in return. "Not at all. Reminds me of our youth." They seemed to laugh softly at some inside joke. Moira felt a sudden jolt in her chest and tried not to let it show on her face. The two got up and went to speak with the druids who were also just getting up. They set up across the room where Theodore and one of the druid women began to untangle Genevive's hair.

After a while of trying to untangle her hair on her own, she slammed the comb down and huffed. Her frustration had nothing to do with watching Genevive sit the way she used to when others took care of her hair. At least that's what she told herself. Untangling her hair used to be one of her favorite parts of the morning. It was relaxing when someone else was doing it for her.

Well, if she couldn't have anyone take care of it, and she couldn't do it herself, it was just going to get worse and worse as time went on. After a moment of hesitation she took her dagger from her waist and carefully cut a piece of her hair away. She inhaled in shock as her hand came away with a length of hair longer than her arm. She watched the strands fall to the ground. Her hair had been the envy of all the other ladies in the court once. Now she was not even a lady at all. She continued to hack at her hair.

"You're going to get an uneven cut like that." Frederick sat down next to her and motioned to the dagger.

Moira glared at him. "I just want it off! I can't manage my hair this long on my own. I don't know how Cassius manages his."

"He's had experience living rough before," Frederick stated. "He's also been on a ship before so..."

With a sinking feeling in her gut she remembered the group of maidservants that used to help her with her hair every day. She had known all of them by name. They had been her friends and they would gossip about the court with her while they tended to their lady's hair. Genevive used to be one of those maids. Now across the room, Genevive was sitting like a lady and having her hair done by a knight. For a split second Moira felt angry that a servant girl, her servant girl, managed to capture the attention of the knight she had her eyes on. Not just him either—she glanced at Frederick—but two knights and one king. Did she have to take all of them?

Then she felt her anger wash away as it was replaced by shame. How could she be so angry that her friend was happy now? Genevive had been her closest friend. She had often tried to make the girl's life easier in Amari, and had lamented often that the servants weren't treated with as much respect as the snotty nobles, especially in Octavian's court. And now look at her. Moira was acting like one of those snotty nobles. She was happy for Genevive, truly. She only wished she could feel happy for her without also feeling just a bit heartbroken.

"Wait here." Frederick stepped away for a moment and came back with a pair of scissors. "I can help with this." Moira turned so that her back was to the knight and he could cut her hair more easily. "You're sure you want to cut your hair so short?"

"It's a nuisance." She sighed.

Frederick laughed quietly. "You know, I had a little sister. She was a lot like you." He snipped away at her hair with the scissors.

"Quite the rebel. She always wore her hair short, much to our mother's chagrin. She always said to her, 'If you want my hair so long, then you wash it!'" He smiled wistfully.

Moira quickly got the sense that something had happened to Frederick's sister. The man had come to Amari alone, seeking a knightship, and he had never mentioned his family before. She didn't ask.

Frederick looked across the room at Theodore and Genevive. "They seem close."

Moira gave him a sour smile. "Afraid of a little competition, are you?"

Frederick gave her a blank stare. "Are you?"

Moira huffed but didn't respond.

"Word around the castle was that Theo had been sweet on you since he became a knight," Frederick said.

Moira was silent for a moment before saying, "Well, obviously that's not true anymore."

Frederick hesitated. "Are they..."

Moira shrugged. "I don't know, they certainly seem like it."

"Do you think Alanor knows?"

"Probably not," she said. "He's worried about other things right now." She looked up at him when he paused his cutting. "Are you going to let her go a second time?"

"That depends," Frederick answered after a bit.

"On what?"

"On her." Frederick made a few more cuts before stepping away. "There. All done."

Moira moved her head from side to side. "It feels so much lighter." She wasn't sure if she was just talking about her hair. She looked at the knight. "Thank you."

He nodded. "Anytime." He held up the scissors. "I should probably go return these."

She nodded and the man walked away. She sighed and stood up, stretching a bit. If she wanted to be done with her chores by dinnertime she had to start soon. She glanced at Theodore and

Genevive one last time before making her way to the upper decks. Best not to get involved, she decided with finality.

✟

"YOU SHOULDN'T SCRUB SO HARD," Nevinon said.

Octavian sent him a vicious glare before refocusing on his task. They were in the galley of the ship. Nevinon was in charge of washing all of the dishes for the day. Octavian had been assigned to scrub and clean the floors. Nevinon had offered to show him how that morning, but Octavian had ignored him and began his task. The warlock had been surprised to see that the man actually knew something about cleaning, though his technique needed some adjusting. At the rate Octavian was going, he would only make the work harder for himself. Though, he wasn't going to offer his help anymore if it would just be met with disdain.

Octavian spoke a little while later. "I see the way you look at him. My son is out of your league, just so you know."

"Piss off!" he shot back. "Alanor is my best friend. Nothing more."

Octavian smirked up at him. "Sure. Well, I suppose it doesn't matter anyway. He's still pining over his peasant wife." The man rolled his eyes. "I'm not an idiot. I know he married her. Suppose he regrets it now that she's all over the other knights."

Nevinon gritted his teeth. "Don't talk about Evie like that."

"Because you're such close friends, right?" Octavian scoffed. "You haven't even spoken to her this entire time. Though I suppose jealousy would throw a wrench in that friendship."

"Evie was a great wife and a great queen." He tried not to let his slight bitterness show as he mentioned the former but the smug look on Octavian's face told him he hadn't been successful.

"And how would you know?" the man asked. "You weren't even in Amari when she was queen, or was that another lie?"

"Evie sat on that throne for longer than you and Alanor combined. If anyone's a royal here it's her, not you."

He felt slightly victorious when Octavian's smug grin was replaced with another glare. They both returned to their tasks in silence. It wasn't until a few more hours of relentless work passed that the silence was broken. Nevinon had almost forgotten that he was not alone in the room when Octavian slammed his scrub into the bucket next to him, sending up a wave of soapy water that drenched the warlock.

"Oi!" Nevinon gasped. "What the hell is wrong with you?"

He was going to throw his sponge at the man in revenge until he saw the look on Octavian's face. It reminded him slightly of the look Alanor would have whenever he was struggling with some painful emotion. Nevinon caught a glimpse of slightly glossy eyes —were those tears?—before Octavian gritted his teeth and looked away. The man silently grabbed his scrub and began to clean the mess he had made with his outburst. It was a while before the man spoke in a quiet voice that Nevinon had never heard him use before.

"I spent my whole life"—Octavian paused like it was hard to get the words out—"fighting for a world where no one could ever push me below my rightful station again. So that any children I ever had would never have to fight for their place in this world at all." He continued his work as he spoke. "Now here I am, on a ship headed goodness knows where. On my knees. Scrubbing the floor."

Nevinon's first instinct was to take over Octavian's job and let him off the hook. Perhaps that would gain him favor in the other man's eyes. He had a brief thought that perhaps Octavian was just giving a sob story in order to get out of cleaning the floor. However, even if he was, Nevinon wasn't heartless. He got down on his knees and tried to take the brush from Octavian. "Let me do it then. We'll tell the others that we both worked."

However, Octavian jerked his hand away from Nevinon. "No matter what you may think of me"—the other man glared at him —"I am not a cheat." He continued to scrub the floor.

Nevinon sighed. It would seem that the father was just as

stubborn as the son. He laid his hands on Octavian's shoulders to stop him, and spoke a spell in a quiet voice. The other man froze before glancing downward and raising an eyebrow at the warlock.

Nevinon gave him a hesitant smile. "Just a bit of cushioning." He stood up. "So your knees don't get bruised."

Octavian gave a slight nod in thanks, obviously uncomfortable over the use of magic. They both returned to their work.

THE NIGHT HAD FALLEN GENTLY, almost unnoticed, until everyone on board the ship began to return to their beds and hammocks. It was humid but not unpleasantly so. At least it wasn't to Cassius, who was no stranger to traveling by ship. Cassius and Solomon had both been given different places to sleep, but they weren't fooling anyone. As soon as the others were asleep he climbed into the hammock with Solomon. He hadn't been able to have a peaceful night's rest without the other man since they had met and come together.

Solomon was still awake and pulled Cassius to his side. Cassius rested his head on Solomon's shoulder, and his hand on the other's chest, feeling the gentle, soothing rhythm of his lover's heart.

"Is everything alright, Sol?" Cassius whispered. Solomon gave him a questioning look and Cassius continued. "It's just that... ever since we came back, you've been..."

"Too clingy?" Solomon winced.

"No, not—I don't mind that you want me so close. I feel the same about you, but I think that maybe this is coming from a place of fear? I just want to know if you're okay, and if there's anything I can do to help?"

Solomon was silent for a bit before answering. "I—I don't think I'm okay, Cass. I watched you die. And it was so quick, not that I wanted you to suffer a longer death"—the man pulled him even closer—"but I didn't get a chance to say goodbye. You were there one second and gone the next. I didn't know who killed you, so I couldn't even distract myself with vengeance."

"I'm so sorry, Sol," he breathed.

Solomon grasped at his hand and intertwined their fingers, Cassius's pale skin contrasting deeply with his. "It's not your fault. You have nothing to be sorry for."

"I left you alone."

"Not by choice. I understand that."

Cassius snuggled in closer, as close as he could possibly get, and after a moment spoke again. "The others say you disappeared a few years after the battle. That they never saw you again and assumed the worst. Did you leave the Isles?"

Solomon shook his head. Cass could tell that it was hard for him to speak of it but he would because Cassius had asked it of him. That was just the kind of man Solomon was. When the other spoke, his words were cut by pain and interrupted by sorrow. "After that day, life just wasn't the same. It was as if the colors around me had bled out. I couldn't live without you. I didn't want to live without you." Solomon brought a hand up to caress his face. "Two years later, on the anniversary of your funeral at the lake, I just...couldn't keep going anymore. I walked into the lake with a dagger...and I didn't walk out." Solomon inhaled. "I just wanted to join you. Wherever you were."

Cassius began to cry quietly and Solomon turned toward him slightly so that Cassius could hide his face in the crook of his neck. "Don't cry for me, sweetheart."

Cassius, after a while of quiet sobbing, was able to get his emotions under control enough to sit up slightly to look Solomon in the eyes, though his face was still wet from tears. "I'll never leave you ever again, Sol. I promise."

"You can't promise me that, love."

Cassius nodded. "I can and I will. Never again. I won't have you suffer like that ever again. This I swear to you."

Solomon gave him an indulgent smile and brought him close again. Cassius sent a quiet prayer to any being who could be listening from above. *Please don't let anything take me from him again.* He repeated the words to himself as they both fell asleep by each other's sides. And if the two clung to each other all the next morning, none of the others would say a word.

✤

ALANOR WAS SWEEPING the deck that evening with his father by his side. His father had stopped grumbling about the chores a few days ago. He had no idea why but he was grateful. Alanor wondered if perhaps one of the others had said something to him. Or perhaps he had just tired of it. Alanor startled when a drop of water splattered on his forehead. He looked up, and noticed that the night sky was now covered by dark clouds. It had begun to rain and the ship started to sway as the waves got rougher.

He looked at his father, who had also noticed the change in weather. "Well, this came out of nowhere."

"Didn't the captain say he was expecting clear skies tonight?" Octavian asked.

One of the crewmen shouted to another, "Wake the captain."

After a few moments of experiencing the ship swing from side to side, the captain made his way onto the deck to take hold of the helm.

Alanor approached. "Is everything alright?"

The captain waved him off. "Don't worry. This ship can handle a simple storm and so can I."

Alanor nodded but he couldn't help but feel uneasy. The storm had come upon them too fast for it to be entirely natural. He had seen too many magical storms in his life to not notice this one. As he turned to his father he noticed that Nevinon, Freddie, and Cass had all come up from the lower deck.

"What's happening?" Freddie asked.

Alanor did not get a chance to answer before shouts went up around them. He looked up to see a swarm of shadow monsters amassing above the ship. They did not attack however. He was distracted by a sound behind him, and he turned quickly to see that Nevinon had collapsed, his hands holding his head as he groaned in pain between Cassius and Freddie, who were trying to hold him up.

"Alanor, look!" His father's voice called his attention. He was pointing into the distance.

One of the crewmen shouted out to the captain from the crow's nest, "Enemy ship approaching from the north, sir!"

Alanor realized that the shadowy figure in the distance that his father had been pointing toward was indeed another ship. It took a few more moments for it to move closer. It must've been moving fast. It came into view and he felt his heart skip a beat.

"It can't be," his father whispered. But it was. The ship approaching them, seemingly ready to attack, bore the Amarian crest on its sails.

He had no more time to analyze the impossibility of it all. Screams went up all around them. The shadows were descending upon the ship. One of the shadows shot directly toward Alanor. Nevinon pushed Alanor out of the way and shot a beam of white light toward it. It seemed to vaporize, leaving nothing behind.

He would've felt more confident at their ability to fight back but there were too many for Nevinon to handle at once. Alanor resisted the urge to take up a sword he saw lying on the ground nearby. He knew that it would be useless against the magical creatures. As Nevinon tried to push back as many shadows as he could, Alanor saw that the others had made it onto the deck. One of the shadows went to attack Nevinon's back.

"Nev, watch out!" Evie screamed. She lifted her hand and a bolt of lightning shot past him, singeing his hair before he could duck, and knocking Evie backward. The lightning hit one of the shadows, pushing it back toward the throng, but not destroying it like Nevinon's magic had.

Evie got back up and looked at her hands. "Oh." She was distracted enough that she didn't notice the monster approaching her from the side. Alanor rushed forward and pulled her back as Moira stepped in front of her, calling out, "Focus, Evie!"

Moira summoned lightning with a spoken spell and shot it toward another shadow, but instead of having the same impact as Evie's lightning, Moira's was absorbed.

"The hell? Why is some magic working but not all?" Moira asked as she summoned a fireball and shot it toward the same monster. This time it seemed to work and it pushed the monster away. Evie tried to throw her hands out several times but her lightning wouldn't come again. "Damn it."

It seemed like the shadows were concentrating on their group, completely ignoring the crew members that were rushing over the deck. Out of the corner of his eye he could see Solomon trying futilely with his sword to push away two shadows that were circling like vultures over him and Cassius. Cassius seemed to be trying to summon his magic too, though Alanor had no idea what help plant magic would be.

"I can't hold them back for much longer," Solomon shouted. "The blades aren't doing anything. It's just like last time."

Cassius shook his head. "There's no ground here. I can't do anything."

Nevinon heard them and shot a bolt of light toward the two shadows above them, destroying them. The warlock was trying his best but there were only so many that he could take at once. Alanor heard a voice behind them. The druids had come up onto the main deck.

"I can help," Stella spoke up. Somehow they could hear her over all of the noise. She turned toward the druids behind her. "You will support me in this."

One of her people called out after her, "No, Stella. There has to be another way." But the matron did not listen. She walked confidently toward the center of the conflict. Alanor wanted to go and stop her but he was busy trying to keep the shadows from getting to his wife, who was still behind him. A shield of light exploded from the matron and encompassed the ship, pushing away all of the shadows.

"No!" he heard Nevinon scream. "Stop her!"

But it was too late. The light seemed to be powered by the woman and she fell to her knees from the effort. Alanor turned toward Evie. "Stay behind Moira." He rushed to the old woman's side, skidding onto his knees beside her.

"What is this?" Alanor asked. "How are you doing this?"

Stella smiled at him but even that seemed to exhaust the woman. She reached out and grabbed him. "Remember, young king"—she coughed—"magic can kill, but it can also protect." She fell over, almost to the floor before Alanor caught her. He could tell instantly that the woman was no longer breathing.

"No!" one of the druid men screamed and ran toward them, pushing Alanor away roughly. He sprawled on the deck from the impact. "Your fault," the man yelled at him. "This is your fault!" His scream turned into a gurgling sound when a shadow enveloped him from behind and bit into him with its large mouth. Blood splattered across Alanor's face. He gasped and scrambled backward. The shield around the ship had failed and the shadows were back. They weren't just going after the group this time. They were attacking everyone, and Alanor spotted some that were even going after the mast and the sails, ripping them to shreds.

The captain was having a hard time keeping hold of the helm. "Those creatures are going to destroy the ship!" he called out.

Alanor got up and moved toward his family to find some semblance of a strategy to take on the monsters around them, but before he spoke the ship gave a mighty jerk beneath him, knocking him to the floor. He looked up to see that the ship bearing his kingdom's crest had crashed their side into the ship and now the two were side by side.

The men from the enemy ship, for it's obvious now that that's what they were, yelled out a familiar cry, "For Amari!" before jumping onto their ship and attacking all of those on board. They cut down the druids in rapid succession. The peaceful people didn't stand a chance against these men. Alanor was too far away to stop them and he was unarmed. He cursed himself for not picking up the sword he had seen earlier. They were being attacked on all fronts now.

"Alanor!" his father's voice came from a bit away and he saw him there holding two swords. Octavian threw one toward him and Alanor thankfully caught it out of the air. He rushed forward and began to take down the men attacking the druids. Only a few of them were still alive. He called out to them, "Go to the lower decks and barricade yourselves there!" They followed his instructions and rushed down the stairs, closing the hatch behind them. He spotted Theodore and Frederick next to him. "Guard the stairs and stop the enemy from reaching the rest of them. I have to go help the captain." The two nodded and he bolted off.

As he made his way across the deck, he saw that Octavian had taken up the fight, back to back with Nevinon. The warlock took care of the shadows while his father took down the enemy soldiers with a cutting precision. He took a second to marvel at the two fighting together before a man with a long sword stepped in front of him. At this close range he could tell that the men were witch hunters, or at the very least they were wearing the hunter uniform. The man grinned at him. "The Supreme Vanquisher has returned! There is nowhere for you to run, sorcerer."

Alanor gritted his teeth and ignored the urge to analyze the other man's words. He would not get distracted by his taunting. The man went to swing at him but was not as skilled as he was. The other man was almost announcing all of his moves before he made them. It only took a few minutes to dispatch the hunter and continue with his trek forward. He finally made it onto the elevated deck where the captain was desperately holding on to the helm of the ship. His second-in-command was helping him as much as he could, but two people could not keep control of the ship while also fending off attacks from the shadows.

"How can I help?" he asked.

"Hold this in place." The captain motioned toward the helm. "That other ship is trying to knock us off course. We're in rocky waters, son. If they push us too far we're going to hit the rocks just southeast of here, and then we're done for."

Alanor ran forward to help while the two men rushed around, trying to stop the ship from veering off course. From his elevated position he could see the other ship clearly. The enemy men had all been dispatched by his knights, though his family was still fighting against the shadows.

There was a man on the other ship, standing calmly as if there was not a battle going on before his very eyes. Alanor could make out only his outline, but the other man was wearing a crown. The shape of it seemed familiar. Could he be the one the men had referred to by his father's title? Then he noticed that there was another group of hunters getting ready to board their ship. He wasn't the only one who noticed.

He watched as Frederick took a stance on the deck and raised his hands. Had the other man figured out his magic as well? Frederick moved his hands upward and outward in a quick motion. Alanor gasped as a large wall of water, large enough to block the other ship from view, rose up from between the two ships and pushed outward, taking the enemy ship and blasting it far enough away that the enemy could no longer board. But the motion also moved their ship too, and Frederick was standing too close to the other side when it jerked. Alanor watched helplessly as Frederick, the first man he ever knighted, fell backward and overboard.

"Freddie!" He was not the only one to call out desperately. Theodore rushed to the side of the ship but was prevented from looking for too long before another shadow sped toward him and the crewman standing next to him. Theodore jumped out of the way but the other man wasn't quick enough. For a second it seemed as if the shadow had been absorbed into the man and had disappeared.

The man ignored Theodore and turned toward Nevinon, and began walking toward the warlock. The man was stumbling like he was drunk with his head tilted to the side. Alanor saw a glint of light come from the man's hands and realized that the crew member held a knife. The man ran at Nevinon, who was too focused on the shadows above to see him coming.

Alanor shouted a warning but the sound of the chaos overpowered his voice. As the man lifted the knife to swing down at Nevinon, his father cut the man down. Octavian did the same to another crew member who came to attack the warlock. Several other crew members began to attack Moira, Nevinon, and Evie. The knights did their best to protect the three without killing the crew members, except for his father of course, who was cutting them down left and right without hesitation.

"What's happening to my crew?" the captain asked.

Alanor was about to respond when a shadow came down fast from above toward the captain's second-in-command, who was standing to their side. It seemed like the shadow had been absorbed into the man, just like with the other crewmen. He was close enough for Alanor to see that his eyes had turned black. The man lunged at the captain and knocked him out with a punch. The helm gave a jerk. Alanor was having a hard time holding on without the captain's help. He had never steered a ship before.

He was holding on for dear life when he felt a burning pain in his gut, as if the air had been punched from his lungs. He knew immediately that he had been stabbed in the back. It was the same feeling he had experienced when Kal had stabbed him during the battle at Bergen Pass. The wheel slipped out from his hands and he collapsed to the floor.

The possessed crewman took hold of the helm and started steering the ship in a different direction. They were being steered to crash directly into the rocks in the water. Alanor groaned as he tried his best to get up and stop the man, but he was bleeding heavily and it seemed that his limbs had stopped responding. The others were too busy defending themselves to even notice.

The ship gave an almighty shake as it crashed into the rocks in front of it. Alanor tried to hold on to something, anything, as the ship tilted to the left, but his efforts were futile. The ship was flipping over. Alanor saw his father and Evie being pitched into the ocean, before he himself hit the water.

The impact knocked the rest of the air out of his lungs. It was like that time he had jumped into a lake in late November, as a stupid teenager in Amari. It was freezing. His limbs weren't moving. He couldn't swim. He tried to open his eyes but he couldn't see anything through the dark and the salt water stung his eyes. He was sinking downward and he was powerless to stop it.

He was going to drown in the middle of the ocean. He wondered if his family was in the same position. He had seen his father and his wife being pitched into the water as well. Though perhaps they were still able to swim. Alanor sent a prayer up to any gods that were listening to keep them safe, as he was no longer able to. He'd be abandoning them to their fate a second time. It seemed that in terms of him fulfilling his duties he would always be doomed to fail.

He was sinking lower and lower, the rough current dragging him through the water. He couldn't even tell which way was up now. He could feel the cold seeping into his bones. Then he couldn't feel anything at all, and everything went dark.

CHAPTER 11

THE DOPPELGÄNGER

His eyes blinked open. Alanor took a hesitant step forward and looked around. One second he had been drowning in the ocean and the next he was in this place. It looked like a forest, though he couldn't see past a certain distance before his surroundings became blurry, almost as if he was in a dream. He was standing in a clearing.

Had he somehow been transported to a different place? Was this Nevinon's doing? He heard rustling in the bushes not far from where he was standing.

"Who's there?" he asked.

There came a noise like bells ringing from behind him and he turned only to come face-to-face with—himself. Alanor scrambled backward. The other man, who wore his face, stood there calmly watching him. There were differences between him and his lookalike.

The other man had a large set of antlers sprouting from his head. The antlers were decorated with blooming flowers and vines. His eyes were completely golden and glowing. While Alanor was wearing the dirty and ripped clothing he had fallen into the ocean with, this other man wore a flowing green garment covered by a coat of different furs. It was then that Alanor noticed the fact that his clothes were dry. He reached a hand behind himself to see if there was still a stab wound there, even though he could not feel one.

He startled when his lookalike tilted his head. "You will not find a wound, young king. It was healed before you even arrived."

"Who are you?" he asked. "And why do you have my face? What do you mean my wound was healed? By whom? And where even is this place? I was just in the ocean, and now I'm in some forest?" The questions spilled out of his mouth but the other man looked at him without an expression, though somehow Alanor thought that the other man was amused.

"Are you not still in the ocean?" his lookalike asked.

"What the hell is that supposed to mean?" Alanor took a step backward. "Is this some sort of illusion?"

The other man smiled. "Perhaps. Perhaps not."

"Enough with the cryptic speak," he said. "Just tell me where I am and how to get back."

"You wish to go back?" the other man questioned. "Into the ocean where you are drowning? You do not ask for me to take you away?"

"My family is in that ocean," he said. "I will not abandon them, not unless I am forced to. Look." He held up his hand placatingly. "I don't care who—or what—you are. Just send me back."

"Who said you were ever away?"

Alanor growled in frustration. "I'm not playing these games anymore. Send me back."

There was a long pause before the other man nodded. "Very well. But hear this, young king." The man's eyes glowed a brilliant white, reminding him of Nevinon. Whoever this man was, he was probably just as powerful. Alanor did not find that reassuring. The man opened his mouth to speak. but Alanor did not just hear the man's voice but rather a chorus of voices that he couldn't pinpoint as male or female.

"The shunvora will rise.

The shunvora will rise and Alexsantari will burn,
When the godchild sets foot on Pithikarian soil."

In a blink, the forest and the man were gone, and he was back in the freezing cold waters of the ocean. He broke the surface with a gasp of air. His head was above the water and his weight was being supported by Theodore and Nevinon. Nevinon was shaking him and Alanor coughed up what seemed to be an endless amount of water. They were trying to keep afloat and keep a hold of each other in the rough, murky water. Though it appeared that the shadows had gone, and the ocean seemed to be calming down a bit.

Alanor was startled when a person popped out of the water in front of them. It was Freddie.

"Where's my father?" Alanor asked.

"He entered the water a bit that way." Nevinon motioned. "He hasn't surfaced."

"Wait!" Frederick called after him but he didn't stop to listen before he dove underwater again. He tried to search for a figure but it was too dark. He couldn't see anything. Suddenly a bright light filtered through the water. Alanor looked to the side to see Nevinon underwater holding up a magical ball of light that illuminated the world beneath the surface. The warlock pointed frantically past him, and Alanor turned to see his father floating listlessly a few meters below with an object that glinted gold held tightly to his chest. He swam down, pushing himself further than he thought he could. His lungs felt like they were going to burst but finally he reached his father. Nevinon was right behind him and they pulled his father upward.

They broke the surface, coughing. The man was unconscious but still had a death grip on the object in his hands. At this close distance, Alanor could see now that it was his king's crown. His father also had their seals around his neck.

"He must have water in his lungs," Nevinon said.

"Here, let me help." Freddie had materialized next to them again. He placed his hands to his father's chest and moved them upward. Alanor stared in awe as a stream of water moved out from his father's nose and mouth, clearing his lungs. His father startled into consciousness and started to cough, but at least he was inhaling.

"I guess you figured out your power," Alanor observed.

"You mastered it pretty quick," Nevinon said.

Freddie smiled. "This is going to sound crazy but there was this voice that was telling me how to use my magic and then everything, I mean the magic, was as easy as breathing." The man looked at Alanor. "It's the craziest thing. I could've sworn it was your voice."

For a second, Alanor thought about the thing with antlers that had worn his face and spoken with his voice. Had that been a vision of some sort? Were the two connected?

Theodore had swam over to them. "Pretty handy power, especially how you just blasted the other ship back."

"Yeah, it would've been epic if I hadn't knocked myself overboard in the process."

"Can we save the chitchat for some time when we're not drowning in the middle of the ocean?" his father gasped.

Alanor looked at the debris around them. "Have you seen anyone else? Genevive? Moira? The other knights?"

Freddie nodded. "They're on the other side of the wreckage. I've already helped them and they're looking through the water for any survivors from the crew or the druid clan."

"Helped them with what?" Nevinon asked.

"With a way to avoid drowning. You need to relax while you're submerged. You guys haven't changed because you're too tense," Freddie responded.

"What?" Nevinon spit out some water.

Freddie nodded. "Just trust me. Go underwater and relax."

"That's ridiculous," his father sputtered. "You just want to drown us."

Before he could protest, Nevinon was already taking a deep breath of air and plunging downward. Freddie followed him. A few moments later they both surfaced. There was something different about them but Alanor couldn't put his finger on what it was.

Nevinon looked at him. "Freddie is right. Do what he says."

His father was shaking his head frantically, but Alanor had always trusted Nevinon, and not once had the warlock failed him. He nodded to Theodore, who was ready to follow his lead. He took a deep breath and separated himself from his father, submerging himself in the cold water.

As he tried his best to relax, he realized that the wound in his back was definitely gone. So it hadn't been a dream? He had almost chalked it up to some weird near-death experience but that the knife wound had been fatal. He was distracted from his musings by a sharp pain followed by numbness in his legs, as if he had a sudden cramp that spanned his entire lower half.

He couldn't stop himself from letting out a surprised gargle as his legs fused together. There was a pain behind his eyes and then the world lit up around him. He looked down to realize that he could now see through the water as if he were on the surface, but what he was seeing was not comforting in the least. He had a tail now, a long fishtail where his legs should be. It was at least a meter longer than his legs and covered in dark blue scales. There was a small ridge of rough fins down the back of the tail.

He made a few jerky moments as he figured out how to swim with a tail instead of legs. He noticed he had short strong fins coming out of his forearms. They were sharp to the touch. His hands were also slightly webbed now. As he made all of these observations he spotted Theodore a bit farther away going through the same process. They stared at each other in shock before Alanor pointed upward and Theodore nodded.

He broke the surface and noticed that his father was still fighting to stay afloat, but it was obvious that he was getting tired fast. Alanor knew that telling him about the transformation would only make him fight harder to stay above water. They needed to take advantage of this new ability, and get away from the wreckage as soon as possible. He looked into the distance where the other ship had been. It was gone now but that didn't mean that it couldn't come back. They would be sitting ducks in the water.

"Theo, Nev, go and help the others find any survivors." The two nodded and disappeared under the surface. "Father, you need to submerge and relax like they say."

Octavian shook his head. "No. No, I refuse."

"Please," he begged. "Trust me."

Octavian sent him a desperate look.

"Trust me," he repeated.

His father sighed before giving in and letting himself be dragged underneath the waves. Alanor followed him and watched as his father went through the same transformation. His father realized what was happening and let out a scream, accidentally inhaling water. Instead of choking however, it seemed as if he could breathe normally underwater.

Freddie swam up next to them, and pointed toward his neck. He had gills on each side. Alanor brought his hands to his neck and found his own set there. His knight motioned for him to breathe, and Alanor did so with trepidation. It seemed that the gills would allow him to breathe normally underwater. His father appeared troubled by the transformation but with a look of determination began to swim down toward the sea floor. Alanor wondered what the other man was thinking but his father soon returned with a leather satchel around him. He tucked his king's crown safely inside and sent him a small unsettled smile. They surfaced once more.

"We need to find the others," Alanor said.

It was much easier to stay afloat now, and they looked around to try to see through the waves and the debris of the shipwreck.

"Look, there they are." Freddie pointed.

Genevive, Moira, and the rest of the knights were struggling to help some of the survivors. It looked like a very small mix of both crew and druids. They swam over to join them. Alanor couldn't help but notice how easy it was for him to slip through the water now. They reached the others in seconds. It seemed that they had been the last ones that Freddie had helped because the others had all transformed. Alanor felt something ease inside of him at the sight of his family safe and alive. Though his use of the word *safe* could be debated.

Genevive swam closer and Alanor noted that she was wearing a shirt, though obviously not hers. Alanor wondered for a brief second about what had happened to all of their clothes. She called out to him, "We can't see the captain. I think he slipped under."

"Stay here," he called. "I'll find him."

He dipped under water and noticed the captain a few meters away. The man was struggling to swim with little success. Alanor quickly made his way over and pulled the man up to the surface.

"Thank you," the captain gasped. Alanor didn't respond but he pulled the man toward the others.

"Is that everybody?" Nevinon asked.

"Everyone that wasn't cut down during the fight, I think," Freddie responded.

"What now?" Cassius asked.

"We need to get out of here before that ship comes back," Alanor said.

"Look!" Freddie said. In the distance there was what appeared to be a capsized rowboat. The same one that had clung to the side of the ship for emergencies and disembarking without a port. The knights went and flipped it over, bringing it back.

"It's seaworthy," Theodore said. "Everyone get on." They helped the druids and crew climb aboard but with silent consensus, they decided to stay in the water.

The captain coughed before speaking. "There's an island a bit a ways east of here. It's inhabited. But how will we get there? We don't have an oar and it's too far away."

"We'll pull the boat while we swim," Freddie said.

"Are you crazy? You can't swim that far," the captain said.

"I guess we'll find out." Freddie smiled.

Alanor nodded. "It looks like we don't have any other choice." He grabbed a loose rope that was floating in the water and with help from the others they tied it to the boat.

Solomon grabbed the rope. "We'll take turns."

Alanor went underwater and started swimming east. With their new tails, Alanor and the others were able to move through the water extremely fast, even with them pulling the weight of the boat behind them. They reached the shores of the island after about an hour of swimming. The captain and the rest of his crew plus a few druids, just a small number left over from the original list of passengers, got out onto the rocky shore while the group pulled themselves up to sit on the rocks. There was quite an awkward silence as the survivors looked at their tails.

The captain shook his head. "Goodness, mermaids, real actual mermaids."

"I think we're mermen actually," Cassius stated.

"I think we're an abomination," Octavian said. "What the hell is this?" He pointed at their tails.

"Now, now." Cassius smiled. "If you want to call yourself an abomination I'm not going to disagree, but don't include the rest of us in your sentiment. I think my tail is majestic." Cassius lifted his tail and waved it a bit.

Alanor ignored his father's comments, turning toward the survivors. "Will you be okay here?"

The captain nodded. "There should be a settlement over there." He pointed toward lights in the distance. "We'll be fine. So I suggest you get out of here soon if you don't want to be seen like this."

"Will you tell them about us?" Nevinon asked.

"No," Jacob said. "You saved our lives. We are in your debt." The man shook his head in shock. "I had thought you were powerful sorcerers to have the witch hunters after you. I certainly hadn't imagined this."

"Yeah," Alanor mumbled, "neither did we."

"We won't tell anyone." The captain looked back at the others and they nodded their agreement. "Thank you for saving us from those monsters. We would have been dead without you." They started walking toward the town lights.

"I think we're the ones that put them in danger in the first place," Theo commented once they were gone. "Those shadows are following us."

Cassius nodded. "And did you see the way they possessed the crew? That was new."

"And alarming," Alanor added.

"Agreed," his father said. "I find this extremely alarming. Did you see how the ship had sails with our crest? How they yelled 'For Amari' before boarding our ship?"

"There's more," Alanor said. "One of the hunters mentioned how the Supreme Vanquisher had returned. I saw a man standing on the other ship. I couldn't make out his face but he was wearing a crown."

"Supreme Vanquisher? Isn't that you?" Cassius asked Octavian.

Octavian nodded. "It's a title that was given to me during the Great Purification."

"You mean when you slaughtered hundreds of my kin?" Moira asked bitterly.

Octavian did not respond to the question but continued, "What's more important, is who the hell is using my title to take control of the hunters."

"This could be really bad," Nevinon said. "I thought we were just dealing with a semi-organized group of hunters. But if they're all acting under a leader—"

"And one who knows who we are," Moira added.

"Then we're in big trouble," Octavian finished.

"Do you think someone is impersonating you then?" Nevinon questioned.

"Or just someone trying to steal our legacy," his father said. "It's been a long enough time that someone could claim to be descended from me and therefore this person could take over the hunters uncontested."

"Either way," Solomon chimed in, "I don't think we're going to figure it out here. I'm more concerned with us having fishtails now."

His father nodded in agreement.

"I'm just grateful we didn't drown," Moira commented dryly. "Freddie, how did you know what to do?"

"It's wild." The knight shook his head. "I just heard a voice telling me what to do. And it was Alanor's voice. That's how I created that wave. But when I fell into the ocean, it was the first time I've been completely submerged since we came back. I didn't feel panic. It's like I felt...I don't know, at home in the water."

"That's how I felt when I started growing those plants in the forest," Cassius said.

Alanor looked down at his tail, remembering that gut feeling and the bright light he had seen the first time the shadows attacked. "There's something else. You said you heard my voice. When I was in the water, I think I had a vision of some kind."

His father stared at him with a horrified look. "You've been having visions?"

"No," he said. "I don't know what it was honestly. But I saw someone else there, and they looked like me." He proceeded to explain to the others what he had seen and the words the man or being had recited.

"shunvora." Nevinon looked lost in thought. "Why does that ring a bell?"

"Oh," he remembered, "there was the sound of bells before this person showed up." Alanor shook his head. "Look, maybe it was nothing. Maybe it was just the lack of air. I'll let everyone know if I see anything else."

"That's weird," Freddie noted. "I think I heard bells too when the voice spoke to me. What does that mean?"

"Who knows?" Alanor looked to Nevinon only to see him

discreetly wiping away a line of blood under his nose. The others hadn't noticed.

"Another nosebleed?" he whispered.

Nevinon sniffed. "I'm fine." Alanor didn't have time to question him before someone else spoke.

"So what now?" Genevive asked.

"Well, we're already halfway to the mainland," Freddie said. "Why don't we just swim there? All we have to do is keep going southeast and we should hit the shore soon considering how fast we can swim. Then we can just follow the shore until we hit the city of Tamlinn. That's the capital, right?"

"I don't see what else we could do," said Cassius.

"It might also be safer," said Theo. "Maybe those creatures can't get to us in the water."

Alanor looked over the group. "Any objections?"

"I thought this was a monarchy," his father said.

"Is that an objection?" he asked dryly.

His father sighed. "I just want to get to the mainland so we can start researching what the hell is happening to us."

"Likewise," Nevinon said, looking extremely disturbed to have agreed with his father on something.

"It's agreed then," Alanor said. "Let's get out of here before the villagers come."

With a little effort they got into the water again and started swimming away.

"DID YOU CAPTURE THEM?" the deep growling voice came from the mirror. The man stood in front of it staring at the ground, not daring to meet the eyes of his liege.

"Well?" the voice commanded. There came an excited chittering sound from the creatures surrounding him. The man fell to his knees. "No, my liege."

"No?" the voice growled. "You mean to say you have failed? Again?"

"We managed to wreck the ship, but we were pushed away in the water and our ship took on damage. By the time we reached the wreckage there were no signs of them."

"Spare me your excuses!" the voice shouted. "How hard can it be to capture a group of hopeless mundanes when I have given you an army?"

"I do not believe they are all mundane, my liege. Some of them seemed to have some sort of power. More of them than we expected."

"It is of no consequence. You will track them down again."

The man looked into the mirror, meeting red eyes. "What if they perished in the wreck of their ship?"

The voice growled again. "They will not have perished. They have been blessed by divine magic. I can almost taste it. It sends ripples across the Veil." The shadowy creatures around the man began to yip and laugh before the voice silenced them with a hiss. "They will have survived and you will capture them. I will not suffer another failure. If you do not succeed, I will send our friends to feast upon you, and I will choose another champion."

"Yes, my liege." The man bowed. "Although"—he gave an audible swallow—"I may have a plan to get them to walk right into a trap. One that would waste less resources."

The mirror was filled with a vicious smile and the room erupted into yips and manic cheers again. "Go on."

CHAPTER 12

TAMLINN

The group had been swimming for a while. Even though they were fast, the mainland was far away. It didn't help that they kept on stopping. It was amazing being able to swim so smoothly through the water, but being able to see the ocean world so clearly through their new eyes was indescribable. They swam over fields of seaweed and coral reefs. It was fascinating. They marveled at all the different fish they could see.

Freddie was having the time of his life. He had picked up swimming with a tail faster than the others had. He would zoom ahead and twist and twirl in the water, performing tricks as he waited for the others to catch up. Alanor found it increasingly adorable.

Nevinon often strayed from the group to look at the different sea plants and animals. Most likely thinking about their healing properties, Alanor mused. Even his father seemed amazed. It was like looking into another world. He wondered if there were others out there with tails and what they would do if they encountered them, though he thought the chances of that were pretty low.

The seafloor beneath them began to turn into rock as they continued swimming. Ahead of them was a field of underwater caves and deep trenches. As if agreed upon they all swam slower, not being able to see very well past certain tall rock formations that reached up from the seafloor. It was as if they had entered some underwater canyon.

Alanor felt a spike of anxiety. Something bad was ahead. He stopped and tried to call out to the others, but he was not able to speak underwater. Before he could do anything else, a large tentacle, as if that of an octopus but much larger, rose from one of the trenches below them and wrapped itself around Genevive, who had been at the front of the group.

Genevive let out a scream that was muffled by the water around them. Freddie and Theodore were there to grab on to her arms, and stop the creature from pulling her down into the trench. Alanor rushed forward and tried to pry the creature's arm away from Genevive's tail. It was of no use. Whatever this thing was, it was strong.

Alanor realized that its strength was the least of their problems when the thing rose out from the trench. It was huge. Larger than two ships put together. He remembered hearing of this mythical creature from one of his tutors as a boy. It was a kraken. And they were at its mercy.

The knights began to fend off the creature's other arms as Alanor continued to try to get the arm off of Genevive. It was obvious that they were out of their element. Though with their tails they could move fast, none of them had any idea how to fight underwater. Their strikes weren't as powerful, and they had to consciously think of every movement they took.

Nevinon took to flinging rocks from the seabed into the kraken, trying to distract it. It was working but the creature's grip was not slipping. He spotted a glint of gold from the trench but did not look away from Genevive, who was twisting, trying to help him dislodge the creature's arm.

His father appeared by his side with a dagger that he had taken out from the satchel holding Alanor's crown. The man took the arm that was wrapped around Genevive and with a few quick motions cut it off from the rest of the creature. The kraken writhed and let out a loud, angry sound that echoed through the water.

Alanor motioned to the others to follow him quickly. They swam as fast as they could away from the creature, and when it seemed obvious that they were not being followed, they finally stopped. Alanor did a quick headcount to make sure that none of his group had disappeared. They were all alright. He slumped in relief. Genevive gave him a tight hug and nodded her thanks to his father. They continued swimming after a few moments of resting and reorientating themselves with the direction they needed to go in.

They encountered an island on the way to the mainland sometime during the night after a whole day of swimming. They pulled themselves halfway onto the shore after they checked to see that there was no one around.

"Wow, that was wild," Cassius said.

"What was that thing?" Genevive asked. "It almost got me."

"A kraken, if I'm not mistaken," Alanor responded. "I recognized it from some myths I've heard."

His father nodded. "Did you see what it was guarding?"

"No." He shook his head.

"Gold," Nevinon said. "And lots of it. I spotted it when the creature came out to attack us."

"That kind of money could set all of us up in whatever city we wished," his father said wistfully. "Heck, it could even be enough to go back and rebuild Amari."

"I would go for option one," Cassius said. "Less paperwork." His father rolled his eyes.

"I would go for the option that doesn't get us eaten by an underwater creature," Genevive said before turning toward Alanor. "So what do we do now?"

Freddie faced the group. "We could get out of the water here, but I think we should keep swimming to reach Tamlinn. It shouldn't be that far away now. Maybe another half day of swimming."

"What about food and water?" asked Solomon. "I don't know about you guys but I'm hungry and thirsty."

Alanor nodded. "I am as well. We can stop here for a few hours to rest and such."

"We can search for a source of fresh water to drink," Theodore said.

"Only one issue," Cassius said. The others looked at him questioningly. "How exactly are we going to get our legs back?"

Alanor looked down at his tail, which was still in the water. He had no idea how they even had tails in the first place, so how were they going to figure out how to change back?

"Well," Frederick said, "we all got our tails in the water, right? So maybe we just have to get out of the water completely before being able to change back."

"Worth a shot." Cassius turned and began pulling himself through the sand and out of the water. "This is a lot harder than it looks," the knight groaned. Once he was completely on land however, it took only a few seconds for his tail to turn back into legs. It was weird to watch and Alanor would have a hard time explaining what he just saw to anyone else. Cassius was also still wearing the clothes he had been wearing when he fell into the water.

"How peculiar," his father observed, very obviously disturbed.

"That's one way of putting it." Cassius looked down at his legs before looking up at the others. "Come on, let's go find some water. I'm dying of thirst over here."

They all moved out of the water and onto the sand, going through the same transformation as Cassius. Alanor wobbled as he got used to being on two legs again after spending so long in the water. Nevinon fell over onto the sand with a yelp, causing the rest of the knights to double over, laughing.

After regaining their senses, they walked farther inland. It seemed all they could talk about was their underwater experience. They were hungry and thirsty but it didn't seem to matter much to them. Even their brief brush with danger wasn't enough to tamp down the amazement at the rest of their experience.

"It was incredible down there! I've never seen anything like it before," Nevinon said.

"Must take a lot to surprise such an old sorcerer," Moira teased him.

Nevinon stuck out his tongue at her before pausing. "Hey, did you cut your hair?" Alanor noticed that she had. How long ago had she cut it?

Moira shook her head before walking past them both. "Men."

"It was awe-inspiring," said Freddie.

"Maybe your magical element is water?" Theodore asked.

Alanor noticed his father tense when the others mentioned magic but he relaxed a few seconds later and turned toward Alanor to whisper, "It really was breathtaking."

"It was, wasn't it?" He smiled.

"Hey, Evie," he heard Cassius call out. "Did you use lightning on the ship?"

"I don't know what happened," Genevive said. "I put my hand out and then lightning shot out of it. But I tried it again and it didn't happen."

"It probably only happened because you were in danger. Maybe if we keep trying you can learn to manage it though," Moira suggested.

"I'm not sure," Genevive responded. "Maybe it would be best if I didn't try again. Wouldn't more magic draw more attention?"

"Hey, guys!" Solomon called out. "There's a stream over here. It's fresh water."

They all rushed toward the stream. Alanor kneeled down to drink, a little farther away from the others so they wouldn't all crowd the same place. Before he could drink though, he was distracted by his reflection.

Alanor had never been a vain man before, though he had certainly had his moments in his youth. He had been wanted and admired by most of the kingdom, even by some from other kingdoms. The golden prince eventually became the golden king, the nickname referring not only to his status but also to the fair hair he had inherited from his mother, along with her blue eyes. Never vain no, but always befitting the title of king. Now though...as he looked into the water, all he could see was a man who would never even be let into a castle, let alone allowed to rule it.

His hair was knotted, and despite having been in the water for so long, it was so full of sand, dirt, and dried blood that he looked brunet instead of blond. His clothes looked like they had been through the wringer, because they had, and it was obvious so had he. Tears, holes, stains, and loose threads. He looked more like a vagabond instead of a king. Just a runaway.

The sound of laughter broke his sudden melancholy and he looked up. Cassius had splashed Moira with water and she had retaliated, catching him and Solomon. Nevinon splashed them both with a wave of his hand, scolding them, "Oi, you guys are going to dirty up the water before we can drink."

Alanor gave a soft smile. At least he still had his family with him. Alanor looked back down and broke through his reflection with a cupped hand. After they all drank their fill, they returned to the beach. They were no longer thirsty but any food they wanted would have to be hunted down.

"We can just wait until we get to Tamlinn to buy some food," Solomon said.

"How are we going to buy food?" Genevive asked. "We don't have any money."

Cassius shrugged. "I could just grow some again now, and later."

"We can also fish much easier now, I'd imagine," Freddie said.

Cassius knelt and grew some more bushes of fruits with a few instructions from Nevinon. He also took the time to grow a few daisies, which he plucked from the ground and tucked behind Solomon's ear. It was the first time Alanor had seen the usually stoic man blush so. They all ate, and this time when Alanor offered his father some fruit, Octavian ate without comment.

They slept on the beach and when dawn came they got back into the water and started swimming.

They hit the mainland in a few hours and they swam along the shore, far out enough that they wouldn't be spotted or come into contact with any people. By nightfall, they had reached the shores of Tamlinn. The city was farther inland and was separated from the shore by a small area of caves, though they could see the walls of the city from where they were.

"I think we should stay the night in one of these caves," Theodore said. "It'll be suspicious for a large group to enter the city at this hour of night. If they'll even let us in through the gates. And we'll never find enough rooms for all of us now anyway."

"Maybe we can do what Freddie said and fish in the morning," Nevinon suggested. "Then we can walk into the city as merchants or fishermen. No one will blink an eye."

"We don't have a net to fish with though," Solomon pointed out.

"I could make one," Nevinon offered, "if we have any spare cloth around."

"We lost everything in the wreck," Genevive said, "except for Alan's crown thankfully."

Alanor felt bashful for a moment over everyone making a fuss about his crown. He wondered if any of them realized that they could sell the crown for enough money to live off for quite a while.

"Can't you just"—Cassius wiggled his fingers—"magic up a net?"

"Magic doesn't work like that," Moira said.

"Actually," Nevinon said, "I think I might be able to. But it would be a temporary spell, since I would have to hold it the entire time we needed the net, and it would disappear once I let go."

"We'll need water too," Solomon commented.

Octavian gave him a look and pointed at the open ocean.

Solomon laughed. "For drinking, I mean."

Moira shook her head. "We can head into the city to use the wells but...I wonder." She turned toward Nevinon. "Hey, Nev, is there a spell to turn ocean water into drinking water?"

Nevinon thought about it for a moment before replying, "I mean, I haven't heard of one, but I could probably do it without a spell. And if not, I'll just create one."

Cassius started. "Create a spell?"

Octavian stared at Nevinon weirdly. "And you can just create your own? On a whim? I haven't heard of that before."

Nevinon rubbed his hands together. "Mostly because it seems like I'm the only one that can, at least that I've heard of. I don't know why."

Alanor knew that it was a sore subject for his friend so he cut in. "Either way. If you can provide us with fresh water without having to go into the city tomorrow morning, it'll be a huge help."

Nevinon nodded. "I'll try my best."

"Could I help?" Freddie asked eagerly.

"Sure." Nevinon seemed glad to have the help.

Theodore held a hand up. "Remember that we have to keep our heads down and keep the magic to a minimum. We don't know if there are hunters here, or if the people will be accepting or not. The last thing we need is to be arrested."

"Don't worry. I know how to be careful about it." Nevinon glanced at Octavian.

Alanor looked along the coast. "Right then, that sounds like a semblance of a plan. We can discuss it further in the morning. Let's all pick a secure location and rest for the night."

The others agreed. They picked a cave that was a little ways from the shore, not easily spotted from the road past the rocky hill leading into the city. Even though they were sleeping on the rough, hard ground, with not even grass to soften the floor, they were all asleep in short order. Alanor was exhausted and he imagined that the others felt the same. He had never swam for so long. It took him only a few moments to fall asleep.

Nevinon looked on in shock as Frederick managed to lift a sizable amount of water out of the ocean. After a few tries they realized that any water Freddie could move was fresh water. Apparently he wasn't able to manipulate anything mixed in with the water, like salt. Freddie let out a cry of celebration, and Nevinon helped him levitate the drinkable water into a basin he had created.

Moira was looking at Freddie in shock. "How on earth did you do that?"

Freddie shrugged. "I honestly have no idea. I just repeated the same thing I did on the ship. I do feel a bit tired though."

Cassius approached to drink out of the basin. "Ah, finally. You would think we wouldn't be so thirsty surrounded by water all day."

Nevinon shook his head laughing. The others quickly followed suit, and after they had drunk their fill, the group crowded around Nevinon as he got ready to create the net they would use for fishing. He sent a nervous glance up at the group, specifically toward Alanor. Nevinon had never been able to do magic seamlessly when others were watching. Growing up in a kingdom where magic was illegal would do that.

He focused his intent and pulled down the energy inside of him. A few seconds later he was left with a sizable net in his hands. It was made of glowing streams of golden light and was obviously magical. They certainly wouldn't be able to bring this net into the city, but maybe it would still be useful for fishing. He handed it off to Solomon.

"So," Cassius started, "has anyone ever gone fishing before? With a net?"

Everyone shook their heads and Freddie shrugged. "Well, I'm sure it can't be that hard, right? We'll just find a school of fish and, ah, sneak up on them." He looked up at the others. "It can't be much more different than hunting on land, right?"

The knights around them nodded and Cassius responded, "Right."

Nevinon turned to Moira and Genevive, who were standing behind him. "I don't think this is going to go very well," he whispered. Moira snorted and rolled her eyes.

Nevinon's prediction turned out to be right when several hours later the knights came back out of the water, drenched, with nothing to show for their efforts. Alanor sighed in frustration. Cassius dropped the empty net on the sand, where it disappeared when Nevinon let the spell go.

"Maybe that wasn't the right call," Alanor said.

"No kidding," Cassius huffed. "I can't believe those little buggers are so fast. How do they know when we're coming?"

Alanor looked up at the sun. "It's just after noontime. Maybe we should just head into the city anyway."

"We should eat something first," Cassius said. "Who knows when we'll be able to eat next after this."

"But we didn't catch any fish," Frederick said.

"Screw the fish," Cassius said with a wave. "I prefer fruits anyway."

With no other remedy, Cassius and Nevinon grew food for the group once more. After growing a few bushes, Cassius swayed where he stood. "Whoa." He brought a hand to his head. "Why do I feel lightheaded all of a sudden?"

"It's your magic," Moira said. "You've been using a lot of it recently. It's magical exhaustion. Using magic saps your energy."

"But I've seen you and Nevinon use more than that amount of magic in one go before," Cassius protested. "And I've been using it this entire time with no problems."

Moira laughed. "Yes, but I've been using my magic for years. And Nevinon for longer than me. You'll be able to use more of it, the more you practice. It's like a muscle. Think of it like knight's training."

"Speaking of knight's training," Alanor cut in, "I was thinking that we should start up training again."

"We would need new swords," Theodore said. "All the ones that we had were lost in the shipwreck. All we have is one dagger." The knight motioned to the blade that Alanor's father had held on to.

"Well, we don't have money for swords," Evie said. "Nor for armor."

"I doubt we'll be able to make enough to buy everyone armor," Alanor said, "but we should be able to soon in order to get everyone a sword. We all need to be armed. We'll have to keep our heads down until we can get our hands on some weapons to defend ourselves with."

After lunch the group made their way to the city. It wasn't long before someone gave voice to what they were all wondering.

"How are we going to pay for rooms?" Genevive asked.

Theodore placed a comforting hand on her arm. "Well, we have until nightfall to figure it out."

"And if we don't, we could just come back to this cave," Solomon said.

Alanor shook his head. "We can't keep moving in and out of the city. It'll look too suspicious. The last thing we want is any bad attention."

Cassius shrugged. "We could always sleep in some alleyway if we can't find rooms. I've done it before after some of my most epic party nights." The knight sent a smirk and a wink at Nevinon. The warlock made a show of shaking his head.

Octavian sputtered, "Sleep on the streets? Like rats? You must be joking." He turned to Alanor. "You can't really have knighted this man."

Cassius rolled his eyes. "Oh yeah, like sleeping in a cave is any better."

Octavian huffed. "At least there no one will have to see us in such a shameful state."

Alanor held up his hands placatingly. "Look, we'll figure it out in the city. It's not like we don't have skills. There must be someone looking for guards. Nev is a physician. We can all read.

I'm sure we'll find some kind of work before the day is done. Enough to pay for at least one room for a night. We can crowd into a room. It'll be uncomfortable but it'll be better than sleeping out in the open streets for sure."

The others nodded. Nevinon turned toward his king. "Do you think we should split up? That way we can cover more ground and we won't attract as much attention as one big group."

"I'm hesitant to have us separate," Alanor admitted, "but you have a point. We'll split up into pairs once we enter the city."

Nevinon sighed and hoped that the blinding sun overhead would dry out their clothes before they crossed the city walls.

NEVINON WALKED down the crooked cobblestoned street, trying to avoid bumping into the crowd around him while also keeping an eye on Octavian, who was keeping pace with him. Originally Nevinon had hoped that he would be paired up with Freddie at the very least, but luck was not on his side. Octavian wanted to get access to the library records in order to try to find any information about what was happening to them, these shadow creatures, or Safehold. And they had found out from one of the city guards that the library was in the same direction as the physicians' guild.

They found the guild first, on one of the smaller streets shooting off from the main one. He checked to see if Octavian was following, which he was, before entering the building. They stepped up to the desk where two men were speaking. They were obviously physicians themselves based on their robes.

"Excuse me," Nevinon called for their attention. "I was wondering if there were any spaces available for another physician?"

The man looked at him for a brief second before turning speaking directly to Octavian. "Well, of course we have space. I'm John, by the way. It's a pleasure. We can never have enough physicians. There are so few of us who are actually trained in these matters. And there are hundreds of people that come to live in the city every week now." John glanced at Nevinon before smiling at Octavian. "I'll have someone show your...assistant...where to set up your things."

Nevinon and Octavian stood there silently for more than a few seconds. Octavian glanced at him before responding, "I'm not the physician. He is." Octavian pointed at him.

The two men behind the desk looked at Nevinon for a few moments before bursting out into laughter. John turned to the other. "Is that right? Look, Max, this child thinks himself a real physician."

The two laughed even harder. Once they had stopped, John turned toward the warlock with a pitying look. "You may have been regarded as a physician in your small speck of a town, boy, but we practice actual medicine here. You'll have to learn how to do the job properly before you could ever call yourself a physician. Though we are willing to hire you as a physician's apprentice."

"Small speck of a town?" Octavian's hands were clenched in fists, his knuckles turning white. Nevinon placed a hand around Octavian's wrist. The last thing they needed right now was a fight.

"How much is the pay for a physician's apprentice?" he asked.

"Half as much as a fully qualified physician," the other man—Max—responded.

"Very well," Nevinon agreed.

Max nodded. "You'll start today then. One of our helpers will tell you where to set up and explain your tasks for the day." Max gave a farewell to John and walked out the door. While John went to go find a helper, Octavian pulled him aside.

"An apprentice? But you've already been trained. Juniper was one of the most well-renowned physicians on the Isles," Octavian protested.

"This is the only guild in the city," Nevinon whispered. "I'll take what I can get. We need the money. This isn't the first time I've been underestimated because I look too young."

Octavian paused for a moment before speaking. "You know, Juniper was a close friend of mine. Did he know about...you?"

Nevinon nodded. "You must know that he had magic too. But you let him live."

"He gave it up when it became illegal."

"Not all of us can be lucky enough to be able to stop," Nevinon said.

"It's an addiction," the man insisted.

"It's innate."

"Whatever." Octavian straightened up. "I should get going then." He looked at Nevinon. "The library is only a few streets away. If one of these men gives you trouble..."

"Looking to be my savior now?" Nevinon raised an eyebrow. "What a refreshing change of pace."

"Hardly," Octavian snorted. "It's just that Alanor would be pissed at me if something happened to you while you were with me so, you know, don't die." And with that he turned to leave the building.

"Likewise," Nevinon threw back before Octavian was out the door, disappearing around the corner. He turned back to the empty front desk and sighed. Nevinon had fond memories of his apprenticeship under Juniper. Somehow he knew that this wasn't going to be as pleasant. This was going to be a nightmare.

Genevive and Moira were walking arm in arm through the town square. Despite them wearing somewhat ratty clothing, the crowds parted for them. No matter how they were dressed, they both exuded the energy of noble ladies. Though, Genevive thought to herself, it had taken her many years to perfect that image. She had often imitated the way that Moira had acted when she herself was learning. She saw a group of kids playing in the corner of the square and sighed.

"What's wrong?" Moira asked.

Genevive looked at her. "Us, I think." She leaned in close to whisper, "We've been back for more than a month now, I think, and I haven't had my menses. I mean I haven't had one since I got older, but my body is younger now so I thought that maybe..."

Moira snorted. "Well, good riddance."

Genevive sighed again. She supposed it would've been a hassle to deal with while on the run, especially in a group of mostly men, close friends though they were. Her sad face didn't go unnoticed.

"Does it bother you?" Moira asked.

Genevive shrugged. "I don't know. Maybe I would've liked to have children again at some point."

Moira stopped dead in her tracks. "Again?"

Damn it all. Genevive looked around to make sure that no one could hear, even though it wouldn't have mattered since no one knew them, before whispering, "Yes, again."

After a pause they kept on walking. "With Alanor?" Moira asked. Genevive shook her head. "With Theodore?"

Genevive winced. "Alanor doesn't know. We were married years after Alanor's death."

Moira whistled and was silent for a while. Genevive wondered what she was thinking and hoped she wouldn't tell the others. Moira looked at her before speaking. "Well, you can always pick up a stray child off the streets. If you're possessed by temporary insanity, that is."

Genevive smiled and looked at her. "Children are wonderful."

"Children are demonic parasites." Moira gave a mocking shiver.

Genevive laughed. "Skies above, Moira. Agree to disagree."

Moira smirked. "I'm just glad Octavian can't pawn me off to the highest bidder anymore, because they're all dead, good riddance." She looked at Genevive. "You don't know how lucky you are, to have married someone you loved. Twice."

"Unfortunately, I know exactly how lucky I am. I tried to make things better for other women when I took the throne but..."

"Let me guess, the council of bitter old men blocked your every suggestion?" Moira rolled her eyes.

"They wouldn't listen to me," she huffed. "I thought it would be better after I had married Theo, but then they just turned to him for orders instead of me."

"Not surprising in the least." Moira shook her head. "Would that I had been born a man. I'd've conquered the world by now." Genevive nodded empathetically.

"Or at the very least dethroned Alanor," Moira continued.

She gave a mock gasp. "You speak treason, my lady."

"I don't just speak it, my lady." Moira stuck her chin up in an exaggerated stance. "I threaten it."

Genevive laughed. "You're incorrigible." Moira smiled and they continued walking.

After a while Moira spoke again. "Are you going to tell Alanor soon?"

"I should, yeah." She sighed.

"I would do it sooner rather than later," Moira said. "You know how he is about lying."

"I'm not lying," she defended herself. "I'm just...holding off."

"I know." Moira nodded. "But you know how he is."

She sighed again. "I just don't want to hurt him. He obviously still thinks of me as his wife. How do I tell him that I married and had kids with another man? One of his closest friends?"

Moira shook her head. "I have no idea. I don't envy your position." Moira paused. "Well, maybe I do just a little," she whispered. Genevive knew immediately what Moira was referring to.

"You know, I am sorry."

"For what?" Moira asked.

"For marrying Theodore. I mean, I'm not sorry I married him, but I know it must hurt you and I'm sorry about that," she said.

Moira nodded. "I know. But I don't blame you. I mean, how could I? I was dead. It wouldn't have been fair to expect him not to have been happy with someone else. And I'm glad you found happiness too."

Genevive hesitated before speaking again. "Why did you never tell me about your magic? I could've helped. Or at least been there for you. I always blamed myself. What kind of a friend was I that you felt you had no one to turn to? So much so that you—"

"Offed myself?" Moira finished for her after a pause. "I didn't want to put you in danger. And it wasn't your fault. I was just...a wreck, that's all."

"Well, I want you to know that you're not alone," Genevive emphasized. "I know the situation with Theo will probably make our friendship a little rocky, but I'm always here for you."

"Thank you. I suppose I'll just have to get over you and Theo." Moira smirked at her. "Unless you're going to get back with Alanor. Or Freddie."

Genevive groaned. "Ugh, Freddie too. Why is my life so complicated?"

Moira laughed. "Just tell them all to go screw themselves then."

Genevive laughed. "I just might."

Moira stopped her from walking forward with a hand on her arm. "Hey, look." She pointed down an alleyway. "You said you wanted kids, right? Well, maybe you can have a whole hive of them."

Genevive looked down and saw a building that was clearly marked as an orphanage. She turned back to Moira. "A hive? They're not bees."

Moira shrugged. "Might as well be. Come on, I'm sure they'll need help here."

"I thought you didn't want kids," Genevive said.

"Just because I don't want any of my own doesn't mean I won't help kids in need. Besides, we need to find something to do, right? Might as well stick together," Moira said. Genevive smiled and they walked toward the building tucked away in that small alley.

Alanor slumped against the back of the bench that he was sitting on. He and Theodore had gone toward the east of the city. They had heard rumors that there were more jobs available there since it was closer to the city's ports. It was as good of an offer as any. But after so much walking they just had to take a short break.

He turned toward Theodore, who was sitting next to him. "I've been meaning to ask... When we were in the tunnels I—not that I care, I was just curious—but I did notice you and Genevive were quite close. Were you searching for something together?"

Theodore nodded. "We just grabbed her queen's seal."

"Ah." He hesitated. "Has Genevive said anything to you?"

"Like what?" Theodore asked.

"Well, it's just that I expected her to be happy when we found each other again," Alanor started, "but this entire time she's just been cold to me. You were there with her the entire time before Amari fell. I was just wondering if she had ever said anything that would explain this."

Theodore shifted in his seat, looking off into the distance. If Alanor didn't know any better he would say that the man looked extremely uncomfortable. But that couldn't be the case, could it? Why would speaking of this matter make his first knight so stand-offish? Maybe she had said something after all. He remembered then that Theodore and Genevive had grown up in the same household. They were friends, weren't they? So if Genevive had somehow fallen out of love with him, then Theodore would know. So why wouldn't the other man tell him then? Perhaps out of loyalty? Alanor had no idea.

"Theodore, honestly what do you think? Do you think I shouldn't keep trying? Am I barking up the wrong tree?" he asked desperately.

Theodore hesitated. "Look, I just think we—you—should give her a little more time. That's all. Maybe we should speak about something else."

Alanor nodded knowingly. It had to be their friendship. Perhaps they had grown closer as friends and now Theodore's loyalty had increased more toward Genevive. It made sense then, that if Genevive had confided in Theodore, that Theodore would not tell him anything about what she said. He would not push the other man to betray her trust.

"Very well then." A thought occurred to him and he smirked at the knight. "So what about you and Moira, huh? No luck for you either?"

"I mean, I haven't approached her or anything."

Alanor sent a shocked glance his way. "What? Why not?"

Theodore sighed. "I'm just not sure if...I want a relationship right now."

"But you've always loved her. Ever since we were kids. And now that you have a chance, you're no longer interested?"

Theodore looked at him. "It's just that our position is too volatile right now. We have other things to focus on."

Alanor turned, feeling chastised. "Right, of course." He coughed. "We should focus on finding a way to pay for a room tonight." Alanor paused before asking, "Any ideas?"

Theodore shrugged. "We're both skilled with swords. I heard Cassius, Frederick, and Solomon were going to the city guard's training grounds to see if they could find anything. But maybe we should try somewhere else just in case that doesn't pan out."

Alanor nodded. "Right, well"—he stood up—"let's continue east, I'm sure we'll find something there."

"Oh, we should also ask around to see if anyone needs help with their records, like accounting work." Theodore seemed to remember something.

Alanor sent Theodore a questioning look. "Who is this mysterious accountant that you know?"

"Genevive," the knight said simply.

Alanor paused. "Since when does Evie do accounting work?"

Theodore gave a wistful smile. "Keeping up with the financial records was Evie's favorite part about being queen and managing the citadel. It helped that she was very passionate about making the other nobles pay their fair share of taxes. She's got a great mind for maths."

"Huh." Alanor said nothing else as they continued to ask around for work. How could it be that he had been married to the woman for five years and had never realized this? It bothered him that Theodore apparently knew his own wife better than he did. Alanor wondered if there was ever any hope for his marriage at all.

ALANOR AND THEODORE had in short order found work for a merchant who needed a couple of guards for his inventory after he had been robbed. It had been mindless work for a few hours. At the end of the day, they had both been paid their share and sent on their way. They headed back to the market near the city gates where the group was supposed to get together at the end of the day. He wondered how the others had fared and he was more than slightly anxious to see if they were alright. This would be the first time that they had been separated in a major way since they had come back. The thought of something happening to one of them had kept him distracted all day.

It didn't take long to reach the market. Alanor noticed that they were the last to arrive except for Nevinon. He looked at his father in alarm. "Where is Nevinon? Did something happen to him?"

His father shrugged. "I left him at the physicians' guild shortly after we entered the city. They took him on as an apprentice."

"An apprentice?" Cassius asked. "But he's a full-blown physician."

"I know," his father said.

"What about you?" Theodore asked. "Did you manage to get a job in the library? Did you find anything about those shadow creatures or Safehold?"

"They hired me as a scribe," his father said bitterly, "but I didn't get a chance to look for anything. They had me working supervised the entire time. It's going to be hard to get in to see those records and books without getting clearance first. Also the place is huge. It's going to take me a while."

"Well, I don't think we have anything to worry about when it comes to money anymore," Cassius said cheerily. "Freddie, Sol, and I have been hired as guards for the city hall. We even get paid extra to train the guards. They were impressed with our skills."

Alanor let the pride show on his face. "Of course they were impressed with your skills. I was the one who trained you after all."

"Oi," Cassius protested, "I was pretty handy with a sword before I even met you, just so you know." The other knights in the group laughed.

"Ah, Genevive," Theodore started. "Did you and Moira manage to find anything?"

Genevive nodded. "We did actually. We were hired as caretakers and administrators of the orphanage at the center of the city."

Alanor saw a look shared between Theodore and Genevive but wasn't able to decipher it in time. Theodore spoke again. "You did always like working with kids." The man almost sounded wistful again, more saddened this time. Genevive sent the man a smile but it looked more like a grimace.

"Look, here comes Nevinon," Frederick said.

Nevinon saw them and rushed over. "Thank all of the gods that today is over. I can't believe I have to go back there tomorrow."

"Rough day?" Frederick asked.

"You have no idea," Nevinon said. "I spent the entire day doing useless work and having all of my suggestions shut down like I'm some newbie who doesn't understand what the hell they're doing. At least in Amari, back when I was an actual apprentice, I was learning and practicing and helping Juniper with his workload.

And he always respected my opinions. All they had me doing today was all of the work that no one else wants to do. It was enough to make me want to break my vows and strangle one of them."

"Yikes." Cassius winced. "Rough luck, mate. But did you get paid at least?"

"Yes I did," he said. "What about the rest of you?"

"We all got hired as well," Alanor said. "But we'll fill you in on the way to the inn. Theodore and I spotted one on our way here. We better make our way there before all of the rooms are taken for the night."

"Do we have enough to pay for a room?" Moira asked.

"More than enough I think," Solomon said.

"Remember that we also have to buy food too," Genevive said. "There will be other unforeseen expenses too, trust me, especially if you knights want to arm yourselves eventually. Armor and weapons do not come cheap. The first thing we need is new clothes. The ones we have are all tattered at this point," Genevive said. She turned to his father. "I don't even know how you got into the library."

"Well, it's open to the public," Octavian said, "so I don't think they could have stopped me from entering."

"Also," Nevinon said with a smile, "you can take the king out of a king's clothing, but Octavian still walks like a noble."

"Thank you." Octavian nodded.

"I'm not entirely sure that was a compliment," Nevinon responded.

Octavian rolled his eyes then looked at Genevive. "We can go into the markets tomorrow to buy cloth for clothing. I'm assuming you know how to sew. I don't think I'm going to be much help."

Genevive raised an eyebrow at him. "Well, I can always teach you if you don't want to sit around doing nothing."

Alanor cut in before his father could respond with a cutting comment. "We'll worry about all of the expenses when they come up. For now let's just worry about getting a roof over our heads tonight. Come on."

The group walked through the evening crowds until they found the inn that Alanor had mentioned earlier. The inn had a tavern on the first floor, much to Cassius's enjoyment. Alanor, Cassius, and Octavian decided to go up toward the bar, while the others grabbed a table for them to eat dinner at. Behind the bar stood an elderly woman with curly gray hair.

"Well, aren't you just the finest woman I've seen in all my life." Cassius leaned on the bar counter. "Won't you do me the pleasure of having a drink with me?"

"Seriously?" his father asked. "You're incorrigible."

The elderly woman laughed and smiled at Cassius. "I would love to have a drink with such a spry young man."

"I'm afraid he's taken, ma'am," Alanor said. "But we would like one of your rooms for the night."

The woman laughed again and told them the price of the room plus how much dinner would cost for everyone. They did have enough to pay, but it had been more than what he was expecting. He supposed that the prices to stay in the middle of the city were higher than they would've been in the small towns he had visited before. It's true that he had never had to pay for lodging in the citadel of course, since he had lived in the castle. Alanor pushed down the thoughts. Thinking about his old home would only bring back feelings of bitterness, and he didn't need that. He needed to stay focused on the now.

The group ate dinner in relative silence, all of them exhausted. They had spent the morning fishing to no avail, and the second half of the day working to the bones in their given menial jobs. Once they had eaten dinner, they all piled into the same room. There was a small bed that was large enough for two, and Alanor quickly gave it to the ladies in the group. The rest of them would sleep on the floor. At the very least it was more secure than camping in the wilderness, and that thought made it easier to sleep even though he was not yet used to the discomfort.

A FEW DAYS later Alanor was sitting in the fairly empty tavern having breakfast next to his father. Everyone had already left for their jobs, which meant that Alanor didn't have to hide the look of frustration on his face. Each person in the group had been working harder than they ever had in their life but every day most of their pay had to go toward their room and their food. Not to mention that after that first day they all had to spend quite a lot on new clothing, just so that they wouldn't be thrown out of the jobs that they had been lucky enough to find. At this rate it seemed like they would never make any progress upward. All the money they earned was just spent immediately.

Alanor sighed. He had never known that it was so difficult to live as part of the working class. He wondered how it was possible that there had never been a riot in Amari. If he had to continue this way for much longer Alanor thought he would surely lose his mind. As a boy he had always romanticized the thought of running away to someplace where no one would recognize him, where he would earn everything based on merit and not just his name. But he realized now that reality was a lot rougher than his romanticized dreams.

Sure they were making a decent enough amount of money that they could survive, but it wasn't enough to move them past just survival. Certainly they were not living the way they used to in Amari. Their first life had been one of kings, queens, and knights. Now they were living like poor peasants, and though Alanor was grateful that they were able to survive at all and hadn't been caught by hunters yet, it certainly grated.

He turned toward his father. "No luck with those records yet? There has to be something on those creatures, right? Or at the very least on the existence of Safehold?"

"I've only been able to check out the books in the library briefly for a few moments," his father said, "and none of them had any mention of anything relevant to our situation. I doubt we're going to find anything honestly."

"How the hell are we supposed to figure out what the hunters are after, and why they're hunting us down, if we can't even find anything on those monsters that they're sending after us? Or the place they're looking for? We don't even know why we came back in the first place," Alanor said.

His father shook his head. "I have no idea, but something tells me the situation is going to get dire if we don't figure it all out soon."

He sighed. "Well, we'll just have to keep trying. It'll take some time but I'm sure we'll find something," Alanor said, not knowing if he was trying to convince his father or himself.

"Keep trying?" His father huffed. "What are we going to do, Alan? Live in an inn, all nine of us to a single room, while we work useless jobs forever?"

"I don't know, Father," Alanor said. "A few weeks ago we weren't even alive. We just need to settle down for now before we figure out what to do."

"What we *need* is a way to finally get ahead of these hunters," his father said. "Gain some sort of edge over them. I don't think it'll be long before they come for us."

Both of them started when one of the other patrons of the tavern sat down at their table. "Did I hear one of you mention those witch hunters?"

Alanor and Octavian shared a wary glance.

"I can't wait till they get here," the man continued. He appeared to be a fisherman.

"The hunters are coming here?" Alanor asked with wide eyes.

The fisherman nodded. "Oh yeah, the council of the city invited them. You see, we haven't been able to get any shipments from other ports and the fish supply has almost disappeared. It's a disaster. Fishing provides almost half of our food. If this continues...we'll have a civil war within these walls pretty soon."

Chapter 13

The Secret Affairs

His father narrowed his eyes. "What's causing the shortage?"

The man looked at them in shock. "You haven't heard?"

"Heard what?" his father asked.

"About the sea monster." Alanor sent an alarmed glance at his father. "None of the ships that have gone out to defeat it have come back. And it's blocking off ships from reaching the port. I hope those hunters can do something about it though."

Alanor felt a sinking weight in his gut. "When will they arrive?"

"Oh, no one knows for sure," the man continued. "They'll arrive when they're able, I suppose." One of the barmaids waved the fisherman over. "And that's my meal. Nice meeting you folks."

As soon as the man was out of earshot, his father turned to him sharply. "I told you that we would be in danger sooner or later. Alanor, we have to do something."

"I know." Alanor nodded. "But right now the others are out already and I'm going to be late, I have to go. The last thing we need right now is to lose a source of income. We'll need to share this with the others tonight."

Before he could fully stand up his father grabbed on to his forearm. The man hesitated before saying, "Just...stay safe."

Alanor nodded. "You too."

The two stood and parted without another word, each moving in opposite directions toward their places of work. He couldn't believe this was happening again. They had just settled down somewhat in the city, and now the hunters were coming back. Would they have to run again and go through the same thing somewhere else? It seemed like they just weren't getting a chance to get their feet under them before they were knocked down again. This time it would be different, he swore. He wasn't going to let these hunters send them packing again.

THAT NIGHT the group had discussed the matter, though they hadn't reached any accord other than to continue as they had been. It was probable that if the hunters were just coming to deal with the sea monster problem that they wouldn't even enter into the thick of the city, though Alanor was hesitant to believe that that would be the case. But currently they had no real home, no weapons, and no allies. All they could do was hope that the hunters would leave them be, or, at the very least, wouldn't notice them. They just had to keep their heads down.

After dinner they had all retreated to their room. Though it was a small space, everyone had already found their spots. Alanor was resting on the bed with his back against the headboard. Moira and Evie were using the cloth they had bought to sew some more clothing for them.

Solomon approached them. "I could help with that." He motioned to the cloth.

"You know how to sew?" Moira looked at him skeptically.

Solomon gave a nod without commenting further. She gave him a needle and some cloth. Cassius and Freddie joined him.

"As a boy, I helped my mother make our clothes every year," Cassius explained.

"Maybe I could help," Alanor suggested tentatively.

Genevive gave a gentle laugh. "Alanor, you don't know how to sew."

"You're likely to give us all shirts with three sleeves instead of two," Cassius teased.

"Well, I could learn," Alanor grumbled.

"Here." Genevive patted the chair next to her and Alanor sat down. She quickly showed him what she was doing with the needle and thread, before giving him his own set. After several failed attempts and quite a few stabs to his fingers, he looked up at the others with a huff. They were trying to stifle their laughs.

"Not so easy, is it?" Nevinon asked.

"It's quite difficult actually. I don't know how you avoid stabbing yourself with the needle."

"It's called precision, Dollface," Cassius said.

"And practice," Moira said. "If you had been a lady at court, you would have been forced to learn this, instead of being able to prance around stabbing things with a sword."

"Don't act like you didn't do both whenever you wanted." Alanor laughed.

Moira smirked at him. "I always get what I want."

Alanor shook his head. He gave the cloth and needle back to Evie, before he managed to butcher the cloth they had bought with their hard-earned money. He spotted his father sitting alone, looking out the window, away from the rest of the group.

He stood and walked over to him. "You know you don't have to be all alone here. And I doubt we need the guard watch right now. You could join us."

His father scoffed, "And do servants' work? No thank you. I've been humiliated enough since we left the Isles."

Alanor paused before responding, "I don't think servants' work is humiliating. It's necessary. We should be thankful. And besides"—Alanor sat down next to his father—"we're no longer at court. They aren't servants."

His father looked back at the group and shook his head. "They're your people. Not mine."

"They would welcome you if you wanted to join them."

"They all hated me when I was king, and for good reason too probably," the man grumbled. "The only reason that I wasn't left behind on the Isles is you."

Alanor shook his head. "I don't think they would have abandoned you."

"I beg to differ. I just don't see what my role in this group is. I'm not king and I don't know how to work manually like the others do. What is my purpose? We don't know what brought us all back, but it's evident that the thing we all have in common is you. But you don't really need me anymore, so why am I here?"

"Of course I need you," Alanor said.

"Do you really? Or do you just think that you do?"

"You're my family. You help me just by being by my side and supporting me." Octavian didn't respond but Alanor hoped that he had assuaged his father's fears. "Besides, you're not the only one wondering about their position in the group."

His father raised an eyebrow at him.

"I haven't exactly always lived up to the expectations set out for me as king. Especially not since we came back. Hell, even before we came back. I'm not sure how you managed for decades. I don't know how I could ever stand in your shoes."

"You can't."

The look of shocked hurt must've been obvious on his face because his father continued, "I meant you can't because they're mine. Get your own damn shoes, kid."

Alanor gave an exasperated smile. His father tilted his head. "Besides, it's not like you can melt down my shoes to make your own."

"You're still mad about that?"

"Who said I was mad? I'm not mad at all." They both laughed and Alanor was grateful to have broken his father's tense mood.

They were interrupted when Solomon approached. "Theodore has just come back from the bakery. He brought some pastries before the shop closed for the night. Come on." He motioned them toward the table at the other end of the room.

Alanor stood up and helped his father to his feet. Alanor inhaled the wonderful smell of warm pastries, and hoped that some good food and conversation would be enough to distract him and his father both from melancholic thoughts.

NEVINON SENT a wary glance over the crowd. He had left the inn that morning with Cass and Freddie in order to buy some supplies from the market. He was about to join the other two when he spotted a man at the other corner of the market square. He was obviously a noble and Nevinon's eyes focused on the bag of coins that was hanging from his waist.

Exactly how much gold did the other man have in that bag? Would it be enough to buy arms for everyone in tne group? It would be so easy to take it with magic. All he had to do was cast a spell to make it harder to notice his presence and sneak up on the man. With another swift spell he could cut the bag from the man's waist and disappear, never to be seen again.

The man probably didn't need the extra money anyway, and with the extra coin he could finally provide something of value to his family. They wouldn't need to keep struggling anymore. Nevinon couldn't help but feel that their situation was his fault in the first place. If he had known that all of them were going to return, he would have planned accordingly.

He went to take the first step but he was grabbed by the arm. He looked to the side to see Freddie giving him a disappointed look. "I know what you're thinking. Don't do it."

"Why not?" he asked. "This could solve all of our problems."

Cassius joined them and nodded. "Yeah, we could become rich in no time at all like this."

Freddie shook his head. "Theft would just create new problems. More serious ones. Especially if you're using magic," he whispered the last word.

Nevinon gritted his teeth. "If you think I won't steal to keep my family safe..."

"Stealing would only put us in more danger," the knight protested.

Nevinon sighed as he watched the man with the bag walk away from the square. He had lost his chance. He turned to his friend. "We can't keep going like this."

"Yeah, Freddie." Cassius lifted an apple to his mouth and took a bite. Nevinon wondered when the man had bought himself apples since there were no fruit vendors in this market. Cassius continued, "We could become a really successful crime gang. I think we'd have an easier time of it too, honestly."

"We'll figure it out," Freddie said in a gentle tone. He turned to Cassius. "Without resorting to crime. We are knights after all."

Cassius laughed. "We haven't been knights since we left Amari."

"Being a knight is more than just a position at court, Cass," Freddie protested.

"Alright, alright." Nevinon held up a hand. "Stop arguing. I get it. Look, we have what we need. We should just head back."

The two knights nodded and they made their way back to the inn. Freddie and Cass went to take the things they had bought upstairs. Nevinon spotted Octavian at one of the tables and sat next to him, ignoring the other man's sigh of annoyance.

After a few moments, Octavian tilted his glass in his direction. "Drink?"

"No thanks. I don't drink."

Octavian raised an eyebrow at him. Nevinon explained, "I might lose control of my magic if I get drunk."

Octavian nodded and enjoyed his drink while they sat in

silence. After a while Nevinon spoke again. "Do you think I'm a bad person?" He continued before Octavian could respond, "Not because of the magic. Just because...because I'm willing to do bad things to keep us safe. To keep Alanor safe."

"Bad things?"

Nevinon shrugged. "Theft...murder, the works."

Octavian took a sip of his drink. "I wouldn't hesitate either if it was about keeping my son safe."

"I'm not sure it's good for me to be agreeing with you about something. Bad for my psyche," Nevinon said.

"Piss off." Octavian laughed. "Anyway, I think it's normal to want to do anything we can to keep our loved ones safe."

Nevinon nodded and they sat in silence for a while. If anyone had ever told him years ago that he would actually enjoy sitting next to Octavian at a tavern he would've wondered if they had been drugged. Yet here they were, not murdering each other. Who would've thought?

When the others arrived, Nevinon headed up to their room to sleep. Perhaps it had been a good thing that he had listened to Freddie. At the very least theft would've made Alanor extremely disappointed in him. The man wouldn't have wanted to use stolen money anyway. The rest of the night, Nevinon wondered if there was actually a way for them to escape their situation with their honor intact. Sometimes he wondered if he even had any honor left to begin with.

Alanor spotted Nevinon walking up the stairs of the tavern with a frown. The other man had seemed strangely somber after his trip to the market. Nevinon had been sitting next to his father, and Alanor wondered if the man had said anything. Alanor approached the table and sat in the seat that the warlock had vacated.

"What's up with Nevinon?" Alanor asked.

His father huffed. "Do I look like his keeper?"

Alanor hummed and figured he would find out later. However, he had been meaning to speak to his father all day. He had forgotten what it was like to turn to him for support. After their conversation last night, Alanor had wondered if he should approach the man about a different issue. His father had not only been king, he had also been married.

Alanor turned so that he was facing the man. "I—need your advice."

"Gods, I don't know when I became the advice guy," his father mumbled then shook his head. "On what?"

"Evie."

His father waved for him to continue.

"I know she wouldn't have been your first choice for my wife" —his father snorted in agreement—"but I love her very much. She's an amazing woman. But for some reason, she just doesn't want to be with me anymore." Alanor leaned backward in his chair. "It would be easier if I knew why exactly, but I don't, and it's been driving me crazy."

His father put his drink down and stared at Alanor for a bit. "Are you sure you want to be with her?"

Alanor narrowed his eyes. "What kind of question is that?"

"I'm asking because—" His father sighed. "Genevive went on to be much older than you, right? About my age, if not older actually. She must've gone through things and changed as a person. I'm wondering if you really want to be in a relationship with her as she is now, or as she used to be. Are you sure that you're not just reaching for a relationship with her because that's what feels familiar to you?"

"I—what?" Alanor sputtered. "Okay, yes, she might've changed a bit, but she still seems like the same Evie to me. If she's changed then how am I supposed to get to know her as she is now if she won't let me?"

His father shrugged. "Why do you want to be with her?"

"Because I—I love her," he said.

His father paused. "That's it?"

"What the hell do you mean, that's it?"

"Look, kid." His father gave him a deadpan stare. "Aside from the fact that you married a peasant, I'm sure you two were great and all back in the day"—the man gave an eye roll—"but from where I'm standing right now, neither of you really knows the other. I see the way you are with Nevinon. Genevive doesn't seem to know you like he does. Theodore and Moira seem to know her better than you do, which is saying a lot considering Moira hanged herself shortly after I died—"

"What's your point?" Alanor interrupted.

"My *point*," his father emphasized, "is that you can't claim to love someone you don't know. You can't just say 'I love her' and have it be true, Alan. You can't love a stranger. So either take the time to actually get to know the woman you claim to love or accept the fact that you only feel like you love her because you used to and that's what's familiar."

His father picked up his drink and finished it in short order before placing the empty glass down. "And you know what? If she doesn't let you get to know her as she is now, obviously she doesn't feel the same way about you." The man stood from his chair. "If that's the case, I suggest you get over it and move on. We have more important things to be worrying about."

Octavian walked away and up the stairs to their room. Alanor spent the rest of the night tossing his father's words around in his head.

✤

It was noontime and Genevive had arrived early that day from her work in the orphanage. She had been one of the first to return from her job. She went up to the room and sat on the bed with her back against the wall, sewing up a rip in one of the knight's shirts. She looked up when the door opened and Octavian walked in. The man still intimidated her quite a bit, despite her many decades as queen.

The man paused at the doorway. "Good evening, Genevive."

"Good evening...Octavian." It was weird to be on a first-name basis with a man who had once almost banished her because of his son's interest in her. And the man who had been her father-in-law.

Octavian paused and nodded awkwardly before entering the room.

"Still getting used to not being called Your Majesty?" she asked. The man nodded and she continued, "I'm getting used to it myself."

Octavian looked at her curiously. "You were Alanor's queen. I suppose my efforts to deter him were futile."

Genevive laughed silently. "If anything they encouraged him."

Octavian shook his head before nodding his head at the spot next to her. "Do you mind?"

"Not at all." She scooted over a bit so that the man could sit. They were silent for a while before she said, "It's not easy, ruling as a widow."

"No it is not," Octavian agreed.

Genevive looked down at the cloth in her hands. "Alanor wants to get back together again. He doesn't understand." She realized then that perhaps it wasn't a good idea to discuss this with the father of the man in question. "I don't know why I'm telling you this."

"Maybe because I understand. You lived for most of your life without him. You mourned him," Octavian said in a gentle tone she had never heard from him before.

Genevive nodded. "And now it's all for nothing. All those years, mourning, ruling Amari. Now the kingdom is gone and we can never go back."

Octavian didn't say anything for a bit until he sighed. "You know, when I was a boy, the kingdom was overrun and I had to run from the citadel."

"The warlord Vasilios, right?" she asked.

Octavian nodded. "I was raised by a friend of my father's. King Dimitri was his name. He was the King of Risvall, which used to be its own kingdom. And I spent the next decade learning how to fight and lead. I raised an army and I reconquered Amari when I was only twenty years old."

Genevive stayed silent and waited for the man to continue. She had never heard that much about the power struggle for Amari before Octavian had become king. It had been before her time.

"Strange," the man said, "to think of all that time spent dedicating my life to a kingdom that doesn't exist anymore."

She nodded in agreement. Octavian continued, "I met Anastasia in Risvall. She was Dimitri's daughter. We fell in love, so of course we married as soon as I was crowned king. After her father died we were able to unite our two kingdoms."

Genevive smiled. "Alanor married me shortly into his reign too."

There was a pause before Octavian spoke again. "Being a widow is hard. Ruling a kingdom even more so. But doing both is..."

"Nigh on impossible?"

"Almost." He smiled. "Though I imagine it was harder for you. Not being of noble blood."

"And my being a woman. The councilmen didn't like that."

Octavian nodded to concede the point. "No, I imagine they didn't. I swear those bastards only served to make ruling the kingdom more difficult." They shared a laugh.

Genevive looked at him. "You never remarried."

Octavian sighed, "No, I loved Ana. There was no one else for me, not in marriage." Octavian sent her a searching look. "You remarried?"

She hesitated before nodding. "Yeah."

"I'm guessing my son doesn't know."

She paused. "Are you going to tell him?"

"Are you?"

"I'm just waiting for the right moment." She shrugged.

"I'm familiar with the feeling." He huffed. "Word of advice, since apparently that's who I am now, the right moment doesn't exist."

Genevive sighed. "I don't want to hurt him."

"You're going to hurt him even more if you keep it from him for much longer."

"You're one to talk, you know. It's not like you haven't kept a secret of this magnitude from him too," she said against her better judgment. Genevive regretted it immediately. She shouldn't have brought it up, but it had been something that she wondered about for years after Alanor's death.

Octavian tilted his head. "I don't know what you're referring to."

She paused for a moment before responding, considering her words carefully. "When I became queen I went through all of the historical financial records in order to teach myself what I needed to know about the kingdom's taxes and such. I went through all of Alanor's reign and then decided to go through yours as well since he had only ruled for a short period of time." Octavian's eyebrows grew more furrowed as she continued. "I found some interesting payments. Ones made on a regular basis directly from your vault. Several of them."

The man turned away and grew silent for a while. She had almost gone back to her sewing before he spoke. "Are you threatening me?"

"No. I only ask that you extend some understanding. Let me tell him when the time is right, and I will extend the same courtesy to you." Genevive noticed the other man's clenched jaw and she hoped she hadn't just made a mistake.

The man went to speak again but was interrupted by the door opening. Solomon came into the room and spotted them sitting on the bed and gave a curious smile. "Am I...interrupting something?"

Octavian planted a smile on his face. "Oh, haven't you heard? It's the first meeting of our new community group, Widows United." The man stood from the bed. "Nice chat," he said, and left the room without sparing her another glance.

✠

NEVINON WALKED through the narrower streets that led to the library, following as Octavian led the way. The other man had told him Alanor had assigned him to search the library that morning while they were eating breakfast. Nevinon had been a bit miffed that Alanor hadn't told him himself, but he noticed Alanor had been putting himself under more pressure at his job these last few days. Most likely because of the news that hunters would be arriving soon.

The warlock admitted that it made sense for him to go alongside Octavian. After all, he was no stranger to research. He wondered if he'd be able to find books that mentioned the ritual he had used during Samhain, and if he'd be able to look at them without Octavian noticing. Probably not though. The older man had the eyes of a hawk.

"The library is this way." Octavian motioned. "There are two guards posted at the door so keep your head down."

"Won't they see us?" he asked.

"There are enough people passing by and going in and out that it shouldn't be a problem," Octavian said.

Nevinon took a few moments to cast a spell on them, one that would push others to glance away from them. It wouldn't stop the guards from seeing them if they were too obvious or noisy, but it would help them stay under the radar. The glare that Octavian sent him told him that the other man had not missed the sensation of magic on his person.

"You don't think magic is exactly the kind of thing that's going to get us noticed?"

Nevinon huffed. "It was just a look-away spell. Relax." Octavian didn't say anything in response. Not long after, they arrived and entered the library without any problems. The guards didn't even notice them. Nevinon let go of the spell.

"The section on magic is over to the right." Octavian led the way.

"You would think that they would have gotten rid of these books considering the oncoming presence of hunters in the city, no?" he mused.

An unfamiliar man's voice interjected. "This land was accepting of magic long ago but has recently turned toward suspicion due to the presence of witch hunters and their propaganda." They turned to see a man dressed in modest dark robes.

"This is one of the librarians," Octavian explained to Nevinon.

"You've come in on your day off. And you have brought a friend. Are you sure I can't help you find what you're looking for?" the man asked.

"I think we'll be fine, thank you," Octavian responded.

The librarian gave a nod. "As you wish. If you change your mind I will be up front." The man walked away.

"Are you sure it was the best idea to brush his offer of help off?" Nevinon asked.

"What were we supposed to say? 'Hello, we're looking for information on something that could've brought us back to life a century after we've died, and that has given us magic and fishtails. Oh, and also we're looking for information on mythical shadow monsters that absorb magic. By the way, have you heard of a magical safe haven called Safehold?' They would have kicked us out, if not reported us to the guards standing right outside." Octavian pointed.

"He did seem sympathetic to magic," Nevinon argued.

"Better safe than sorry. We should keep this in-house," Octavian said.

"Well, then." Nevinon looked at the vast number of books on magic that the library held. "We'd better get started."

They began to pull tomes from the shelves and flip through them. It was going to be a long day. They read in silence for several hours at one of the tables tucked into the back. It was just as Nevinon had expected. No mention of Safehold or the shadow monsters. No mention of anything his mother had ever shared with him. It didn't surprise him.

His mother had never been to the mainland, and he had always believed that she had made up all of those stories. It was something to instill hope in a young boy with magic growing up in a hostile world that would see him killed, nothing more. The hunters were chasing a nonexistent myth.

Nevinon couldn't even find any ritual with a resemblance to the one he had performed in Amari during the few moments he flipped through those tomes when Octavian left the table to grab more books. All of the binding spells he could find with remotely the same purpose were completely different. He rubbed his eyes. He needed a break from the books. Octavian looked up at the same time, apparently feeling the same way as he pushed away the book he had been reading.

"Any luck?" he asked.

"Nope." Octavian shook his head.

Nevinon sighed and opened the next book, which was a compendium of mythical creatures. He looked through the table of contents. No mention of shadows, but Nevinon paused when he spotted a familiar name. He flipped to the indicated page and there it was. A whole section on krakens.

"Hey, look at this." He pushed the book over to Octavian. "I think I might have an idea on how to fix our situation."

Octavian paused, skimming over the entry, then looked up at him with a smirk. "For once I agree with you."

Nevinon smiled and leaned forward. "Imagine if we can find a way to get all that gold. With that kind of money we can finally get out of that inn, and instead of working jobs all of us can focus our efforts here in the library. Between all of us it'll be much easier to search for the information we need."

"And we can finally arm ourselves," Octavian added.

He nodded. "Exactly."

"There's something else I've been thinking about since we passed that trench," Octavian said.

"What?"

"Do you think there could be more of those out there?" the man asked.

Nevinon shrugged. "I mean, ships go down all the time. I'm sure a lot have precious cargo on board."

Octavian seemed enchanted by the idea of amassing such a large fortune. "If we can get our hands on even just a fraction, we could be rich. More so than we ever were in our first life. And all without going to war. We just have to figure out how to haul it all onto land." Octavian brought a hand to his chin. "The trench is so far out and there's only two of us, since I'm assuming that we won't be involving the others."

He nodded. "Alanor and the rest would only try and stop us."

"There's a lot of gold in that trench. How could we bring it all back? We'd need to take so many trips it's unfeasible. Not to mention the very large sea monster—"

"Kraken," Nevinon interrupted.

"—kraken that's guarding it. But there has to be a way to get it done."

Nevinon thought for a few seconds. "Perhaps magic can help."

Octavian narrowed his eyes but nodded for him to speak. "How?"

"I can enchant several bags to be able to hold more things inside them, as well as be lighter. The spell is simple enough."

Octavian gave a slow nod, apparently not so put off of magic anymore when money was on the line. "The idea...has merit."

Nevinon laughed. "Wow, it really hurt you to say that, huh?"

Octavian grimaced. "Don't push it."

"What about the kraken though?" Nevinon asked. "This page only describes it, not how to fight it."

"I have enough money saved up from my work here to buy a sword. The others would be pissed if I spent it all, but if we recover this gold then it won't matter. I can distract the kraken while you take the gold," Octavian suggested.

"But the last time you all fought the creature underwater wasn't exactly a resounding success. That kraken was pretty fast," he pointed out. "Is fighting with a sword even the same underwater as it is on land?"

"Do you have a better idea?" Octavian asked.

"Um, I can help you take down the kraken with magic too. I think I flipped through a book here on water magic. I'll try to find it again. I'm sure there are spells in there that can help. It'll be harder for the kraken to take both of us," he said.

Octavian gave a stiff nod and Nevinon sighed. "Are you really going to be able to work with me if even the slightest mention of magic has you on edge?"

Octavian visibly gritted his teeth. "I will do what I have to do. I'm sure you will too."

"Why do you hate magic so much anyway?" he asked.

The man glared at him but didn't say anything. "Right. Subject off-limits, got it," Nevinon said.

Octavian shook his head. "Let's just figure this out, alright?"

They went back to the bookshelves to find anything that would help them take on the kraken and retrieve that gold. It would finally be a step toward removing the threat of the hunters from their backs. They spent hours combing through the books and only left once the library was about to close for the night.

They exited the building, turned a corner, and walked right into a crowd of witch hunters. There were a dozen of them, in hunter uniforms. They seemed to be in an argument of sorts with the guards who normally worked in the city. "Well, I don't care what your schedules say. You can take it up with our superiors when they get here. There's another convoy coming from the Isles soon. Unless you'd like to deal with your food shortage on your own?"

One of the guards held his hands up. "Now, now, let's not be too hasty."

Nevinon ducked his head, walking past them as quickly as he could without arousing suspicion while they were distracted. Octavian had followed suit, and pulled him into an alleyway as soon as they were out of sight.

"Damn it all. The hunters have arrived," the man whispered.

"Yeah, I noticed," Nevinon said.

"We have to get back and warn the others."

Nevinon nodded in agreement. "And we need to go after that gold. Tonight if possible."

Octavian held up what seemed to be a sheathed sword that Nevinon hadn't noticed the other man holding earlier. "I think I can help with that."

"Where did you get that?"

"Never you mind," Octavian brushed him off.

"Did you take that from one of the guards? How did you do it without them noticing?"

"Let's just get back to the others. I'll hide this behind the crates in the alleyway behind the inn and grab it before we leave the city. Come on." Octavian looked out into the street, and when he motioned that the way was clear, they started walking toward the inn at a brisk but not running pace. A few minutes later Nevinon was leaned up against the side of the building, out of breath. Octavian was next to him and checked around the corner. "It's all clear. We need to act normal."

The warlock nodded and the two entered the tavern. Nevinon spotted the knights at the other end of the room. Octavian gave them a signal that he didn't recognize, but the others started making their way toward them and Octavian grabbed him by the arm. "Upstairs. Come on."

The two rushed up the stairs. Moira and Evie were already in the room, and Moira noticed their tense stances. "What's going on?"

Octavian shushed her and they waited for the knights. Once

everyone was in the room Octavian spoke, directing himself to his son, "We've got a problem. There are hunters in the city."

"You're shitting me," Cassius cursed.

"We're not." Nevinon nodded. "They're guarding all of the entrances and patrolling the streets. Though it looks like they're having a bit of a conflict with the local guards." He turned toward Cassius, Solomon, and Freddie. "You didn't hear anything about them arriving today?"

"Not a thing," Freddie said. "But maybe it's because we're mostly guarding city hall."

Alanor nodded. "If they're here for the sea monster then they would stick to the outskirts, especially in the side of the city facing the port."

"If they're here for the sea monster, then what are they doing patrolling the streets?" Octavian asked.

"Protocol maybe," Theodore said.

"Do you think they're after us or the sea monster?" Genevive asked.

"I don't know," Nevinon said, "but we overheard that another large group of them is scheduled to arrive soon from the Isles. I'm assuming that they've come to apprehend us as well as take out the kraken."

"I thought that there weren't going to be any ships arriving from the Isles in a long while," Solomon commented.

Octavian shrugged. "Well, they found a way. It's going to be a risk walking through the city every day. We can do it, we just have to make sure that we blend in seamlessly."

"There's too many of us," Moira said. "They're going to spot us sooner or later, especially if more are coming."

"Did the two of you make any progress in the library?" Solomon asked.

Octavian shook his head in the negative. Nevinon silently marveled at the other man's ability to lie, though he supposed he wasn't any different.

"Damn it," Alanor cursed. "We need to arm ourselves immediately." He turned toward Nevinon. "Isn't there another way to find the information we need?"

Nevinon hesitated. "I can ask around, but with the hunters arriving it's more than likely that all druids or magic users have gone underground or have left the city. We're not going to find anything that way either." He thought for a moment. "There was one of the librarians we saw today. He seemed sympathetic to magic and knowledgeable too. We can go and ask him tomorrow to see if he knows anything," Nevinon suggested.

"Yeah, maybe he'll tell us what he knows," Octavian said sarcastically, "or maybe they'll just report us all to the hunters and have us all burnt alive."

"We can't take the risk," Alanor said. "Maybe I can get my hands on a few weapons. Theo and I will be accompanying our employer to city hall tomorrow. I'll see if I can get into the armory. Father, Nev, continue in the library tomorrow. If you think they suspect you, leave and come back immediately." The two nodded.

"You're not going to...steal weapons, are you?" Freddie asked. "Alanor, you've never—"

"I will protect this family," Alanor interrupted firmly.

"Alan, if you get caught tomorrow..." Genevive started.

Alanor didn't look at her. "I'll be fine. We should stay up here tonight, and only leave the room if necessary. If the hunter presence becomes too strong in this city we might have to leave eventually."

Hopefully Alanor wouldn't have to put himself in danger if he and Octavian succeeded tonight. Nevinon caught Octavian's gaze and the man gave him a nearly imperceptible nod. He knew then he had asked the right person to come with him to face the kraken. Someone who was also willing to do anything for his loved ones.

Nevinon waited until he could see the moon high in the sky through the window and hear the steady breathing of everyone sleeping around him before he started to get up silently. Out of the corner of his eye he saw Octavian doing the same. The best plan was to sneak away in the middle of the night. That way none of the others would try to stop them, and they would have a head start on finding their way to the trench. They had nothing to go on but the general direction they had come from, so he figured it would take some time to actually find the place. Nevinon was almost to the door when the last voice he wanted to hear called out.

"Going somewhere?" Alanor asked.

CHAPTER 14

THE KRAKEN

A warm light filled the room and Nevinon squinted to see that Moira had lit a candle. Alanor was sitting up, perfectly awake, while the others were slowly starting to come to.

"Is there something you'd like to share with the rest of us?" Alanor stared at them both with veiled anger in his eyes.

"Damn it, golden boy," Cassius groaned. "Did you really have to wake us all up? Maybe they were going to go shag."

Octavian sputtered, "We were not!"

"No, of course not," Alanor said. "Instead you were sneaking off to do what exactly? On the same night that hunters arrive in the city."

Nevinon held his hands out placatingly. "Alan—"

Alanor interrupted him with a sharp glare. "If the next words out of your mouth aren't a truthful explanation, I don't want to hear it."

Nevinon inhaled and spared a glance at Octavian before confessing. "We were going out to get the gold from the kraken." Octavian huffed and shook his head. Alanor was shaking from rage. Nevinon had rarely ever seen him this angry before.

"How dare you? Both of you." Alanor seemed to be trying to keep his voice down. "What if you had died out there? The two of you would've just disappeared in the night, never to be seen again. Gone without a trace. Do you have any idea what that would've done to us? To me?"

Genevive nodded and sat up on the bed. "This was really reckless of you. I can't believe you weren't going to say anything to us."

Theodore nodded his agreement. "We can't function as a group if we don't trust and confide in each other. We can't make decisions like this without running it by everyone."

Nevinon sighed. "But none of you would've agreed."

"I resent that assumption," Cassius protested.

Octavian rolled his eyes. "At least we're actually trying to do something that will help keep the group safe. We're not making any progress. We're just stalling before the hunters get to us. I mean"—the man threw his hands up—"we might as well just hand ourselves in at this point."

"Facing a sea monster on your own isn't the answer though," Freddie said.

"No," Cassius agreed. "But what if we faced it as a group?"

"I'm not keen on getting almost eaten by that thing again," Genevive said.

Cassius shrugged. "We've faced beasts before. Granted that was all on land, but if we work together we can do this. I hate to agree with Kingface over there—"

"Oi!" Octavian protested.

"—but I would absolutely love to not have to sleep on the floor anymore."

Solomon rolled over and sighed, "And buy ourselves some actual arms. The ones from the city's armory are low quality and we have to return them at the end of every day."

Freddie turned and gave a slight smile to the group. "I'm sure I could help."

"I'm on board," Moira said.

"I'm not." Genevive shook her head and Theodore nodded his agreement with her.

"Well." Cassius smiled. "Majority rules."

Octavian practically growled, "If you hadn't noticed, this is not a democracy." Then he turned to look at Alanor, who hadn't moved or said anything in a while. Nevinon couldn't read the look on his face, which worried him. But after a few moments of Alanor and Octavian staring at each other, Alanor finally sighed.

"You know, if we're that desperate for money we could just sell the crown and the seals. They would fetch us a large amount of money without putting us in danger," Alanor said.

The chorus of protests rose up immediately. "Are you out of your mind?" Octavian asked.

"Absolutely not." Nevinon shook his head.

The others voiced their objections and Solomon sat up to look at Alanor. "It wouldn't be a good idea, and not just because of what that crown means to us, but also because it would signal our presence in the city, considering the seals bear the crest of Amari and the crown is recognizable."

"Fine," Alanor said. "Kraken it is. The extra resources wouldn't hurt. But we take what's left of the night to rest and we'll have an early morning to plan it all out. If we're doing this, we're doing it right." Nevinon felt a smile bloom on his face and Alanor shook his head at him. "Everyone get some sleep." He nodded at Moira, who blew out the candle and plunged the room into darkness once more. Nevinon took up his spot again and hoped that this would be the last night they would have to sleep on the floor.

✚

THAT MORNING the group got up extremely early, only a few minutes after the first rays of sunlight had entered the room. Nevinon, and Moira with some direction from him, enchanted a few bags to be able to carry more than they should while they all ate breakfast. He took a moment to hide the fact that it caused him another nosebleed along with some lightheadedness. At this point Nevinon was starting to get concerned.

It seemed that every time he used his magic it caused him physical stress. It was something he had heard could happen to other magic users if they overexerted themselves, but it had never happened to him before, and the feats of magic he was performing now were way less magic than he had used before in the past. It had all started with the ritual. Nevinon felt a sense of foreboding that he tried to push down as he rejoined the others.

Octavian had gone out in the morning, supposedly to get his sword, but the man came back with two swords in hand and quickly passed one to his son. Nevinon wondered if he had taken the second sword as well, and marveled at the older man's ability for theft.

They had also managed to purchase a few daggers, which were handed out to the rest of the knights. Once they left the inn, they split up to be able to evade the hunters that were patrolling the streets and the city gate. It didn't take very long to meet up outside the city and begin walking toward the shore. Nevinon took the opportunity to share some of the water spells he had found the previous day with Moira.

Once they were at the shore, they quickly got into the water. The girls left their shirts nearby so that once they transformed they could put them on. It left them with less mobility but they had no other options. Alanor had briefly argued that the girls should stay behind, but had dropped his argument when both of them had slapped him upside the head. Besides, they needed Moira's help and both of them were safer with the knights than left behind in a city crawling with hunters.

After they got into the water, they swam in the general direction that they came from, hoping to pass the trench before noon. It didn't take long to find it, but they had to take a few moments to decide which direction to go in. Based on what some of them remembered, they chose to go northwest.

They swam for a while before they heard what could only be

described as a muffled roar in the distance. They quickly hid behind some rocks and columns that surrounded the seafloor. Nevinon peeked his head out from behind the rock to see the distant outline of a huge kraken a bit farther up the trench.

He looked back at Alanor, who gave the signal for them to split up. They would attack the monster from different sides. Moira, Freddie, and Nevinon would wait on the sidelines in order to help the other knights with magic while Genevive and Theodore would take the bags and start to fill them up with gold while the monster was distracted.

The knights split up, rushing the kraken from both sides. Octavian was the first one to get a strike with his sword. From his vantage point Nevinon could see that the cut hadn't been deep enough. The man swam in the opposite direction, leading the kraken far enough away from the trench that Genevive and Theodore were able to slip downward. Nevinon followed, with Moira and Freddie by his side. They stopped directly above the trench, ready to guard it from the monster if it returned.

He looked downward. This close up, he was able to better see what was actually at the bottom of the trench. It was a shipwreck. The pieces of wood were strewn all around the scene. Barnacles had grown all up the side of the ship. It had obviously been there for a long time. There was a large pile of gold coins that could be seen around the ship, spilling out of broken wine barrels. Perhaps the ship had belonged to smugglers? He thought back to what Octavian had mentioned the other day. If there were more ship-wrecks like this then—

He didn't have time to finish his thought before Freddie pulled him out of the way of an incoming tentacle that had been about to smack him into the rock. The kraken had grown wise to their plan of distracting it while they took the gold at the bottom of the trench. It had rushed backward in order to guard its trea-sure. Freddie had tried to warn him, but being underwater he had not heard him. They had to find a better way to communicate.

Freddie pushed his hands outward and with the water around

them pushed the kraken away from the opening of the trench. Nevinon and Moira backed him up with their spells. He spotted Cassius, but instead of rushing toward the monster, he was swimming toward the ocean floor. The man laid his hands on the sandy rock bottom. In a few seconds it became obvious what Cassius was doing when seaweed grew from the seafloor and wrapped itself around the kraken.

The beast roared and flailed its limbs, ripping through the seaweed and bringing down an arm toward Cassius. The knight dodged out of the way seconds before the kraken crushed the rock underneath where he had just been.

Alanor rushed forward and with a swift swing upward, he cut off one of the sea monster's arms. Octavian was able to cut off another while Solomon cut at the next arm that lashed out with his sharp arm fin.

Meanwhile Nevinon focused. Cassius had the right idea. If he could bind the monster with magic, then they would be able to get all of the gold at the bottom of the trench without injury. He remembered the way he had created the fish net with magic. There was no time or ability to explain to Moira what he was doing so he was on his own.

He had enough magic to power the spell but for how long he had no idea. He called on his inner energy and moved his hand outward. Magic spilled out from his fingertips and coalesced into ropes of golden light that shot out and bound all of the creature's arms, anchoring it to the seafloor. He gave a hand signal to Freddie, hopefully conveying that they had to hurry.

Freddie nodded, and he and Moira rushed into the trench to help Genevive and Theodore. The other knights stayed close to the monster on standby. He looked down to see Freddie and Moira using their water magic to pick up as many gold coins as they could and move them into the bags at a faster pace. Once they had all of the coins in the bags all four of them rushed upward and out of the trench.

Just then the bindings on the creature failed, but they had

what they came for. Alanor gave a sharp gesture in the direction of the city. They would have to make a swim for it. The creature roared and lashed out with one of its limbs. Nevinon could see that it was about to hit Octavian from behind. Nevinon rushed toward him and pushed him out of the way. The monster's arm crashed into his side and he felt all the air leave him in a rush that left him feeling choked and nauseated. Octavian grabbed him and pulled him forward, distancing them from the beast. Freddie and Moira pushed the monster backward one last time, and they were able to speed away, swimming as fast as they could. After at least an hour of swimming, when they were sure that the monster was no longer following them, they surfaced.

Nevinon groaned out his discomfort, bringing a hand to his side. Thankfully it didn't seem like the monster had broken any of his ribs, but he would certainly have a nasty bruise for at least a week or so. If he didn't spontaneously heal again, that was.

Octavian came up next to him and stared at the warlock in mild shock. "You saved me. Why?"

Nevinon huffed. "Don't think much of it. It was mostly just instinct anyway." Octavian gave him an indecipherable stare. Nevinon moved toward the others, who were celebrating their victory already.

"We're rich," Cassius whooped. "We're rich, we're rich, we're rich!" The man laughed and draped himself over Solomon, who returned his embrace.

Nevinon shook his head but smiled like the others. Finally. It had felt like too much time had passed since their last victory. Maybe this would be a turning point. They would be better able to manage the threat of the hunters now and perhaps even find a more permanent solution to their situation. It had been a rough few weeks, but for the first time in a long while Nevinon felt like things were finally looking up. He followed the others as they swam back to shore with a new lightness in his heart.

⚘

They had arrived just before sunset. Thankfully they had gotten into the city before curfew. Alanor noticed that the hunters had taken to guarding the city gates in droves once they shut for the night. They split up again to bypass all of the hunter patrols. Even though they were still under direct threat, Alanor could feel a bounce in his step. Finally he had done something that would help support and protect his family the way a king should.

With this new money that they had, they would no longer need to work in such tedious, purposeless jobs. They could buy swords and armor and begin to train again. They could even buy land if they wished. Alanor idly thought about a house with enough rooms for all of them. Not a palace or a castle as he had been used to, but something that was theirs, that no one could take away.

The group met up again in the tavern, and after they had taken the bags of gold and stored them safely in their room, which Nevinon had shielded with a pretty heavy locking spell, they had all gone to celebrate on the first floor. Alanor had ordered a hefty meal for everyone and drinks all around. Something eased in his chest, a tension that he had been carrying since they had left their homeland.

After they had eaten, some of them split off to join different groups of other patrons as the tavern filled up for the night. His father was up by the bar, enjoying a stiff drink while conversing every now and again with the man sitting next to him and the bartender. Over at the other corner he could see Nevinon, Moira, Genevive, and Theodore having a hushed conversation with two individuals who were wearing cloaks.

He picked up the few extra drinks that he had ordered and moved to the table where the rest of his knights were sitting.

Cassius motioned to the drinks. "You better have gotten one of those for yourself, Dollface."

Alanor smiled and picked out the smallest glass and brought it up for a small sip. The other knights laughed and Cassius groaned, "Oh, come on, man, loosen up a little."

Alanor shook his head, smiling. "I'm here, aren't I? Besides, you shouldn't be getting drunk either."

"At this point I'm wondering if I can get drunk." Cassius looked down at the empty glasses in front of him. "I've had so many drinks. I really should be at least tipsy by now."

"So about swords," Frederick interjected, continuing the conversation that the knights were having before Alanor rejoined them. "We can get our swords directly from the blacksmith that supplies them to the city guard. We won't have to custom make any so we could probably get them tomorrow from his stock."

Cassius grinned. "That is of course as long as Alanor and Octavian don't want to jam-pack their swords with jewels and gold."

Alanor rolled his eyes. Cassius knew full well he hated ostentatious weapons and armor. They were meant to be used practically, not for decor. "We can go get the swords tomorrow so we can start training as quickly as possible," Alanor said. The knights groaned and he continued, "And we can quit all of our jobs." He laughed when they cheered.

Solomon nodded. "We should also look into getting better rooms from now on."

"Actually," Alanor said, "I was thinking about buying a house." The three knights looked up at him in shock.

"Buy a house?" Frederick asked. "Here in the city? Are you sure we're not rushing? What about the hunters?"

"Well, think about it," he said. "We can get a house near the city gate that leads to the shore. We would have more privacy that way."

"He is right," Solomon agreed. "There would be less chance of someone seeing something they shouldn't and reporting us for it."

Cassius held his hands up. "As long as I finally get to sleep on a bed instead of the floor, I'm all in."

"Cheers." Freddie raised his glass and the others followed suit.

Alanor smiled. "We'll see about trying to find a house, hopefully with nine rooms, tomorrow. Maybe we'll get lucky."

Frederick coughed, "Eight rooms."

"What?" Alanor asked. Freddie motioned with his head to the two men sitting next to him and Cassius sent him a wink.

"Right." Alanor smiled. "Eight rooms. Though"—he made a show of thinking for a moment—"you might need the extra room for your ego." Alanor laughed as Cassius kicked him under the table.

His laughter was interrupted when a sudden wave of nausea hit him unlike anything he had ever felt before. His eyesight became so blurry that he could not see, and he felt himself knock over his drink. When his vision finally cleared up, he gasped. Somehow in a split second he had traveled to the other side of the tavern, but he could still see his own body frozen in movement at the table with the other knights. To see himself from an external perspective outside of a mirror was extremely discomfiting, and reminded him somewhat of the vision he had experienced during the shipwreck.

Cassius was waving a hand in front of his face—well, his body's face—which was strange, because when Alanor brought a hand up, his features felt different. His nose was bigger, and when he looked down he could see that these hands were not his but somebody else's. There was a ring on his ring finger, one he had never seen before.

He jerked to the side when he felt hands on his arm, and he turned to see a woman sitting next to him. She looked at him with a concerned glance. "Are you alright? You've gone pale all of a sudden." The woman lifted a hand to feel his forehead then she came closer to his face. "Honey? Why are your eyes blue?"

There was no chance to respond, not that he would've had any idea what to say, before the nauseous feeling came back. It faded in a few seconds, as did the temporary blindness, and he blinked to find himself back in his own body.

The other knights were staring at him. "Are you okay?" Cassius asked. "You kinda stopped responding there for a second. Where did you go?"

"No idea," Alanor mumbled. Even though he was afraid, he turned very, very slowly to look in the direction of the vantage point he had had after the episode of nausea. He could see at a table on the other side of the room there was the same woman who had been sitting next to him fussing over a larger man who was holding his head as if it were in pain. The man had the same hands that Alanor had seen when he had looked down. He was even wearing the same ring he hadn't recognized. Alanor turned away quickly before they could see him staring. What the absolute hell had just happened?

The other knights were still staring at him concerned, but he was saved from having to explain when Nevinon plopped down into the space next to him.

"Alanor." His tone was serious and caught the attention of everyone at the table. "You need to hear this."

Nevinon nodded at Theodore, Genevive, and Moira, who brought over the two cloaked individuals who they had been talking to. Once they were all sitting down at the same table, Alanor nodded for Nevinon to explain.

Nevinon glanced at the two strangers who Alanor could now see were a man and a woman dressed in clothing similar to those worn by the druids they had met on the ship.

"This is Rose and Cedar. They're the leaders of one of the small groups of druids in the city," Nevinon whispered. "They told us that they know where Safehold is."

Cedar nodded. "We are very blessed to have a seer amongst our group. She has deciphered from her visions that the entrance to a magical safe haven lies in the city of Ozokeld."

Alanor felt his eyebrows rise. Ozokeld was on the other side of an ocean separating the mainland from a vast continent that lay south. It was infamous for the large temple that stood in the center of the city.

"And why would you be telling us this?" Solomon asked.

"We were tasked by the elders to go out into the city and try to find other magic users. With the increase in witch hunters, we were told to find anyone who might want to come to Safehold with us, so that we may protect our people as best as we can," Rose said.

"How did you find us?" Cassius asked.

The woman pointed slightly with her head at Nevinon. "Your friend is very powerful. We could sense his magic from leagues away. It took us a while to find you here in this crowd."

The man nodded. "We are going to be taking a boat to Ozokeld in a fortnight or so. We'll cast off from the eastern port then head south. If you have need of us, your friend"—he nodded at Nevinon—"knows where to find us."

"We will have to leave now if we want to be off the streets by curfew," the woman said as she and her friend stood up.

Nevinon stood. "Thank you for sharing this information with us. If you're in need of help, you know where to find us as well."

The two left and their spot was taken by Octavian, who had seen all of them sit down at the same table, and had left the bar to join them. "What was that about?"

"Those two claimed to be druids that knew where the entrance to Safehold was. They said it was in Ozokeld," Theodore explained.

His father narrowed his eyes. "We've been looking for Safehold for a while now and then all of a sudden two people show up with the exact information we're looking for?"

Alanor nodded. "It was extremely suspicious to me too."

Moira glared at his father. "They were obviously druids and they even had magic. So they wouldn't be working with the hunters."

"You don't know that for sure," Cassius said. "I mean, the hunters are working with those shadow monsters that have attacked us twice now. And those things couldn't be anything other than magic. We don't even know if Safehold is a real place. What if those druids were just loons?"

Moira leaned forward. "We don't know why or how we came back. Maybe this is it. Maybe we're meant to go to this place and help them."

Nevinon shook his head. "This could finally be our chance to get ahead of the hunters. If this information is circulating in the city it's only a matter of time before they find out. If we can make it to Safehold beforehand we can—I don't know—warn them or something."

"But Nev," Genevive protested, "we don't even know if this place is real. You told us it was a myth and we haven't found any information about it in the library or any other mention of this place, aside from the hunters who are after us and suddenly these two druids."

"I don't like it at all," Alanor agreed. "The timing is way too convenient. And I don't like the fact that they know exactly how many of us are here and where we're staying. Tomorrow with the money that we have, we'll get a new place to stay. Somewhere far away from this inn. We'll leave the jobs that we've taken and focus all of our efforts on the library. We'll see if we can find proof for ourselves that this Safehold is in Ozokeld."

"With this new information we might have some more luck in our search." His father nodded. "But I doubt it. My gut tells me that those two are lying. There's no way they would approach a group of strangers and just blurt out the exact location of their safe haven."

Nevinon glared at the man, but before he could speak, he was interrupted by a commotion coming from the back room behind the bar. It seemed like there was a fight going on, and muffled yelling could be heard by all of the patrons of the tavern. Not wanting to be involved, most of the people cleared out rapidly.

Alanor stood. "All of you go and wait in our room upstairs. Cassius and Solomon, with me." Even though Cassius had drunk a lot, he seemed completely sober and Alanor knew the man had participated in his fair share of tavern brawls. Plus Solomon's stature would discourage anyone from attacking them.

They made their way past the bar and toward the back room. They entered a small kitchen with a back door into the alley behind the inn. The yelling was coming from the alley, and they stepped out the back door to find the owner of the tavern yelling at a little old lady who, from the look of it, was extremely poor.

Cassius grabbed the owner by the arm and pulled him so the man was facing the knight. "Hey! Did no one ever teach you any manners?"

"Manners?" The man huffed and pulled his arm away. "This woman was stealing from my establishment."

Alanor looked at the old woman who seemed barely able to defend herself, let alone attack anyone. "And what exactly did she steal?"

"Excuse me?" the owner asked.

"What did she steal?" Alanor glared at him. "You said she was a thief, so what did she steal?"

The man didn't answer but the old woman spoke up. "Only some food, sirs. Bread and cheese. I was only hungry."

The owner turned and yelled at the woman, "And the two bottles of mead that you were carrying out?"

The woman looked up, panicked. "I was only going to sell them. I needed the money."

"Those were my two most expensive bottles!" the owner growled. "We all need more money. You—"

"Have you recuperated the two bottles?" Alanor interrupted.

The man glared at him. After a moment he responded through gritted teeth, "Yes."

"Then it seems the only thing the woman actually managed to steal was the food she ate, all of which can be replaced quite easily, I would imagine, for a tavern owner as yourself," Alanor said. "I suggest you return to your 'establishment,' before I let all of your patrons know exactly the kind of person you are."

"I won't stand for this," the man said. "You're lucky I'm not allowed to throw you out right before curfew. But tomorrow at the earliest I want you and all of your ilk out of my inn!"

"Consider it done," Alanor said. "Now you'll excuse us."

The man huffed and walked back into the kitchen, slamming the door and locking it. They would have to go around to the front to get back inside.

"Nice guy," Solomon commented sarcastically.

The old woman sniffled in front of them. "Forgive me, sirs. I didn't mean to cause any trouble."

"It was no trouble at all, ma'am," Alanor said. "Are you still hungry?"

The woman tried to shake her head but the growling from her stomach betrayed her.

"Give me a moment." Cassius walked a bit down the alleyway behind some piles of boxes and a few seconds later came back with a large basket of fruits. Alanor could tell that the knight had grown some of them with his magic since they were out of season. "Here." Cassius held out the basket to her. "Take this. Eat what you can and sell the rest."

The old woman gasped and took the basket carefully before looking at them with tears in her eyes. "Thank you. Thank you."

"No need to thank us, ma'am." Solomon smiled. "We're just doing our jobs." The woman thanked them again before walking out of the alleyway with one last grateful glance.

Once the woman was out of earshot, Alanor turned toward Cassius. "Are you sure that was wise? You could've been seen."

Cassius waved him off. "We're the only ones here. I saw the basket next to a few small crates, and there was a patch of dirt right there, and I figured why not?"

"Either way," Solomon said, "the hunter patrols will be around soon. We don't want to get caught outside, so let's go join the others." Alanor nodded and followed the other two as they walked around to the front and back into the building.

✣

That morning Alanor and the others packed up their things and left the inn before dawn to avoid an encounter with the owner. He had filled the rest of the group in on what had happened the night before. Those who had jobs split off to go and quit, with Theodore having offered to pass on the message for him to the merchant, meanwhile Alanor went to go ask in the market about any properties that were for sale.

It took a few hours of asking around but he found a vendor who was selling a small manor house for relatively cheap. When Alanor asked about the low price the man explained that the previous owners had a business that relied heavily on the sea trade and that they quickly lost their money when the trade stopped. The price also reflected the position of the house. It was outside of the city walls, making it undesirable for most buyers. Alanor however thought that would be an upside. The hunters would stick to patrolling the city and the manor was closer to the shore anyway. The price would barely put a dent in the gold they had retrieved.

The man offered to take him to the house so he could see it for himself and Alanor agreed. He ducked his head as they passed the city gates, where the hunters were looking over the crowd. It took a short walk along a road leading away from the walls of the city before they reached the house. It was large enough for all of them, though it had six rooms instead of eight. Cassius and Solomon would have a room together, the ladies could have another, and he supposed that the remaining pair would be decided later on. Aside from the rooms there was a modest kitchen that opened into a dining room, and the sitting room was just outside the dining room.

He immediately gave the full sum to the vendor and the man handed over the deed and left. Alanor would soon go and find the others, who had decided to meet up again in the same market from their first day in the city. For now though he was content with exploring the house, and he felt something akin to peace settle over him. While he was a knight, Alanor found himself tired of the constant uphill battle that they had been fighting to survive these past few weeks. Alanor hoped that this would be a step forward for his family. Their own little safehold, he mused, no battles necessary.

NEVINON HAD QUITE gladly quit his job, if one could call it that, as a physician's apprentice. The other men in the guild had laughed when he handed in his resignation, commenting that they had known a boy like him wouldn't have the mettle to become a physician. Nevinon tamped down the instinct to burn the entire building to ash in response. That would send the hunters into high alert, and besides, there were people inside who had actually come here for medical help.

Instead, Nevinon was comforted by the fact that he was already a practiced physician and now he could spend his time better taking care of his friends instead of doing the busywork of these arrogant men. He left and met up with the others. Alanor was already there with the deed to their new abode. The group left the city while Alanor described the house to them. Nevinon smiled at the look on his friend's face. It struck him suddenly that it had been a long while since the last time he had seen Alanor excited.

As they entered the house, he felt a soothing sensation. He relaxed, not having realized the tension he had felt before. It must have resulted from some combination of not having a secure roof over their heads while also being in close proximity to a large army of witch hunters. Theodore offered to bunk with Freddie and the others went to claim their rooms. Nevinon found himself in a room on the first floor, next to Alanor's. He wanted to be close in case there was an emergency. The only downside was that it was also close to Octavian's room. Though they had been quite civil with each other lately.

The house was furnished somewhat but they would still have

to buy certain things. He went back to the kitchen to find Octavian there running his hands over the bare dining table. It was a rough thing, not even polished, but the man didn't seem to notice or care. He appeared relieved, almost. Perhaps Nevinon had not been the only one feeling the tension of being on the run.

"Color me shocked," he said. "This must be the first time you've ever been in a kitchen."

Octavian huffed a laugh but didn't respond. Instead he looked down. "A table." Octavian sounded amazed. "I should not be this happy over a simple wooden table."

Nevinon approached and sat down on one of the chairs. "But you are."

"But I am." The man nodded.

"Why?"

Octavian gave a small smile. "Because it's mine."

"Because it's ours," Nevinon corrected.

Octavian paused then nodded again. "Ours."

"Oh, by the way." Nevinon took something out of his pocket and tossed it to the other man, who caught it in a single hand. "Here. It's one of the bags we used for the gold. I made it smaller and put it on a cord so you could wear it around your neck. It's still enchanted to fit larger things inside it."

"What for?" Octavian examined the bag.

"For Alan's crown and the seals," he answered. Octavian nodded and put the makeshift necklace on and tucked the bag beneath his shirt. They both looked up when a noise came from the doorway.

Freddie walked in and paused when he saw them. The man had a look on his face like he had been caught. There was a strange movement in the knight's shirt.

"Why is your chest wriggling?" Octavian asked.

"Oh." Freddie looked down at his chest then back up. "Sometimes it just does that."

"Really?" Nevinon stifled a laugh.

There was more frantic wriggling at the noise. "Yeah." Freddie nodded. The man tried to hide the hissing coming from his shirt with a cough.

"So there isn't an animal in your shirt right now?" Octavian asked.

"No, I—uh"—Freddie took a step back—"woke up with a cold this morning. Think I'll go back to my room. Bye." The man turned and left the room. Nevinon shook his head and laughed. The other knights walked into the kitchen, taking seats themselves.

"Have any of you noticed that no matter how much we drink we can't seem to get drunk?" Cassius asked.

"We or you?" Theodore asked.

Cassius shrugged. "Well, am I the only one who's tried?"

Octavian leaned back in his chair. "I haven't really felt anything from the alcohol I've been drinking."

"Then why drink?" Alanor asked.

"I like the taste of a good whiskey," the man said simply.

"Huh." Genevive joined them, "Actually now that you mention it I didn't get tipsy last night like I usually do."

"Lightweight," Nevinon teased her.

Alanor smiled at him. "Look who's talking, Mister 'I've never had a drink in my life.'"

He held his hands up. "I never drank because if I get drunk I'll lose control of my magic. I assume."

"You assume?" Cassius asked.

"Well, I mean I've never tried," Nevinon said.

Cassius gave a mock gasp. "Oh, that is so on our to-do list."

"Right, enough chitchat," Moira called down. "We need to head to the market for supplies. I think I noticed a small town, or really a village, just down the hill from here."

Alanor and Theodore decided to go back into the city to buy swords and other weapons and armor. "Chain mail, if I can get my hands on it," Alanor added.

Nevinon sighed. He could see a close future of bandaging scrapes and cuts as the knights got started with their training again. Before leaving, Alanor mentioned that practice would have to wait until the day after tomorrow, since he wanted them all to go to the library one last time to research the lead on Ozokeld. Nevinon retired to his room, where he spent the rest of the day sleeping, waking up briefly in the evening only to eat dinner with the others.

The next morning the group got up early to head into the city. Nevinon wondered briefly what Alanor would do if they didn't find any information on Ozokeld today. Either way, he was excited to take another look at the spell books that he had found in the magic section. He had gone through all of the spells that had been useful underwater but now he was curious to see what he could find for other elements. Maybe those would help him teach the others in the group more about their specific magical elements.

They made it through the main gate without any problems and Nevinon noticed the distinct absence of any hunters. A sense of dread rose up inside of him as they got closer and closer to the courtyard outside the library and the crowd grew thicker and harder to move through. The crowd was thickest around the courtyard and the group had to muscle their way through in order to see what was happening. The sound of drums reached them before the sight of two pyres set up in the middle of the courtyard. There was to be an execution.

CHAPTER 15

THE EXECUTION

Nevinon's memory took him back to his first years in Amari, where he had lived under Octavian's reign. He hadn't seen an execution like this since the man had died. There was a stage set up next to the pyres, where two lines of witch hunter ranks stood at attention. A man wearing a commander's uniform stood in front of them and paced back and forth across the stage addressing the crowd.

"People of Tamlinn, it is with great pleasure that I announce to you all that we have been successful in routing out the magic users that have been infesting this city." The man gave a victorious grin.

The commander gave a motion and two witch hunters dragged out an old woman who had tears running down her face. Nevinon felt Cassius gasp next to him. "Alanor." The knight reached out to grab his king's arm. "That's the old woman that we helped the night before last." Alanor was staring at the scene in wide-eyed horror. He nodded his recognition.

"This woman"—the commander pointed—"has been accused of witchcraft. She has been found in possession of fruits that were poisoned with magic. Thankfully, we noticed that these fruits were out of season and therefore could not have been grown by natural means. This is how deep the infestation is. It is even in our food!"

There were outraged gasps from the crowd and Cassius brought a hand up to his mouth. Out-of-season fruit. Nevinon turned to Cassius. "Oh, Cass, you didn't." But the warlock could see clearly that he had. Nevinon had not been vigilant enough. He should have told them how imperative it was that they were careful with their magic. The woman was tied to the first pyre while she protested that she hadn't done anything wrong. Her words fell on deaf ears.

Cassius went to step forward but Solomon and Theodore held him back. "She's innocent," Cassius whispered frantically.

"It doesn't matter," Nevinon said. "Even if you go up there, they'll kill you both and then the rest of us too."

Moira nodded. "You need to calm down. They'll be looking at the crowd for dissenters."

"This isn't right." Cassius shook his head.

"Of course it isn't," Nevinon agreed, "but we can't do anything or they'll kill all of us. We are outnumbered."

The commander on the stage continued his speech. "The hunters have reached new successes under our Supreme Vanquisher." Nevinon glanced at Octavian, who had his hands curled into fists. "We will continue to root out the magic that plagues our communities. We have also found today a traitor amongst us. Those who would sell the souls of innocents to be corrupted by the poison of magic do not deserve our mercy."

The hunters brought out one of the librarians. Nevinon immediately recognized him as the man who had appeared open to magic when he had last visited the library with Octavian.

"This man," the commander continued, "was safeguarding an entire collection of spell books and magical records. Waiting for the right moment to poison our communities once more."

The librarian spoke out in a clear voice even as he was being tied to the pyre. "I am not guilty of anything but ensuring that our generation and future generations are informed. The books do not have magic. They only speak of it."

As the man spoke, another group of hunters brought out boxes and boxes of books and scrolls. It couldn't be, but Nevinon knew that the hunters would never leave magical resources untouched.

"Good gods. They're going to burn the books." Genevive gave voice to his greatest fear. Their only resource against the witch hunters was about to go up in flames.

The commander pointed at the pile of books that now lay in front of the two pyres. "They speak of it without warning the reader of the evils of magic. In fact, most of these promote the use of it."

The librarian huffed and looked down on the commander with a disappointed gaze. "Perhaps because the evils of magic are falsified."

The commander turned to the crowd with a smile. "There you have it! Confession of his guilt." The commander faced the librarian. "You will not spread your poison any longer."

Nevinon felt a push to do something, say something. To stop what was happening, even though logically he understood that nothing would stop the hunters once they got started. He thought of the two people in front of him, neither of which actually had magic at all. Even if magic was a crime, which it wasn't, these two were innocent.

He thought of the books that were spread carelessly around the two pyres as kindling. Perhaps one of them contained the answer to their problem. Priceless information about Safehold or the monsters that they were up against. Every spell and piece of information that would disappear from common knowledge forever if these books were burned. However, there was nothing he could do if he didn't want to put his family in danger.

"This can't be happening." Alanor shook his head. But it was happening. Nevinon spared a thought to what he could do as a distraction with magic. But he knew, deep inside he knew, that doing so would only push the hunters to capture and kill more innocents. The commander lit a torch and in quick succession lit the two pyres alight. The group watched in horror as the flames grew higher and higher, and Nevinon turned his head.

Alanor pulled at his arm. "We need to leave."

"Alan." Cassius's voice was rough.

"Now," Alanor commanded. Nevinon turned and grabbed Cassius by the arm and started pulling him through the crowd and back toward the main city gate. He spared only a few glances behind to make sure that the others were still following. It was a miracle that he didn't break out into a run, only avoiding doing so in order to not draw attention.

The next few moments were a blur. Nevinon felt a pain in his chest and he could barely focus as they left the city and made it back to their house. The house that had felt so peaceful yesterday now felt oppressive, like a cage. They were not safe here, not as long as the hunters continued to oversee the city. The group filed into the dining room and Nevinon slumped into a chair as Alanor, Octavian, and Theodore locked and barred the front door. It would not help them feel safer. Cassius had drawn his knees up to his chest and Solomon put his arms around the man. Aside from Cassius's sobbing that it was all his fault, and Solomon's unsuccessful attempts to comfort him, the group spent the rest of the day in that small room in horrified silence.

A FEW DAYS had passed since the execution. The group had not gone back to the city. Instead the knights had gone out daily to hunt since Cassius could not bring himself to use his magic at all. The man had secluded himself in his room and only Solomon managed to get any response from him.

Today however, Alanor had brought out the weapons that he had bought previously. He and Theodore had gotten swords for everyone, though he knew that neither Nevinon nor Genevive would know how to use them, so he had gotten daggers for both ladies and Nevinon. He had also gotten a second blade for his father, smaller than a sword but longer than a dagger.

The execution in the city had only emphasized their need to restart their training. The hunters wouldn't be slacking, so they wouldn't be either. Alanor wondered briefly if Cassius would be able to join them today, and he hoped that Solomon would encourage him to. Nevinon had protested when Alanor gave him a sword.

"I have no idea what to do with one of these," he said. "I'd be better off just using my magic."

"And what happens when you get into a situation where you can't use your magic, and you still have to defend yourself?" Alanor asked. Nevinon sighed.

"Don't worry." Alanor gave a slight smile. "I'll teach you some basic moves during training. You'll at least be able to defend yourself long enough to get away."

"Fine." The warlock held his hands up.

The knights grabbed their weapons and headed to the beach where they would train. Genevive stayed behind, as she had offered to prepare lunch for the group. Alanor made a note to train her up on how to use her dagger at some point. Cassius had joined them but hadn't said a word the entire way. Nevinon plodded behind them, though Alanor made sure that he wouldn't slip away to return to the house. Moira had also decided to join in. The other knights had been hesitant to go up against a lady but their attitudes quickly turned around as she thrashed them during the practice drills.

Alanor decided to pair Theodore with Nevinon. After all, Theodore had been the one to train him when he had been a young squire. Then he had started to spar against his father. Very rarely had the two ever taken up arms against each other, even during practices. It wasn't the done thing to have the king and prince fight each other in front of their subjects. Alanor was interested to see how his father fought.

He was also interested to see how his body held up against his own training regimen. His current body was slightly younger than the one he had died in, and though Alanor was sure that for some it would be a boon, for him it was a nightmare. He had lost significant muscle mass in the last few weeks. He would have to train his body and his muscles from scratch all over again. Not to mention the fact that he was used to overcompensating for the different injuries he had received over the years.

He didn't seem to have those anymore, not even the scars, and he was sure that he would need to train for a while to get used to using a sword again. Alanor wondered if it was even worse for Theodore, who had lived even longer than he had and was missing quite a few decades. The man commented as much as they took a water break.

"All of those years of training down the drain," Theodore complained. "Not that I don't love being young again."

"Hear, hear." Octavian held his flask up.

"But honestly," Theo continued, "we look like boys that have never been trained before when we spar."

Alanor nodded. "It's frustrating to say the least. It'll take some time to build up muscle again, that's for sure."

Theodore sighed. "Well, I suppose if we don't want it to take centuries we should get back to it."

Alanor nodded and they returned to the sand to spar again.

"You ready, kid?" His father grinned.

"Absolutely." Alanor smiled. They started their mock duel and Alanor found himself straining to keep up with his father. The man moved in unexpected ways and his reactions were extremely hard to predict. He figured that the opposite was true for him, considering that his father had seen all of his tournaments and duels. Alanor noted that it was twice as hard to defend against his father when the man had two weapons in hand. He needed to get his hands on a shield.

"I had never seen you wield two blades before in Amari," he mused. Maybe conversation would distract the man.

"Ah." His father didn't even pause his movements. "I might've mentioned before that I was born left-handed. I had to learn how to fight with my right hand as a knight so I ended up able to fight with both."

"I had no idea." Alanor was almost too late in lifting his sword to parry a blow. He tried to feint to the left but his father always seemed to see past his maneuvers.

"It's not something I publicized. Something unexpected like that could give me the advantage in a fight. Kind of like this—" In a sharp move, his father tilted his blade and then Alanor's vision was abruptly blinded by the sunlight. He felt a foot hook behind his ankle and a well-placed shoulder shove pushed him to the ground.

He shook his head and tried to blink the dark spots out of his vision. "That was dishonorable," Alanor huffed and stood from the ground.

His father shook his head. "Honor doesn't exist in war. There is only victory or death."

"This isn't a war," Alanor protested. "We're just sparing."

"Life is war," his father said.

"I think I would rather die with honor than live without it."

His father stared at him with an indecipherable look for a moment before turning to walk away. "Then you're more foolish than I thought, kid."

Alanor shook his head and went to partner with Frederick. He made a note of observing his father more in the future. Then maybe he would stand a fighting chance against the older man.

The knights trained for the rest of the morning, though Nevinon had left to return to the house halfway through. They drank their fill of water as they walked back. The knights had done surprisingly well, though they were all a bit rusty. In a while they would be back up to par.

The practice had also done a bit to ease Cassius's suffering. The man's grief had been overtaken by a look of determination. If they weren't the murderers of innocents, Alanor would almost feel sorry for any hunter who would encounter Cassius in the future. The man looked ready to avenge that poor old woman and then some.

When the house crept into view, Cassius said to the others, "Hey, has anybody noticed how we seem to be healing from injuries pretty instantaneously? That's kinda weird, right? What's up with that?"

Alanor turned back with a curious glance. "Oh, I thought it was just me. I mean, I've been stabbed and—"

"Stabbed? What do you mean stabbed?" Cassius asked in shock.

His father grabbed his arm to stop him. "When was this?"

Alanor sighed, "On the ship. Right before it capsized."

"You gotta share these things with us, Alan," Theodore said.

"It's fine." Alanor shrugged them off, uncomfortable with all the sudden concern. "I'm fine. Look, let's just get back to the house, alright? I'm hungry." He tried not to notice the skeptical glances that his men exchanged.

They made it to the house in short order. When Nevinon had left them on the beach he mentioned helping Genevive make lunch, but that was not what they were doing when they all entered the kitchen. The kitchen that was now filled with glowing butterflies. Genevive and Nevinon were giggling as they stared up in awe.

"What is all of this?" Alanor asked. Out of the corner of his eye he could see his father back up as some of the glowing butterflies approached him.

Nevinon laughed. "Relax, they're just butterflies."

"Yeah, magical butterflies. Who knows what they could do," his father muttered as he swatted some away, though the butterflies didn't seem to mind.

"They're obviously going to eat you, Octavian." Moira held up her hands so that one of the butterflies could land on her arm. "I've never seen magic used like this before. Is there a spell for this?"

Nevinon shook his head. "Nope. I just wanted them to appear and they did."

"It was amazing," Evie said. Alanor couldn't remember the last time he had seen her so surprised. "We finished with lunch so we turned to sewing. Nev was helping me but we ran out of cloth. He started duplicating the clothes that we had already made with magic."

"She asked me what else I could do with my magic and this was the first thing that I thought of," Nevinon continued.

"Butterflies?" Cassius asked. "You, my friend, are such a softy." He placed a hand on Nevinon's shoulder. The warlock laughed at the teasing but his smile lessened when he saw the looks on the rest of the knights' faces.

Alanor was quick to reassure him, "It's not a bad thing, and they're very pretty, but it worries me when you use magic so often. I don't want you to be seen and reported. What happened to those two the other day..." He trailed off.

Nevinon gave a somber nod. "Don't worry, I know how to keep my magic a secret. I'm not going to go around making butterflies in the middle of the city."

"What else can you do with magic?" Theodore approached one of the butterflies carefully.

Nevinon perked up again, seemingly happy that one of the knights was curious about his magic. The warlock went to respond but the only thing that left his mouth was a choked sound. Alanor looked on in panic as Nevinon's eyes rolled back into his head and the man collapsed to the ground.

EVERY THOUGHT in Nevinon's head was destroyed by a sudden blinding headache. One moment he had been standing and the next he was on the floor. He brought his hands up to his temples. It felt like someone had slammed something hard into his head. For a brief moment he thought he could smell something rotting.

THE FEAST IS NIGH

A loud voice echoed in his head, followed by manic laughter.

THE SLAUGHTER IS COMING

MUST EAT

SO HUNGRY

SLAUGHTER!

WE FEAST WE FEAST

_SO_

HUN—

—GRY

"Nevinon!" A shout jerked him out of the waking nightmare and the voices faded away. The knights were looking at him in deep concern.

Alanor held a napkin to his face. "Nev, your nose is bleeding. Again."

Nevinon took the napkin and quickly cleaned up his nose. The voices had come again. He had no idea where they were coming from. They didn't sound like other magic users, or human voices at all. It made him feel uneasy in a way that nothing else ever had.

"What the hell was that?" Cassius asked.

"Nothing," Nevinon protested but he could see from the looks on their faces that they weren't going to let him get away without explaining this time. "I just—I think I'm hearing things."

"What kind of things?" Solomon asked.

"Like voices in my head," he whispered. He half expected Octavian to chime in with an insulting comment about him going mad but the older man just looked down at him in shocked seriousness.

"Voices?" Theodore asked.

"Look, it's probably nothing. Just something I drank." Nevinon could tell that they didn't believe him. Granted he wouldn't have believed himself either.

"I think maybe we should get you to bed." Genevive helped him sit up. "And don't you even think about skipping dinner tonight."

"I'm fine, I swear," he said.

Solomon sighed. "You and Alanor both need to relearn the definition of the word *fine*."

Cassius nodded. "I agree."

Nevinon sighed. He was hoping that he wouldn't have another one of those episodes in front of his friends. He had no idea what to do to make them stop. They had to be a warning of some kind, some sort of omen. If only he knew where those voices were coming from. He resigned himself to a night full of uncomfortable questioning from his friends, not that he would have any answers for them.

Alanor nodded at the others before speaking. "No more magic."

"What?"

"You heard me," the man said. "This is happening to you every time you use magic. Don't think I haven't noticed. It's doing something to you."

Nevinon groaned, "I thought we were over this."

Alanor shook his head. "I'm not talking about magic as a corrupting force. But even Moira has mentioned that using magic can take a lot out of someone, and it seems to be taking the life out of you, Nev."

Theodore helped him up onto a nearby chair. "Is this at all usual for you?"

The warlock sighed, "No. I've never had this much difficulty with magic. Or...I suppose it's not difficulty with the magic, just the aftermath of it. I don't know why this is happening." He hated to admit it out loud.

"Maybe it's a result of whatever brought us back," Octavian suggested.

"Maybe." Nevinon looked down at his lap. It made the most sense. Nevinon thought back to the vision he had had of his mother. Had he irreversibly damaged his own magic with the ritual? Nevinon pushed down the urge to throw up as he doubled over.

"Okay, that's enough." Solomon walked over and picked him up with little effort and started walking toward the warlock's room. "Let's get you to bed. And you're going to rest there, Nevinon, you hear me?"

He was too exhausted to protest.

THE FEELING of any progress being made through their knights' training was stripped away when a couple days later they heard that a ship had arrived from the Isles with backup for the hunters. Due to their success during their first witch trial, the hunters had been ramping up their search for magic users. There were now twice as many men patrolling the city and they were even spilling out into the countryside.

Nevinon couldn't help but feel that sooner or later the hunters would stumble upon their house and all hell would break loose. He felt like they were trapped in a corner and it was not a feeling he enjoyed at all. He felt completely helpless. Not to mention the fact that he hadn't used his magic since his episode the other day. All he could do was prepare for the worst.

When the group had woken up, and everyone had gone to the kitchen for breakfast, Alanor had paired Moira and Octavian to go into the small town nearby to replenish their food stores. Nevinon had no idea why Alanor would pair those two up. Moira had been completely ignoring Octavian as of late, not that he didn't understand why. Nevinon wondered if the presence of the hunters even impacted him at all. Octavian was not a man who wore his feelings. He was the hardest to read from the group, aside from Genevive when she was angry, which was rare. Perhaps Alanor wanted them to make amends. Nevinon doubted that it would work.

However, he quickly volunteered to accompany the pair. "I'm interested in building several medical kits. Just in case something happens. I'll need to buy several tools and herbs." Alanor nodded his approval, and the three headed toward the small town.

"Did you know," Moira began, "that the magical peoples of the Isles used to call you the Blood King?"

Octavian glanced at her. "I'm aware."

Silence reigned for a few minutes until Moira stopped and turned around to face Octavian. "Why do you hate magic so much?"

Octavian gave her a blank stare until finally he sighed. "I suffered much at the hands of sorcerers as a boy." Nevinon was surprised the man had actually spoken on the subject.

Moira raised an eyebrow. "Are you going to expand on that?"

"No."

Nevinon broke their staring contest when he pointed to the town in the distance. "Look, let's just get what we need. You two can hash this out later."

"You can't tell me that you don't want to know why," Moira said. "That you don't want to understand."

"It doesn't matter." He shook his head.

"How can you say that?"

"Because I'm tired." He sighed and motioned to Octavian, who was watching their exchange. "Because there is nothing he could ever say that would justify the pain he's caused our people."

"Then why don't you just kill me where I stand?" Octavian asked.

"Because the cycle of revenge will only cause more people more pain," Nevinon said before turning to Moira. "I'm not saying we should forgive him or forget what he's done." He looked at Octavian. "I could never forgive you for indiscriminately murdering my people. But we need to move on, and no, I'm not entirely sure what that looks like. What I do know is that if we get caught up in revenge and start attacking each other, then we'll only be doing the hunters' work for them. And I don't plan on making their lives any easier if I can help it." With that he walked away from the other two. Moira and Octavian joined him shortly and they spent the rest of the walk into town in silence.

When they arrived at the town they were shocked to see the place had been completely ransacked. The doors to all of the houses were open, and Nevinon could see that the insides had been torn apart. As they walked pieces of ceramic and clay crunched beneath their feet, most likely from vases or plates that had been smashed. People all over the town were cleaning up the disaster. As they got closer to the market, they saw that all of the stalls had been torn down and destroyed with all manner of goods and food strewn around the square haphazardly. The people seemed despondent.

"Excuse me," Octavian called out to one of the villagers. "What happened here?"

The villager paused his sweeping. "The hunters came through this morning. They've started to patrol outside of the city and they're searching everywhere now for any signs of magic."

"They can't just destroy everything," Nevinon said.

"Who's going to stop them?" The villager shook his head in a desolate manner and walked away.

Nevinon turned to share a look with Moira, and the woman grabbed Nevinon and Octavian by the arm and dragged them into a small alleyway between two houses. "We're going to stop them," Moira said.

"How?" Octavian asked.

"They should have a headquarters here, right? Like in Maydon," she said.

"Right." Nevinon nodded. "Maybe we can sneak in and do something to disrupt them."

Octavian gave a stiff nod. "I'm in."

Nevinon gave him a look. "You? Do you actually want to stop the hunters?"

Octavian turned toward the warlock. "I'm sick of hiding away in that house like a coward, waiting for the other shoe to drop. If they're after you, they're after my son, and if they're coming for my son, they better be ready to come for me too."

Moira gave a vicious grin. "Let's take the fight to them instead."

"What are you thinking?" Nevinon asked.

"Well, the hunters are fond of fire, right? Why don't we give them a taste of their own medicine?"

CHAPTER 16

THE COUNTERATTACK

"Wait a moment." Octavian brought a hand up. "We can't just attack their headquarters. They'll think it was sorcerers from the city and then they'll think they're on the right track and increase their searches and patrols. I wonder if there's a way to get them out of the city."

"Well, they're looking for Safehold, right?" Nevinon asked. "Remember those two druids? They said that it was in Ozokeld. What if we were to send the hunters in the other direction instead? North. We could even leave a trail leading north so that the hunters follow it out of the city."

Octavian nodded. "We can work with that. We'll figure out the finer details later. But whatever plan we come up with, we'll have to implement it soon. Before the hunters decide to search our house too." With that settled, they headed back to the house, creating a more solid plan for their attack on the way.

Nevinon peeked over a crate that he and Octavian were crouching behind to check on the entrance of the hunters' headquarters. They had snuck into the city just before curfew, as the sun set behind the horizon and bathed the city in darkness. Moira had split off. Her job was to set fire to the docks and head north. She had said she had an idea on how to drop the false lead. Nevinon hoped she knew what she was doing.

Once Octavian and Nevinon had reached the street just before the headquarters, they had taken down two of the hunters on patrol. Nevinon had put them under a sleeping spell and concealed them in a hidden alleyway. He hoped beyond hope that his magic wouldn't act up, but he did feel a little nausea creep up on him. Thankfully it was manageable. They had taken the hunters' uniforms and dressed in them. Nevinon tried not to think about wearing the insignias of the people who had hunted him his entire life.

"Any moment now," Octavian whispered. Once the hunters realized there was a magical attack on the docks they would sound the warning bells and most of the hunters would leave their headquarters, giving them their opening.

The bells started ringing only a few minutes later and the hunters rushed out of the headquarters en masse, supposedly to try to stop Moira's attack. Nevinon hoped that she stayed safe. Once most of the hunters were gone, Nevinon and Octavian took their chance to sneak into the building. There weren't even any hunters on duty guarding the entrance. They would pay for their negligence.

Most witch hunter headquarters were organized in the same way and Octavian was the most familiar with the layout. He led the way to the armory, where the man picked up a few small daggers. Nevinon raised an eyebrow but didn't comment. Then Octavian waved him toward an open corridor. "The filing room should be somewhere around here. It'll hold their records and paperwork." It took only a few seconds to find the right room, since the door was open.

"Come on." Nevinon pointed to the cabinets on the far side of the room. "I want to find out if there's any information on Safehold and what exactly they know about it." They began to open drawers and sort through papers as fast as they could. Octavian took the files on the right while Nevinon took the left and they worked their way toward the middle.

"Let's see if they also have anything on those creatures they were working with," Octavian said.

"We haven't seen them since the shipwreck." Nevinon closed the first drawer, realizing it contained only financials, and moved onto the next one.

"Maybe because it's too dangerous to bring them near such a large city," Octavian suggested. "But they could still be working with them."

That was probably true, though Nevinon would prefer to never have an encounter with those monsters again. He saw Octavian slow down and pull out some papers from a lower drawer.

"What is it?" he asked.

"Letters," the man replied absentmindedly. "Apparently from the Supreme Vanquisher. They have the Kovian seal on them."

Nevinon paused. "That could be faked, right?"

"That's not what alarms me."

"Then what?"

Octavian looked up at him. "I recognize this handwriting. I can't place where I've seen it before but I definitely have."

"How is that possible? Everyone else from Amari is dead."

Octavian shook his head. "I don't know." He put the letters aside. "Let's keep searching."

It took only a few more minutes for them to meet in the middle. Nevinon slammed the last cabinet closed with a bang. "There's nothing here. It's been too long. We need to move on to the final phase of the plan."

"Wait." Octavian moved toward the door. "I want to search the commander's room."

"Octavian," Nevinon tried to call him back but the man left the room. Nevinon followed. "If we tarry any longer we might get caught."

Octavian continued walking down the hallway. "Just a bit

longer, come on. If this follows a normal layout then the commander's rooms should be…here!" Octavian motioned him into a room and closed the door behind them. The room was sparsely decorated, with only a plain cot for a bed and a desk covered in paperwork. Octavian began to search the desk.

"Find anything?" he asked after a few moments.

"Nothing of import," Octavian responded, though apparently he had found a sack of gold and silver coins, which he slipped into his belt with a shrug. "We might as well."

"We're not here to rob the place," Nevinon gave a scandalized protest.

"No." Octavian smiled. "Just to destroy it, right?"

"Speaking of…" Nevinon moved toward the door and opened it, waiting for Octavian to follow. "Onto the next phase then."

Once Octavian was in the hallway, Nevinon summoned a ball of fire into his hand and set fire to both the commander's bed and the desk before leaving the room. He set fire in every room they came across, including the records room. Everything went up in flames quickly and they rushed to exit the building the same way they had entered it. Thankfully there were still no guards at the door. Nevinon took a gasp of fresh air once they were outside. He stumbled a bit and leaned up against a wall.

Octavian noticed he had lagged behind. "Are you alright?"

He nodded. "It's fine, just a lot of magic all at once." He had never had problems with a few fireballs before, but he supposed this was his new normal.

Octavian put Nevinon's arm around his shoulder and supported the man. "We need to leave. Now."

Nevinon nodded and they made their way quickly through the city. Thankfully no one tried to stop them, most likely because they were still wearing hunter uniforms. They met up with Moira on the way to the house, stumbling a bit through the darkness. They didn't want to bring any attention to themselves from the city walls by creating a magical light so they made do with the moonlight.

"How did your side of things go?" Octavian asked.

"I managed to set most of the docks on fire," Moira said, out of breath. "I tried to avoid as many casualties as possible. Once the hunters arrived on the scene I headed north. I let one of them almost catch me and ranted at him that the hunters would never get near Safehold since it was safe atop Zarakish." That was one of the tallest mountains in the north of the mainland. It made for a decent lead. Hopefully the hunters would feel the same way.

"That was a risk," Octavian said, "but nice job."

Moira smiled. "Thanks. What about you guys?"

"We didn't find anything." Nevinon smirked. "But their headquarters is turning to ash as we speak."

Moira laughed and the other two joined as they finally reached the house. Nevinon hushed the other two and then entered the house as quietly as possible, only to find Alanor waiting for them in the kitchen with an angry look on his face.

The room was smothered in silence for a long while. The rest of the group was there as well, with varying looks of concern. Nevinon forced himself not to gulp audibly. Octavian took a step forward so he was standing slightly in front of Nevinon and Moira. "Alan."

Alanor visibly gritted his teeth. "Do you have any idea how afraid we've been? We wake up to the sound of the city warning bells going off and we can't find any of you in your beds. Where the hell were you?"

"We wanted to retaliate against the hunters and try to find any information they had at the same time," Moira said.

Alanor predictably did not take it well. "Are the three of you insane? You could've been caught and killed!"

"Did you find any new information?" Theodore asked.

Octavian shook his head. "No, but we did manage to set some false leads. The hunters now think that Safehold lies north of here."

"And burning down their headquarters will decrease their foothold in the city," Nevinon said.

Moira nodded. "We're not safe as long as the hunters are here."

Alanor sighed and pinched the bridge of his nose. "I understand that, but what the three of you did was incredibly reckless. This is just like that time you and Nevinon almost snuck out that night to face the kraken alone. We need to start working as a team and stop keeping these plans from each other."

"Only if you promise to actually listen to what we say," Nevinon said.

"Don't I already do that?"

"Not always," he disagreed. "Sometimes you think you know best and won't listen when we disagree with you."

Alanor nodded and then slumped into a chair. After a moment he spoke. "I'll try to do better then, if you promise to do the same."

"I promise," he said. Moira and Octavian nodded too.

"Gods," Alanor sighed. "The three of you hoard secrets like dragons hoard gold."

"There are no more dragons, Dollface." Cassius smiled. "Didn't they all go extinct centuries ago? Anyway I'm just glad the hunters got some payback. It's the least of what they deserve." The knight sent a mock glare their way. "Shame on you guys for excluding me though. A second time."

Genevive cut in then in a slightly interested tone, "So...what actually happened?"

Moira smiled and launched into telling the story of what went down, with Octavian explaining their side of things. Nevinon went to sit down next to Alanor.

"You really need to stop scaring me like that," Alanor whispered.

Cassius let out a whoop when Octavian threw the bag of coins onto the table with a flourish.

Nevinon nodded and reached out to take Alanor's hand in his. It had been a risk, but a worthy one. They were safer now with the hunters distracted. Nevinon could only hope that they would soon take the false lead that Moira had planted and leave the city. The group continued to listen to Moira's avid retelling of the night until dawn broke.

ALANOR WALKED through the small market, exchanging coins for the food that they would need in the coming days. The others hadn't been able to buy food from the fishermen's village so they had been forced to go into the city. Theodore and Solomon had come with him.

As he walked the market, he pondered what they were going to do about their situation. The hunters had not left after their headquarters had burned down. Instead they had ramped up their chokehold on the city even further. If things continued they would have to sell the manor house and leave the city. It was the last thing Alanor wanted to do. They had only just settled down. However, Alanor knew that he couldn't neglect to explore other options just because he didn't want to be on the run again.

The group had been discussing the offer that had come their way from the two druids they had encountered. There was still time to join them on their voyage to Ozokeld. Alanor still had his doubts though. That encounter had been too suspicious to be coincidental, and they hadn't found a single shred of evidence that Safehold, if it was a real place, lay in that direction. So he had sent Nevinon, Moira, and his father to the city hall that morning.

Rumor had it that a large part of the library's tomes and scrolls were being moved there to be protected. He hoped that they would find a way to get access to those books. It would be the very last attempt to research Safehold before they had to make a decision about leaving or staying.

Alanor dreaded the upcoming conversation. He knew that the others would look to him to have the final say. A king should have the answers and be decisive. Alanor just felt scared and it terrified him to death. He couldn't let the others see how much he had been shaken by the execution they had seen. It hadn't been his first time witnessing an execution, but this one had been different. He had been having nightmares of burning ever since, or even worse, watching his family burn and not being able to do anything about it.

He was shaken out of his thoughts when he heard a conversation start between a merchant he had just bought from and the man running the stall next to him.

"Did ya hear 'bout that reward this mornin', Benet?" The merchant called.

"Aye." The other man, Benet, responded. "A lot of money for sure. Not certain what I'd do with all of it."

The first man laughed. "You'd never get your hands on it anyway. You've never been in a fight a day in your life."

Alanor walked back toward the vendor. "Excuse me. Did you mention a reward?" Alanor wondered if there was a certain tournament or something similar taking place in the city. He had been training with a sword every day for a while now. He wasn't back up to the standard that he was in Amari, but he could certainly win a fight, especially if his opponent was untrained. Perhaps this was how he could provide a way for his family to live in peace again. With the added gold from a tournament they could easily leave the city and set up somewhere else, something that Alanor was starting to think was inevitable. Even better, this solution would be solely provided by himself, proving his worth as a leader and as a king.

"Thas' right," Benet said. "It's the talk of the town this mornin'. The hunters came through last night and announced that they were rewarding anyone who came forward with information about a certain number of suspicious individuals."

"If you're interested," the first man said, "you should go take a look at them posters that the hunters put up on the side of the cobbler's shop, over there." He pointed toward a building on the far side of the market. "They've put up those posters everywhere. I haven't gone to look and I won't. I won't be looking for trouble anytime soon. Those damn hunters can do their jobs on their own."

"Right. Thank you." Alanor walked away as quickly as possible without arousing suspicion. He tried to keep his face down. He felt a knot form in his stomach and his suspicions were confirmed when he grew closer to the wall where the posters had been hung.

The posters showed nine images of each member of their group with their names written in bold under each one. His eyes caught on the capitalized "WANTED" printed above the faces of his family. He remembered the same drawings from the search he had conducted in Maydon. The hunters were after them and they wouldn't stop until they were all caught.

Alanor turned and moved away from the building, keeping his head down, hoping that no one would notice him. He made it back to where the others were standing. "We need to leave now," he whispered to them.

"Leave? But we haven't gotten everything on the list," Theodore protested.

"Theo. Now," Alanor said. Perhaps the others could tell from his voice that it was serious, because no one raised another protest as they moved to leave.

"We need to go to city hall, get the others, and leave the city," he said. The others nodded and they started toward the center of the city. All Alanor could hope for was that they would make it back out alive.

NEVINON FLIPPED another book shut with an audible thump and ignored the dirty look that one of the librarians sent him. They had managed to get access to the collection inside city hall only when he had told the head librarian that he was there with his "assistants" in his capacity as a physician researching cures to an illness he was trying to treat. Of course, in between the medical books, he had also pulled any book that had a reference to magic or Ozokeld. He didn't have high hopes of finding anything considering the amount of time they had already spent looking and the fact that most of the books on magic had been burned, but somehow he was disappointed anyway. He looked across the table at Octavian, who was looking just as frustrated.

"We're never going to find anything," Nevinon said. "We've been through almost every book that references Ozokeld. We haven't come across even a mention of anything we're looking for."

"Well, if you want to give up, you can go and tell Alanor that." Octavian didn't look up and kept reading.

"We haven't found anything useful. What's the point of continuing? It's one thing for all of us to develop magic, but I've never heard of anyone growing a fishtail before. I had never heard about Safehold or these shadow creatures from anyone other than my mother either. If Safehold is real, it must've been kept extremely secret. We're not going to find anything written down. Our best hope is to join the druids who are traveling to Ozokeld."

"It's not that I don't agree with you, because I do. We can't keep coming here to research," Octavian said. "Especially not to look up something as incriminating as magical creatures, and Safehold. We're going to get ourselves reported and arrested." Octavian closed his book. "But I don't think we should just blindly trust two strangers that showed up with the exact information we were looking for at such a convenient time. We have no proof that they were telling the truth."

"The druids are a secretive people," Nevinon said. "Things are often spread in the magical community by word of mouth. It would make sense for these things to not be written down for safety measures. Maybe they even have information on those shadow creatures. But we'll never know if we never ask," Nevinon huffed and leaned back in his chair. He spotted Moira coming back to the table with a pile of books. She sat next to him.

"Hey," Moira caught their attention. "I just spoke with some of the scholar apprentices. Guess what I heard."

"What?" Nevinon asked.

"There's a whole battalion, at least half of the hunters in the city, that will be traveling toward Ozokeld in a few days. They've hired some of the apprentices to accompany the ship. Apparently the hunters need their help deciphering some maps or something. The commander of the expedition, as well as his captain, is due to meet them here any minute now."

Octavian sat up straight in his chair. "There are hunters coming here now, and that's not what you lead with?"

"We need to leave." Nevinon went to stand up but Moira pulled him back down.

"Why leave now? This is the perfect opportunity to find out what the hunters are planning."

"If they catch us we're screwed," Octavian said.

"Then let's not get caught. Come on, there's a section of the second floor that overlooks the tables where they will be meeting. We can see everything from up there."

Nevinon was hesitant to take the risk and it seemed like Octavian was thinking along the same lines.

Moira continued, "Don't you think this information would be important to bring back to the group? Know your enemy and all that."

Octavian sighed. "Fine. I suppose even if we're caught, the two of you could just blast your way out of any situation, right?"

Nevinon gave a nod. "Gods, if Alanor finds out about this, he'll kill us."

"He should be grateful that we're as bold as we are," Moira scoffed. Nevinon thought that Alanor would probably call them reckless again, but he kept that thought to himself.

They stood up and followed Moira to the second floor. They crouched down near the railing that overlooked the tables on the main floor. A few minutes later three men dressed in hunter uniforms walked in. Their leader was none other than the

commander who had ordered the execution in the library courtyard not so long ago. Nevinon felt Moira tense up next to him.
Two librarians and their apprentices met hunters at one of the
tables. They seemed tense as well, more than likely feeling bitter
against the men who had killed one of their own.

Two groups exchanged stilted greetings but were speaking in
low tones. They wouldn't be able to hear anything like this.
Nevinon discreetly called on his magic and focused on his intention. Moira and Octavian jumped slightly when suddenly they
could hear everything that was being said downstairs loud and
clear.

"What was that?" Octavian asked.

"A spell to amplify sound. Shh, listen," he whispered.

"What exactly are you looking for in Ozokeld?" one of the
librarians asked.

"Upon the orders of the Supreme Vanquisher, we are tasked
with finding the entrance to a legendary place, a place of magic. It
is said that there is a treasure to be found at this entrance. We are
to bring back this treasure, as well as find ourselves a way through
this portal," the commander said.

Moira turned and whispered, "How did they find out about
Safehold being in Ozokeld?"

"And what's this about a treasure?" Octavian asked.

"Is all you ever think about gold?" Moira asked.

"Only when gold can help us destroy the enemy," Octavian
responded, "Besides, think about what the hunters could do if
they suddenly had access to a large sum of money."

Nevinon responded to Moira's original question, "Perhaps
they heard the rumors that were spread by the druids? Though,
why wouldn't they have taken the lead we dropped as seriously?"

They refocused on the conversation that continued below
them.

"Which legendary place do you speak of?" the head librarian
asked. "I have never heard of such legends before. Not centering
on Ozokeld."

"It is a place only referred to by the name Safehold, where those infected by magic escape to. A place of demons and criminals. It must be destroyed for the good of all humanity," the commander responded.

The librarians shared a skeptical look. "And you are convinced that such a place exists?"

The commander glared at them. "Whether or not it exists is of no matter to me. I am tasked with finding it, therefore we will try our damnedest to come back with good news. I'm sure I don't need to explain to you the consequences if we come back with bad news." The commander waited for the scholars to nod before continuing, "Then we will meet at the docks in a week."

The hunters left and Nevinon backed up from the railing. They hid behind a bookshelf so they couldn't be seen. Moira spoke first. "Do you think Safehold is actually in Ozokeld? This is the second time we've heard about the two being related."

Nevinon shook his head in bewilderment. "Why would my mother tell tales of some mythical place so far away? My mother never even left Amari, let alone the Isles, and somehow she knew about this place across the sea on the other side of the mainland? And why wouldn't she tell me where it was, if it did exist?"

Octavian was about to say something when Moira gasped and pointed toward the entrance of the library, where they could see Alanor and the others walk in.

"Shit," Octavian cursed. "We can't be seen all together here like this."

They rushed downstairs as fast as they could without being seen, and once the group was all together Alanor motioned for them to follow. "We need to leave immediately."

"You took the words right out of my mouth," Octavian responded.

They left the library, keeping their heads down. There were more than a few stressed-filled moments as they headed out of the city and back toward their house.

"There's a bounty on our heads?" his father asked.

They had just arrived back at the house, and Alanor was trying his best to keep calm. "Yes. It looks like the new troops have come back with orders to capture us. I don't know how we're going to keep living here with so many hunters out looking for us. And now the entire city is going to be joining the hunt just to make money."

"Well, thankfully a lot of the troops are going to be leaving soon. Within a week," Moira said.

"What are you talking about?" he asked.

"We overheard a conversation in the library. The hunters have orders to find the entrance to Safehold. I guess somehow they heard the rumors of it being in Ozokeld. There's supposedly also a treasure at this entrance that the hunters are after," his father responded.

"And did you find anything new about Safehold?" Alanor asked but he could see from the look on Nevinon's face that the answer was no. The warlock shook his head.

"I swear with all of this business surrounding Safehold, you'd think we would have heard about it before we came back," Theodore commented.

"There's something else," his father said.

"What?" Alanor asked.

His father looked at Nevinon and Moira. "When we were at the library we didn't just overhear the hunters say they were looking for Safehold, they also mentioned that they were receiving orders from the Supreme Vanquisher again."

Alanor sat straight. "The same man who organized the attack on the ship."

"Apparently so," Octavian said.

"Well, I say we should go to Ozokeld," Moira said. "Anything that the hunters could want is bad for us. We should go and find a way to stop them or get there before they do. If this place is real, we could warn them that the hunters are coming."

"I'm still not sure that this Safehold is a real place," Octavian said. "But getting our hands on that treasure, if it exists, would certainly be a huge help. We can never have too many resources."

Nevinon sat up again. "And if this Safehold is a real place, maybe we could be safe there from the hunters. Maybe we can find out why these shadows are after us. Maybe we could even find out why you all have magic now and how we were all"—he shook his head—"turned into merpeople for some reason."

"Wait a minute. Wait a minute." Alanor held his hands up. "We don't even know if there is a Safehold or even a treasure. It could be just a story. If the hunters will be leaving soon, then we'll be safer here than going to the place where they'll be following us. Why would we put ourselves in their path? We should be doing everything to avoid them."

"So you're saying we should stay?" his father asked.

"At least we'll be safer here than in Ozokeld."

"How much longer can we live in this house doing nothing? We're just sitting ducks here," his father said. "If I have stay here for another week I'm going to lose my mind, Alan."

"You should be thankful we have a place to stay at all," Alanor said.

"Alan, we're not making any progress here. We're here to find information on what happened to us, but there's nothing in the library about people coming back from the dead, about the shadows, or about Safehold. Maybe by following this we can finally figure out what's happened to us," Freddie pointed out.

"If there's no treasure and there's no Safehold, then we can come back and stay to your heart's content," Octavian said. "But if there is a treasure, then that combined with what we've already gained from the shipwreck can help us fight back against the hunters. Maybe we could even go back to Amari. Start over. Push the hunters out of our lands and take back our kingdom."

Alanor shook his head. "Amari is gone, Father, and even if we rebuild the castle the people will still be gone. It won't be the same. It's too dangerous to go back. And it's too dangerous to go to Ozokeld."

"It's also pretty dangerous for us to stay here, Alan," Evie said. "It's only a matter of time until we're known to the people of the town. Some people in the city already recognize us. How long until they realize that we match the people that the hunters are looking for? Just because some of the hunters will be leaving doesn't mean all of them will. We still have to deal with that bounty."

"I say we go too," Cassius said. "Those druids are already headed there, right? We could just join them and get there before the hunters do. If the hunters have arrived and we haven't found anything then we could just leave and go somewhere else."

Cassius looked at Solomon, who backed him up. "He has a point. We'll be stronger in numbers."

"What about our home here? We've just started getting back up on our feet. We're just going to leave all of our things behind?" Alanor asked.

"Better that we lose our things before we lose our lives," Genevive said.

Alanor stared at the others until he sighed. "Well, I suppose I'm outnumbered." Once again they'd be losing their home. He felt like a boat lost at sea. "The druids said they'd be leaving tomorrow night so we'll spend one more day here so we can prepare to leave." He pinched the bridge of his nose. Where would they go when they ran out of places to run to?

Nevinon watched Alanor shake his head and leave the room, calling back to the others, "If we're leaving for who knows how long, then we might as well squeeze another training session in."

With that settled the group broke apart, with the knights grabbing their weapons. Genevive accompanied the knights, who wanted to show her how to properly throw a dagger. Nevinon and Moira stayed behind to take care of dinner, though considering the fact that Moira had never cooked a meal in her life, Nevinon figured he'd be handling most of the work.

He began to cook the fish Alanor had brought back from the city in the oven while he chopped up some vegetables. Moira was silent, leaning against the counter and staring out the window into the distance. Nevinon could tell that she had something on her mind and waited for her to speak up. Maybe she was nervous about sailing toward Ozokeld. Nevinon felt the same apprehension.

"What do you think about Octavian?" she asked. Nevinon paused his chopping and sent her a questioning look. "I mean," she continued, "do you think he's a good man? I've always thought of him as this evil tyrant who murdered people like me. And he still fits that image somewhat, but ever since we came back he's been more and more..."

"Open-minded?" Nevinon asked.

"Yeah." She looked down. "I know that he still thinks magic is bad, but he helped us during our counterattack and he, I don't know, doesn't seem to want to kill us."

Nevinon waited for a bit before speaking. "I think he's going through a shift in the way he sees things. Before he was so set in his opinion but I think the fact that you have magic—" Moira rolled her eyes but Nevinon insisted, "No, it's true. He loves you like a daughter. It must've hurt him to hear that you had magic and eventually"—he swallowed—"killed yourself because you couldn't keep living a lie. Plus the fact that Kal, the head of the organization he founded, a man he trained, grew up to murder his son based on Octavian's own principles." Nevinon shook his head. "Him being around us and seeing us use our magic for normal day-to-day things and realizing that our magic hasn't corrupted us has helped. I think he's really starting to maybe change the way he sees magic."

Moira didn't look at him when she spoke. "Are you sure that magic doesn't corrupt? That it doesn't turn a person evil?"

"Of course I'm sure." Nevinon looked at Moira with wide eyes. "I've had magic my whole life."

"But you've killed people before," she insisted.

"When I've had to."

"And you've used dark spells before?" she asked.

"When I've had to," he repeated in a quieter voice.

"Then," she continued, "how can you be sure that magic hasn't made you do those things?"

Nevinon didn't respond for a few moments. "Where is this coming from, Moira?"

She sighed and turned away. She paced the kitchen a few times before stopping and facing Nevinon. "What would you say if I had done something horrible when I was in Amari?"

"Define *horrible*."

Moira swallowed and looked away. "Hiring an assassin."

"An assassin?" He felt himself give a quiet gasp. "To kill who?"

Moira's response was barely a whisper. "Alanor and Octavian."

The knife dropped out of Nevinon's hand and hit the floor with a loud clang that had them both jump in fright. Nevinon didn't say a word but stared at Moira like he had never seen her before. Nevinon had also suffered under Octavian's reign but to have gone to such lengths would've never occurred to him.

"You have to understand," Moira begged, "I thought it would free magic. Free our people."

"Why Alanor?"

"Because I thought he was just like his father." She shook her head. "I was alone and desperate."

Nevinon bent over to pick the knife off the floor and placed it quietly in the sink.

"Alanor's birthday was the perfect opportunity for someone to sneak into the castle." She looked away. "The man was supposed to kill Alanor and then Octavian. I wanted Octavian to suffer, to see his son die. To feel the same pain he had caused countless others. But Octavian leapt to Alanor's defense."

"Octavian took down the assassin but the man had already landed a fatal blow. A stab wound through Octavian's chest," Nevinon recalled that night. He and Juniper had been dealing with a few sick patients so they had missed the party. His mentor had never forgiven himself for not being there to save his old friend. Even though Nevinon hadn't mourned Octavian's death, Alanor had. Nevinon had often wished he had been there that night to save Octavian, if only to save Alanor from his pain.

Moira rubbed the palm of her hand into her eye. "When I saw him, Alanor, draped over his father's body like that..." She sniffled. "I had never seen him weep like that. He called for help but no one ever came. The assassin had taken out the guards. It was horrible." She was silent for a long time before whispering, almost to herself, "He reached out to me. In his final moments, Octavian reached out for me, but I stayed in my chair, and then he was dead, in Alanor's arms."

Nevinon had no idea what he could say to the revelation so he said nothing. Moira eventually continued to fill the silence, "I felt so guilty. I had murdered a man. A man who had taken me in after my parents died and raised me." She gave a bitter laugh. "And the worst part was that nothing changed. Magic was still illegal. Our people were still being hunted. It was all for nothing." She looked at Nevinon. He could see the echoes of desperation in her eyes. "Eventually I couldn't take it anymore," she said, "so I ended things. Felt the life drain out of my body, and then I woke up in that lake."

Nevinon needed to say something. Anything. But he couldn't get any words to come out of his mouth. A few seconds later Moira turned around and left the kitchen. Nevinon heard the door to her room close shortly after. The woman had just confessed to regicide and treason. What the hell was he supposed to do with that information? He stood there for what felt like an eternity before the smell of cooked fish hit him. He took the fish out of the oven and, without anything else to occupy his mind, picked up a new knife and went on with making dinner.

A part of him hoped that the knights would return soon to give him a distraction, but the other part of him balked at the idea of having to face Alanor and Octavian so soon. Alanor hated it when Nevinon kept secrets, but the warlock didn't think this would be something he could ever reveal to the other man. It would rip the group in two. He felt a brief surge of anger directed at Moira. Why did she have to go and confess this to him? Forcing him deeper into the shadows he had fought to free himself from so long ago. He could feel himself drowning in all of his secrets. He continued cutting the vegetables.

NEVINON WAS STANDING on the hill watching Amari burn to the ground. Everything he loved was burning to ashes. The castle was being ripped apart by shadow creatures that descended upon the citadel. He could hear the screams of people calling out as they attacked. Then in an instant, the fire was gone and so was the castle. The cries had gone silent. There was only a blackened crater left where his home should have been.

The shadows were still there though, in the sky circling. With nothing else to feast upon they turned their soulless eyes to him. Hundreds of them rushed toward him. He knew that if they reached him, they would devour his magic until nothing else was left. He tried to run but his feet had sunk into the ground. No matter how hard he pulled he seemed to only sink further.

The first of the shadows were upon him. He raised his arms to defend himself against the vicious claws, but no such attack came. When he looked up again he was on the beach outside the house where they had been staying. His feet were no longer stuck in the ground and he scrambled up.

"Nevinon," a woman's voice came from behind him.

He spun around, and gasped. Before him stood his mother,

looking not a moment older than the day that she left. She was even wearing the same clothes he had last seen her in. She had looked the same the night she had appeared as he performed the ritual that brought Alanor and the others back.

"Mum," he whispered.

"There is danger ahead, Nevinon." When the woman spoke it was not with his mother's voice, but rather an echoing of a vast number of unidentifiable women's voices.

"You are not my mother," he said.

"There is danger ahead, Nevinon," the woman repeated. She pointed behind him. He turned around to see the house engulfed by roaring flames, burning everything in its wake. All of their belongings. Everything they had worked toward. Then he could hear the sounds of his dear friends crying out. Screaming for help. He covered his ears with his hands, and he turned back toward the woman.

"Why are you doing this? Who are you?"

"The answers you seek, the truth of who you are lies in wait." The woman once more pointed behind him, but instead of seeing the house when he turned around, on the beach stood a massive building held up by vast columns of marble. It was a temple. Nevinon knew enough from his readings that this was the Temple of Ozokeld.

"Nevinon!" He could hear Alanor's voice calling him from someplace that he could not see.

"What does this mean?" he asked the woman.

The woman did not respond. Instead she faded from view as if she had never been there in the first place. Then he felt himself being shaken.

"Nevinon!" He opened his eyes to find Alanor sitting next to his bed. "Are you alright? Were you having a nightmare?"

Nevinon groaned and sat up. "I think I was having a vision."

"Well, whatever it was caused you to levitate everything in the house. I think Moira was having a vision too. She almost set fire to her own bed." Alanor helped him get up and walk toward the kitchen where the others were sitting. On the far side of the room, Theodore was helping Moira sit down and handing her a blanket to cover herself with and a cup of tea.

Nevinon wiped the sweat off his brow with the back of his hand. "I really need to get my magic under control. I haven't had outbursts like this since I was a teenager."

"Maybe it just needs a while to settle after coming back," Alanor said.

"Maybe." He was doubtful. He hadn't actually "come back" like the others. His magic had never acted out like this after he had learned to control it. It was disheartening. And terrifying. Nevinon was starting to wonder if he needed help. "What did Moira see?"

"She saw the house on fire," Alanor said. In an instant, Nevinon felt sick.

"I saw the same thing," he admitted. "And I saw the Temple of Ozokeld. I think the dream was a message for us to go there."

"We need to go there immediately," Moira cut in. "If we don't leave soon something bad is going to happen. We should leave now."

"It's the middle of the night. We can't just up and leave. There aren't even any ships leaving right now," Octavian said.

Moira shook her head. "We should swim there. And we should leave now."

Nevinon nodded. "I agree."

"At the very least we should sell the things that we have instead of abandoning everything," Octavian said.

"Can we truly not wait until morning?" Alanor asked. "The last time Moira had a vision it took a while for the attack to actually happen. Maybe we have more time than you think we do."

Nevinon hesitated. "I don't know. You can never really know with visions. But perhaps you're right. It would be a bad idea for us to be unarmed. I would hate to leave everything behind."

"We can pack everything up tomorrow, just like we planned. We'll go into the city market one last time, a different one far from where the posters were hung, and sell everything that we're not taking with us. And then we can leave tomorrow evening with the druids. That's less than a day." Alanor looked at Moira. "Do we have enough time?"

"I'm not sure. Last time we did but I don't know if this time we will," she said.

"What exactly is the threat we'll be facing if we stay too long? Do you think the shadows are coming again?" Solomon asked.

"I'm not sure." Moira pulled the blanket closer.

Theodore rubbed her arm. "Come on, let's try to get some sleep before the sun comes up." Moira nodded and he helped her up the stairs. Her legs were still shaking. Nevinon felt quite weak in the knees too.

Solomon approached Alanor and Nevinon. "Maybe we can get an early start on selling our things."

Alanor nodded. "I'm going to stay up and start separating things we won't bring. Hopefully we'll be able to sell the house too. We can set out for the city earlier. Oh and let's try not to leave any candle unattended, just in case." When Solomon walked away, Alanor turned back toward Nevinon. "Try to get some sleep, Nev. Who knows what tomorrow will bring."

Nevinon nodded and, after assuring Cassius and Freddie that he was alright, returned to his room. He doubted he'd be able to find sleep again. Who had been the woman in his vision? Had it truly been his mother?

THE GROUP WAS FILLED with a sort of frantic energy that morning. Everyone was disturbed after the dreams that Moira and Nevinon had experienced during the night. Breakfast was had in silence. Everyone ate faster than usual. Before the sun had come up, Alanor and his knights had set aside a variety of things they needed to sell. While the others stayed behind to pack their belongings, Alanor went out to the market with Cassius and

Solomon. He wasn't able to find the merchant who had sold them the house and he resigned himself to losing the money they had spent on it. Perhaps they had been too hasty in their purchase, but what was done was done.

They stood at the market selling what they could for the better part of the morning, keeping their faces down, but they were tense all the same. At any moment anyone could recognize them from their wanted posters. If that happened they would be lucky to make it out of the city alive. Everything was going smoothly until Alanor noticed that there was a young boy at the corner of the square staring at them. He waited a while before checking again. The boy was still there. He seemed to be trying to hide the fact that he was quite obviously keeping track of them.

Alanor turned to Solomon and whispered, "Have you noticed that young boy looking at us. He's behind me at the corner of the square."

Solomon nodded without looking. "Mm-hmm, he's been there for a while."

"I don't have a good feeling about this."

Cassius spoke up from his other side. "Maybe he's just a kid." Though even he sounded doubtful.

"Yeah, or maybe he's an informant," Alanor said. He looked back toward the kid. The boy now seemed to be looking at the wares of some merchant. Alanor was about to look away when suddenly a cloud of black engulfed the boy. He blinked but what he saw didn't change. It seemed as if the boy had been surrounded by a shadow. Were the shadow creatures here? Alanor waited to see if the boy would be possessed, but it didn't appear like the shadow cloud was doing anything other than enveloping the boy. Still, the presence of the black cloud induced a certain anxiety in him.

"Do you see that?" he asked the others.

"See what?" Cassius asked.

Then it was gone. The shadow cloud had faded into nothingness. No one else had noticed the thing. Was he hallucinating? It was enough to make him afraid. He turned toward Cassius and Solomon. "I think we should leave now. We've made enough for the trip, haven't we?"

Solomon nodded. "Yes, but we haven't sold everything."

"It doesn't matter." Alanor shook his head. "We'll leave it behind. We should leave now. I don't like the fact that we're being watched."

The moment they started preparing to leave, the boy up and ran out of the square. The knights shared a look and rushed out of the square like they had the previous day. Alanor felt the pounding of his heartbeat. Perhaps he should have listened to Moira this morning.

Even before they crested the hill overlooking the beach and the house, he knew that something was wrong. There was a cloud of smoke in the air coming from where their house was located.

CHAPTER 17

THE TEMPLE OF OZOKELD

The knights dropped what they were holding and unsheathed their swords. They rushed over the hill.

There was a pillar of fire roaring out of the house they had lived in for the past couple of weeks. The rest of his family was on the beach fighting against a large group of hunters. They were outnumbered by a large margin. Nevinon was there slinging spells at the enemy and that seemed to even the odds for a while, but Alanor could see from their position on the hill that there were more troops of hunters coming from the other side of the beach. They would be surrounded soon, and he didn't know how long Nevinon would be able to keep up without fainting again.

They rushed down the hill and into the fray. Alanor was able to take out three hunters in quick succession. It was not enough. They could not be captured. Who knew what the savages would do to his family?

"Into the water!" he yelled. "Everyone into the water now."

He wondered whether the others had even heard him over the shouting and the clanging of swords, but he could see that Nevinon had turned to blast aside the soldiers standing between them and the sea. Out of the corner of his eye, he saw one of the hunters plunge a sword into Solomon's chest.

"No!" Cassius shouted. Moira took down the hunter and Cassius dragged Solomon into the water with him. The man was unconscious and Alanor hoped beyond hope that he was alright and that he would heal just like Alanor had during the shipwreck.

Alanor and Nevinon stayed on the beach fighting until all of the others had made it into the water. Then the warlock covered them both as they followed. They transformed quickly. Alanor had to drop his sword, and the money pouch that was dragging him down, in order to swim out fast enough as arrows pelted the water's surface.

The group swam until they were far enough away that the hunters arrows could not reach them.

Cassius was cradling Solomon's body to his. "Sweetheart, please wake up." The unconscious knight had not transformed. Without doing so the man would not be able to breathe under-water and they would have to make their way back to the shore. Alanor could see their enemy's backup had arrived, doubling the already overwhelming number of hunters. There was no way back.

His attention was brought back to the group by the sound of a hacking cough. He turned to see that Solomon had regained consciousness and he breathed a sigh of relief. Cassius gave an elated cry and practically launched himself at the man.

"Alright, alright, give him some space, Cass." Freddie pulled Cassius back. Solomon took the opportunity to submerge himself and surfaced a few moments later, having successfully transformed.

Alanor turned to look at the shore as the group helped Solomon gain his bearings. He watched on in silence as their house, and all of their belongings within, went up in flames. The swords and the gold they had had on them were lost beneath the waves, too close to the hunters to recover. They would need to leave soon, but none of them could tear their eyes away from the sight of everything they had worked for burning to ashes.

"Were you able to salvage anything?" Alanor asked the others. They shook their heads.

"I hope Timmy got out okay." Freddie sniffled.

"Who the fuck is Timmy? Did I miss a child living with us?" his father asked.

"Timmy was the snake," Nevinon said. Alanor hadn't even noticed a snake in the house but Freddie always had a way with animals.

"We weren't able to grab anything before the hunters attacked. Not even the gold we had saved," Evie said.

There was nothing that Alanor could say in response so he didn't say anything at all.

"We should leave soon. Those hunters are not just going to stand there and let us swim away," Nevinon said. "They're bringing boats onto the beach now."

"What do we do?" Theodore asked.

Alanor felt something he very rarely experienced as a wave of rage washed over him. "We're going to Ozokeld. If they exist, we're going to find Safehold and the treasure that lies at its entrance. I don't know what the hunters want but I am sick of running away. Whatever it is that they want, they're not going to get it. Not on our watch."

"Hear, hear," said Moira.

"Let's hit those bastards where it hurts," Cassius said.

"So are we swimming there? It's a long way," Solomon said. "We can still go to the port where the druids will be leaving soon."

Nevinon nodded. "We should at least go and warn them that the hunters will be on the beach."

"Alright," Alanor agreed. "Let's go."

It only took them a bit of swimming to follow the coast until they hit one of the smallest ports of the city, the one where the druids were set to depart from. It was already getting dark when they poked their heads out of the water. The two druids were there on the docks next to a small boat. Alanor narrowed his eyes. That boat was too small to brave the waters of the Arlian Sea that lay between Tamlinn and Ozokeld. Perhaps that had been the only thing they'd been able to get their hands on?

Nevinon swam forward to approach, but Alanor gasped and grabbed at his arm to hold him back.

"What?" the warlock asked him. Alanor had stopped the man when he saw a cloud of black encircle the two druids. It was the same type of cloud that had surrounded the informant in the city.

"Wait," he said to Nevinon. "Just wait."

"What are you talking about?" Moira asked. Alanor shushed her frantically. The others stayed silent.

"What are we waiting for?" Cassius whispered.

"Good question," his father added. Alanor didn't respond.

Then Moira gave a gasp. "Hunters." Indeed there were hunters moving down the docks toward the druids.

"We need to warn them." Nevinon tried to pull away, but Alanor didn't let go. "Alanor, they're going to kill them."

Alanor doubted that, and his fears were realized moments later when the leader of the team of hunters shared a salute with the druids, who responded in kind. The hunter seemed agitated, pointing out toward the sea. The druid man shook his head and shrugged. Then the group shared a gasp when the two druids shrugged off their brown robes to reveal hunter uniforms underneath. He pulled on Nevinon's arm and submerged himself so he wouldn't be seen. The others followed suit. They surfaced quite a distance away, where a large rock formation blocked them from view.

"It was a trap." Nevinon sounded out of breath. "It was all a trap. But they had magic."

"The hunters have shown that they won't hesitate to use magic against magic users." His father nodded gravely. "It makes sense. Something about that original encounter never sat well with me."

"Nor I," Alanor admitted.

"How did you know for sure though?" Genevive asked. "You held us back. What tipped you off?"

Alanor shook his head. There was no way he'd be able to explain it without sounding like he was losing his mind. "It was just a feeling." He changed the subject in order to distract them. "I think it would be better if we swam to Ozokeld."

Freddie pointed behind them, out to sea. "The city should be in that general direction."

Alanor nodded and the group disappeared beneath the waves.

THEY HIT the shoreline of the continent in just about a day. The adrenaline that had pushed Alanor to swim at a speedy pace was fading now, leaving him feeling drained. He wondered if they had traveled faster this time because they were anxious or just because by now they were better at using their tails. The underwater landscape began to change and the fish became more colorful as they swam south. The blue color of his tail had become lighter and more vibrant as well. Moira's tail had a reddish tint now, and Cassius was sporting a few sea-green stripes in an irregular pattern. He wondered what had caused the change.

They pulled themselves from the water once they reached a cove that was near what seemed to be one of the main roads. It was certainly large enough. If they followed it south it would hopefully lead them into the city. It was a lot hotter here than it was in Tamlinn. The air was dry and it was more difficult to switch from breathing underwater to breathing on land. They took a few moments to rest once they were out of the water.

"They're not going to stop, are they?" Genevive broke the silence with a whisper. "They're going to keep hunting us."

His father nodded. "Unless we do something to stop them."

Alanor sighed and looked down at his bottom half, where his tail had transformed back into legs. "What can we do aside from grasping at straws, trying to find a mythical place that probably doesn't exist?" He scoffed. "A safe haven for magic? That's not the kind of world we live in."

"Alan's right," Theodore said. "We don't even have any of the money we managed to save. We're back on square one."

Solomon nodded. "I'm just afraid that the hunters will have salvaged our gold from the house. Who knows what they would do if they got their hands on that kind of money."

His father turned toward him. "We built ourselves up once and we can do it again."

"Now who's being naive," Frederick said.

His father sent a glare at the knight. "It's not naivety, it's determination. You should try it sometime."

Freddie went to respond but Alanor held up a hand. "For goodness' sake, not now."

"We should stay the night here," Cassius suggested. "We need to rest."

"No," Moira disagreed. "We need to get to Ozokeld as fast as possible."

Alanor nodded and stood up. "Sounds like a plan. Let's get a move on. I want to reach the city before it's dark."

By the time they had started walking down the road they were sweating from exertion. They spotted the city after a few hours on foot. The walls towered before them. Alanor's feet were burning, but he couldn't be the first to say he needed a rest. That would make him look weak in front of the group. Thankfully, Nevinon always noticed when Alanor needed a break, because the warlock called to the others that he couldn't walk any farther. Everyone took that as a cue to collapse onto the ground with no further warning.

"If I have to take another step in my life it'll be too soon," Cassius huffed.

"We've walked farther distances in Amari," Alanor said.

"Not in this heat we haven't," Theodore protested. They were all silent for a while just trying to catch their breath.

"So once we get into the city, what's the plan?" Solomon asked.

"Maybe we should ask around, see if anyone has heard any

legends of this Safehold. Or we could do what we did in Tamlinn and go to the library to do some research. A city this big? They've got to have one," Freddie said.

"You guys always want to do research," Cassius groaned. "When do we get to fight something?"

"We just fought half a battalion of witch hunters, Cass," Freddie responded.

"Well, that was yesterday, today is today. I say we go to the closest tavern. I haven't had a good drink in ages, and chances are that we'll probably get more information there than at any library. Our experience at Tamlinn just proves my point," Cassius said.

"And with what money are you going to buy yourself a drink?" Evie asked. "We've got none of it left."

"We don't have time to ask around randomly. The hunters are set to arrive soon, and they probably moved up the day they were set to leave Tamlinn because of what happened yesterday," Octavian said. "They'll be here soon and we need to find wherever that treasure is before they get to it or capture us."

"We need to go to the main temple," Nevinon said in a flat voice.

Theodore looked at the warlock. "You sound pretty sure of that."

"I saw it in my vision, remember?"

"Moira, did you see it in yours?" Theodore asked.

"Doubting me so soon, Theo?" Nevinon asked.

"I'm just looking for confirmation," Theodore assured him.

Moira shook her head. "No, but I trust Nevinon's instinct. Besides, there could be any number of scholars at the temple. Maybe there's someone there we need to talk to."

"I doubt we're going to find the treasure in the middle of the temple. There are people from all over that go there every day," Octavian said. "Hell, even my parents made the pilgrimage."

"They did?" Alanor asked.

Octavian nodded. "It was before I was born though."

"You don't talk about them a lot," Alanor commented.

His father didn't say anything but he stood up. He offered his son a hand and pulled Alanor up alongside him. "If we're going to get to the temple today we should go now. It's almost sundown."

"We should probably rest for tonight and go early in the morning tomorrow," Alanor said.

"What about the hunters?" Freddie asked.

"They're not going to get here in a day. It takes longer than that to sail across the Arlian Sea. We can rest for the night."

"Where? We can't afford an inn and there's not enough time left in the day to make up what we need," Evie pointed out.

"We can offer our services. It might not work but we might as well try," Alanor said.

The group arrived in the city just as the sun was going down. They were kicked out of three inns before they found one that was willing to let only three people stay in exchange for them cooking dinner for the patrons.

Nevinon was the best cook amongst them so it was obvious that he was going to be one of the three, along with Evie, who was also experienced in the kitchen. The others suggested that Alanor be the third person to accompany them since he was the group's leader, but he wasn't going to leave Moira without a place to sleep.

The knights could sleep anywhere, but it was improper for a lady to be on the streets at such a late hour. Though he didn't mention it out loud because he knew Moira would punch him if she knew what he was thinking. Alanor and the knights left the inn.

"We could sneak into the city stables and leave before morning," Cassius suggested. "I've done that before."

At this point Alanor was so tired that he couldn't think of another alternative, so he simply nodded. It was easy enough to do since there was no one there, and they lay down amongst the hay to sleep. He lay down next to his father, who was staring up at the ceiling with an annoyed look on his face.

"This is my life now," his father complained. "From being the king of one of the most important kingdoms on the Isles to sleeping in the stables."

"It's just for one night, Father," he sighed.

"And what about tomorrow night? And the night after that? We can't keep going like this, Alanor."

"Where did all of that optimism go?" Alanor asked. "Let's just get through this one day at a time."

His father was silent. Alanor shifted uncomfortably. He felt something small move beside him. He looked down and yelped when a rat ran over him and his father and disappeared into a hole in the wall, though his father had no reaction other than to huff a humorless laugh. It took a long while for Alanor to settle down into a restless sleep.

ALANOR and the others woke up early in the morning to avoid being caught in the stables, and the others at the inn had woken up just as early.

"How was it?" Alanor asked.

"It was fine, you?" Nevinon responded.

"Same. Though I think my father found it too demeaning." Alanor tried not to think of how many rats must've crawled over him while he was asleep.

Nevinon rolled his eyes. "That man would find anything except for absolute power demeaning."

Alanor laughed, "Too true."

The group made their way to the temple and sat outside on the front steps until the doors opened and they walked in. The main entry was empty aside from a young man who was arranging a pile of papers at the front desk. Cassius approached without hesitation and Alanor followed him, hoping the knight wouldn't say anything that would get them thrown out.

"Hello, beautiful." Cassius smiled. "We're looking to speak

with whoever is in charge of the temple today. We have some questions for them."

Alanor groaned internally at Cassius's forwardness. The young man gave them a look-over, and his face scrunched up in distaste when he spotted their clothes. After a short battle, contact with ocean water, a whole afternoon of walking down a dusty road, and a night of sleeping in the stables, Alanor couldn't imagine that they looked very dignified.

The man looked up and motioned for them to follow. "Right this way." He led them through a few hallways before knocking on a set of large wooden doors that were carved with delicate details.

"Elder Marcus," the young man said as he opened the door, "there's a group of people wishing to speak with you." The boy nodded for them to enter and walked off.

The room they entered was quite ostentatious, with many expensive-looking furnishings and decorations of gold and marble. It contrasted deeply with the man sitting at a desk in the center of the room, who was dressed in simple robes.

"Good morning." The priest looked up from the scroll he was reading. "Is there something I can help you all with?"

"Yes," Alanor said. "We've...heard some stories of a legendary place here in Ozokeld. Supposedly, there is a treasure to be found in this place, as well as the entrance to a magical world referred to as Safehold. We were wondering if you had ever heard any such stories before."

Elder Marcus tapped his fingers on his chin. "I've not heard of this treasure or of this Safehold, but the legend of an entrance to another world does strike a chord. Forgive me for being cautious, but this information has been kept guarded for quite some time. It really should only be shared with certain...individuals."

Without more prompting, Nevinon held up a hand and formed a fireball that dissipated after a few seconds. "Merry meet."

The priest smiled. "Likewise." The man stared at Nevinon for a few long moments. "I have not met anyone with that much magic within them in all my life. It's enough to overwhelm the senses. However, you are not the first with such power to grace these halls. Please sit, make yourselves comfortable." The man pointed to the benches and chairs in front of him.

As the group sat down, the priest began to speak, "I've been dying to tell this story for ages. My great-grandfather was also a priest here. It runs in the family, you see." He smiled. "And my father always told us this story of something that had happened when my great-grandfather was just an apprentice here, oh more than a century ago, I'd say. One day, in the ritual chamber, a woman and a man appeared out of thin air from between the obelisks at the back of the room."

"My goodness, how is this not spoken of more frequently?" Octavian asked.

"Well, the priests have always been a very secretive group of people. We won't lie if we're asked, but we don't often go out of our way to speak of such things with the public. Now"—Marcus turned to Octavian—"there have been some accounts of very powerful sorcerers traveling short distances with magic, but it was obvious that these two had come from a faraway place. And the location they appeared in was notable, because it is believed that two obelisks can create portals to other worlds. Anyway..." The priest waved off his tangent and continued.

"This man and woman were a couple. They were sorcerers and powerful ones at that. The woman was pregnant. They had the air of running from something. The man explained that they had been transported to the ritual chamber from another part of the world, but none of the priests believed that. Magical travel across the world? Nothing like that had ever been done before or since. It is just impossible for magic to do something like that. Or so they thought."

Alanor noticed Nevinon shifting on the bench next to him, but he refocused on Elder Marcus's story. "So what did they believe?"

"Many of them, including my grandfather, mind you, believed that they had come from another world. Of course, we have no proof of that, but nevertheless it is what the priests at that time believed."

"Why?" Nevinon asked.

"Well, I remember my father mentioning that their clothes were very strange compared to what everyone in the city was wearing. The woman's skirt stopped at the ankles, she was barefoot, in fact both of them were, and she had a shirt that seemed more like a woman's undergarments. It was a band of fabric around the chest, showing her midriff. The priests at the time thought it very indecent. And a decorated sash across the chest and over the shoulder that flowed behind her like a veil. The man was wearing a tunic that was apparently quite fitted"—Elder Marcus raised an eyebrow—"with a very large white fur coat. Their heads were adorned with vines and greenery. A very strange duo indeed.

"The clothes they were wearing would have been very expensive. So that stood out to my great-grandfather because it was very rare at the time to see clothing made of such rich fabrics, embroidered and decorated with beads and jewels, especially fur this far south. All the bells and whistles. It was as if they were royalty."

The priest lifted a cup from his desk and took a sip before looking up again. "Oh my, how rude of me. Would any of you like a cup of tea? One of the servants can bring up a tray for us."

"No thank you," Alanor declined. Cassius gave him a betrayed look and Alanor glared back at him.

Marcus continued with his story. "They also had a last name in the way that many peasants don't. Their behavior was strange. They seemed surprised at many things that were ordinary to people in the city, and they seemed skittish, which added to the perception that they were running from something.

"They stayed here for many months. The priests had allowed them to stay in one of the studies in the building across from here, where all of us live." Marcus pointed out his window.

"And now here's where it gets really curious." The priest

leaned forward. "Just before the woman was set to give birth, they both disappeared. The man came back only a year later, without his wife, no child in sight, and refused to say anything about what had happened. My great-grandfather thought that perhaps they had died. The man went to the ritual chamber and never walked out again. He disappeared just like he had appeared."

"Then, to my great-grandfather's surprise, the woman came back twelve years after her husband. She seemed distraught. Considering that she had nary a child with her, the priests assumed the worst and did not ask her much at all. She went to the ritual chamber and disappeared just like her husband did. And no one has seen them here ever since." The group was silent for a while just absorbing the story.

"That's wild," Cassius said.

"Did they mention any names?" Theodore asked.

"Oh, let me think." The priest closed his eyes for a moment. "Ah yes, their names were Janus and Vesta Ambrosius."

As the others continued to question the priest, Alanor felt Nevinon go rigid beside him. "What's wrong?" he whispered.

Nevinon started and turned toward Alanor. "That was my mother's name."

"Vesta Ambrosius?"

"I never heard her last name. I didn't think she had one. But her name was Vesta."

Octavian had been listening and leaned in slightly. "Do you think it was actually her?"

"I don't know," Nevinon said, "but the timeline fits. Maybe it's just a coincidence."

Octavian scoffed. "Heck of a coincidence."

Alanor focused again on the conversation the others were having with the priest.

"Now, you'd best not be asking just anyone about this, lest people think you're witches. Magic is not as welcome as it once used to be," the priest warned.

"Did they leave anything behind?" Moira asked.

"Not anything they had appeared with, but they did leave everything in their study. It was the first time anything like this had ever happened here so the priests have kept it intact since then, hoping to figure out where exactly the two had come from."

"Could we see this study?" Octavian asked.

"If you think you can figure it out, you're welcome to look through it. It's the highest room in the building across the street, the only room on the top floor. It has a great view of the bay. Let me go grab the key." The priest stood. "I'll be just a moment."

Once Elder Marcus had left the room, Genevive turned toward the others. "What are we hoping to find in this study?"

"Anything that can help us find this mythical entrance to Safehold will be helpful. Maybe it really is the ritual room of this temple," Octavian responded.

"But there is no treasure in the ritual room," Cassius said.

"Maybe the treasure is just a myth," Alanor said.

"A myth created by who?" Moira asked. "Can this really be what we're looking for? It seems like the priests haven't told anyone about this and yet somehow the hunters back on the Isles had heard legends of this place? Maybe this has nothing to do with Safehold. It's just a different magical place."

"Then why did I see this place in my vision?" Nevinon asked.

"Either way," Octavian cut in, "it won't hurt to check out this study. We have no other leads right now."

Alanor nodded. "You're right. We'll search the study, see if it hides anything of use, and then decide what to do next."

ALANOR LED the way up the spiral staircase leading to the study at the top of the building's tower. They unlocked the doors with the key that Elder Marcus had given them. It was a circular room surrounded on all sides by large open windows. Needless to say, the view was breathtaking.

The room, on the other hand, was pretty sparse. The only

part of it that was cluttered was the desk. It was overflowing with all sorts of papers and scrolls. They started searching the room. Evie and Freddie searched through the armoire in the corner. Solomon, Theodore, and Cassius looked through the other side of the room, checking the walls and the floor for hidden nooks, while the rest of them searched through the pile of papers on the desk.

By the time the others had finished, they had made it through only a fraction of the paperwork. The Ambrosiuses had done research on all sorts of things, not all of them about magic. It seemed like they had done extensive amounts of research on different places, not just on simple cities, but also on kingdoms throughout the continent, the mainland, and the Isles. In fact, there was an inordinate amount of research on Amari specifically.

"More coincidences?" Octavian gave Alanor a look.

"No, I think we've moved past coincidence at this point," he responded. Nevinon gave a silent nod.

"Look." Moira held up a black leather journal. "It looks like they were keeping a diary."

"Does it say anything useful?" Octavian asked.

"I'll have to read through it." Moira began to flip through the pages.

"Well," his father's voice suddenly took a strangled tone, "I hope you can read fast." He pointed out the window toward the port.

Alanor approached the window to get a better view. Out near the bay he could see a dozen warships headed for the nearest port. There was a black cloud above them, darkening the sky so that it looked almost to be sundown. That was odd. There hadn't been any signs of a storm coming this morning. He refocused on the ships. They were quite obviously witch hunters, displaying their insignia on the sails. The hunter insignia was not the only symbol present however.

"The Amarian crest," Octavian said. "The same as the ship that attacked us on the way to the mainland."

288

"Good gods, there's a whole fleet of them," Freddie said.

"So someone's not just using Octavian's title," Solomon said. "Someone is literally pretending to be King of Amari."

"Regardless," Octavian said, "there's a whole lot more of them than there is of us. And it won't take too long for them to find us. We need to find a lead or we need to go now."

"Moira, how's it going with that journal?" Alanor asked.

She was frantically flipping through the pages. "I'm looking, I'm looking... Oh!" She waved them over. "Come look at this. All throughout the journal they've been referring to the place they came from as home, but look at this passage. It's written just a few days before they left Ozokeld."

Octavian took the journal and began to read out loud, "'We have decided to leave Ozokeld. Vesta will be going into labor soon. Originally we thought that just moving into the mundane world would be enough to escape the threats of home, but we are too close to the portal here. It would not be safe to have our son in a place where he could be so easily found. So we must leave. There is a kingdom in a faraway place called Amari. Magic is illegal there. No one would think to look for our son in such a place. With that settled there's really only one disagreement between Vesta and me. We cannot stay in the mundane world for too long. This place is too devoid of magic. But we cannot bring the boy to Safehold with us. It would be too dangerous for him. We are afraid that we must leave him behind.'"

"They mentioned Safehold. So is the ritual room in the temple really a portal to another world?" Cassius asked.

"Apparently so," Theodore said.

"Is there"—Nevinon hesitated—"any mention of when the boy was born?"

Octavian flipped forward through the journal and then froze and nodded.

"Well, what does it say?" Alanor asked.

Octavian looked up at Nevinon briefly before reading out, "'It is the morning of Yule. Our child has been born. Like we predicted it is a boy. He is hearty and healthy. The boy already shows signs of magic. He has been floating his toys above his crib. While we are obviously proud of his magical prowess at such a young age, we are worried also. We chose this place, Amari, because no one from Safehold would find him here. But now we fear that we might have put him at a greater risk.'"

Octavian paused before continuing, "'The witch hunters of Amari are not known to be merciful toward those with magic. I am worried about what will happen to the boy once we leave. And we will have to leave at some point. I can already feel the pull. Vesta hasn't yet, and I hope that she won't for a while. Perhaps she will be able to stay with him. She does not want to speak of such things. And I do not want to spoil her happiness. So instead of speaking of these important matters, we occupy ourselves with finding a name for our son. We were so worried about our boy needing protection that we almost forgot that the boy also needed a name. Hopefully we will come to an agreement on a proper and fitting name for him soon.'"

Nevinon gave an audible swallow.

"What's wrong?" Moira asked him.

"My mother's name was Vesta. And I was born in midwinter, or at least that's what my mother always said. That I was born on the morning of the solstice. On Yule."

"It could be talking about anyone though, right?" Cassius asked. "I'm sure there are many babies born on Yule."

Octavian shook his head. "No, not right. Look at this next passage." He read out, "'Vesta and I have finally decided on a name. Nevinon Janus Ambrosius. A strong name for one such as he.'"

"Janus Ambrosius?" Nevinon breathed. "I have a last name? And a middle one too?"

"Wait, better question, your parents are from Safehold?" Freddie asked.

"Maybe that's why your magic is so strong," Moira said.

"Guys," Solomon caught their attention. "The witch hunter

fleet has reached the port. They're disembarking. I don't know where they're going first but I'm sure that the temple is high up on that list of potential locations."

"We should head to the ritual room," Evie suggested. "We know that that's where they came through."

"What if we can't find this portal? There's obviously no treasure in the ritual room. And if we can't activate the portal to this magical world, then we'll be cornering ourselves. Maybe we should leave the city," Octavian said.

"No. We've come too far to just let the hunters get whatever they want now. We need to get to that room first," Alanor said.

"Agreed." Nevinon held out his hand for Octavian to give him the journal. "And I want to know what the hell is going on with this. If my parents are really from Safehold—"

Alanor nodded. "Let's get going."

Before leaving the room, Nevinon took the journal and hid it in his jacket pocket and grabbed a bag. It took only a few seconds for him to shove a great quantity of papers from the desk into it. The warlock shrunk the bag and fitted it into one of his pockets, hidden away, then they rushed out of the room and down the stairs.

They burst through the front door and sprinted toward the temple. It seemed as though they had entered another city. The streets were empty. The people had most likely gone to their homes to hide from the fleet of witch hunters flooding into the city. The temple was also abandoned, though perhaps that was a good thing considering that they needed to get into the ritual room. The room was very easy to find, being the largest in the temple. It was empty aside from two large obelisks at the back.

"Okay, now what?" asked Cassius.

"Now we—" Alanor was interrupted by a sharp pain in his gut that caused him to double over. When he looked up he saw the others were in pain too.

"What's happening?" Octavian groaned.

Before anyone could respond, a blinding pain resonated in

their heads. Alanor could barely keep back the cry of agony as he collapsed onto his hands and knees. He could hear voices in his head, growing louder and louder, accompanied by manic yipping and giggling.

Tasty souls ready to be devoured...
I'm hungry, so, so hungry...
The feast begins—soon...soon...
Hungry... Hungry...
DEVOUR!

He gritted his teeth as that last scream echoed through his mind. He instinctively clapped his hands over his ears, but it was of no use, given that the sounds were not coming from around them.

"It's the shadows. They're coming," Nevinon groaned.

He felt sick to his stomach. The stench of rotting flesh surrounded them. The taste filled their mouths and Alanor retched.

The shadow creatures glided into the room through the ceiling. They were circling the group but they did not attack. The pounding headache continued to get worse. The doors slammed open, and around fifty hunters flooded the room, surrounding them easily. From what he could hear, there were more men waiting outside. Alanor saw Nevinon try to attack them with his magic, but he was weak from the mental attack.

It took five hunters, but eventually they managed to clasp iron manacles on Nevinon. The situation was hopeless now. No sorcerer or warlock could use their magic when cuffed in iron. Alanor was lying useless on the floor, unable to help. The hunters put them all in chains and dragged them so they were leaning against the wall on the left side of the room.

A man dressed in a commander's uniform, but wearing a hood that hid his face, walked in and the other hunters moved out of his way. He moved until he was in the center of the room, then raised his hands.

"Now you may feast!" the man called.

Alanor flinched as the shadow creatures dove downward. But they did not attack them but rather descended upon the hunters. The witch hunters transformed before their very eyes, the same way that the crew of the ship did when they were leaving the Isles. Their eyes turned fully black, and their mouths were overtaken by deranged smiles. All of the possessed hunters turned toward them. Now that the shadows were within the hunters, the group could no longer hear their voices and cries. Alanor felt his headache recede slightly.

The only hunter who had been left alone was the commander, who now approached the group, clapping slowly. "My, my, how the mighty have fallen."

The man reached up and lowered his hood, revealing shock white hair and a familiar face, wearing the crown that his father had been buried in.

"Kal," Alanor breathed.

CHAPTER 18

FAMILIA QUAM OMNIA

"A commendable effort, but I'm afraid you're no match for the shunvora. They have been waiting so patiently to feed on your magic." Kal grinned.

"How is this possible?" Alanor asked.

"You didn't think you were the only ones who came back now, did you?" Kal crossed his arms and approached until he was looking down on Alanor.

"That's how the hunters knew about us," Solomon said.

Kal gave an amused smile. "Correct. When your dear friend Nevinon ripped a tear in the Veil... Well, my master is not one to turn down such a lovely opportunity." A tear in the Veil? The Veil between worlds? Alanor looked at Nevinon, but the warlock was focused on Kal.

"You've allied yourself with these beasts?" Octavian gave the traitor a disgusted look. "And allowed them to take over your men?"

Kal shook his head. "I'm not their ally, *Your Majesty*, I am their commander. And they were so gracious to accompany me to our world, don't you think? Especially when I promised them a tasty meal at the end of it all. The hunters were just collateral damage."

"You brought them here?" Nevinon asked.

Kal scowled. "Don't speak to me, you filthy sorcerer. It's only natural that the shunvora would follow me. We have the same goal after all. These creatures devour magic." He motioned to the possessed men around him. "Once I have access to Safehold I will set an army upon this world and the next and purify it from the evil that you sorcerers bring. I will destroy magic once and for all."

Kal paused and looked at Octavian. "That is what you wanted, isn't it? And it is I, not your golden son, who will finally achieve what you've always dreamed of."

Nevinon scoffed. "You cannot destroy magic as much as you cannot destroy the sky above us. It is in the very air that we breathe. In the earth that we walk over."

Kal shook his head. "Not if I destroy it at its source."

"What source?" Alanor asked.

Kal ignored him and looked at the enthralled hunters around him. "Get the circle ready and prepare our captives for the ritual."

"What source, Kal?" his father repeated his question.

Kal sighed and turned toward Octavian. "Safehold is the last bastion of magic. Its source lies within."

"That's why you've been looking for this place?" Alanor asked.

Kal smiled. "Oh no, I've known where the entrance has been all along. My master told me. But I needed you all to get me in. You see, only those with Safehold blood or magic can cross the portal, and unfortunately the shunvora cannot cross the protections. I sent them after you to capture you. I have no idea how you avoided them twice, but it is of no matter. I do not mind getting creative." He smirked. "I eventually decided that it would be much more poetic to lure you here."

Nevinon scowled. "You arranged for those fake druids to find us and lead us here."

"And that's why the hunters didn't take the bait we set," Moira said.

Kal laughed. "Zarakish? Please. It was a good try, but yes, all I needed to do was get you here. And even though you didn't join my 'druids,' you still found your own way to the temple." He started clapping. "Congratulations."

Kal bent down so he was face-to-face with Octavian. "To seal the deal I made sure my men mentioned a treasure when you were there to 'overhear.' I knew you wouldn't be able to resist the possibility of a score big enough to reestablish your standing in the Isles. That is after all what is most important to you, isn't it? Your standing? Your reputation?" Kal spoke in a soft, bitter voice and his father scowled at the man. Alanor wondered where Kal's animosity had come from since the knight had always seemed to worship Octavian.

Nevinon glared at the man. "If the shadow creatures can't cross the protections on the portal how are you going to fulfill your mission? And who is this master that you speak of?"

Kal paid no mind to Nevinon, still staring at his father. Octavian gave a twisted smile. "I never took you for a mindless follower, Kal."

Kal's face scrunched up with rage as he shouted, "My master was the only one who gave me the power I needed to come back and achieve my purpose! To bring about the destruction of magic once and for all." He turned toward Nevinon, his voice returning to its previous volume. "As for how I'm bringing the shunvora into Safehold"—he spread his hands wide, motioning to the crowd of possessed hunters behind him—"the portal cannot perceive them when they are within living vessels." Kal smiled and lowered his arms. "And now you may be wondering how we're going to bypass the blood or magic requirement. I believe that is something that you can help me with."

"We won't help you, you murderer," Moira called out.

"Oh, you think you have a choice?" He laughed. "We will use your filthy magic to get in and then I will kill you all again. And I will wipe magic off the face of the earth if it is the last thing I do. However"—he paused—"I am not without mercy."

Kal knelt in front of Octavian. "You, the first Supreme

Vanquisher, the one who trained me, the most formidable enemy of magic. We can find a way to rid you of this evil. To cure you. And we can stand side by side as we take on evil together. The way you were never able to with your *son*," he spat out the word, "who was weak against the corruption that magic wrought."

Octavian glared at the man. "You say you are against magic in the midst of preparing for some ritual? And you've allied yourself with these creatures who are clearly magical?"

Kal shrugged. "If I must surrender myself to evil in order to defeat it, then that is what I will do. You are the one that taught me that. The ends justify the means."

"Is that why you waged war against your homeland? Is that why you murdered my son?" Octavian asked.

Kal scowled. "Yes! I did it for you. For us. For our legacy!"

Genevive laughed. "You're a hypocrite. All you did was weaken Amari, you bastard. It was your fault that the kingdom was later overrun by barbarians."

"I'm not the one who weakened Amari," he shouted. "You were. You all were."

Octavian called out to the man, "This is madness, Kal. I'm not even sure if I was right to do what I did in the first place. Perhaps I was wrong. Perhaps magic is not the evil that I always thought it was."

Kal gave a shocked huff and stood up. "It is too late then. You have been corrupted. The real Octavian would never submit to magic." Kal had a faraway look in his eye now, as if he was looking through them. "The real Octavian would want me to stop him from becoming a monster." He turned and began whispering to himself. "And I don't need all of you to get through the portal."

Kal looked at a nearby hunter with a crossbow and motioned to Octavian. "Kill him."

"No!" Alanor shouted.

The hunter raised the crossbow at his father, but Octavian surged to his feet and, despite the chains that restricted his movement, tackled the hunter, wrestling the crossbow from his grip.

He quickly pointed the weapon at Kal before any of the other hunters could get to him.

"You disappoint me, Kal," Octavian said. "You don't even have the courage to kill me yourself."

Kal had turned a pale shade but stood his ground. "And you, Your Majesty? Are you ruthless enough to kill me? Me?"

Octavian didn't shoot though, he just stood there. His father gave an audible swallow. His hands were white from the pressure of his grip.

"SHOOT HIM!" Alanor screamed. His father didn't move.

"They don't know, do they? About all of the secrets that you're hiding. But I know." Kal smiled and then scowled. "And I know that I'm not the only one."

Octavian's eyes widened with fear.

"Look out!" Nevinon called but it was too late. Two hunters had snuck up behind Octavian and tackled him to hold him down again.

Alanor made eye contact with his father as the hunters adjusted his manacles so his hands were behind his back. His father mouthed *I'm sorry* to him.

One of the possessed hunters approached Kal, but when he spoke it was with a decidedly not-human voice. "The circle is ready."

"Excellent," said Kal. "Then we shall finish preparing now."

Kal and his hunters gathered around them. The front group approached them with daggers. Kal took a blade from one of his men and stepped up to Alanor. He winced as Kal slashed at his upper arm. Kal laid his hand over the wound, and Alanor watched on in disgust as Kal smeared the blood on his face. He noticed that all of the hunters were doing the same with the others as they looked on in shock.

In short order all of the hunters had their faces painted in blood. Alanor looked at his friends and noted that while all of them had had their arms cut, no one seemed to be in danger of bleeding out soon.

The hunters then dragged them to the center of the ritual circle that had been drawn on the floor. Kal took out a scroll from his jacket and held it up unfurled in front of Nevinon.

"You will speak the spell."

Nevinon glared up at Kal. "No."

Alanor felt someone pull his head back by his hair and place a blade at his neck.

"You will speak the spell or your dear king will die. Again."

"Don't do it, Nevinon," Alanor said. But even as he said that he knew that Nevinon would. He always would. Anything for family.

The hunters removed the iron manacles from the warlock's wrists. Nevinon sent him a glance that shouted both hopelessness and determination, and he took the scroll from Kal's hand. Nevinon unfurled it, and with a furrowed brow, spoke aloud a short sentence: "'Let the gates of Pithikar be opened to her children.'"

The circle glowed with bright white light. The wind began to howl around them, though Alanor had no idea where it came from. For a moment he thought he could hear voices over the wind, whispering something that he couldn't perceive. And then, for just a moment, almost imperceptible, the distant sound of bells. The light overtook his vision to where he could no longer see, and the ground rippled beneath him, sending him tumbling to the floor, which he could feel now had been replaced with what felt like grass. When he could see again they were no longer in the ritual room.

Alanor did not think they were even in Ozokeld anymore.

They were positioned on top of a cliff that overlooked a vast area of land. He could see some large buildings that were fashioned in the same style as the temple in Ozokeld, and a city that surrounded a large castle in the middle of a valley. In the far distance, there were what seemed to be several floating islands. And there were creatures flying over the city, magical ones for sure.

"Dragons?" Nevinon gave a shocked gasp.

"Finally." Kal held his arms up. "Victory is within reach. Come forth, my warriors of darkness."

The skin of the possessed hunters seemed to bulge and move until from each man a shadow creature burst out, leaving behind a shattered corpse. The group was covered in the blood of what used to be a battalion of witch hunters. He heard a scream but he did not know from whom. The shadows were even larger here, and they circled above like vultures, but they seemed to be trying to hide from the sunlight, using each other for shade.

Kal pointed toward the group. "Kill them!" he ordered.

As the creatures descended, a beam of white light burst through the mass of black. A few of the creatures were incinerated. The lights had come from the right, and Alanor could see a group of people headed toward them in tight formation. One of them sent another beam of light at the shadows. The creatures were now hesitant to approach Alanor and his friends.

Kal looked at Alanor and growled, "I will face you another day, traitor. And you will die by my hand again. Permanently this time."

The creatures descended upon Kal, but not to attack him. They circled their commander, and with a swirl of black smoke, they were gone.

Alanor and his friends were left, handcuffed on the ground, in the middle of a circle of carnage. The group of sorcerers that had saved them had now reached them. They were wearing black outfits, knee-high boots, and long cloaks that flowed in the strong gusts of wind that blew over the landscape.

"Thank you," Nevinon called out to them. "What are you—" The warlock was cut off as the sorcerers pulled them all onto their feet roughly.

"Invaders. They must be," one of them accused.

The man holding Alanor shook him forcefully. "You're under arrest. All of you."

"Arrest? Arrest for what? We were the ones being attacked," Octavian said.

"For threatening the safety of Pithikar." The man holding Alanor responded, "Traveling through the portal is illegal. And allying yourself with the godless or with a horde of shunvora is punishable by death."

The man turned to another. "Put them to sleep." The other man snapped his fingers and Alanor felt a sudden wave of exhaustion pull him under. Alanor tried to resist but it took only a few seconds for everything to go dark.

As the sun rose, light filled the grand room and made it nearly impossible to notice the golden magical glow. The priestess only noticed when she turned to see the head oracle sitting up with her head held high and her eyes open wide. The priestess gasped and reached out to the woman standing next to her, the high priestess.

"A new prophecy?" the priestess asked. The two women moved closer to the oracle, who began speaking once more in her raspy voice.

"The shunvora will rise.
The shunvora will rise and Alexsantari will burn,
When the godchild sets foot on Pithikarian soil."

The oracle continued with the second half of the prophecy, then inhaled and her eyes cleared. The two women looked on in shock as they became the first to see the oracle's natural eye color since the elder had taken her post.

The oracle looked on in fear. "The prophecy. Its foretold events have commenced. The godchild. He has entered Pithikar. The shunvora are coming to devour us all." The oracle gave a final gasp before falling back into her dormant state with her eyes closed.

Silence reigned for a few moments before the high priestess

spoke. "All of our efforts were for naught. This can only spell destruction for our people. We must alert the council of elders."

The priestess nodded and rushed out of the room to send the warning. The high priestess walked toward the edge of the staircase leading down from the temple, and she looked out over her homeland, feeling a wave of dread take over her as she whispered to herself, "Pithikar is in danger."

ALANOR CAME to with his head pounding. He raised his hand but paused when he felt the manacles on his arms. The chains clinked as he pulled himself into a seating position. His face was itchy from the gore that still covered it from when the shadows burst from the hunters.

"Finally awake, Dollface?" He looked up to see Cassius in the cell across from his.

"Piss off, Cass," he responded mindlessly. His father was lying down on another cot on the other side of his cell.

"How long have we been here?" Alanor asked.

"No idea. It was daytime when we came through the portal but it's dark now and we've just started waking up. Everyone's accounted for. They still have us in irons. Nev doesn't seem to be reacting too well," Cassius said.

"I'm fine," Nevinon's voice groaned in a way that told Alanor he was obviously not fine. "At least I'm awake. Moira hasn't come to yet."

He couldn't see Moira from where he was sitting. The chains weren't long enough for him to get too close to the wall of bars facing the other cells. Alanor looked at his father. The man was staring at the wall emotionlessly.

Without even a warning Alanor felt fury overtake him. Here they were in some far-off magical land. His family, trapped in cells and chained like common criminals. Nevinon in pain and Moira in goodness knew what condition. Alanor had no idea who was even holding them or how the hell they were going to get out of this one. Kal was still alive and free to wreak havoc. And it could've all been prevented.

"You had a direct shot. You could've taken him down and you didn't. Why?"

No reaction. It was like his father hadn't even heard him.

"You had my murderer in front of you," he shouted, "and you let him go. Have you nothing to say to me? Look at me!"

His father turned his head to look at him briefly but still he did not say a word.

"Secrets, he said. What did Kal mean? What are you keeping from me?" Alanor asked. "You've put us all in danger, and you don't think I deserve to know what for?"

Nothing. His father continued to stare at the wall.

Alanor huffed, "Lies, lies, and more lies. You and everyone else. Is there not a single one of you that hasn't been keeping something from me? Is it my fate to constantly be surrounded by people who keep important information secret? Friends and family who don't trust me?"

"I trust you," his father said in a quiet voice.

"Not with the truth."

The man didn't have a response and Alanor turned away, not able to bear the sight of his own father. The sound of footsteps drew his attention. A man wearing the same uniform as the men who arrested them, except for the green coloring of the inside of his cloak, walked up to their section of cells. The man had his hand held up with a glowing ball of golden energy levitating over it, lighting up the passageway.

The man's eyes scanned over them. "Who is the leader of your group?"

"I am," Alanor called.

His father sat up as the man approached their cell. "What do you want with us?"

The sorcerer narrowed his eyes at Octavian. "I suppose I could ask you the same question. As you have been informed previously, traveling through the portal is illegal. And allying yourself with the shunvora is punishable by death. And as far as we can tell, you lot helped the invasion that came through this morning."

"We weren't helping them," Evie said.

"Exactly," Freddie said. "If we were their allies then why do you think they would put us in chains?"

"That's not for me to decide." The man shook his head. "You will face trial once the council of elders has gathered."

"This has all been a big misunderstanding," Alanor said.

"I've heard that one before." The man threw one last glare at them before he started to walk away. The sorcerer paused in front of Nevinon's cell. "Are you alright? Do you need the help of a healer?"

"What I need," Nevinon coughed, "is to get these chains off of me."

"The chains aren't coming off until you serve trial," the man said.

"Then I'm not going to get better until I serve trial," Nevinon responded.

The man raised his magical light to see Nevinon better. Alanor could now see that his friend was obviously in bad shape.

"What have you done to him?" Alanor asked. "Those cuffs are hurting my friend."

The man looked back at Alanor. "Those cuffs are just magical dampeners. They're not supposed to cause pain."

"Well, obviously they are causing him pain."

The man looked back at Nevinon before nodding. "I will speak with my captain." He rushed down the corridor and out of sight.

"Nev, are you alright?" Alanor could have smacked himself for asking such a stupid question.

"I'm fine, Alan," Nevinon breathed. "Though I've never had this reaction to iron before."

"That's not usual, is it?" Cassius asked.

"No," Nevinon groaned.

Alanor was about to speak again when he was interrupted by the sound of Moira screaming.

"Moira," he called. "Is she hurt? Who's in the cell with her?"

"I am," he heard Theodore's voice call out. "She's alright. She's just shaken up. She's had another one of her nightmares."

"It was bad." Moira's voice was shaky. "It was very, very bad."

Alanor felt a weight sink in his stomach. "What is it? What did you see?"

He heard Moira sob before she responded, "The destruction of everything. This world and our world. It was Kal, and another man. They summoned an army of those monsters. No, more than an army. Their numbers were vast and innumerable. Enough to outnumber the population of any kingdom, I think. They fed on all of the magic of this world and the next. Without magic the world will perish."

"Did you see anything that could tell you when this is going to happen?" Theodore asked.

"No."

"Are we sure it was a vision and not just a nightmare?" Solomon asked.

"Sol," Cassius scolded.

"I'm not trying to be dismissive, I'm just trying to be sure," he responded.

"It was a vision. It's going to happen. I'm sure of it," Moira said.

"Damn," Freddie said. "That doesn't sound good at all. We weren't even able to fight against fifty of them. How are we going to stop him? An army of those things? He's too powerful."

"I don't know. But we'll figure it out," Alanor said.

"We should run," Nevinon said. "There has to be a way back through the portal and into our world. We should get away from Kal as fast as possible."

"I never took you for a coward, Nevinon," Alanor said.

"My job is to keep us safe. And we are safest far away from Kal," Nevinon said.

"And it's my job as king to stop Kal. Like it or not he was a citizen of Amari, which makes his actions my responsibility. And if he is going to unleash hell on both this world and our world, then it is our obligation to do whatever we can to prevent him from doing so."

"Maybe we should tell these people what Moira has seen," Freddie said.

"And put ourselves under more scrutiny?" Octavian protested.

"If an attack of such magnitude is imminent, then we need to tell them. They must have some sort of defense system, right? They knew what those things were," Freddie said.

"Don't forget that they will ask us how we know that information," his father said. "Who knows what they'll do to Moira if they find out that she's a seer." Alanor heard a click and turned to see his father drop his manacles to the ground. "Finally."

"You know how to pick locks?" Cassius asked.

Alanor looked at his father, who knelt before him and started fiddling with the cuffs on his wrists. "What are you doing?"

"We're getting out of here." With another click Alanor felt his cuffs give and they fell away.

"And going where exactly?" Theodore called.

"Anywhere but here," his father responded.

Genevive stood as his father opened their cell and they approached the others. "Octavian, we don't know anything about this place."

"If you want to stay around waiting to be sentenced to death, be my guest." His father shook his head. "But I am leaving."

"Unshackle Nev first," Alanor said. In short order they were all free and out of their cells. Nevinon was taking in huge gulps of air like he had been suffocated. They started walking in the direction the sorcerer in uniform had gone in, as that's where the exit must've been, when a high-pitched voice called out.

"Hey, could you guys let me out too?"

Alanor started and turned to see a short bearded man standing in one of the cells that had been next to theirs. He had two short luminescent green wings that spread from his back.

"Who are you?" Cassius asked.

"I'm Gavin."

"Have you been here this whole time?" Solomon looked at the man with a raised eyebrow.

"Oh yeah." Gavin had a smile on his face. "I heard everything. Working with the godless to bring about the apocalypse, huh? I dig it."

His father turned to Alanor and made a gesture asking if he should let the man go. He motioned for his father to wait and then asked, "What are you in here for?"

Gavin laughed. "Oh, I'm a thief! And a murderer. Gavin the slasher, that's me. If you ever want something stolen or someone murdered, I'm your guy."

"The slasher?" Theodore whispered to the group.

"Why should we let you go if you're admittedly a criminal?" Genevive asked.

"Well, hey." The man scratched his head. "You guys seem to really not know the lay of the land. If you wanna take your chances, I can't wait to see you die. Maybe if you take me with you, you'll just die another day."

Freddie frowned. "You seem to be pretty enthusiastic about watching us die."

Gavin grinned. "I'm pretty enthusiastic about watching everyone die, including myself!"

"Okay." Freddie turned. "We should not let this man out under any circumstances."

Cassius shrugged. "I don't know. I kinda like his vibe."

"We could use some allies right now," Solomon pointed out.

"Oh, I've never been one for allies. All of my allies seem to die fast, hee hee." Gavin grinned.

"Really?" Alanor asked dryly.

Gavin nodded. "Because I kill them! Usually with a knife in the back. That's always where they least expect it, tee hee."

"So you've just lived your life alone with no loyalty?" Moira asked.

"Loyalty?" Gavin waved them off. "The only person I'm loyal to is the Queen of Ishwick. She's a pretty nice gal. We've got a pretty good thing going, rebelling against the elders and all. Fuck those old squares! And"—Gavin smirked—"she's pretty open to outsiders and outcasts."

"Sounds like what we are right now," Nevinon pointed out.

"I can take you to her if you want to meet her."

"Are you going to stab one of us in the back?" the warlock asked.

"Prolly." Gavin nodded.

Moira narrowed her eyes at him. "Not if we stab you first."

"Ooh." Gavin seemed delighted in a disturbing way.

"Well, we outnumber him so we could probably handle it if he tries to attack one of us," Alanor whispered to his father.

"And we do need to get out of here," the man said before moving to help Gavin out of his cell.

Gavin waved them down a different tunnel. "Come on, the exit is this way. I should know. I've been here before. Many times. They just can't get rid of me." He led them through numerous passageways and then through a small gate, with a lock that his father picked, that led outside of the building. Alanor took in a breath of fresh air and hoped that the darkness of the night would cover their escape.

"Where to now?" Genevive asked.

Gavin pointed to the tree line in the distance, across a small field. "Into the forest. I hope you guys have good survival instincts."

Alanor exchanged a glance with Nevinon. Trusting this man was not ideal, but neither was staying in a place where they had already been assumed to be criminals and might be sentenced to death. He looked back at the prison and then forward toward the forest that was so clearly magical it even seemed to glow with small colored lights. After a few moments Alanor realized that the lights were coming from certain plants and insects. Wonderful. They weren't even in the same world anymore. The rest of the group had already gone ahead. He followed but paused at the tree line. Who knew what was waiting for them there.

"Alan."

He looked at his father, who had reached a hand back for him, and Alanor shook his head. "I won't let anyone, especially not Kal, destroy this family a second time."

"I'm with you." His father nodded. "Now let's go. We need to keep moving."

Alanor grabbed his father's hand. The older man pulled him up a short incline and they all disappeared into the forest.

Deep in the darkness, in the void that was not empty but full of cavorting and yipping shadows, a pair of fangs tore into a piece of rotting flesh.

The thing opened its mouth in the mimicry of a smile. Too many teeth. Too sharp. Drenched in gore. With a massive clawed hand, it wiped away the black ooze that covered its face.

"Soon."

The series isn't over yet!

If you'd like to be notified when the next book comes out sign up to my email newsletter. PLUS get your FREE 200 page workbook of word search puzzles with themes like Dungeons and Dragons, Mythology, Magic, and Fantasy.

· · ·

CLICK HERE to get your free puzzle workbook! Or scan the QR code below.

If you enjoyed the book, please leave a review! Your reviews mean the world to me.

ALSO CHECK out my website here to learn more about me and learn about any new releases.

www.milenadelgadolaborde.com

LOVE you all and see you next time!
- Milena Delgado Laborde

www.ingramcontent.com/pod-product-compliance
Lightning Source LLC
Chambersburg PA
CBHW022023310726
48972CB00006B/1784